CROWE

Wade Gustafson

Copyright © 2008-2022 by Wade Gustafson.
All rights reserved. Revised edition.

This is a work of fiction. Names, characters, places, and incidents either are the product of the author's imagination, or they are used fictitiously, and any resemblance to actual persons, living or dead, business establishments, events, or locales is entirely coincidental. The scanning, uploading, and distribution of this book via the Internet or via any means without the permission of the author is illegal and punishable by law. Please purchase only authorized electronic editions and do not participate or encourage electronic piracy of copyrightable materials. Your support of the author's rights is appreciated.

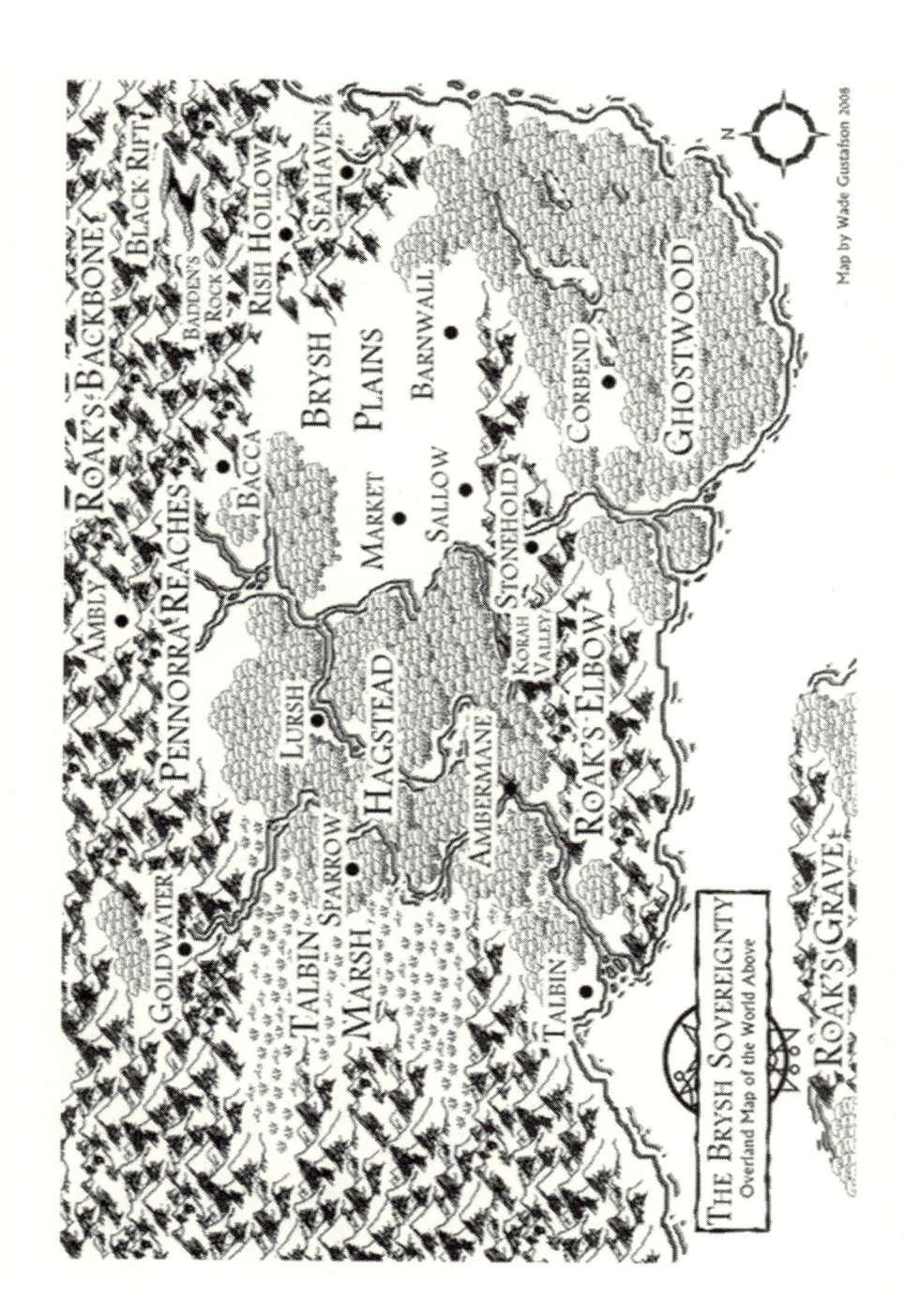

Crowe

Crowe

The Brysh Sovereignty
Subterranean Map of the World Below

Map by Wade Gustafson 2008
Not drawn to scale, passages under 10 meters wide have been omitted.

Labels: Garuk Tunnels; Black Rift; Roak's Forge; Lava Lake; Unknown Garuk Territory; Garuk Tunnels; To Amber Gem Mines; Chasmarrud; To Stonehold; Blocked Cavern; Magmanera Road; Garuk Massacre; To The Blue World; Subterranea

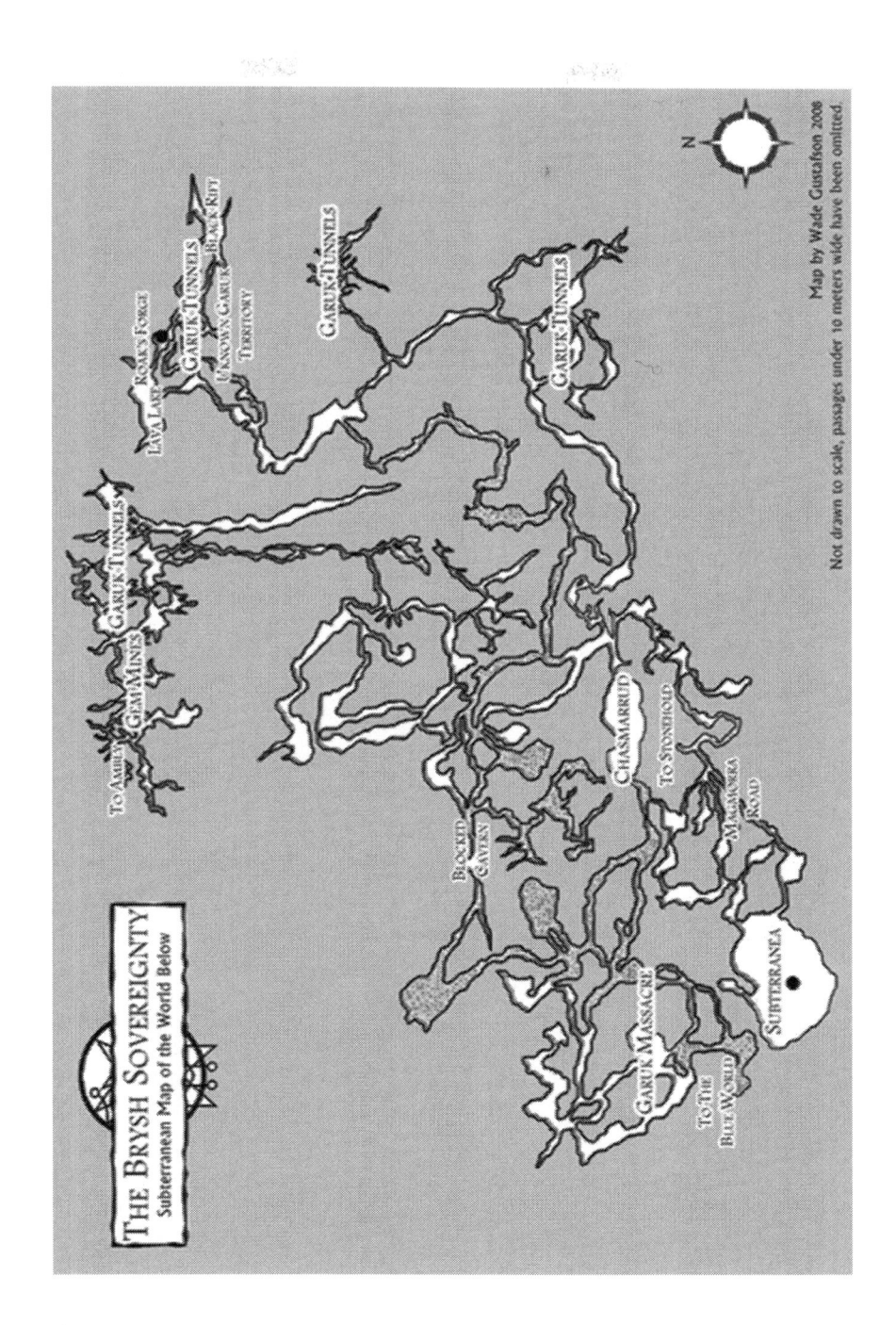

Chapter 1

They never spoke of it directly, for it hung between them like a dark shadow.

Death.

Mortality.

Odderly felt a surge of relief wash over him as the last of his students filtered out of his classroom. Eager to be on their way from their final lesson of the cycle, the youths restrained their excitement, taking care not to disturb the intricate glasswork that occupied the surface of every table crowded into the small space cleared between the empty shelves. While most of Odderly's books and alchemical tools had been neatly packed into crates the week before and readied for the inevitable transfer to the great Undercity of Subterranea, the vast contraptions of shining glasswork and the liquids in them remained untouched. Most of the projects were harmless student works, however there were a few projects that were quite volatile in nature.

The door closed quietly as the last student, a bug-eyed boy often teased for his obsessive interest in alchemy, took his leave after a mournful last look into the room. The only sound that remained was Odderly's heavy breathing and the dripping and bubbling of the colorful liquids as they eased through spiraling glass tubes and dropped into simmering flasks suspended over the low flames of everburning candles. What remained here were concoctions best not jostled, their transmutation wisely left undisturbed until the mixtures reached a state in which they could be safely handled.

It was one such mixture to which the herb master hurried. Hidden away in a seldom-used corner of the classroom and partially covered with old, moth-eaten linen was an old still where a seemingly inconsequential blue fluid dripped into a clear flask. A magically warmed pebble glowed orange within the flask to keep the fermenting serum at a steady temperature. For a full month it had remained there, a daily test of the dusky, red-haired alchemist's patience.

Odderly crouched down and examined the potion. Another day, maybe two, and he would be certain of its potency. Unfortunately, he could afford to wait no longer. A message had arrived by carrier crow earlier in the day and Odderly's every thought since had been of his dying friend. Were it not that he was still watched by warders, even all these cycles after Asher Crowe was extricated from the university and declared an outlaw, Odderly would simply have skipped his final day of instruction and faced the reprimand with his usual dour demeanor. He could have taken the serum and made his escape from the university under the cover of night. He could not, however, risk drawing such attention to his departure. Nor could he risk being followed. Asher Crowe was, after all, more than *just* an outlaw. He was the most notorious outlaw in all the Brysh Sovereignty, a man wanted more dead, than alive. Odderly's former friendship with *the* Asher Crowe remained a reason for the Lord Martyr's men to scrutinize any out of place conduct to this very day.

Sweeping his long hair out of his eyes, Odderly lifted the flask from its place and transferred the precious mixture into a dented tin canteen, which he corked and secured in his medical case. It would have to do. Crowe had been too long without an injection. Though the message he had received was written with intentionally deceptive references to the health of her family goat, an animal that did not even exist, Claudia had made no effort to disguise her worry.

Out there all alone, Odderly thought as his mind conjured an image of Asher Crowe's young granddaughter sitting at the relic's bedside. *That old goat is all the poor girl has left.*

Odderly quickly crossed the room and had his hand on the dingy brass handle of the door when he heard the clapping of boots coming down the hallway outside. There were voices, and Odderly mouthed a curse when he recognized one in particular.

Warder Mankoff.

"A troublesome man on the best of days," Odderly muttered under his breath.

Mankoff was making his rounds again, and Odderly did not have the luxury of time to spare entertaining yet another inspection. Especially not when Mankoff always made a point to interrogate Odderly about his past associations and end every conversation with a veiled threat.

Odderly retracted his hand the way one might after touching a hot kettle. He turned and darted away on the tips of his toes, just making it into the cover of the menial space that served as his office when he heard the lock turn. Odderly closed the thin office door quietly behind him only an instant before the warders stepped into the classroom and patronizingly called out his name.

Odderly hastened to the tall, latticed window and looked outside. He was at once thankful that his classroom was on the ground floor in a little visited corner of the east wing where the trees and shrubbery were oft neglected by the groundskeepers. Nobody saw him drop out of the open window, and in moments he had stepped clear of the foliage and joined the crowd of students and faculty alike who milled about the open courtyard.

———••———

"Off to check on Widow Tillembrook again?" the ostler asked when Odderly ducked into the shack aside the stables.

The homebound woman had often served as a convenient excuse for Odderly's frequent absences from the university. Well on in her cycles, the old crone was left a sizable inheritance by her late husband and was among the university's most generous benefactors. Her estate was several hours ride outside of Ambermane, which justified an overnight excursion, and in the same general direction as Crowe's cottage. The fact that Odderly had not so much as seen Widow Tillembrook in several cycles did not settle well on his stomach. But the widow was well known to be something of a shut in and Odderly doubted that she had shared more than a few foul words with another living soul since her husband had died.

"Aye, once more before I leave her in the care of my juniors," Odderly answered. "Should any of them be brazen enough to face both the winter *and* the widow."

The ostler chuckled and repeated the usual oratory about getting Odderly's stiddleback saddled up, but he did not otherwise inquire as to the meaning of Odderly's barb before shuffling outside. Winter was coming, and in a world where a single year spanned a lifetime, the change of seasons meant a significant change of lifestyle for all the Brysh. Odderly, like all the others who were young enough to forge a new life in the World Below, was expected to take refuge from the coming twenty-five cycles of winter in the safety of the great undercity. In another few weeks he would be meeting with the wizards of Fire Falls to accept tenure at the subterranean academy. Those who would remain behind were either too old to suffer such a transition, or among the Lord Martyr's selected custodians who would tend to the needs of the elderly and Ambermane University itself until the Brysh populace returned to the World Above in the distant spring.

As he waited, Odderly paced about impatiently. Twice he wiped sweat from his face with the grimy red handkerchief that he always kept close at hand. Frequently he pressed his face against the foggy glass of the shack's windows to make sure that no warders were headed his way.

Where in Shadow is that damned ostler?

Odderly's eyes looked up to the gray clouds gathering overhead. He knew that winter, when it came fully, would be merciless and unforgiving. It was getting cold already. Unnaturally cold, according to his reckoning. At last, the shadow of the ostler fell across the window and Odderly stepped back, turning his attention to the door.

"She's all ready for you," the ostler muttered when he ducked back inside. "Have a safe ride, Master Flack."

Odderly nodded and muttered something of a thank you as he

stepped back outside. He found his stiddleback tethered to the hitching post and patted the fat old beast on the side of its long neck. He reached a hand up to her equine-like head so that she could take in his scent and recognize him. With cataracts filming each eye, Odderly suspected that the beast was all but blind and ran her route solely on trust that Odderly would not march her into a ravine or anything that might eat her.

Never one to anthropomorphize, Odderly had never bothered to name the stiddleback though he often called her with some reference to her girth. The beast was fat, gravidly so, with long skinny forelegs and knobby knees that barely seemed able to hold up her own weight, let alone his. As Odderly rounded his mount her much shorter back legs buckled, and she lowered her tailless rear quarter to the ground so that Odderly could throw his medical bag into the wicker saddle basket. Slipping one booted foot into a stirrup he pulled himself up onto the padded saddle and adjusted himself where a man must to ensure a painless ride. He reached high up over her stiddle, the raised hump anatomically positioned over her front shoulders, so he could take the reigns.

The ostler, who had followed Odderly outside, unclipped the tether and stepped back when Odderly tapped the stiddleback's ribs with the tip of his boots. He would ride hard, but not until he had slipped out of the university without notice and was safely beyond the reach of those who might cause further delay.

———••———

Odderly spurred his bloated stiddleback and turned southward, riding into the sparse woods. He would keep clear of the road now, choosing instead a familiar route along game trails through the Hagstead Forest until he reached a sheltered dip between two low hills. From there, the trees thinned out into a vast stretch of grasslands.

A cold wind whipped through the ringbarks, tearing the withered oval leaves off the black-and-white banded giants, and Odderly felt moisture on his skin. He turned his gaze up to the dismal gray sky visible through the interwoven branches rushing overhead. It would rain before long, and he had forgotten his traveling cloak in his rush to sneak away from the university without being noticed. Not for the first time, or the last, he was certain, Odderly cursed Mankoff's name.

Unfortunately, there had been little time to properly prepare for the ride ahead of him. Asher Crowe's very life depended upon him, and Odderly's loyalty to the reclusive outlaw took precedence above all things, especially something as trivial as personal comfort.

As the cloudy, blue-gray sky darkened into night, Odderly wiped the rain from his face and slowed his mount. He brought the stiddleback to a trot and directed the hairless beast across a shallow stream. Tall flowering pine mixed with ringbarks on the other side, and not too far into the woods Odderly could make out the distinct shape of the cottage. Firelight could be seen flickering inside.

Claudia heard the stiddleback approach, but she did not turn to the door until she heard footsteps walking across the sheltered wooden porch. *Odderly is finally here*, she thought.

When the rugged alchemist opened the door and stepped inside, Claudia let out an exasperated sigh and got up to fetch him a warm blanket. Odderly took the seat that Claudia had vacated and sat his saddle basket down beside him.

"How has he been doing?" Odderly asked in lieu of a greeting.

"He is more feverish than normal," Claudia said, taking a seat on the edge of the bed where her grandfather slept. "He's hardly stirred all day and I was beginning to worry that you had trouble on the road. I was about to do it myself."

Odderly paused and raised a brow at Claudia.

Claudia had known Odderly for a long time, and her fear of needles was not something she'd been able to keep secret from him. She smirked and looked away.

"No, no trouble on the road. Just the usual goings on at the university." Odderly began unpacking small wooden cases from his basket. "Warder Mankoff is on the rampage again, and it was all that I could do to get away without being noticed since he's made a point to aggravate me all week."

Claudia bit her lip as she watched Odderly assemble a syringe and draw a bluish fluid from out of a dented canteen he pulled out of his medical case. He flicked the syringe with a grubby finger and tiny bubbles of air floated up through the fluid. After a moment, the fluid began to glow radiantly. He slowly pushed on the plunger forcing the serum to rise and bead on the point.

"Looks about right, and it'll have to do," Odderly muttered. "Are you ready, Asher?"

Claudia's gaze turned toward the old man stretched out on the bed before her. Her grandfather, Asher Crowe, would soon be celebrating his 108th cycle. Nature dictated that he should have died of old age more than thirty cycles ago, but he had been *preserved* during that time by the regular injections administered by the rugged alchemist at his bedside.

The glowing serum was Odderly's own special blend of herbs and magic, ironically brewed at the very university that wanted Crowe dead. The serum could potentially fuel a man through life indefinitely, one day and one injection at a time.

"It's not that I'm afraid to die," Crowe had told Claudia on more than one occasion, "rather that you are simply not ready to face the world without me."

Claudia was now fourteen cycles, fast becoming a woman, but not one yet. Her grandfather had taken her in when her father failed to return from the Pennorra Reaches after the garuk had sacked Ambly, the small mountain village where Claudia had been born. The garuk, a savage cave-dwelling people, had been pushing back the Brysh border for fifty cycles. The attack on Ambly, however, was the first time that they had come in such force and number as to do much harm. Few people survived that horrid day.

Sitting now at her grandfather's bedside Claudia looked every bit like her mother at the same age. She was a pretty lass, thin and small, with light blonde hair falling over her shoulders. She also had her father's intense gray eyes.

Claudia watched Odderly carefully, fascinated by the magic that the dusky, red-haired herb master used each day to keep her grandfather alive. She knew how to brew the life-sustaining serum, but her stomach tightened as she watched Odderly prepare to administer the injection.

Claudia turned away when Odderly finally pushed the needle through her grandfather's jaundiced skin. Claudia dreaded the day that she would have to give her grandfather the injections herself, so not a day passed that she was not thankful that Odderly had given up his own personal ambitions to tend to his old friend.

Crowe moaned and stirred in his sleep. He opened his eyes as he woke and tried to speak, but his voice was weak, and Claudia was unable to make out what he was trying to say. From the look in his eyes and the expression that he wore, Claudia could see that the serum was burning painfully within him.

It took several minutes for Crowe's pain to subside and the magic of Odderly's serum to take effect, but when it did the change was miraculous. Claudia watched the deeply set wrinkles around her grandfather's eyes fade away. The lines that had creased his brow lightened, and his eyes became vibrant and alert – the eyes of a man sixty cycles Crowe's junior.

Crowe pulled his elbows back under him and eased himself up a little from the bed.

"There now, how are you feeling, Asher?" Odderly asked as he ruffled his hair with the blanket to dry it. His voice was thick with worry.

"Better now, my friend. My strength is returning again," Crowe said as he stared at them in turn. "What ever would I do without the two of you?"

———•—

As the sun set on the western horizon Claudia and Crowe sat together on the old porch swing where they could clearly see the cloud-streaked sky. The storm had moved on, and several of the World Above's sixteen colorful moons could be seen hovering overhead.

It was on that bench where Claudia and her grandfather spent the evening in the way that they spent most evenings together. With Asher Crowe passing on a lifetime of knowledge and memories spanning each of the World Above's twenty-five cycle seasons, and Claudia Kobb carefully committing each tale and fact to memory.

Having been born a season after the Bjoran Revolt, Crowe had accumulated countless secrets. His stories, recounted first hand, often predated the First Lord Martyr's rise to power and the founding of the Brylands. Sometimes it was hard for Claudia to see her grandfather as the historical figure present in his stories. But it was true that Crowe had been a powerful warder in his youth, and at one time a daring adventurer. He was the same Asher Crowe who once crossed the Easterly Sea when a rare conjunction of the moons released their grip upon the turbulent waters of the World Above. The same Asher Crowe who had once led an expedition into the ruins of Roak's Grave. Her grandfather had seen more of the World Above than any hundred other men combined. In a world where a single year spans a lifetime, men like Asher Crowe who could attest to seeing the same season twice in their lives, simply did not exist.

Crowe's legacy was to pass on a complete year of history to his granddaughter. It was important to him that Claudia know the truths of the world, rather than the sanitized record of history found in books written to soothe the egos of the Lord Martyrs and the High Warders who penned them.

Claudia knew that it was her grandfather's hope that she would follow in his footsteps. He had often challenged her to learn to use her mind and her intellect rather than facing the world with a sword in one hand and a handful of prayers in the other – the way that her father had done.

Under her grandfather's tutelage Claudia had advanced quickly in her magical studies and she could easily outspell mages several cycles older than her – even those who had received *proper* training at Ambermane University, the Bryland's premier educational institution for wizardry. Her grandfather had been instructing her for six cycles now, and with Odderly teaching her the more technical aspects of science and alchemy Claudia's potential was limitless.

Claudia would have done exceedingly well at the prestigious university, but her grandfather had been afraid that she would end up consumed and polluted by the politics of the place just as he had been when he was a student there nearly a hundred cycles before.

"There will be a day not so far from now when I'll not be around to guide you, my dear," Crowe said abruptly.

Claudia looked at him, alarmed by the sudden change of subject to one that she hated to discuss. "Nonsense, Grandfather," she said. "With Odderly's serum you'll still be around when I am your age."

"And what if I am not?" Crowe asked.

"Well, I . . . I don't know," Claudia answered. "I suppose that I would leave here."

"And where would you go?"

"Ambly."

"But Ambly is no more. The garuk burned the village to the ground and there is nothing there now, save for the ghosts you've left behind."

"I would like to see it again, none-the-less, Grandfather. I would..."

"You would climb Roak's Backbone and walk into the Pennorra Reaches to find the same death that your father found there," Crowe interrupted.

Claudia looked up at the old wizard with tears welling up in her eyes. No matter how many times they had this discussion, Claudia always had to fight to block out the thoughts of her father's death from her mind. Not knowing what truly happened after her grandfather had taken her to safety weighed heavily on her. Even though six cycles had passed, her dreams were still haunted by images of the day that Ambly fell.

In those nightmares she would see her father riding a stiddleback into the advancing ranks of savages. In those nightmares Claudia had watched her father die a thousand horrible deaths. In every dream she would see her grandfather standing at Badden's Rock, where he hid something in a small hollow beneath the boulders. If there was meaning in this seemingly unrelated event, Claudia had yet to realize it.

"He could still be alive," Claudia argued.

"And he is more likely dead. You must accept that fact, Claudia, if you are ever to fully invest yourself into wizardry." Crowe shook his head in dismissal and narrowed his eyes at Claudia. "There is no room in your studies to harvest false hopes."

"But why do you think it is that I study so hard, if not to one day be able to evoke magic that will help me to find my father," Claudia paused, "or at least learn what really happened to him!"

Crowe started to say something, but instead let out a deep sigh. Claudia looked away and brushed away the tears that had found her cheeks. She felt her grandfather's hand take hold of her shoulder and she tensed. A moment later she accepted a warm embrace as her tears turned into outright sobbing.

A few minutes later, Crowe stood up and started to walk away. He paused at the cottage door and looked back over his shoulder. He studied Claudia for a moment and then turned, his words trailing behind him, "the world stands to gain too much from you, Claudia Kobb, for you to be ruined by grief."

Claudia heard her grandfather go back inside. She sat there for a long while, gently rocking forward and back on the porch swing, left alone with her thoughts.

Chapter 2

Far away, deep within the World Below, more than two hundred shouting garuk surrounded Horace Kobb. He was fenced in with a massive guskar, and as hunchbacked as the hairy black-skinned humanoid was, it still towered over Kobb by more than two heads.

This particular guskar was a recent acquisition. It was the best fighter in Pulgra's stable. Kobb could hear the familiar guttural sounds of the fat garuk stable master's voice shouting above the crowd. Pulgra was certain that his pockets would soon be lined with gold, but more importantly, that this battle would prove once and for all that Atta's prized Brysh slave was merely a weak human from the World Above.

It was well known, even to the gladiatorial slaves, that Pulgra wanted to stab at Atta's pride; that Pulgra wanted vengeance for the loss of more than a dozen of his best fighters, including a pair of rare euum giants that had fallen before the Brysh slave only a few days earlier.

Kobb saw the guskar stomping toward him and pushed Pulgra's ranting out of his ears. Within the magma-forged fighting pit Kobb dove down into the mud just in time to evade a powerful arc of the guskar's spiked club.

In an instant, Kobb was back on his feet. The garuk spectators cheered and threw dirty water into the arena. With each passing moment, the footing became more treacherous as the bloodstained soil turned to mud. Kobb's long gray hair was caked to his face and something in his back had twisted during the roll. As he sprang back up to his feet, he brought his short spear up and lunged forward as pain burned in his spine. As a man of fifty cycles, Kobb was simply getting too old to be a gladiator.

The spear point landed perfectly. It found an opening in the guskar's rotting hide armor, in the depression between the arm and the shoulder, but with the pain of his back overwhelming him, Kobb didn't have the strength at hand to push the sharpened stone through the guskar's thick skin.

The blow did make the fat stable master wince, however, until Pulgra realized that the strike had done little to slow his newest champion. Pulgra rose from his carved seat and howled madly, thrusting a clawed fist into the air.

"Your human grows old and feeble, Atta!" Pulgra taunted.

Folding her arms over her exposed breasts, Atta idly picked at the gray tooth that stuck awkwardly out of her mouth, even when it was closed. Atta watched the gladiators calmly. She had given her aging Brysh slave a garuk title, *Lor Sarkka Rah*, the Gray Swordsman. It was rare for a stable master to bother for the slaves of the garuk seldom survived the garuk gladiatorial games long enough to earn any degree of fame. But this one, captured six cycles ago during the most successful surface raid in garuk history, had simply refused to die. In fact, *Lor Sarkka Rah* had outlived many of his slavers, having been the property of four separate stable masters before Atta had won him for her own.

The guskar grabbed hold of the spear shaft and used it for leverage, fully lifting Kobb off the ground as he maintained his hold on it. It swung the spiked club and hit Kobb square in the face. Kobb felt his nose shatter. A single spike pierced deeply into his cheek, and he could taste the blood running down into his mouth and shaggy beard. He was dazed, but somehow, he managed to catch sight of the guskar raising the spiked club for a killing blow.

Lor Sarkka Rah curled up his legs and kicked hard at the guskar's abdomen, but it had little effect. Kobb was forced to let go of the spear and fall onto his back to avoid the sweep of the club. And though the guskar missed, a wispy patch of Kobb's hair was ripped from his scalp as the spiked club sailed past.

Without Kobb's head to absorb the strength of the blow, the guskar spun around a little too far; it tried desperately to regain its footing in the mud, but it slipped, twisted, and exposed an unprotected flank.

Kobb hit the ground hard, but he realized that this was his opportunity to end the fight and bring down the massive guskar. He bit his tongue to stave off the pain of his back and quickly got back up to his feet. From across his back, he drew a short, broad-bladed sword and sprang forward.

He plunged the point of the sword into the guskar, felt the resistance of its tough skin, and then the blade pushed through. Kobb felt the resistance give way and the blade then sank effortlessly into the soft insides of the creature. He grunted and turned the blade upward in search of the lungs.

The sudden absence of breath silenced the guskar's pitiful wail. Pulgra came up to his feet again, cursing and shouting as he threw his mug into the fighting pit.

In that same instant, the guskar's spiked club came around and Kobb took the blow hard enough for three of the iron spikes to become lodged in his sword arm sending Kobb spinning around in excruciating pain. Kobb lost his grip on his sword and staggered down to one knee, clutching his wounded arm to his chest.

A shower of dirty water was thrown down into the fighting pit as the cheering above intensified. Gold nuggets began to be exchanged among the garuk. Pulgra was at the edge of his robuck-hide stand, gripping the lava stone rail and shouting curses as loud as he possibly could.

Had the guskar the strength left to yank the spiked club free, it would likely have taken Kobb's arm at the elbow. But the massive guskar staggered and fell backward, losing its grip on the haft of the club. Fighting for each shallow breath, it merely sought to reach around to its side and pull the blade free. Fumbling blindly in search of the impaled blade, the guskar's mouth opened and closed frantically with each attempt to draw in enough air to breath.

Kobb made it up to his knees and used his free arm to pull the club away. Waves of pain shot through his arm as the long spikes slowly slid free of his tissue, one tug at a time. Kobb could tolerate no more when the spikes pulled free and blood poured openly from the wound – he screamed.

Water came down from the crowd in torrents as the howling cheers of the garuk reached a crescendo. Both gladiators lay bleeding together in the pit, each trying to swallow their pain long enough to rise and end the life of the other.

"It would seem that your guskar champion will sleep in Shadow tonight," Atta said in her guttural language, the words rolling off of her tongue with a tone that openly displayed mockery. She grinned and gestured to the arena with a toss of her head as Kobb staggered up to his feet.

Lor Sarkka Rah fumbled with the buckle of his belt as he fought to unstrap it. He finally managed to yank the belt free and held one end of the leather strap in his mouth while he wrapped the other around this arm in an effort to stem the flow of blood. His eyes fluttered, and his body was pale with shock at the grievous wound. Growling under his breath and drawing upon a reserve of energy somewhere within him, Kobb clambered back up to his feet knowing what must be done.

"Enshalaan," Kobb whispered.

Kobb left the dying guskar bleeding in the mud and stumbled away. He almost fell two times, but at the side of the fighting pit he found a crudely carved lava stone pedestal that held a box decorated with bits and pieces of bone and broken skulls.

A new wave of excitement washed over the crowd of garuk spectators as the cavern suddenly fell silent. All around the arena, all eyes watched in quiet anticipation of the moment to come.

Kobb became detached from all of it. With each step, Shadow seemed to draw closer to him. He fought hard to simply remain conscious and standing, coherent of his surroundings. Shaking away the confusion that was beginning to settle in his mind due to blood lack Kobb swayed and tried to keep his balance. He looked up to Atta for confirmation. The ugly garuk female grinned at Pulgra and then slowly nodded.

Kobb reached forward and wrapped the hand of his uninjured arm around the prominent euum tusk that served as the handle of the lid of the box.

He opened it.

Kept within the box was a long, simple-looking dagger. The dagger was old and worn with rust-colored bloodstains dried to the surface of the blade. It might have appeared entirely insignificant, if not for the desiccated demon's heart tied to the pommel with dried roshae gut.

Insignificant. Nothing could be farther from the truth. This blade, *Enshalaan*, was passed around among the garuk stable masters as a trophy. *Enshalaan* was always used to make the killing blow, for those slain with such a weapon would not find judgment in the afterlife; their souls were sent directly into Shadow, to empower the shade that was bound to the blade.

It was the victor's duty, reward, and pleasure to make that final killing stroke, for *Enshalaan* took good care of those who wielded it.

Kobb took up the old blade. *Enshalaan*, he thought.

Kobb could sense the spiritbound demon in the blade. Kobb felt a presence in his mind and he knew that *Enshalaan* was acknowledging the hand that wielded it. Holding the dagger in his hand, Kobb felt somehow comforted.

For a moment, Kobb forgot about the madness all around him. He forgot about the silent garuk spectators who watched him, and the guskar who had nearly killed him. He no longer felt the all but unbearable pain of his nose, back, and wounded arm. All that mattered to him now was *Enshalaan*.

"Before it dies!" Atta shouted from the crowd, bringing Kobb back to his senses.

Kobb could feel *Enshalaan's* pulse beating in his mind. The demon's heart thundered with anticipation, with hunger for the taste of freshly drawn blood. It was eager to lay claim to the guskar's soul.

Kobb summoned a reserve of energy within him and stalked back across the muddy fighting pit to the fallen guskar. It now fought frantically for each shallow breath as its lifeblood pooled in the muddy water around it.

Kobb placed a well-worn boot on the guskar's shoulder and shoved it over onto its back. He crouched beside its head and raised *Enshalaan* to the guskar's neck.

In his head Kobb felt the demon's presence. *Enshalaan's* thirst was all that mattered, and the demon was insatiable.

With a sudden jerk of his hand the blade sliced into the guskar's neck. It sliced smoothly, with almost no resistance, as if it was cutting nothing more than soft, freshly baked bread. The smooth slice of the enchanted blade caught on the bone of the guskar's neck. Blood came freely from the lethal wound. *Enshalaan's* pulse throbbed suddenly and, in his mind, Kobb could hear the demon's unmistakable laughter.

Enshalaan's pulse beat so loudly in Kobb's mind that each pulse brought him physical pain. Soon though, the guskar's blood began to crawl toward the blade, which seemed to drink of the guskar's life blood. The dried section of the demon's heart began to moisten and fill with color—renewed life. The pain subsided. *Enshalaan's* pulse synchronized with Kobb's pulse and pleasure replaced pain.

Kobb reveled in the feeling, taking comfort in the familiar warmth that began to run through his body. He found that the stinging pain of his back, and the throbbing of his arm became more of a warm tingle before becoming numb all together. He closed his eyes, lulled his head back, and then fell over into the bloody mud.

Kobb winced only slightly as he felt his spine pop back into place. Even the terrible wounds from the spiked club began to pull themselves together, the flesh mending. Kobb slumped forward and turned to one side. He lay there, listening to the guttural chanting of the garuk.

Lor Sarkka Rah!

Lor Sarkka Rah!

But soon, all of this faded away into muted silence as Kobb lost himself to *Enshalaan's* healing euphoria.

Chapter 3

Unusual silence marked the dawn as Claudia found her way out of uneasy sleep. Most days she woke to the voices of her grandfather and Odderly talking down the hall, but not today. Her dreams had been particularly disturbing, and panic filled her. She was up in an instant, wide-awake, and running barefoot from room to room.

"Grandfather?" Claudia called out.

"He's not here!" Odderly shouted from somewhere.

"Odderly?" Claudia shouted as she descended the stairs that led into the basement larder.

"Aye, down here!"

The darkness of the basement stairwell was in stark contrast to the torch lit larder that Odderly had converted into a makeshift laboratory last cycle. Claudia could see him hunched over his worktable with his back to the stairs. His attention was focused intently on his work.

Great contraptions made of interconnected tubes, vials, lenses, and bubbling liquids covered nearly every flat surface of the room. Many of these were still a great mystery to Claudia. One small still in the corner, however, she knew quite well for it was where Odderly had shown Claudia how to brew the serum herself. Even now, her first precious batch of the life-sustaining fluid simmered within a clear glass tube suspended over a candle flame. The mixture catalyzed with prolonged heat; it would not be ready for several more weeks.

"Where is . . ."

Odderly snapped a finger up over his shoulder signaling for Claudia to be silent.

She obeyed and moved quietly to his side, gracefully slipping around the tables and glasswork that crowded the room. Peaking over Odderly's shoulder she discovered that the headband he wore was actually a leather crown fitted with wires and bolts to suspend a large magnifying lens directly in front of his face.

"They are . . . very delicate . . . when they are moist like this," Odderly explained. His words were drawn out by the complexity of his task.

Before him sat a handful of dead red and white salamanders. Claudia had often seen them on the bedrocks of the stream outside of the cottage. A puddle of milky water surrounded the salamanders and a line of the slimy substance ran to the edge of the table where it dripped now and then onto Odderly's leather boot.

In his hand Odderly held a small metal tool that was sharp on one side and fitted with a tiny scoop on the other. Claudia watched intently as Odderly pried at the edges of each individual eye to loosen them from the orbits, and then she grimaced when he gently scooped each eye out and tapped it loose in the small glass dish that sat off to the side. Extracted eyeballs glistened within the dish.

Odderly turned around to face Claudia and smiled. The large round lens magnified and distorted his leathery face so much that Claudia couldn't help but laugh. It made it look as if she could plunge her whole arm through the space between his two front teeth.

"What's so funny, child?" Odderly asked, his face scrunching into deep creases as he raised a furry red brow.

That of course, only brought on a second chorus of laughter. "Take that silly thing off and talk to me!" Claudia managed between her chortles. "What are you doing, and where is my grandfather?"

"He's gone . . . to run some errands, and what I'm doing," Odderly said, "is scooping out the eyes of salamanders."

"Well, I see that," Claudia said. "Why?"

"Spell components," Odderly answered.

"For?"

"For . . . for a farseeing spell."

"You taught me that the eyes from a bird of prey were used for clairvoyance spells," Claudia said.

"Well, ideally yes. But we're far too close to winter now. There won't be birds around here for another thirty cycles or more if you believe what Asher says about winter. So, I have to improvise. Magic is like that, Claudia. There is always room for improvisation." Odderly paused for a moment, extracting another eye. "Now aren't you going to ask me why I chose to use salamanders instead of say . . . ringtail fox, or rabbit perhaps?" He removed the magnifier and sat it on the worktable.

"That was going to be my next question, actually," Claudia said as she looked down at Odderly's magnifier, "but I think I already know the answer."

Odderly leaned back in his chair and began wiping his hands clean with a red handkerchief. When he was finished, he thrust it back into his pocket and looked at Claudia expectantly.

"Well, in addition to the roots, sulfur, and salts needed for most clairvoyance spells, the eyes of an amphibian are symbolic representing the elements of both land and sea, therefore acting as a bielemental focusing component."

"Yes." Odderly grinned. "Go on."

"And you're keeping them moist because water is not just a universal solvent, it is a universal lubricant; the field of view will be extended further than you would normally be able to see with a dry substitute component?"

Claudia stared at Odderly, who looked silently back at her. She expected either a confirmation or one of Odderly's lengthy, and often tangent-filled explanations as to where her logic had failed.

"Well?" Claudia asked. "Am I right?"

"Right as rain, child," Odderly said with a wink.

Crowe was amazed at the general sense of chaos that had spread throughout the university. It had been more than fifty cycles since he had set foot into the Township of Ambermane, let alone the university itself and little appeared to have changed. The same old ivy-coated buildings towered over the surrounding campus wall that divided the township from the university grounds, and while the faces of the students and faculty that he passed in the magically lit halls had changed, their countenance and bearing remained the same as those of his era.

Crowe was born almost thirty cycles after the wizard Ambermane had brought an end to the Bjoran Revolt and united the Brysh clans, beginning an age of relative peace. Not long after, the University of Ambermane was founded and by the time that Crowe was old enough to attend the university had grown larger and more noteworthy than the village that surrounded it, and the Fire Falls Academy of Magic in Subterranea that predated it.

Crowe remembered Ambermane University as a tranquil place of learning during his childhood, and later as the place where he cast his *Oath* aside and turned forever from being a servant of the Lord Martyr to an outlaw and enemy of the sovereignty.

Each turn brought back a distant memory. And with them came a bitter taste in Crowe's mouth. If only the Second Lord Martyr had been less of a fool, Crowe would not have been forced to act against the headmaster whom he believed had become the vessel of an Ambraic shade. But as a warder, it had been Crowe's duty to protect the Brysh people, even if doing so meant that he had to sacrifice his own future. Crowe was a wanted man now, the most wanted of men, and so he pulled the hood of his academic robe low over his face and moved with long, purposeful strides in an effort to avoid drawing any undo attention.

With so many people filling the halls there were potential enemies all around him. This visit, however, carried with it a special purpose. And it was one that could wait no longer. To Crowe, it was worth the risk in returning to the university he had once called home.

Crowe rounded the corner of an arched hallway and walked outside onto a grassy expanse beyond. The courtyard was wooded and shady, painted in shades of green with cobbled paths connecting the numerous buildings.

The swiftly flowing Goldwater River cut the courtyard in half, thinning where it ran around both sides of a large island held between its banks. Visible there, was the largest structure of Ambermane. It was just a non-descript tower with a rounded peak, demonstrating much less grandeur in the architecture than the buildings clustered together on the west side of the river. But the tower was quite special to Crowe. It was the greatest technological marvel of Brysh society found in the World Above.

The Ambermane Observatory was formed from granite blocks brought by boat from the Village of Goldwater in the north, and it was only as wide as was needed to keep the spiraling steps inside manageable for those who climbed to the peak of the tower where a mammoth brass cylinder gleamed in the sunlight. The observatory held the single most powerful magnifier in the Brylands, and with it the scholars and wizards of the university were able to study the sixteen moons that orbited the World Above, even the green moon, *Lyria the Timekeeper*, which was the smallest, but also the most brightly reflective of the moons. *Lyria the Timekeeper* was so named, as it was the moon that marked the passing of Brysh aging cycles. Traveling around the World Above in an elliptical orbit, it became visible as a bright green sphere only one night out of every three hundred and sixty-five.

Crowe stopped just shy of the granite bridge that spanned the river. He looked down at the mud, crouched, and drew his old wand from its sheath. Crowe pushed the tip of his wand into the mud and drew a perfect circle, within which he drew several sharply angled symbols with circles on the ends. Crowe sprinkled some yellow powder that he had prepared the night before over the magical symbols and then spoke the words of power needed to enchant the glyph.

Letting out an overly loud yawn Odderly cocked his head to the side and asked, "did you finish reading the scrolls that I had given you?"

"Yes, two nights ago," Claudia answered as she took a seat next to

Odderly at his workbench. "Does Grandfather know that you gave them to me?"

Odderly laughed. "You know as well as I do that Asher has his ways of knowing just about anything he wants to know."

Claudia frowned, remembering the lecture she had received about trust and integrity last cycle when her grandfather had confronted her about picking the lock of his private study to get a peek at some of the spell books that he kept inside.

When she had asked him how he had known that she had picked the lock, her grandfather whispered to her, "the books told me that you were looking at them."

Odderly laughed out loud. "In this case, yes, he knows. He is the one who asked me to sneak them out of the university library to give to you."

"Grandfather?" Claudia exclaimed.

"He's stubborn and set in his ways, Claudia, but you'll have to forgive him for that one of these days. He asked me to give them to you so that you'd finish reading them before you knew that he had a part in getting them to you."

"I don't understand. I've been griped at for six cycles to forget all about Ambly and the garuk, and set my focus on my studies . . . that I should leave the past behind me . . . seize my future, and all that hogwash!"

"He always has good reasons for doing things the way he does," Odderly said. "Those scrolls are one of the few recounts of what the warders found when they returned to Ambly. They are graphic, and terrible, but an honest enough journal of what happened. Asher wanted you to understand what your father faced there to make sure that the rest of you were able to get out of the Pennorra Reaches alive."

"Why?" Claudia scowled. "So, he can lecture me again about the terrible way that my father was killed?"

"No," Odderly said. He leaned forward and stared Claudia in the eye. "He wanted you to be prepared in case he has been wrong all along."

Crowe

The interior of the observatory chamber was painted black. Softly glowing balls of magical light had been placed all around the inside of the chamber to recreate the exact placement of stars and moons in the night sky. The depth and complexity of the stellar recreation stole Crowe's breath as he stepped into the starchamber. It was an exhibit of fine Brysh wizardry one hundred and fifty cycles in the making.

Located in the center of it all was a complex system of gears, within which was interwoven a series of steam chambers and coal ovens. Behind these, massive gears churned. Powered by burning coal, steam, and a little magic, the massive mechanical device was able to rotate and aim the colossal brass magnifier at the night sky through a portal in the rounded roof.

It was through this invention, the observatory telescope that the fine magical art of astromancy was born. Asher Crowe had been one of the early pioneers in the field, but he was a young man the last time he had been here, and at that time only a small portion of the sky had been magically duplicated.

"You've kept busy over the cycles," Crowe shouted, addressing a willowy old woman cleaning the fine lenses at the eyepiece of the machine.

"Roak's hand," the old woman called out. "I'd been told that Asher Crowe had been killed twenty-two cycles ago. You look rather good for a dead man, Asher."

The woman climbed down from the observation platform using a series of ladders to get to the ground. She crossed the distance between herself and Crowe and swallowed him into a powerful hug.

"I've missed you, Yssa," Crowe said as he looked down shamefully. "More than you'll ever know, and certainly more than you'll ever believe. Knowing that I would miss you was the hardest part in deciding to do what I had to do."

"Then you shouldn't have done it and left me here," Yssa said, pulling abruptly out of the hug and folding her arms across her chest. "Do you realize what you've put me through? It was ten cycles before the Lord Martyr decided that I had nothing to do with what you'd done, and another five before I was allowed anywhere near the observatory again. That's fifteen cycles that you owe me, Asher."

Crowe stood silently and let Yssa express the feelings she had been unable to let out for such a long time. He had not told Yssa when he had decided to break his *Oath*, and knowing that she would talk him out of doing what he felt he must had forced him to leave without ever giving her the chance to say goodbye. His subsequent self-exile had no doubt put anyone who had called Asher Crowe a friend under the scrutiny of the High Warders. Yssa more than any other, for times were different then and it was well known that they were courting.

"Well," Yssa yielded. "I can feel the magic about you, Asher, and you look sixty cycles younger than you should. Maybe those fifteen cycles are fifteen cycles that you can give back to me, eh?" Yssa smiled.

Crowe nodded. "I can indeed."

"What are you talking about, Odderly?"

"He doesn't believe that you are right," Odderly said. "But Asher said that it was high time for him to prove to you once and for all that your father is dead, before . . ."

"Before what?" Claudia asked as she sat up straight. Her usual enthusiastic smile suddenly gave way to a trembling lip. "What aren't you telling me?"

"The serum isn't working anymore, Claudia. Not like it used to anyway."

Claudia paled.

"I've been having to brew it stronger for the last few weeks, and it is causing him a lot more pain than he lets on. He's also been keeping an extra syringe on him and giving himself little boosters when he feels that he needs them to catch his breath. All in all, it's taking its toll on him."

Claudia sat down on a nearby stool and let her shoulders droop. She stared at the floor as she struggled to swallow the news of her grandfather's worsening condition. She felt ill and she was unsure of what she should say, or what she could hope to do. At last she looked at Odderly with tears welling up in her eyes.

"I don't think he'll be able to do it much longer, and I think that the only reason he hasn't let himself sleep in the Light is because he doesn't think you are prepared to accept his passing when you cannot even accept your father's. So, he's . . ."

"He's what?" Claudia whispered.

"He's gone back to the university."

Yssa led Crowe out of the observatory tower and across a second bridge to the far side of the river. There were no buildings there, just a buffer of ringbarks, but as they reached the tree line Yssa drew her wand and waved it through the air. The space between two stands of trees wavered and shimmered for a moment and then a small cottage wafted into visibility as the magical shroud was blown away like a heavy, swirling fog.

"You've hidden it!" Crowe said with a chuckle.

"Well, you taught me a long time ago that invisibility was much more easily woven over things that don't move than over things that do." Yssa frowned as she led Crowe up the porch steps. "And after you left, I couldn't think of anything more worth hiding than my own front door. I guess that I became something of a recluse after you left, Asher. A lot of us did."

What splendor the cottage lacked on the outside carried over to the inside, but Yssa's home was comforting in a rustic kind of way. The furnishings were simple, and most had knitted blankets thrown over them. Yssa had decorated with a number of plants that Crowe recognized as having a wide variety of medical and magical properties when used correctly.

Crowe took a seat at the small kitchen table while Yssa added a log to the stove. A wave of her wand brought forth a low-burning flame by which she began to prepare some tea.

"You've mustered up a lot of courage, or gone quite mad, to have come back to Ambermane," Yssa told Crowe after bringing the water to a boil.

"Well, as far as anyone knows I've been dead for more than twenty cycles. The last anyone would have known of me would have led them to Ambly, which is long gone now. Besides, even if I did pass anyone who knew me back then it is doubtful that they would recognize me now. I was a much younger man then, and the magic of my serum keeps me looking a lot younger than I should. Though, truth be told, I feel as old as I ever did." Crowe shrugged. "At any rate, I'm dying, Yssa. What could they possibly do to me now, even if they still wanted to bother?"

"Oh, trust me, Asher, they would still bother. Your name still comes up an awful lot around here and the fact that you were responsible for the death of a former headmaster will never be forgotten." Yssa looked back and raised a brow. "Did you know that the students are now required to write a parchment on you each cycle?"

"On me?" Crowe laughed. "So much tadoo over an old man."

Yssa shrugged and handed Crowe a cup of hot water and a silver tea dipper. "You weren't so old then, Asher. Nor so modest."

"Well, as usual, the Lord Martyr has buried the truth of what really happened. It is not like it was the headmaster anymore; it hadn't been for a long time, Yssa. He was a demon, Yssa. He was possessed by the shade of an Ambra."

"Not according to the books in the library. He was merely Headmaster Collinhodge, and very highly respected. The books say that you broke the oath and turned your wand against him, so the fact remains that if the warders knew you were here, they would be blasting down my door right now."

"Bah! All lies."

"Bah to you," Yssa said as she sat down and dipped her tea into the hot water. "So, then what is worth the risk you have taken in coming here again?"

The two of them talked for hours about Claudia and her father before their conversation turned to the more personal aspects of their own lives. Neither had married, though Crowe had two sons and a daughter, all of whom he survived. When the conversation came at last to the subject of Crowe's breaking of his *Oath* and self-exile, he at last fell silent not knowing how to justify having made such a rash and life-altering decision without having first consulted Yssa. Crowe shook his head and sighed.

"I would have stood with you, Asher," Yssa said.

"I was afraid that you'd talk me out of it, especially knowing that the Lord Martyr had denounced my petition for the High Warders to look into the matter."

"I would have trusted your judgment." Yssa stared at her tea for a long moment before she looked back up at Crowe. "We could have led different lives. We could have spent our lives together."

"I wish that I had done things differently, Yssa." Crowe looked up to Yssa and blinked away the building tears. "I wish that we had grown old together," he said.

Chapter 4

Haverstagg stood at the open window of his home watching the languid fall of snowflakes outside. Cold air blew in on a gentle breeze, carrying with it the promise of the changing season. People were everywhere outside, filling the cobblestone streets between each of the low stone buildings of Barnwall in a bustle of activity.

Haverstagg was no child at forty-two cycles, yet he had never seen snow. He stared outside enthralled by the phenomenon, trying to imagine what the village, and the World Above, would be like in the coming cycles. Twenty-five cycles of winter were on their way. Everything would change.

Can this really be happening?

"The seasons are changing," Hannah said as she stepped up behind her husband and wrapped her arms around him. "All this fuss will soon be over, and the streets will be empty."

Haverstagg closed his eyes and took a deep breath, inhaling the scent of his wife. "I'm not sure if we're ready for this, Hannah. It doesn't feel right. Like it's not really supposed to be happening."

"Of course, it is supposed to be happening. I remember my great grandmother telling me stories about winter. She said it would come again in my lifetime." Hannah slipped around Haverstagg and allowed herself to be pulled into his embrace. "But I know what you mean. It is hard to accept that everything we've taken for granted throughout our lives is changing. Before long Barnwall will stand mostly empty and we'll all have started anew in the Undercity of Subterranea."

"Not soon enough," he said after a moment. "I talked to Old Man Milliam over at the brewery this morning and he said that he's not going to leave. The Kembles too, and their boys." Haverstagg looked down at Hannah who was a full two heads shorter than he. "Maybe we shouldn't go? Maybe all the warnings about winter are just old stories told by our grandmothers."

Hannah grinned. "You're not afraid to live underground, are you?"

Haverstagg's eyes narrowed. He was a proud man, and Hannah always knew how to prod him. It was part of why he loved her. When they had first wed, Haverstagg was only a laborer who worked with the roshae in the fields. She had convinced him that he deserved better and pushed him to strive for more. Now, ten cycles later they owned their own land and the hops that grew upon it.

"I'm not afraid," Haverstagg said. "I just feel so out of sorts knowing that we've worked so hard for so long, and now we're just going to walk away from all of it."

"We're not just walking away from the farm, Hav. We're leaving it behind for our children." Hannah's grin spread into a beautiful smile. "You've promised me a baby, husband. And I mean to make you keep your promise once we get settled."

Hannah let go of Haverstagg and crossed the room, which had been filled with all the comforts they had collected over a lifetime together. The house was empty now. With such a long journey ahead of everyone Haverstagg had sold his two old stiddleback for a great profit. This, together with their life savings, was enough for them to start over in Subterranea and leave a fitting inheritance locked in the basement larder for the children that they hoped to conceive. Not everyone would be so lucky.

Hannah took an envelope from a small wooden box sitting on the mantle and returned. "This morning when you left, I wrote a letter to leave behind. I know that we'll both be back one day and that we'll still see our grandchildren raised here, but that's a long way away and just in case something happens to us I . . ."

Hannah opened the envelope and looked at Haverstagg to make sure she had his attention. He closed the window shutters and turned around, nodding to her.

"My babies," Hannah began reading. "The first snow of winter fell today, and your father and I set out for our new lives in Subterranea not knowing when we would be home again. We hope that we are with you now, maybe even with you and your own babies." Hannah looked up and smiled at the thought. "But if we are not, no matter what has happened, know that we both love you with all of our hearts. You have no doubt filled our lives with happiness and joy. It is with great pride that we leave to you the home where we fell in love and where we dreamed together of having children – of having you.

"The land and fields surrounding this house are deeded to your father. If you seek out the village reeve, he will be able to grant you legal ownership of our holdings. In the larder below you will find our worldly belongings including enough preserved seed to sow the hop yard twice over and provide for yourselves, and for our grandbabies."

Hannah looked up again before she continued. "A word of warning. We hired a wizard to protect your inheritance. The larder door will open only by the hand of our bloodline. Do not let anyone else touch it before you do.

"We hope that you find as much happiness here as we did. And if we are not here with you now, know that we are waiting together in the Light, and that we will surely see you again."

Hannah handed the letter to Haverstagg and wiped the tears off his cheeks. She waited for him to read the words himself and then kissed him, tugging on his stiffening lip with her own.

"You're a poet," Haverstagg whispered. "But we'll be reading this to them together when we come back." Haverstagg returned the letter to the envelope and put it back into the box, which he sat back on the mantle. "Come then, my love. The least painful wound is that which is quickly made."

Haverstagg hoisted the heavy pack and bags that had been left by the door onto his back and took a moment to mentally prepare for the daunting journey ahead.

Crowe

Before Crowe's unexpected arrival, Yssa had decided that she would remain in Ambermane for as much of the winter as she would live to see. She was simply too old to start over in Subterranea and too stubborn to make the long journey when so few cycles remained ahead of her anyway. Fate would cast her generation as the caretakers of the university until another generation returned to reclaim the grounds when the relentless winter had finally passed.

But now, Yssa questioned her future. Asher Crowe was alive! Not just alive, but alive and back from hiding. Yssa had dismissed her love for him a very long time ago, but the evening spent in his company had rekindled emotions in her that she had cast away as youthful optimism.

We can still have a life together! Yssa thought as she busied herself adjusting the settings of the giant telescope. It was as if a new future was now open to her and she couldn't help but feel once again like that young schoolgirl who had fallen madly in love with the dashing Warder Crowe.

Yssa's only dismay came in the form of a lithe figure that strolled casually into the darkened starchamber. Warder Mankoff, who was nearly the same age as Yssa, would also be remaining behind and the thought of having to endure the man's presence for the rest of her days was troublesome to say the least. She decided then and there that after she helped Crowe's granddaughter use the telescope, she would leave Ambermane behind to be with him.

"Already prowling around, are you?" Yssa called from inside the gearwork of the telescope. "I figured that I'd have at least a few weeks of peace before you began coming around here."

"Must you always be such a bitter woman?" Warder Mankoff asked as he ran a long finger along the side of a polished gear.

"Well, Mankoff, you know my reasons for hating you. For hating *all* of you."

"None of that matters now, Vand. The winter has finally come, and you and I are destined to find our ends together." Warder Mankoff tugged at his gray-streaked moustache, "more or less."

"Less would be preferable to me," Yssa said as she slid out from beneath the gearwork. "Really, Loris, I find your presence here offensive."

"Is that so?" Warder Mankoff asked, his eyes wide with surprise at such a venomous statement.

"Yes, that *is* so, and if you want to run back to Subterranea and tell the Lord Martyr that I said so, then so be it. I'd rather rot in a pit then spend my last days with your shadow looming over me."

"That would be preferable to my company?"

Yssa dusted off her breeches and paused to consider her reply, "definitely."

The sun had set by the time Crowe returned to the cottage. Before his feet hit the wood of the porch the cottage doors flew open and Claudia stormed outside. Crowe could tell by her deeply etched scowl and flushed skin that she was livid.

"How could you go back there?" Claudia shouted as Crowe crossed the porch. "You know that the warders would just love to get their wands on you!"

"I had to make some arrangements," Crowe answered, taking a seat on the porch swing and letting out a deep sigh. He looked at her with a straight face, though he knew it would take more than couth to calm her.

Odderly appeared at the doorway. "She's been all a fuss since I told her."

"And did you tell her *everything*?" Crowe asked. He knew that Claudia had a way of cutting through Odderly's defenses like butter.

"Not *this* time. Though I did finally have to stop talking to her all together."

Claudia spun around to glare at Odderly and then stepped in front the swing. "I just don't understand why you went back there, and why you hadn't told me that the serum wasn't working like it used to."

Crowe looked up and scowled at Odderly.

Told her that, did you?

"You told me that you would never keep secrets from me."

"And I won't," Crowe retorted. "In time you will know every secret that I've ever had to keep, but I can't just tell you them all at once and fill your head with needless worry." Crowe looked to Odderly. "We always knew that eventually I would start to develop a tolerance to the serum. We just didn't know that it would begin to happen after only thirty cycles."

"Well now *I* know, and I can help Odderly refine the formula. There must be other herbs . . ."

"No, Claudia, there isn't the time now. The first snow has come. I saw snowflakes falling as I rode out of Ambermane."

Odderly raised thick red brows. "Really?"

Crowe nodded. "Do not forget that I was born a winter child. I've seen firsthand what the World Above will be like next cycle, and there will be no more herbs. None at all, only dormant trees and ice."

"Then what are we to do? Just watch you die?" Claudia threw her hands up in frustration.

"No, not that," Crowe whispered. "I went to the university to speak with an old friend." He paused, thinking of Yssa. "More correctly," he started again, "I went to the observatory to see Vand Yssa."

"Yssa?" Claudia's anger melted and she blinked. "Yssa, as in . . ."

"Yes!" Crowe snapped, cutting off Claudia before she could say anything more. He hoped that his narrowed glare was enough to hold Claudia's tongue.

Crowe managed a glance at Odderly who leaned on the doorframe of the cottage, smiling. Odderly knew Yssa, of course, but Crowe had never confided in his friend that he and Yssa had once been lovers.

Odderly's face twisted up into a smile so big it almost reached ear to ear. Crowe did his best to conceal his embarrassment. As curt as he came across to most people, Crowe knew himself to be a sopping romantic. While he had told Claudia all about his courtship with Yssa, he could not help but wince at the thought of Odderly knowing those private details. Crowe had befriended Odderly when he was but a boy, but there were some things that a man simply did not discuss with other men.

"Shut up, you!"

Odderly laughed. "I didn't say anything!" He put his hands up defensively and backed into the cottage. A second later, Odderly's head peeked back out. "I'll just be downstairs if . . ." Crowe and Claudia both shot him an icy glare. Odderly left laughing heartily, and the door closed behind him.

"Odderly's work downstairs has something to do with the observatory, doesn't it?"

Crowe nodded.

"And the war scrolls he took from the library?"

Crowe nodded again. "You are becoming a fine young woman, Claudia, and I am immensely proud of you. But there is one thing that you must come to terms with before I die. Yssa has agreed to sneak us into the observatory tonight so that we might consult the most distant knowledge stars and find closure to the question that I fear is consuming you."

"Into the university?" Claudia's eyes glittered brightly. "All of us?"

"Yes. It will take all of us. Yssa to align the telescope, myself to evoke the farseeing magic, and you to provide the force of will and longing that we might find an answer in the stars."

"And Odderly?"

Crowe smiled. "Someone has to watch the door."

———•———

Hannah had been spared the burden of the load and was fortunate that Haverstagg was truly a bear of a man. He easily carried the loads of three average men, and he considered the weight he felt on his back to be only mildly uncomfortable.

The couple walked in silence for a while, following closely behind a caravan on route to the Undercity of Subterranea, the capitol of the Brylands. Directly ahead of them swayed the arses of two fat stiddleback. The animals formed a line two wide, and six head deep. When one of them defecated before his eyes and Haverstagg was forced to walk around the steaming pile of dung, he at last broke the silence.

"Disgusting animals, stiddleback," he said to his wife.

And truly, Haverstagg believed his own words. Shaped much like a fat, bloated stag with overly long front legs and a long curving neck, stiddleback had a massive hump positioned just over their front shoulders that served as a second stomach for storing chewed food and water.

In ideal conditions, the *stiddle* was full, hard and firm beneath the hairless black hide of the animal, but the animals that they had been following were not so well nourished and their stiddles *whooshed*, *swashed*, and *gurgled* audibly with every step.

"Yes, but in another two days you'll be wishing that you hadn't sold the old mares that we had. You'll be wishing that they were carrying that load on your back," Hannah said.

"No, no, that wouldn't do. We might never be returning to Barnwall, but one day, after we've passed on, our daughter will be claiming our home there. It wouldn't do for her to inherit an empty house. What we have left may not be much, but it will be a fitting enough dowry and get her through a season or two. Better that we sold the beasts than everything else." Haverstagg adjusted the weight of the pack and intentionally looked away from his wife as he let his words sink in. He smiled at her silence and rambled on. "Besides, demand is high, and they sold for a lot more than they were worth."

Hannah stopped dead in her tracks. She wiped snowflakes off her face and stared at Haverstagg. People moved around them, and the line of stiddleback gained some distance.

"A daughter?" she questioned.

"Aye."

Haverstagg started walking again and Hannah moved to keep up with him.

"You'd not want our first born to be a boy? You'd not want to have a son?"

"Both, aye. Maybe even a bunch of both. As many as we can afford to keep, but I was thinking a daughter first, as heir. A family needs a woman to hold it together and keep everyone's heads on straight," Haverstagg said in a calm tone.

"A bunch of both?" Hannah said through smiling lips.

"Aye, it is what you've always wanted, is it not?"

"Aye, but you always said that we'd not be able to afford a single child without having to turn them out to help in the fields, and here you are with all this talk of having a bunch of them."

"Well, things are going to be different now I reckon, when we arrive in Subterranea. We may not be able to bring the farm with us, but industry is different in the World Below. A man would be a fool not to choose me to work the mines and tunnels down there. I'll put my back and arms behind a pickaxe and bring home more than enough money to maintain a nice home for you to chase around a bunch of babies."

Haverstagg had to try hard to keep his usual stoic expression as he looked down to his wife. He knew that she had been filled with anxiety about the change of seasons, and while they had talked a lot about what life would be like in the undercity they had not often spoke about children.

Hannah was virtually aglow by the prospect of starting a family, and it made Haverstagg feel good to know that his hard work these past cycles was paying off. It would not be long before they were reestablished in the undercity. Working the mines would be back breaking work, no doubt, and dangerous in its own right, but the subterranean miners were paid well.

———•———

They moved swiftly down the arched hallways of the university. Each of the three had much to lose should they be found here. For Crowe, the consequences were obvious. There was not a warder in the Brylands who would not jump at the chance to gain fame by killing him. For Odderly, the punishment would be only slightly less severe. But for Claudia, being caught now would mean that she would never learn the truth about her father.

Getting inside the university had been simple enough, but always, they were the ones walking against the crowd. While a few of the older masters would remain behind, the state of affairs on the university grounds much resembled the happenings of the township itself; people were packing their things and departing. It was only the general pervading sense of chaos that made Claudia feel that they might just accomplish what they had come here to do without any trouble.

And then it happened. Claudia saw a group of warders walking directly toward the three of them, and the warder's faces were red and furious.

"Just keep walking," Odderly's muttered to Claudia.

Ten paces ahead of them the warders ducked into an open doorway and began shouting at someone inside. Relief surged through Claudia's veins, bringing a sudden chill.

"What is that all about?" Claudia whispered to Odderly after the threesome passed by the room.

"Whatever it is, it has nothing to do with us. And if they are busy back there then that is good for us. Warder Mankoff was with them, and that is truly a stroke of luck for he is the most troublesome man that we'll find here."

They quickened their pace and rounded another corner. As they did, Crowe bumped into a young student and sent the boy's armload of books toppling to the floor. In an attempt to avoid suspicion Crowe crouched down and helped the boy pick up his books. There was a moment when the two looked up to each other, and despite Crowe's raised hood, he locked eyes with the boy.

"I'm sorry," said the young mage. "I couldn't' see where I was going. I'm supposed to return these books to the library before I pack the rest of my things."

"No worries," Crowe said kindly, "and no harm done. Run along now."

The encounter lasted for only a moment, but as they continued to walk through the magically lit halls Claudia found a new level of fear rising inside her. She prayed silently that her grandfather had not been recognized.

A few minutes later the trio passed through the inner doors of the building and stepped out into the leafy courtyard. It was twilight now but rising taller than the trees and any of the surrounding buildings Claudia could make out the shape of the observatory tower across the river.

"Is that it?" she asked, looking up at the tower.

"Yes," Crowe answered.

As they walked, another building off to the south caught Claudia's eye because so many people were gathered around it. "What is that over there?"

"That's the Inquata Building," Odderly answered. "Do not look upon it."

Crowe touched Claudia's shoulder and whispered in her ear. "That is where they train warders to hunt down wizards that have gone bad."

Claudia looked again at the small fortress-like building with unease rising in her stomach, and then she quickly looked away. *There must be more than fifty warders outside.*

Chapter 5

Vand Yssa looked nothing like what Claudia imagined she would look like; the obvious had escaped her. Her grandfather had often described Yssa to her, but the descriptions of the vivacious young strawberry-haired woman were now fifty cycles old. Yssa was now gray-haired, bone thin, and nothing like the images that had been swirling in Claudia's mind.

For all the knowledge Claudia had of people throughout history, she had spent surprisingly little time around real people. Well, anyone other than Odderly and her grandfather. It took her by surprise just how old and withered someone could become without the benefit of regular magical anti-aging.

"I'm so pleased to meet you, Claudia," Yssa said as she let them all into the tower. "Asher has told me a lot about you, and I hope that I can be of some help tonight."

With that, Yssa nodded in greeting to Odderly and raised her wand to the door. *"Magus fastoon!"*

The wooden door shimmered only slightly. Claudia recognized the spell. It was common for wizard locks to be placed on doors that the evoking wizard did not want to have opened.

It was tedious, the walk up the spiraling steps inside the tower, and Yssa had to stop twice to catch her breath before reaching a landing where she instructed Odderly to keep watch on the bridge through a window cut in the stone. When they finally reached the top of the stairs

Yssa led Claudia and Crowe into the darkened observatory chamber. She raised her wand a second time and there was a bright flash of light as brilliantly glowing sparks flared into burning globes and streaked up to the top of the starchamber where each split into two, and those in turn split into four, then eight, and so on until the ceiling of the observatory recreated the stars and moons in the sky outside.

When Claudia looked back to Yssa, she was gone, having already moved toward the telescope. Yssa climbed the ladders to the observation platform with surprising skill. She began adjusting dials and levers. The coal ovens flared to life, steam escaped vents along the steam chambers, and slowly, the colossal telescope began to turn and rise toward the ceiling. When it came close to the top of the starchamber, the roof itself split open and the telescope extended out into the cool night air.

Not far away, her grandfather was busy using colored sand to create a circle of power on the floor in the center of the starchamber. Claudia's heart began to race, but her fear subsided. For a moment she forgot that she was on forbidden ground. She forgot about the warders outside, gathered just across the river. She forgot about the student that her grandfather had bumped into in the hall, and she even forgot about her grandfather's growing tolerance for his life-sustaining serum.

When tonight is through, Claudia thought, *I'll finally know the truth. But what then? What if my father is truly dead? And what if Grandfather dies? Will Odderly stay with me or will he go on to Subterranea like everyone else? Will I be left all alone?*

It all began to make her queasy. Her fear returned unbridled, and Claudia began to wonder if maybe they should not have come here after all.

Warders Mankoff, Solias, and Abrashi, all powerful wizards in their own right, had spent far too long trying to explain to Master Epsnill that he could not take his entire classroom or personal library with him when his caravan left for Subterranea.

"It will all be here, exactly as you leave it, when you return in the spring," Warder Mankoff argued.

"I'll be sixty-four cycles in the spring," Master Epsnill protested, "and I'll need all of this if I am to teach in the undercity!"

"I assure you, Master Epsnill," Warder Abrashi said, "that the library at Fire Falls is well stocked. We have everything there that you will need. You may take your personal things, and if there are any books that you truly prize you may take those as well, but . . ."

"But I *prize* my entire library!"

Warder Mankoff was growing angry. He was not accustomed to people arguing with him, and he had thus far faced almost nothing else this day. He turned his head as a young student sheepishly entered the classroom.

"Warder Mankoff," the boy said meekly. "Might I have a word when you have a moment?"

"Allus," Warder Mankoff said to Warder Solias. "Will you please *help* Master Epsnill pack a single crate and escort him to his caravan." With that, Warder Mankoff turned away from the argument and strode over to the boy.

"I'm very sorry to bother you, Warder Mankoff, Sir," the boy whispered.

Warder Mankoff crouched down by the young student, whispering into his ear "No, believe me lad, you are rescuing me, and it's a rescue that I'll not soon forget!" He winked at the boy. "Now what can I do for you?"

Claudia was unprepared for what she saw when she put her eyes up to the eyepiece of Yssa's telescope. The beauty of the colorful moons in the starry night sky had always awed Claudia, but it was not a moon, nor stars, that she saw in the telescope. Instead, her view was of a very distant, but beautiful cloud of blue, yellow, and green gas.

"I don't know what to say, Yssa, this is so beautiful," Claudia managed. "What is this that I'm looking at?"

Yssa moved up beside the girl and spoke softly. "It's not what you are seeing that is important, but what yet remains to be seen. That cloud is a distant galaxy, one that neighbors our own, and holds billions of stars surrounded by billions of worlds. Some, I presume, are much like our own world, but others are most likely quite different."

Crowe began climbing up the extended ladders to the observation platform. When he arrived, he too was out of breath. He crouched next to Claudia and pulled a small glass dish out of his cloak. He unscrewed the lid and placed the dish on Claudia's leg.

"Be still now," Crowe said to her.

Claudia recognized the dish, as she had seen Odderly filling it with the salamander eyes the day before.

"This will feel a bit odd, and it might even be a tad painful, but you'll get used to it quickly," Crowe said as he sprinkled salts, sulfur, and a mixture of herbs onto the eyes and began to mash them into a thick paste with his finger. "Think of that cloud in the telescope as a scrying bowl, just like any other that you would use to evoke clairvoyance."

Claudia nodded.

"Astromancy is different than other forms of magic, and you won't be able to make out much of what you are seeing, but I have enspelled the sands on the floor to help us see what you see. Just keep your focus on your father and consult the stars that you will see in that cloud just as you would the stars around our own world to learn someone's fortune. Do you understand?"

"I think so," Claudia said, though the concept was much for her to take in.

Yssa bent down and whispered in her ear "Just trust the magic, child. When you feel the magic in your eyes, look through the lens and think about your father. Ask yourself where he is, and the magic will do the rest."

"Is that right?" Claudia asked her grandfather.

Crowe nodded. "Are you ready?"

"Are you certain that it was him?" Warder Mankoff asked the young student.

"Quite certain," said the boy. He opened a thick leather-bound book that he carried to a chapter about Asher Crowe. The drawing of Crowe was old but made with a skilled hand. "This is the man that I passed in the hall. Master Toom had us write a parchment on him last cycle."

"And you are certain that he was walking with Master Flack? Herb Master Odderly Flack?"

"Yes Sir, and a young girl, I think. I presumed her to be a student being that she was with Master Flack, but she had her hood drawn. I only saw Asher Crowe's face because he helped me pick up my books when I dropped them."

Claudia almost squealed when her grandfather smeared the paste of salamander eyes into her own. It burned painfully, but she balled up her hands and dug her fingernails into the palms of her hands to stave off the pain. It was worth any amount of pain to take this chance and prove once and for all that her father had survived the Battle of Ambly.

"Don't blink it out!" Crowe snapped.

Crowe raised his long, skinny wooden wand to Claudia's face and uttered, *"occulossa farvissa!"*

A bright flash erupted in front of Claudia's face and the mild burning in her eyes became an intense searing pain. But before she could even scream the pain was gone and she became disoriented as everything around her went completely out of focus.

She saw the blurry shape of her grandfather, but as she tried to focus on him, she saw his skin zoom into focus instead. She saw giant glistening bubbles of sweat, the massive holes of pores, and towers of coarse white hair. And then her vision sank into him, into muscle, into bone. Her sight then broke through him all together and she began to see the distant observatory wall in the same unearthly clarity.

"Look through the lens." It was Yssa's voice.

And so, Claudia did. But she could not begin to fathom the spatial distortion she saw through the lens. The telescope took her sight to the stars, and the magic pushed beyond that limit, into the distant galaxy. Stars rushed by in long streaks. Planets came into focus and then streamed by as a blur. Whole constellations transformed into solar systems, and then everything became a dizzying blur of space and time; millions of stars sailed by as each second passed.

Claudia began thinking of her father. She recalled childhood memories, and those inevitably cobbled the way to her dreams, her nightmares, and the memories of that horrible night.

Ambly was home to about one hundred families, and as the sun began to set over the small mining village Claudia watched a group of men emerge from the gem mine in which they had been digging. This was nothing new. Claudia was eight cycles of age, and as a young girl she would often wait for her father to step out of the mines from her favorite watching spot where a slanted rock lay against the trunk of a hundred-foot flowering pine.

It was a day like any other, but as the men came out, she noticed that they were not walking with their pickaxes slung over their shoulders as they always did. They were running. Some of them were covered in blood. Had there been an accident?

She saw her father emerge; his eyes went immediately to where he knew that she would be waiting. "Claudia!" *he shouted,* "come girl, hurry!"

"What is wrong papa?" *she asked?*

Her father threw down his pickaxe and scooped her up into his arms. He ran with her toward the village. People were coming out of their buildings, confused, and frightened by the shouts of the miners. She saw her grandfather. She was pushed into his arms.

"The garuk, they've chiseled into the mine!" *Her father told her grandfather.* "They . . ."

All eyes looked up to the ridge. The garuk in the mine were not all that had come. A dark line of savages crested the ridge. Ambly was surrounded on three sides, and a steady stream of savages had begun pouring out of the mine. People were shouting. The men were gathering weapons and saddling stiddleback, the women were running south with their children in their arms.

"Take her and go, Asher, take the road through the Pennorra Reaches, the garuk will be afraid to go there."

Someone had brought her father a sword and was climbing atop a stiddleback.

"The euum giants are superstitious, show them any magic and they'll not bother you. Take Claudia and as many of the village folk as will follow you. Go!"

Her grandfather put a hand on her father's shoulder. "You do not have to do this, Horace, I can get us all safely through the Reaches."

"Not with the garuk giving chase. Just go, make for Lursh. If I don't meet you there or on the road in a ten-day, raise Claudia as if she was your own. I've never believed what they say about you, Asher, you are a good man, and you will raise Claudia to be a good woman."

Her father grabbed them both in a powerful hug and then forced himself to pull away. He raised a foot into the stirrup of the stiddleback that had been brought to him and hoisted himself up to the saddle. He spurred the beast and charged off toward the garuk that were coming from the mine.

Her grandfather mounted another stiddleback and held Claudia close to his chest as he kicked the beast forward.

It was not until they were atop a hill on the south side of the village that her grandfather turned his stiddleback and Claudia was able to look back upon Ambly for the last time. As she did, she saw somehow that her father was surrounded by garuk, spurring his stiddleback through them and slashing down at each one he passed, killing more than he left standing.

A spear caught his stiddleback in the chest; it reared up and twisted as one of its rear legs was cut out from under it. The beast fell and her father tumbled from the saddle. Her father rolled away and came up to his feet, bringing down another three garuk as he did so.

His sword flashed this way and that, and each time it did a garuk fell and blood sprayed across the battlefield that was, only minutes before, Claudia's home village.

He was surrounded, the garuk cautiously approaching, for her father would cut down any who came within the reach of his sword. But then an older, hunchbacked garuk stepped forward from the flames that had begun to consume the village. He was different than the others, he wore lizard skins around his neck and the lesser garuk parted to allow him through.

Her father took on a defensive stance and readied his blade.

But it was not a sword or spear that the garuk shaman raised, it was a staff crafted of a long bone and decorated with small humanoid skulls. With a thrust of the staff a shower of sparking white energy swept over her father. He froze momentarily before his knees buckled and he sagged to the ground. His shoulders slumped and the tip of his blade hit the earth before him. He staggered, and then he fell to the ground in an unnatural slumber.

The garuk shaman said something to the others, pointing at her father with the staff of bones. The others nodded, and two of them took her father and bound him with strips of leather.

The Battle of Ambly raged on, and in its wake, there was little left but ruin. The bodies of those who had fought against the savage raiders were scattered among the bodies of the garuk they had slain.

Claudia could see several garuk following the shaman on foot back up to the eastern ridge. Her father was alive, taken captive. He was forced forward by spear point, encircled by more than a hundred surviving garuk. As the only survivor taken prisoner by the garuk, Horace Kobb was led for miles across the rocky terrain, until the garuk came at last to a massive ravine so deep that everything in its depths was lost to utter blackness.

Claudia felt both Yssa's and her grandfather's hands on her, helping her up and trying to steady her. She didn't remember it, but she must have fallen. Her eyes burned and instinctively she wiped the salamander paste out of them.

"He's alive," she said flatly.

Though her eyes were swollen and blurry, Claudia could make out the shape of her grandfather. He was nodding.

"I believe you, child," he said softly, patting her hand.

When her vision returned her grandfather helped her climb back down the ladders and took her to the circle of power he had drawn with the sand. The arcane symbols were gone, replaced by a three-dimensional formation in the sand that resembled a sculpture that might otherwise have been made on a sandy riverbank.

Claudia had seen the image it represented before, though her memory of the vision was beginning to get fuzzy already. The sand had formed craggy mountains, a broad glacier, and a seemingly endless rift in the ground that seemed to somehow pierce the floor upon which the sand sculpture stood.

It was a magically crafted birds-eye view of the Black Rift of Roak's Backbone, the only place so untouched by the sun that ice could be found year-round, even during the burning twenty-five-cycle season of summer. It was Claudia's map of where she could find her father.

Chapter 6

Odderly remembered standing at this same window once before, during the mutiny of Asher Crowe. Astromancy was a new magical art at that time, and through the distant knowledge stars Crowe had learned a terrible secret; Headmaster Collinhodge, the highest ranking official of the university and a close friend of the Lord Martyr himself, was not Headmaster Collinhodge at all.

There was a time, many generations ago, before written history, or the Lord Martyrs, or the Brylands themselves, that the Roak, the Creator God, walked among the mortals of the World Above. He was a benevolent god who cared for and trusted the people he had created, but not all his creations returned Roak's love.

It was the Ambra, people of the distant southwest that betrayed Roak and slew their creator thinking that they were equal to their god. Atop the Lone Mountain, as Roak lay dying, he cursed the Ambra. At the moment of his death Roak's anger caused the Lone Mountain to explode and magma rolled down the mountainside. His wrath tore the Ambra's land away from the mainland, and he raised the sea around the new island. Roak burned and drowned the Ambra for their treachery, and their spirits were cursed to sleep in Shadow and suffer eternal agony while watching the people of other lands enjoy life that the Ambra would never taste again.

In time, however, Roak's curse began to fade. The people of other lands scarcely remembered Roak or realized why the high mountains of the World Above bore his name. Places such as Roak's Backbone, Roak's Elbow, and Roak's Grave. They were only names, names common to a godless, atheist people.

The *shades* that remained of the Ambra began to grow stronger and rebel against the curse of the creator god. A few, a very few, were able to resist the old binding magic and as spirit, they forced their way into mortal bodies. This act of possession gave birth to *demons*, mortal men inhabited by the shades of the Ambra.

It was such a shade that Asher Crowe had learned possessed the Headmaster of Ambermane University. Crowe was a young warder at that time, but the act of exorcism was strictly forbidden.

Crowe had confided his discovery in Odderly, who was then just a lowly third cycle student gifted in alchemy. Together they had made the long journey to Subterranea to share the dark discovery with the High Warders Council. But the High Warders scoffed at Asher Crowe and said that he was foolish and paranoid to think such things. After all, it was impossible for a man of Headmaster Collinhodge's power and reputation to be dominated by spirit, and so Crowe and Odderly had returned to Ambermane, and the observatory to consult the distant knowledge stars a second time. This time though, Crowe asked the stars to show him a way to destroy or bind an Ambraic spirit, for Crowe could not sit idle while a demon walked the university in mortal guise.

It was on that night that Odderly had stood at this same window, keeping a watch on the Inquata Building across the river. When they left the observatory tower Crowe and Odderly parted ways. Odderly knew that Crowe intended to kill the headmaster that night, and he later learned that Crowe had been successful. The headmaster's body was found the next morning, and the heart had been cut from it.

Remembering this, Odderly understood at once what was happening when he saw magical lights begin to be conjured outside of the Inquata Building. The boy in the hall, Odderly realized, had indeed recognized Asher Crowe.

The warders were coming.

Odderly counted more than fifty glowing lights before he turned and ran up the stairs to warn Crowe that the warders were coming to avenge the murder of Headmaster Collinhodge.

Yssa was the first to see Odderly come running into the dimly illuminated starchamber for her eyes were the most accustomed the dim light cast by the glowing orbs.

"Asher!" Odderly shouted, "the warders are on their way!"

"How many?" Crowe asked.

Odderly paused, no doubt thinking of how to put it. "All of them, I think."

There were no windows at the top of the observatory tower, and no way out save for the single door at the bottom of the stairs. Claudia had overcome her confusion and now regarded Odderly with an expression that betrayed the fear in her heart. She finally knew beyond all doubt that her father was alive, and now the warders were coming to kill her grandfather, and likely her as well.

"What do we do?" she asked, her voice cracking.

There was a loud crashing noise at the bottom of the tower. The warders were bombarding Yssa's wizard lock with magic. Wizard lock or no, few spells could hold up to the combined magical battering of a handful of warders, and Odderly had said that *all* of them had come.

A moment later an explosion rocked the tower.

"They're on their way up here," Yssa stated. She quickly began to recalibrate the telescope to conceal her previous activities.

Crowe looked thoughtful. "Yssa, do you remember the place by Lake Almswell where we first kissed?"

Claudia and Odderly looked at them.

"Yes," Yssa said thoughtfully.

"When you are able, go there and pry up the flat rock that we used to sit on together. I've left something there for you."

"You're *not* leaving me again, Asher Cr . . ."

Crowe raised his wand suddenly, *"spirro sudaban!"*

A spiraling line of green energy swirled out from the tip of Crowe's wand and cocooned Yssa. She did not even have time to finish her sentence before the energy whisked away and she collapsed to the ground rendered unconscious.

"Grandfather!" Claudia screamed!

Shadows blocked the light coming up from the stairs and then magical light washed over the room.

The warders had arrived.

One thrust a staff to the sky and called out the words of a spell. A ball of fire sparked into flame and streaked up to the center of the starchamber where it burned like a tiny stationary sun, dispelling all shadows.

Odderly drew a long iron rod from his back and mumbled something too quietly for Claudia to hear.

"I'm very disappointed in your judgment, Master Flack," Warder Mankoff said from his position at the head of the assembled mob. "And your taste in friends."

Perhaps Warder Mankoff had expected to conversate before securing the glory of having killed Asher Crowe and those he traveled with, but Odderly was less a man of words than action. He thrust his rod toward the group and a wet, *gloop* sounded across the observatory chamber.

A sickly green blob of liquid soared across the chamber, and while Warder Mankoff raised his wand with ample time to conjure a magical shield to protect him, the acid hit it, ate through, and showered the warder's face and body. Steaming and screaming in agony, he dropped to the ground.

Odderly, Claudia knew, was never one to limit himself to standard magic. If it was acid he conjured, it would be acid capable of chewing through any magical shield that was likely to be raised in defense. The warder had underestimated Odderly's cunning, and it had cost him dearly. The others though, were not likely to make the same mistake. They would be more cautious. Claudia and her friends were about to run out of time.

Dozens of wands, rods, and staves were raised as each of the warders targeted Crowe, Odderly, and Claudia. Dozens of spells were unleashed at once; bright lines of energy, flaming balls of pitch, clouds of deadly gas. Claudia's skin felt like gooseflesh as her short life flashed before her eyes.

But the contrails of magic did not reach them.

Crowe raised his own wand and uttered a single word of recall. Claudia felt herself being pulled in every direction at once. There was a dizzying blur not unlike that of having viewed the star field through the farseeing spell. And then she was outside, standing by the bridge that led to the observatory.

"What just happened?" Claudia asked. She turned around quickly, surveying her surroundings.

Odderly began to laugh. "You saw this coming?"

Crowe smiled. "I thought that if things didn't go well, it would sure save Yssa a lot of trouble this time around."

"Roak's hand!" Claudia cursed, "what about Yssa?" She spun around and looked up to the observatory tower. "You put her to sleep!"

"Actually, I made her dizzy, so much so that her mind couldn't rationalize the vertigo. But the effect is the same. Don't worry about her. I couldn't let her get into trouble again on my behalf. She's sleeping now, and she'll be fine by sunrise." Crowe turned away from the observatory tower and began to walk away. "She'll play along and pretend that we got into the observatory by ourselves and that I enspelled her. To listen to Yssa talk, I'm quite a dangerous man and easily capable of overwhelming one tired old lady." When Claudia and Odderly didn't immediately follow his lead, Crowe turned back and looked into Claudia's eyes. "It won't be long before they come looking for us."

"What do you suggest?" Warder Abrashi asked Warder Solias as they squatted next to the sculpture rent of colored sand.

Unlike his apprentice, Warder Solias was a grave, easily angered man, and his face was flush red with outrage at having lost his quarry so quickly. He was reputedly one of the best wizard hunters to have ever lived, and tonight had played out in such a way as to leave a good friend injured, a dangerous criminal on the loose, and a prisoner who was clearly lying about the whole thing.

"It is unfortunate that while Warder Mankoff will be healed, he will be left horribly disfigured. There is little that even magical healing can do for wounds as vicious as those made by acid," Warder Solias said as he looked back to the crowd of wizards tending to Warder Mankoff. "We can assume that Asher Crowe and Master Flack came here searching for something."

Warder Solias regarded the image rent of sand on the floor. "And that they have learned that what they seek lies in the World Below. If the subject of their search is important enough that Crowe would come here, right under our noses, then we would do well to keep them from ever entering the Black Rift."

Warder Abrashi nodded.

"They are on their way to the Black Rift, even now," Warder Solias added, "as certainly as stiddleback are born standing up. We have time. It is a trip they cannot make by magic alone, and the way to the Black Rift is treacherous, especially for a man who must avoid being seen."

"Then we'll wait for Warder Mankoff to recover, so that he may join us on the hunt?" Warder Abrashi asked his master.

"No. Let Loris follow when he is able. While it is most likely that we will catch up to them long before they reach the Black Rift, we must be prepared to deal with them if they do make it into the World Below. We will need a guide, someone who has been down into the rift before."

"That's impossible, Master. Nobody ventures into the rift."

"A man would have to be insane to do so, yes. But I know of such men. Have what we will need assembled and packed on stiddleback by morning. We'll be going to Lursh."

Warder Abrashi stood and looked at his master as if it was he who had gone mad. "Lursh? We'll not be well received. Reeve Boarwind . . ."

"Is an arrogant swine fitting of his namesake," Warder Solias interrupted. With a swipe of his hand, he destroyed the magically created sand sculpture and got up to his feet. "Holes such as Lursh draw men of many talents, and not all have always been on the right side of the law. You will learn, my young apprentice, that all men have their uses."

"Yes, Master."

"Good, then have our stiddleback ready."

"And what about her?" Warder Abrashi turned his gaze to Yssa who was awake now, sitting on the floor by the coal ovens.

"Until we know whether or not she is in league with Asher Crowe have her locked away in the gaol."

"You can't do that!" Yssa protested. "I am a master here! You can't lock me away like some kind of outlaw!"

"You are mistaken Mistress Yssa. A man who you may very well have aided has seriously injured a warder. I have more than enough cause to detain you, and I am quite sure that should the need arise I have sixty witnesses here who will testify to the Lord Martyr that it was your wand and your spell that struck Warder Mankoff. After all, we all know you have no love of the man."

Warder Solias' mouth turned up at the corners, twisting into a wicked grin. "Collect Mistress Yssa's wand, Warder Abrashi, and have her taken to the Inquata gaol. Make sure that you write in the ledger that she is only to be released per my order. That way, if trouble befalls us in the pursuit of Asher Crowe, the High Warders will be able to identify the corpse in the gaol when they return in the spring."

Yssa stiffened.

"This is your one chance, Mistress Yssa, to speak the truth."

Yssa remained silent.

"Very well," Warder Solias said coldly. "Take her away."

Warder Abrashi snatched Yssa's wand from her belt and tucked it into his own. As Yssa rose he took her by one arm and escorted her toward the stairs.

"And Warder Abrashi, make sure that you issue a statement that Asher Crowe has been seen here and attempted to take the life of Warder Mankoff. I hereby place a bounty of one hundred golden flays on his head, and twenty on the heads of any that he travels with or who aid him in any way."

"You can't do that," Yssa said again. "Asher Crowe is one thing, but he is traveling with his granddaughter. She is just a child; she has nothing to do with Asher's past!"

Warder Solias regarded Yssa for a long moment before smiling victoriously. "Asher Crowe has a granddaughter?"

Chapter 7

Opportunities such as this did not happen by accident. Not in the slave pens of a garuk stable. Kobb had awakened to find his head still spinning from *Enshalaan's* healing magic, but he noticed right away that he was surrounded by silence. There was a dangerous stillness in the air, and like he remembered from his former life in the World Above, still and quiet meant that there was danger nearby.

When he sat up, he noticed that the door to his pen was ajar. Atta would never allow this to happen.

Where are the guards?

At all times, night and day, at least one garuk guard could be found sitting across the cavern at the stone slab where the savages played stones. They were gone.

Kobb stood and walked to the gate of his pen. To step outside without direction would mean a terrible beating. Kobb was used to beatings, but he was also used to *Enshalaan* restoring his health when the beating had ended. And so, Kobb waited at the open gate as several minutes passed, but nobody came. And then he detected a peculiar scent in the air.

Blood.

They are all dead.

Kobb stood thinking. It was the only logical answer. And that answer yielded others. Pulgra was here, waiting for him. Why else would his slave pen be left open, but Kobb himself be allowed to live?

Any garuk stable master had more enemies than they could count. Violence was the garuk way of life. But this happening now, with Pulgra here, it could not be a coincidence.

Kobb ventured out on steady legs. Unlike the day of the fight before, he felt strong, sure-footed, almost as if he were a much younger man with the strength and energy of youth. He would see no fatigue today, and beyond the rest he had already taken, he would need no sleep. It was, Kobb began to think, an opportunity unlike any he had ever had before.

Pulgra was waiting, surely, but Pulgra could be killed. Compared to euum giants, guskar, and the other foul things he had faced in the fighting pit, what danger could a fat, bloated stable master pose to a seasoned fighter like Kobb?

No. For Pulgra to have moved against Atta so openly, he must be quite confident that all traces of Atta and her stable can be destroyed this day.

There was danger still; Kobb could feel it inside of him. He could escape, it would be possible, but Kobb could not do it alone.

Enshalaan. I need you, my friend.

Kobb would not leave the dagger behind. *Enshalaan* was more than just an inanimate object, and it was not just because Kobb could feel a hidden sentience in the magical blade. The dagger, and the bound demon, they had long since become a part of Kobb's own identity. They had drawn blood and taken lives together too many times over the last six cycles. Kobb could not hope to explain it, but somehow, he and the dagger had bonded.

If Pulgra was waiting here somewhere, baiting him, then Kobb would take the bait and face the danger head on. But he would not face the trap alone.

There was a time not long after Atta acquired Kobb that he had been taken from his pen in the middle of the night to pleasure his new owner. It was the only time that Kobb had seen more of the cavern complex than he could normally see from the vantage point of his pen or the arena, and as such, Kobb had committed every detail of that night to memory.

In Atta's office cave he had seen the box of bones where *Enshalaan* was kept. *Enshalaan* would be there now, waiting for him. And if Atta had been killed, the box would be unguarded.

Unless Pulgra has the box. The thought unnerved him. *No. Atta would not have left her magical trophy in plain sight. Not with Pulgra's stable here. Enshalaan would be hidden.*

But Kobb was confident that the dagger would reach out to him if it sensed him nearby. It was worth the risk.

Kobb made his way out of the cave where his pen isolated him, but not before prying a burning torch from a sconce on the cavern wall. When he rounded the first corner, his suspicions were confirmed. Sprawled out on the ground before the pens of the common slaves were two of Atta's guards.

Kobb approached the bodies. Though massive, the garuk had been killed quickly, and violently, as had the slaves that they were guarding. The bars on the pens had been bent apart, and the slaves inside slaughtered like the trapped animals they were. The dead garuk too had been slaughtered by whatever massive beast was now loose in the cavern complex. One of their heads looked to have been bitten off, and it was nowhere to be found.

Whatever had killed the guards had left their armor and weapons behind. From the bodies Kobb took a pair of breeches, boots, and a leather belt. The boots and clothing were too large for him, but no matter, each could be drawn tight enough about him to be of use. To the belt he affixed both of the guard's swords. The armor was ripped apart, making it useless even if Kobb had been able to fit into it.

Kobb also found a ring of keys. He did not know whether they opened only the slave pens found here, or if they might open other doors in the stable, but he felt that it would be better to have them than to not.

Out of the corner of his eye Kobb noticed a fleeting movement within a shadowy depression along the wall opposite the slave pens. In a single sudden movement, he drew one of the short-bladed swords and sent it flying pommel over tip for the shadow. There was a chirp of metal striking metal, and then a dull thud. His aim had been true, a garuk hand fell out of the shadow releasing a spear that it had been holding.

Kobb grabbed hold of his torch and ran to the fallen garuk. It was a huge male that had been hiding in a dark patch along the roughly hewn cavern wall. Kobb quickly examined the body lifting the arm and turning it over so he could see the back of the dead garuk's hand; it bore a branded scar that Kobb recognized as Pulgra's mark.

Kobb pried the short-bladed sword out of the dead garuk's chest and returned it to his scabbard and added the garuk's own sword to his belt as well. As he searched the body for anything else that might prove useful a thought nagged him.

Why play this game, Pulgra?

"I'm being herded," Kobb said aloud to himself, realizing that Pulgra wanted Kobb to face whatever new champion the stable master had dug out of the darkness of the World Below. Pulgra wanted to watch Kobb die in combat.

Yssa found the gaol utterly disgusting. She had been thrown in a small room just barely wide enough to lie down in to sleep. In the center of the cell, making that impossible, was a wide privy hole that reeked of urine and feces. It was hard for her to imagine a worse place. The only light came from a little slat in the iron door, and this was barely bright enough to illuminate the rats that shared the gaol cell with her.

With her back to the corner Yssa tried to ignore the rough texture of the stone as it jabbed through her roshea wool shirt. A chill was already setting into her old bones.

"If Warder Solias wants to kill me, he'll not have long to wait!" Yssa shouted, though she did not know if anyone was outside of the gaol cell to hear. "I don't do well with the cold; my breath is already getting heavy!"

Silence was the only reply.

"So much for saving me from getting into trouble this time, Asher Crowe. You should have taken me with you. I would have gone with you. I would have gone the first time you left when we might have had something of a life together, and I would still have gone with you now,"

Yssa lamented. "You shouldn't have left me behind, you old coot."

A shadow moved over the slat, blocking the light. Yssa thought at first that perhaps Warder Solias had come to set her free, or maybe that Warder Mankoff had recovered and come to kill her. But it was just a warden's son bringing her some bread and a cup of water to drink. These Yssa took as they were pushed through the slat in the door.

"What is your name boy?" Yssa asked the young child.

"I'm not supposed ta talk ta the prisoners," the boy said sheepishly.

"Told you that, have they?"

The shadow on the other side of the door shifted, and Yssa could tell that the boy was nodding.

"And why is that?" Yssa asked, taking a sip of the water.

"Because you're a prisoner, and my pa is the gaol warden, and he says that I'm not supposed to talk ta the prisoners."

"Are you allowed to talk to the university masters?"

"Yes," the boy said.

"Well then you can talk to me. I'm Mistress Vand Yssa, I teach up in the observatory. You may even have seen me before."

"You're Mistress Yssa?" the boy asked.

"That's right."

"Then why are you in there, shouldn't you be at ta observatory?"

"I should be, yes. There's been a terrible mistake, and I need you to help me."

"What kind of mistake?" the boy asked.

"Do you know who Warder Mankoff is?"

"Yes. He's not very nice."

Yssa chuckled. "No, he's not very nice. But he got hurt tonight, he got hurt really bad."

"Did he go ta the Light?" asked the boy.

"No, no he didn't go to the Light."

"That's too bad."

"Too bad?" Yssa asked through a grin.

"Yes. I don't like Warder Mankoff. He's always mean to me, and he's mean ta my father."

"Well, he's mean to me too," Yssa said. "Have you ever wanted to do something mean back to Warder Mankoff?"

"Well, I didn't say that," the boy protested, the tone of his voice changing to reflect his fear of speaking out against any of the warders.

"No, no, of course you didn't. But if you've ever wanted to do something mean back to Warder Mankoff, then I know something that you could do that would get him back for every mean thing he's ever done to you and your pa."

"Really? What's that?" the boys' voice changed to a mischievous whisper.

"Well, when Warder Mankoff had me locked in here, they took my wand from me. If you were to bring me my wand, I would be able to get out of here, and that would get Warder Mankoff back for every mean thing he's ever done to you and your pa."

"My pa would kill me if I let a prisoner out!"

"Well, that's just the thing," Yssa said in her most charming voice, "you *wouldn't* be letting me out. I'd get out on my own. And nobody would ever have to know that you gave me my wand. They would all think that I summoned it to myself somehow, and they wouldn't blame you or your pa, but you would be able to get even with Warder Mankoff just the same."

"I don't know," the boy said. "I'll have to think about it."

Yssa mouthed a curse as she heard the boy's footsteps walking away from the gaol cell.

───•───

Jacob returned to his duties and began washing the dishes while he waited for his father to come back. Everything that Mistress Yssa had said made a lot of sense, but he thought that he should wait for his father and then tell him about what Mistress Yssa had asked him to do. That way, his father could decide to help her if he thought that giving her back her wand would be a good way to get even with Warder Mankoff.

He had just finished drying the last plate and returned it to the cupboard when a group of warders came walking into the kitchen.

"Boy!" one of them yelled. "Make me a plate to eat, it's been a long day."

"Aye," both of the others put in. "And prepare it quickly, we're heading to Lursh tomorrow at sunup and we need to get some rest."

"But I just finished doing my chores," the boy said meekly.

The three warders had taken seats at the table in the kitchen and they looked at each other with wide eyes, surprised that the boy had spoken back to them.

"P'raps you didn't 'ear what 'e said," one of the warder's said. "We be takin' a plate, an we be takin' it now. Make it up quickly er we'll tell yer pa that you've been slackin' again, and he'll tan yer 'ide right quick."

"But I haven't been slacking. I've done all my chores."

One of the warders reached down to his belt and withdrew his wand. He pointed it at the boy and whispered something and a pinpoint of bright energy flashed across the kitchen and struck the boy in the bottom of his breeches. Jacob yelped and patted his bottom, which smoked slightly.

"Put down your wand," the leader of the three said turning his attention to the warden's son. "You'll get us a plate now, won't you lad?"

Jacob nodded.

"I'm sorry," he said to the three warders. "Forgive me."

The warders shared a laugh and began to talk about Warder Mankoff and Asher Crowe while they waited for Jacob to fix them each a plate of food. When they ate, they made a point to smear gravy on the table and drop breadcrumbs on the floor knowing that the warden's boy would have to clean up after them.

Jacob took it all with a grain of salt. He was used to the warders being mean to him. They were all just like Warder Mankoff when it came down to it. They all thought themselves better than the wardens who, like the warders, were agents of the law, but unlike the warders were men-at-arms rather than men of magic. They were all mean to his father, and they were all mean to him.

When the warders left Jacob washed their dishes and wet a rag to clean up the mess they had made at the table. When he had finished that, he left the kitchen and walked down the long hall that he had seen Warder Abrashi in earlier that evening after he had brought Mistress Yssa to the gaol. In a room at the end of the hall Jacob found Yssa's wand lying on the desk beside his father's ledger.

"It will serve them all right," Jacob said aloud to himself as he wrapped his little fingers around Yssa's wand.

Kobb moved cautiously through the roughly hewn tunnels of Atta's cavern complex. He knew where each turn would take him, and as he drew closer to Atta's office, he began to grow more and more excited. It might have just been his imagination, but he thought that he could feel *Enshalaan* around every bend.

When he finally came to the door painted with Atta's brand, the door that he knew led into her office, Kobb paused and put his ear against the wood. Silence. He pushed the door open.

Atta's office was immaculately decorated with fine furs and animal hides. It was more or less a circular chamber where the naturally slanting floor of the cave had been carved away to make the floor relatively flat, but the stone underfoot could not be seen or felt for Atta had spread creb furs over every square inch of the surface. The heads belonging to the animals, massive and fearsome looking like a mix between a wolf and a bear, hung on the walls. There were more of them than Kobb cared to count and he paid them no attention.

Torches burned in niches in the walls, and there was a peculiar scent in the air that Kobb had not smelled when he was here the first time. It was reminiscent of flowers. Centered in the room was Atta's desk, if the massive stone slab that rested across two smaller slabs could be called such a thing. The desk was cluttered with parchments scrawled with garuk runes, but while Kobb was fluent in the garuk's spoken language, he could not read their writing.

The parchments were of little interest anyway, and what he had come here for was not directly visible. His pulse quickened.

The box, the box decorated with bones, *Enshalaan's* box . . . it was nowhere to be seen. Kobb saw no other way into or out of the office, so he hurried around the desk. *Enshalaan* was waiting for him here, he could *feel* it. Somehow the demon sensed Kobb's presence, his nearness, and Kobb could feel the blade beckoning him onward.

When Kobb stepped around the desk he caught a round, bulky shape out of the corner of his eye. He spun and prepared to jab the burning torch he carried into the hidden attacker, but as he did so he recognized it not as an attacker, but Atta's body. She lay lifeless on the floor behind her desk with the fletching of three arrows sticking out of her naked chest.

Pulgra had killed her, but he had done more than that. Atta's gray tooth, the one that always stuck out of her mouth at an awkward angle, had been pried out of her mouth. Blood ran down her cheek, and the blood was still wet. Her killer had been here no more than a few minutes ahead of him.

As Kobb stepped over Atta's body intending to search the area around her desk, he stopped suddenly. It was all wrong. He could feel *Enshalaan* pulling at him, drawing him closer, but the strange feeling was calling him away from Atta's desk, toward a tapestry that hung on the wall and displayed the image of, of all things, a beautiful mountain range below a sunny blue sky. Kobb recognized the tapestry as having once hung in the small inn of Ambly.

Kobb grabbed hold of the tapestry and ripped it down from the carved stone wall; behind it, a hollow was revealed, and within the hollow was the box of bones. Kobb felt *Enshalaan's* presence there, but as he reached for it a part of him was irrationally afraid that he would open the box and find it empty.

He wrapped his fingers around the euum tusk and pulled back the lid. *Enshalaan* rested safely within the box. Kobb had never been happier during his time as a slave to the garuk as he was the moment he felt the warmth of *Enshalaan's* hilt as his fingers curled around it.

"It is time to leave, my friend," Kobb said to the dagger, and though no voice filled his head, Kobb was certain that *Enshalaan* was eager to make the journey.

Yssa had almost fallen asleep out of boredom, but when a shadow blocked the light from the slat in the door she came back to her senses. She had given up hope that she would ever see the light of day again, but her hope was rekindled when she saw a tiny hand push through the slat in the door holding her wand.

She got up quickly and took hold of the wand. Everything had just taken a turn for the better.

"Thank you," she said to the boy as he withdrew his arm. "This cell that I'm in, does the back of it connect to any rooms on the other side?"

"No. But there are trees out there," Jacob said.

"Alright. I'm going to leave now, and I'm going to make a lot of noise in doing so. The warders and the wardens are going to come. I don't want anyone to know that you helped me. Do you sleep in this building?"

"Yes," Jacob answered. "My father and I have quarters here."

"How long will it take you to get to your bed and under your covers if you run really fast?"

"A count of twenty maybe?"

"Then I'm going to count to thirty, and when I reach thirty, I'm going to blow this wall apart. You'll be safely in bed at that time. If anyone asks you anything, you tell them that you brought me my bread and water and that was the only time you had any contact with me. You tell them that you know better than to talk to prisoners and that you didn't say anything to me at all, and that I didn't say anything to you."

"Alright," Jacob said. "Mistress Yssa?"

"Yes?"

"I hope you make all the warders really mad."

Yssa heard the boy's footsteps running away from the door and light streamed back into the gaol cell. Keeping true to her word Yssa counted to thirty, gave the boy another ten seconds for good measure, and then she raised her wand to the back wall of her cell.

"*Lorroak fury!*" Yssa shouted as loud as she could.

Chapter 8

Haverstagg and Hannah had long since fallen behind the rest of their caravan. Barnwall was a week behind them, and it had been two days since they passed through the chaos of Market. Already, the road had begun to wear on Haverstagg, so when the red-brown blur spreading across the western horizon began to take on the shape of mountain peaks, his heart sunk even further.

"Maybe you were right about the stiddleback," Haverstagg said as they sat on the roadside prairie eating a light lunch of bread spread over by a thin layer of goat butter and washed down with barralak juice. "Maybe we should have kept one of them. I've been alright thus far, but I didn't think that mountains could grow so high."

Hannah followed her husband's gaze and put a reassuring hand on his thigh. "Well, we can't be more than another day from the mountain inn that the furrier in Market was telling you about. Why don't you split up the pack, and let me carry some of it? You can share the load, Hav, I'll be alright."

Haverstagg stuffed the last of his bread into his mouth and licked a smear of goat butter off his thumb.

"No, that won't do. I can't have my wife acting like a mool. But we might have to spend a few days there. I didn't want to spend any coin on this trip, but I might have to. I can feel the ground rising already, and once we enter that canyon . . ." Haverstagg let his words hang in the air.

Hannah opened her mouth as if she was about to say something, but hesitated, and then raised her waterskin to her mouth and took a long draw instead. The water was warm, and hardly quenching, but she voiced no complaint. Haverstagg watched her carefully pack away the uneaten portion of their meal and relace her boots.

Hours later, the plains were behind them and Haverstagg found himself at his limits. His pack's straps had rubbed his shoulders raw and brought on blisters that had long since been torn open. They had been assured that the Otep-Korah crossroad could not be missed and from there the inn was only an hour up the canyon switchbacks. But the terrain had turned from open expanses of grassland to a craggy valley and though the trail was well marked, Haverstagg began to wonder if they might have missed a fork in the road. It was not quite dark yet, but in the dusky shadow, the valley had been plunged into near perfect darkness, and the burning torch that Hannah carried often did not penetrate the mountain pines that crowded the roadside.

A mile later, Haverstagg's boot caught something in the road. A fallen branch, or loose stone perhaps, but whatever it was it caused a stagger in his step that brought the big man crashing down.

"Hav!" Hannah called, rushing to his side.

"I'm alright," he said as he pushed himself over and struggled to get back up to his feet. "I'm alright, I just . . ."

"Let's stop for awhile," Hannah said, trying to pull Haverstagg and his load upright. "You need to catch your breath. A short rest will do you some good."

"No, we can't be far from the inn."

"Well, I need a rest," Hannah said, finding a seat among some trees at the side of the road. She began unlacing a boot. "I've a stone in my boot, so you might as well take a few minutes. Unless you'd rather press on madly without me?"

"No," Haverstagg said emotionlessly. But he did yield enough to drop the pack and take a seat.

Haverstagg ran his hands through his unruly blonde hair and wiped sweat off his brow. These cursed mountains were challenging his manhood, and with every step he began to think it was a battle that he would lose. Closing his eyes, he leaned his head forward and reached behind his head to rub the soreness out of his shoulders. He never heard them approach.

A moment later Hannah let out a scream, but it was quickly cut off. Haverstagg snapped his gaze in her direction just in time to see her being pulled back into the blackness amongst the trees. He was up in an instant, but as he took the first lunging step toward the brush two shadows came at him from both sides. They were men, he realized, and though he got an arm up to knock aside a thick knife-tipped pole from one attacker, this made him turn his back on the other.

White-hot pain ran through his back, just above his belt and to the side of the spine. He felt the pressure stop, and then was pushed forward as the knife sank deeper into him.

Haverstagg could hear Hannah struggling, screaming as best as she could with an arm around her throat and a hand over her mouth. He tried to stay standing, but the pain overcame him, he went down to one knee and then fell over to his side. He reached behind him to feel the handle of the knife that had was lodged deep in his lower back. He ripped it out, screaming out loudly as he did so.

Hannah's torch had been knocked into the brush by the roadside and the dry tinder under the trees quickly took to the flame. The forest just behind him glowed orange, casting the highwaymen in an ominous fiery glow. There were six of them who stood behind the pole-wielder, and another off to the side who had knotted up his hands in Hannah's hair and pulled her head sharply to the side. Haverstagg filled with renewed rage and vigor as he saw the highwayman lock his mouth around Hannah's soft neck.

The pole-wielder leaned close to taunt Haverstagg in the helplessness of his situation. It gave Haverstagg the chance that he needed. Biting back the pain, he swiped the knife he had pulled from his own back across the air. The pole-wielder was sent spinning backward clutching his face as blood sprayed into the burning bushes.

Haverstagg tried to rise, but in that instant the others were all upon him. He could not be sure how many times they stabbed him with their sharpened wooden poles, but over and over again he felt searing pain rip through his body until it all became too much to bear. His vision failed him, aside from the faint sense of flickering orange light in the blackness. He could smell the smoke and burning pine, and he heard the laughter of the highwaymen as they fled through the trees, but soon all of that was gone and the horror of what those men would soon do to his wife followed him into darkness.

The chatter of birds and the dewy scent of the forest brought Yssa into consciousness. It was dark, though the light of several bright moons cast the forest in dim silvery light. The events of the previous day came back to her quickly and she found herself upright suddenly, crouched within a hollow formed by the exposed roots of a mighty ringbark and sheltered by the surrounding bushes. She knew this place, and had been here before, but in those previous visits it was only to enjoy a walk in the woods outside of Ambermane when she found the stresses of university life wearing her thin.

This time everything was different. Asher Crowe had left her a second time. Oddly Flack had grievously wounded Warder Mankoff. And two dead men were left behind in Yssa's attempt to escape Ambermane.

It isn't my fault, Yssa told herself again and again as she recollected the misfortunate events that had befallen her. *I was defending myself. They would not listen to reason.*

And truly, they had not. Not more than ten minutes after Yssa had blasted her way out of the Inquata Building's gaol, she had been set upon by two wardens and a single over-eager warder. She had pleaded with them, proclaiming herself innocent of what had happened to Warder Mankoff, but it had all been futile.

The warder, a man she recognized but did not know by name, had unleashed a mad fury of spells against her. He had been the first to die. She had thought that the wardens would, in turn, realize the folly of their pursuit. She managed to bring the forest to life against the first. As if every branch, plant, and blade of grass was a vine of strangleweed the forest took him under its control. It was the other one that she had not had the time to deal with so mercifully. Yssa saw the flash of steel in the moonlight, and she uttered the incantation that came to her in that moment of panic as she brought her wand to bear. He never closed the gap between them; he simply ceased to be.

Guilt ran through her. Had she been able to escape without harm coming to anyone else then certainly neither the boy, Jacob, nor his father could be held accountable. How Yssa had gotten a wand with which to destroy the wall would certainly have placed them under scrutiny, but neither would come to any ill. Now, however, Yssa was not so sure. The killing of any man in the Brylands was a crime for which there was only one punishment, but the killing of the Lord Martyr's officials, the warders and wardens, the punishment for such a thing was no less than that which Asher Crowe had lived his life in fear of.

Yssa knew all about the Obelisk of Condemned Souls in Subterranea, even though she had never before laid eyes upon it. To have her ashes placed inside, to have her very soul imprisoned there, well that brought the thought that maybe she would be better to throw herself off a cliff where nobody would ever find her bones.

But that was all nonsense. Although Yssa pretended that she had found comfort in old age and her inevitable demise, she feared death. Too many cycles spent studying the technical aspects of magic had blurred her perception of the theological *Light* and *Shadow* where the good, and the evil respectively find their end. Nothing else of the God Times remained, save for the names associated with mountains, lakes, and the like. The fact that people still believed in the afterlife only demonstrated their need to believe in something other than the nothingness of death. And that nothingness, well that was something she was not quite yet ready to face.

Yssa kept hidden in the cover provided by the foliage and listened to the sounds of the woods for quite some time. The wardens of these parts were skilled woodsmen, and if she hoped to make it out of the Hagstead Forest alive, that meant that there was no room for any lack of caution.

Where can I go? Even if I tried to catch up to Crowe, he would likely be miles away by now and taking a course that was not meant to be followed because certainly he knew that the wardens would be in pursuit.

Even though she knew where Crowe was headed, the Black Rift was almost two hundred miles away, deep inside the garuk and euum infested Pennorra Reaches and while Yssa was a formidable wizardess, she was after all, an old lady who couldn't even hope to make such a journey on her own.

Not unless Asher had taken precautions.

"Indeed, I can," he had said to her that night at her cottage. *"Do you remember the place where we first kissed?"* He had asked her in their last moment together . . . Asher Crowe was the founding father of astromancy, the magical foundation of true divination, had he foreseen all of this?

Kobb no longer moved with caution. Whatever Pulgra had in store for him was a massive beast, that was obvious from the way that the slave pen guards had been ravaged, and there was no way that it could fit into the tight quarters of the narrow passage through which Kobb ran with *Enshalaan* in one hand and a burning torch lighting his way in the other.

Caution was not something he could afford now. While Kobb had no way of telling just how deep within the World Below, he truly was, these tunnels were swelteringly hot, and that meant that the surface of the World Above might as well be a thousand miles away.

Pulgra had boldly taken quite a risk in moving openly against Atta. She had powerful allies among the garuk tribes. And all of this risk, Kobb reasoned, was simply because Pulgra had been driven to such rage that revenge, not only against Atta, but against Kobb as well, was all that mattered to him. Kobb was being routed to whatever place Pulgra had picked out to watch what would be Kobb's final gladiatorial battle in the World Below. He would either die here this very morning, or he would at last fight his way out of the World Below.

With *Enshalaan* firmly in his grip, Kobb did not care what Pulgra had in store for him. Whatever it was, it was the last thing that stood between Kobb and his freedom.

———•·•———

"Should we go after her?" Warder Abrashi asked Warder Solias as they stared at the charred remains of Warder Colm. The burned man lay face down in a trickling brook, a haze of gray ash being carried away from the body by the flowing water.

"No," Warder Solias said calmly from atop his stiddleback. "We do what we had discussed. The bigger prize is Asher Crowe."

Warder Abrashi nodded and reached back into his saddle basket, placing the silver mirror he'd used to scry the location of the missing warder back into its padded compartment. "Shall we throw up a beacon, Master?"

Warder Solias nodded.

From the belt around his waist Warder Abrashi drew a long, smooth wand of lacquered petrified wood. He pointed it to the air, threw a pinch of red powder up before him, and called out the words of a spell. The powder sparked into flame and flew up into the sky leaving a contrail of bright red smoke behind it. The beacon would guide the other warders back to this place so that they could attend to Warder Colm's body.

The two warders kicked their stiddleback in the ribs and pulled them around to head back the way they had come.

Chapter 9

Otep was the first to notice the flames. From high atop the mountainside, the weathered old man stared down to the valley below, concern pressing deep wrinkles into his face. His attention turned upward. There were several colorful moons visible in the night sky, but there was not a cloud in sight.

It was not unheard of for a storm to set such a blaze when lightning would strike a summer-killed pine, but no such storm had caused the fire that was beginning to spread up the mountainside. With the mountain roads being used more and more frequently with the onset of winter, the fire had to have been caused by someone traveling through the canyon. Otep's expression soured. Perhaps the rumors of highwaymen were true.

Dropping the phosphorescent moss that he had just picked into one of the many pouches on his belt, Otep walked back up through the trees to where his mool was tethered. He patted the large boar-like pack animal's hairy hide and unfastened a long, gnarled wooden staff from the saddle basket over the animal's rump. With the staff in hand, Otep returned to where he stood before and looked back down to the valley. From this vantage point he could not see the road, but the orange glow was far more intense now, and the scent of burning pine wafted up the mountainside as ash and burning embers drifted on the breeze.

It was not nature that caused this fire, but nature could be called upon to stop it. Otep thrust the staff up into the air and shouted a loud, repetitive chant in which each verse came more loudly than the one that preceded it until his booming voice began to reverberate off of the canyon walls. The sky darkened and clouds began to manifest. Before long he began to swirl the gnarled head of his staff around in a circular pattern and the cloud cover began to grow black, swirl, and thicken. Forks of lightning could be seen chasing each other through the sky followed by the almost instantaneous clap of thunder. By the time Otep's chanting came to an end, a fierce storm had been born and the landscape for miles around was covered in torrents of pouring rain.

Claudia was miserable. She was not used to such extraordinarily long rides, and she was sick to death of the rain. The storm had come on so suddenly that before Odderly could unpack their heavy traveling cloaks from his saddle basket, she was already soaked to the bone and it did her little good. Sitting behind her grandfather on a stiddleback only slightly smaller than Odderly's and without a saddle basket, she could feel that her grandfather was similarly drenched.

Asher Crowe said nothing as they rode, however at times on the road he whistled unfamiliar songs. For the most part he rode in silence with something of a smile on his face. Whereas Odderly's expression revealed the same discomfort as Claudia's, her grandfather almost seemed to be enjoying the trip, which was more than a little irritating given their current situation.

"When will this storm stop?" she asked.

Crowe looked up to the sky. "This storm will not end until it is willed to end," he said. "There is magic in those clouds."

"Magic?" Claudia asked. "Is it the warders? Are they trying to hinder our escape?"

"More likely that it's the old man of the mountain," Odderly interjected. "They say he watches over these parts. They say he's mad, not right in the head."

"Is he a wizard then?" Claudia asked.

"He was a warder once," Crowe said. "And he's no less right in the head than I am. Naivety comes with youth; eccentricity comes with age."

"But if he was a warder, should we not find another way? The storm only grows worse ahead of us, Grandfather," Claudia said before wiping rainwater off her face and fighting to tuck her wet hair back into the hood of her traveling cloak.

"No, this is the quickest road to where we are headed, and we'll not long have the luxury of being able to travel by way of the roads at all. Word will soon spread throughout the Brylands as to what happened in Ambermane. Besides," Crowe added, "the storm only proves that the old goat is still alive and that we haven't wasted our time in coming here."

Oddly spurred his bloated stiddleback and brought it up beside Crowe's. The sudden jump in pace almost made the beast slip in the mud. "We're taking quite the risk here, Asher. How can you be sure that he will help us?"

"Well, one can never be certain of anything where a wizard is concerned, especially a *mad* one." Crowe smiled, "but regardless of whether or not he will help us, he'll not hinder us." Crowe paused for a beat and then increased the pace of his own stiddleback with a good kick. He began to whistle again, and then paused abruptly, "at least I don't think he will."

Claudia looked back over her shoulder as she and her grandfather trotted away. Oddly had fully halted his mount and his expression could melt ice. It was obvious that he didn't share the enthusiasm that her grandfather did about paying his old friend a visit.

"Asher!" he called after them.

In front of her, over the sounds of the gusting wind and pouring rain, Claudia was almost certain that she heard her grandfather laughing.

The cave had given them both shelter and opportunity. It had served

Palis and his band of highwaymen well for the last month while they had haunted the road between Market and the Otep-Korah Crossroad. Only a few light snowstorms had thus far reared their head, but the sight of a few snowflakes had put the machine into motion. Villagers from all over the Brylands had begun the annual pilgrimage to the refuge of Subterranea. With so few routes through the mountains of Roak's Elbow, Palis had known that the opportunity for banditry would never be better. These last weeks had been very lucrative indeed, but this last encounter had been the first where any of the highwaymen had been hurt.

"I don't believe you let him get your knife," Palis said to his brother, a large man with greasy black hair and only a few remaining teeth. A third man stitched Palis' face back together. "How could you be so stupid?"

"You said that they would be easy prey, Palis."

"And they were, weren't they? All alone on the road, exhausted, lost, and just asking to be robbed. He didn't even have a knife until you gave him yours!"

"I didn't give him anything, I lost my grip on it when he spun around to face you."

"Well, if you'd stabbed him in the right spot, like I've shown you a thousand times, that would have been the end of it all. I honestly don't know why I put up with you, Anvis. I should have left you behind. All you're going to do is get us all killed, or worse, burned at the tip of a warder's wand."

Palis felt the third man tie off the stitches and flinched with grinding teeth. He sat up and slipped his knife from the sheath at his belt. The blade was dirty and pocked with rust, but it was reflective enough in the fire light of the cave that he could see the terrible cut. It stretched from his right cheek to the top left of his forehead cleaving flesh to the bone. At one spot it even crossed over his left eye, but luckily it hadn't blinded him. Still, whenever he blinked or closed his eyes, Palis could see the flash of steel and the burly blonde-haired flatlander's furious face staring up at him with a look that chilled even Palis' hardened resolve.

"It'll heal," the third man said, no doubt sensing that Palis was seething.

"Of course, it will heal, Wick, the point is that it shouldn't have happened in the first place," Palis spat.

Palis' scowl settled on his brother's face. Anvis had always been more trouble that he'd been worth. That is the way it had been when they were children growing up without a father in Corbend, and it would never change. As Palis watched his brother get up and walk out of the cave, he felt his grip on the rusty knife tighten. For a moment, he actually had to restrain himself from putting the blade into Anvis' back and freeing himself from the burden that had plagued him for his entire life. It was only when he saw the big oaf disappear into the rainy night outside the cave that Palis managed to calm down enough to sheath the blade and head back to the secondary cave where the others had taken their booty.

Palis swatted away the moldy curtain that separated the two pockets in the mountainside and finally felt his high spirits return when one of his men handed him a skin of Barnwall Ale and announced that they'd all decided that Palis should get the first ride since he was the one who had gotten hurt in the fight.

"Might kind of you, lads," Palis said to them as he quickly finished off his drink and threw the skin to the side of the cave.

The woman was remarkably beautiful in a simple kind of way, with the body of a brothel whore, (the good kind of whore, not like those back home in the hollow), and a particularly fiery spirit. Despite the helplessness of her situation, she continued to fight against the ropes that had been used to bind her spread-legged to the large rocks and mineral columns in the back of the cave.

Palis began to strip off his breeches as he walked toward her enjoying the cajoling laughter of his friends. He relished the obvious fear and disgust in the girl's eyes. He fell in love with the sweat that had beaded up on her skin, and for Palis, the bloody nose and blackened eye only sweetened the deed. He had been bullied a lot as a young boy. Now those cycles of abuse were long behind him, and Palis was a grown man.

He preferred his women bound and beaten.

Blood had run out of him to mix with the rainwater that accumulated in the low spots around the injured man, but as Otep hunkered down over the body he realized that there was still life left within the unfortunate stranger. The trees nearby were blackened, and Otep's storm had come none to soon, for surely the man had been left for dead and would have been burned alive had the rain not quelled the flames.

"You are lucky to be alive," Otep said to the stranger whose eyes stared blankly up to the rain pouring down from the sky.

The old wizard pulled open the traveler's shirt and examined a few of the wounds. The punctures were deep, and many had pierced the flesh and driven into vital organs. There was little that could be done, but Otep felt obligated to do whatever he could to try and save the traveler's life.

"Amm," Otep said to the mool. The hairy boar-like creature looked over at him. "You run home now."

The mool turned and ran off through the brush.

"Now, my poor friend let us see what we can do with you?"

Otep stood and used the base of his gnarled staff to draw a crude circle around himself and the unconscious traveler. When the circle was closed, he reached into one of his pouches and sprinkled a yellow powder over himself, and then over the traveler, and when he was finished Otep spoke a single word of power. He felt as if he was being pulled in every direction at once as the magic took hold of him. And then both Otep and the grievously wounded traveler were gone.

The trailhead was clearly marked, but Claudia felt no safer when her grandfather turned the stiddleback northward and began leading them into an even narrower valley. The trail quickly turned to gravel-covered switchbacks that frequently doubled back on themselves as they ascended the very side of the canyon wall. More than once the stiddleback slipped on the loose, wet stones, and Claudia dug her nails into her grandfather's ribs for fear of being thrown down the mountainside.

The storm grew worse as they gained elevation, and the wind came in such gusts that the rain was blown horizontally at times so that the hood on her traveling cloak did no good to keep the cold rain from finding her skin. Claudia ultimately had to bury her face into her grandfather's back to find any sort of protection.

And then, just as quickly as it started, the rain stopped. The clouds thinned, and then parted all together revealing the soft blue glow that comes before dawn.

"Well, this is a stroke of luck," Crowe said, stopping his stiddleback just as they came up from the last switchback and found that the ground leveled out at a wide rocky ledge.

"Aye," Odderly said as he came up beside them.

Claudia pried her face out from the back of her grandfather's cloak and saw Odderly gesture ahead of them by raising his scruffy chin. They had reached the top of the switchbacks and passed through a keyhole in the canyon wall, but directly ahead of them was a long arching bridge of natural stone. Given the trouble that the stiddleback had been having keeping their footing on the wet gravel of the trail, she felt her chest tighten at the thought of having to cross the bridge with the rain pouring down and the wind trying to push them over the edge.

"We're not crossing . . . that?" Claudia asked, slipping down from the saddle and carefully treading up to the end of the ledge. Although the rocks piled there prevented her from getting too close to the lip of the cliff, she could clearly see that the natural stone bridge was suspended several hundred feet over the valley floor. From there, she could see the trail that they had just come up, and she didn't want to slip and see it again any time soon. "Surely you jest?"

"It's not far now," Crowe said, he himself slipping down out of the saddle. "We'd better walk them across."

"Grandfather . . ." Claudia said sheepishly. "There has to be another way. You can't be serious."

"This is the only way into the Korah Valley," Crowe said.

Beside them Odderly hopped down from his stiddleback and rolled his hands up in the reigns. "Don't worry, I'll go first."

"Odderly, don't!" Claudia protested as Odderly took his first steps onto the bridge.

Crowe moved to follow, and soon Claudia was alone on her side of the arching natural bridge. She had no choice, she was just as likely to fall heading back down the slippery switchbacks as she was crossing the bridge, and even if she went back, where then was she to go? Squealing with every short step, Claudia quickly crossed the bridge.

It seemed that this trip was testing all her fears. At the other side of the bridge was a massive tunnel that led directly into the stone of the cliff-side. Only blackness lay ahead. Her grandfather and Odderly had already gone inside the dark tunnel.

"This isn't good," Claudia said factually as she slipped her wand out of the sheath on her waist. She waved the smooth, pale wooden wand in the air and said, *"intium orohthem."*

It was a simple spell, one of the first she had learned. The tip of her wand began to glow and the tunnel ahead of her for a little way was bathed in bright white light. Claudia bit her lip and took a step forward into the crack in the stone, but as she did so she stepped on something and felt it crunch beneath her boot. When she moved her foot, she saw that what she had stepped on was a broken humanoid jawbone.

Gooseflesh crawled up her arms. As she looked ahead, she saw that there were bones all over the tunnel. When her eyes settled on a skull that had a wide sloping forehead, a large jaw, and jagged teeth just a short way ahead, she realized that they were garuk bones.

"Grandfather?" she called as she ran down the tunnel.

Claudia was relieved when she caught up to her grandfather and Odderly. She slipped gracefully between the stiddleback and glared up at Crowe. "You could have waited for me!"

"Bah, you would have dilly-dallied out there forever. Now you're here with us. Hardly no time dillied or dallied."

Odderly laughed out loud at the comment until Claudia's elbow found a soft spot between his ribs and his belly.

"These are garuk bones," Claudia said when they passed another pile of remains kicked to the side of the tunnel. "What happened here?"

"There is a valley at the other end of this tunnel that was once home to a garuk tribe," Crowe began. "They had lived here forever, but there was no way out of the valley, so they posed no threat to the

Brylands. Some time between the winter and spring of last year, the ice, mixed with the cold and subsequent thaw, cracked the mountain, making this tunnel."

Claudia looked back the way they had come.

"Well, it didn't take them long to discover the Brylands. There were countless raids. Many people died. And so, some of us were sent up here to put a stop to it."

As they walked, Claudia looked at the bones that littered the sides of the cave. "You did this, Grandfather?"

Crowe said nothing at first, and then, "there are many reasons why I've warned you away from a life in the service of the Lord Martyr, Claudia. There are choices in life that I hope you never have to make. I did what I was told to do, and because of what I did, what happened to Ambly didn't happen to Stonehold."

This hit a nerve inside her, and Claudia stopped walking. Crowe and Odderly looked back at her as she fell behind the stiddleback, but neither said anything to her. After a moment, they began talking to each other, but she was too far out of earshot to be able to make out what they said. She had not been counting the bones, but she did not have to in order to understand that this place was a place of massacre.

For a moment Claudia pictured the garuk, brutal and violent, but no match for wizardry. They stood no chance, and as Claudia's eyes settled on some of the nearby bones, she realized that based on the size of them they must have belonged to a child. The Lord Martyr had done more than send warders here to stop the garuk raids; he had sent them here to wipe the garuk out completely. Man, woman, and child. Her grandfather had done this, this old wizard they were going to meet had done this, and surrounded by the bones of the dead, Claudia could not help but to feel the severity of it all.

But then thoughts of Ambly came to her mind. She was only eight cycles of age when the gem miners of Ambly had inadvertently broken into the garuk caverns. The garuk had come up from the World Below and destroyed everything she knew. Her friends, her family, even her father. All lost. Ambly, gone. But now she knew that her father was alive, somewhere in the Black Rift, and that could mean only one thing. The garuk had taken slaves. Her father was a slave. *What horrors has he endured for the past six cycles?*

Claudia looked back down to the scattered bones with mixed emotions. Children were killed here. Her father was a slave. Hating the garuk should come naturally, but regardless, she found herself pitying them at the same time. *Why does everything have to be so confusing?*

"We're here!" Came her grandfather's voice from down the tunnel ahead of her.

Claudia snapped out of her reverie. With her wand lighting the way she hurried down the length of the tunnel trying not to think any further about the garuk and deftly dodging their remains. When she caught up to her grandfather and Odderly they stood on a giant slab of broken stone that overlooked a massive boulder field. Among the massive mounds of jagged gray stone, built at the lip of a ledge that looked out over a deep and heavily forested valley fed by dozens of waterfalls, was a pretty two-story building that had been painted a bright blue. It stood out oddly and in sharp contrast to the dull gray and ruddy red of the striated rock.

Smoke rose from the chimney of the building. Grass grew around it. There were even flowers growing in long planters under each window. A clearly marked path led to the double-doors of the building, and as they walked Crowe announced loudly, "welcome to the Blue World." His cheerful mood had returned in full.

CHAPTER 10

Perched precariously on the edge of the cliff-side overlooking the Korah Valley, *The Blue World* seemed completely out of place. The boulder field was littered with the bones of dead garuk, and Claudia found herself keeping her eyes directly on the sandy path ahead to avoid having to look at them. The blue-painted walls of the mountain inn and the unequaled beauty of the tranquil hidden valley stood in stark opposition to the reminders of what had once happened in this place. Cheery colors and natural beauty among jagged broken stone and age-rotted corpses.

Crowe handed the reigns of his stiddleback to Odderly and made his way inside. As she passed, Claudia had trouble discerning Odderly's expression while he tethered the stiddleback to the hitching post and conjured water into the trough for the beasts to drink. He obviously knew more about this *Old Man of the Mountain* than she did, and while he had expressed his doubts on the road as to whether or not the old ex-warder would offer to help them, he certainly hadn't expressed any fear of the old man. Yet, there was fear in Odderly's eyes now. Claudia began to think that there were things that neither her grandfather nor Odderly had yet told her.

Saying nothing, Claudia followed her grandfather inside. Beyond the double-doors of the inn waited a square cloakroom that was covered with wooden pegs. Upon a good many of the pegs hung traveling cloaks. Some of these seemed quite old, as if they had been hanging there since the cuts and fabric had been in style. Others were much newer and looked to have spent little time on the road. The odd assortment immediately struck Claudia as just that, odd.

So many cloaks for an inn so out of the way. How could so many people have visited this place, yet left their cloaks behind?

Crowe hung his traveling cloak on a peg and pushed his way through the curtain that separated the cloakroom from the common.

Is this why Odderly seems so afraid of this place now that we're here? Do people who come here not often leave?

A moment later Odderly entered from outside. He closed the double-doors and seemed to make the same assessment of the cloakroom before he too hung his cloak and pushed his way through the curtain.

Reluctantly, Claudia surrendered her waterlogged cloak. As she went inside, she felt her stomach tighten up beneath her shirt. There was definitely more to this place than meets the eye. She glanced back again at her weathered cloak, hoping that it would not be long before she could throw it over her shoulders again and be gone from here.

The common room was not unlike that which would be found at any inn or tavern across the Brylands save for the fact that aside from her own traveling companions and a large mool sleeping by the fire, it was completely empty. Claudia joined her grandfather and Odderly as they took a seat at a small round table in the center of the stale room. While she did not understand why someone would keep swine indoors, the pack animal barely opened one eye to note their presence before it returned to its sleep.

"I've not forgotten *you*, Warder Crowe," came a harsh voice that followed footsteps down the stairs.

Claudia's hand went immediately to her wand, but seeing that her grandfather did not react as if there was a threat, she let her fingers slide free from around it and shifted her legs nervously.

Crowe alone stood up to face the stranger. The man, who came down the stairs, leaning heavily on a gnarled old staff, did not look much different than her grandfather. They both had long gray hair, no beards, and shared the same patterns of wrinkles around their cheeks and eyes.

"Nor I you, Otep." Crowe smiled, throwing his arms around his old friend, "but it is Warder Crowe no more. I strayed from that path a long, long time ago."

The two old men pulled away from their embrace and Crowe guided Otep toward the table where Claudia and Odderly sat.

"You know Herb Master Odderly Flack," Crowe said, throwing a hand Odderly's way by means of introduction.

"Master, now, eh?" Otep said as Odderly rose and took his hand. "We met once before Master Flack, though you probably don't remember. You were just a wee boy then."

"I'll take your word for it," Odderly said. He chewed his cheeks uncomfortably.

"And my very own granddaughter, Claudia."

Claudia stood and gave a polite curtsey from across the table.

"Pleased, pleased," Otep said, smiling at Claudia. "You look every bit like your mother, child. But without her eyes, your father's no doubt. Your grandfather and I go way back. Too far back, I'm afraid."

Crowe nodded solemnly, and an awkward moment of silence filled the already stagnant air of the room.

"But enough of that," Otep said, as everyone retook their seats. He followed suit, pulling out a wooden chair for himself and leaning his staff against the table. He looked to Crowe. "The High Warders haven't assembled here in fifty cycles. So, there are only two things that would bring you back here again, Asher. Either you need a favor, or you've come for a boat."

"Both, I'm afraid," Crowe answered. "But those are things that I'll need to speak with you about in private."

Crowe looked pointedly at Claudia, and she could not help but feel a little bit offended. He was keeping secrets again.

"Of course," Otep said. "You'll be staying the night then?"

Crowe nodded. "If you've a room to spare."

Otep laughed. "This time of year, I get a few stragglers who've lost their caravans and the occasional injured traveler, but people don't exactly rush to take me up on my hospitality these days."

I can see why, Claudia thought. Her mind summoned images of the horrible weather, the winding switchbacks, the frightening natural bridge, and the garuk bones that littered the tunnel and boulder field.

"So, I don't think that will be a problem." Otep looked over his shoulder and called to someone, "Rusk, will you see our guests to their rooms."

Claudia had not thought that there would be anyone else here, but her surprise at seeing someone come walking out from behind another curtain paled to her surprise at seeing that it was not a man that emerged, but a withered old garuk. Her hand went to her wand again, and this time she drew it out to her side and quickly got up to her feet as her mind raced in search of a spell to protect her.

"There's no need for that," Otep assured her, patting his hand down toward the table in a gesture that pleaded with her to lower her wand. "Rusk is quite tame."

Claudia looked back to her grandfather who only nodded. She then turned her eyes to Odderly hoping that she would find support there, but he seemed completely indifferent. Reluctantly, Claudia slid her wand back into its place at her waist.

"It's been a long time, Rusk," Crowe said to the garuk. "You look well."

The garuk nodded to Crowe when he arrived at the table. With this, Claudia turned back to her grandfather; she was about to say something when her words were lost in her amazement as the garuk spoke perfect Brysh with an accent not unlike Otep's,

"Your rooms are upstairs. If you'll follow me . . ."

Odderly stood and thanked Otep, following the garuk as it started toward the same set of stairs that Otep had descended. Claudia cautiously followed them. Her eyes never left the garuk.

A garuk, alive, here of all places? Claudia could not understand it. *And speaking our language?*

"Master Flack," Otep said.

Odderly stopped and looked over his shoulder. "Aye?"

"It was *Herb* Master Flack, was it not?"

"Aye".

"Being that you've all come here expecting a favor, might I ask you one of my own?"

Odderly nodded, turning all the way around to face the old ex-warder. The garuk and Claudia both stopped in their place.

"I am afraid that I do have one other guest at the moment. There was a traveler who was beset upon by bandits on the road. I've done what I can for him, but I am no healer. If you would be so kind, could you . . ."

Odderly raised a hand to stop the ex-warder in mid-sentence and said, "I'll see what I can do."

"Thank you," Otep said kindly. "I am certain that he will be most grateful for your aid."

"And Odderly," Crowe added. "Before you retire for the evening, I'll be needing your attention as well."

Odderly nodded. "Of course, Asher. Just find me when you are ready. I trust the . . . I trust *Rusk* will bring our things in from outside?"

Otep nodded. "Of course."

———•———

Odderly was the first shown to his room. He spoke briefly with the garuk who summarized what had happened to the injured traveler. Claudia stood in the hallway and watched this transpire with great curiosity. The garuk seemed genuinely concerned for the injured man and prompted that as soon as he had a moment to unpack the stiddleback he would show Odderly to the injured man's room. Odderly thanked him, and as the garuk closed Odderly inside his room Claudia realized that she was now all alone with it.

"Your room will be just down the hall," the garuk said as it stepped around Claudia and began to walk away.

Claudia followed, but stayed a good distance behind. She walked with a hand resting on her wand. She had seen garuk before, but she was only eight cycles old at that time and everything happened so suddenly, so chaotically, that the images she had carried of them in her mind didn't seem to fit this *thing* that walked ahead of her. Claudia had dreamed of the garuk the way that she remembered them; fierce inhuman monsters with gray skin, hooked noses, pointed ears, mouths full of fangs, and eyes blood red with the hunger to kill.

Now, right in front of her stood a real, live garuk. It was not human, not even close on the evolutionary scale, but it was no monster either. Its features were broad, primitive even, but it walked like a man, and it talked like a man. It even spoke her language fluently. Maybe if it had been young, its wide girth, hunched back, and long limbs might have made it menacing to behold, but this . . . this garuk . . . just looked tired and old.

The garuk opened the door to her room with a key from the ring that it carried in its pocket. It removed the key from the ring and handed it to Claudia. "You needn't worry about your safety here," the garuk said, "but some guests, particularly females, do prefer their privacy."

Claudia let her hand slip from her wand as she took the key in her hand. She stepped inside.

"There is a privy behind the inn, through the door down by the stairs," the garuk said. "And if you would like a bath, just let me know and I'll draw and heat some water. My room is the last on the right at the far end of the hall."

Claudia blushed, embarrassed by the garuk's kindness and softly spoken words. "That . . . would be nice."

The garuk nodded. "I'll prepare it then, as soon as I bring up your belongings." Saying no more, the garuk turned to leave.

"Wait!" Claudia said sharply, startling the garuk who turned around suddenly, clutching its chest. "Thank you . . . Rusk."

Rusk smiled revealing sharp teeth behind plump dry lips. He bowed low with a motion befitting a courtier, stepped outside, and closed the door.

Odderly sat a black leather case down on the floor beside him as he pulled a wooden chair up to the bedside of the injured traveler. Rusk had brought him his things, and offered to draw a bath, but Odderly thought it better for him to check in on the traveler before indulging in such luxury. Given the state of the man's condition, Odderly was sure that he would not turn away the assistance of a healer, however bad he might smell.

The traveler was unconscious, and when Odderly leaned forward to pull back the roshea-wool blanket that covered him, he discovered that Otep had already stripped and bathed the man, as well as having cleaned and dressed the wounds. There were so many wounds. In Odderly's initial assessment he counted seventeen deep, round puncture wounds on the man's chest, arms, and legs. He turned him slightly, and discovered a knife-like puncture wound near the spine on the traveler's lower back.

"Somebody certainly didn't want you to live the night," Odderly said to himself as he began unpacking small jars of ointments, salves, and vials of medicinal fluids from his case. He laid these out on the bedside table and turned the key on the glass lamp that burned there, raising the wick and increasing the overall brightness of the light so that he could better see what he was doing.

The old mage hadn't done a bad job at binding and caring for the injuries. He had sewn many of them closed, but blood and puss still oozed from the wounds. In some places, the wounds had begun to sour, and the man's pulse was virtually non-existent. His breathing faint and watery. His skin was pale. Odderly knew that despite Otep's efforts, the traveler's organs were decimated and poisoning him from within.

It was tedious work, but one by one Odderly undressed each wound. He carefully snipped the catgut stitching and removed the threads, cleaning each wound with the liquids from his case. In each wound he spread the magical healing ointments, and after he had redressed and resewn the wounds, he covered each with a sterile-smelling salve and fresh wrappings.

The hours went by slowly, but by the time Odderly had finished and repacked his medical case, he was certain that the injured traveler would recover . . . in time.

After the others had gone upstairs, Otep led Crowe through a different curtain where Otep tapped the gnarled tip of his staff against a door that glowed for a moment before it popped open effortlessly.

If Crowe thought that the inn itself smelled as if it hadn't been used nor dusted in fifty cycles, he was sure that the alcove beyond truly had not.

They walked together into a circular room walled with stone where Otep cracked his staff on the stonework of the floor. From sickle-shaped stone sconces built out from the wall, blue flame sparked and crackled to life. The room was bathed with an eerie glow. Several tall-backed chairs that each looked as if they had been carved out of a single piece of rock formed a circle in the center of the room, each facing inward to a shallow well inset in the floor. At the same moment that the torches flared to life, water began to fill the well from the bottom, eating away at the thick layer of dust to leave a pool of crystal-clear water.

The room was once the meeting place of the High Warder's Council. Magical symbols that consisted primarily of circles etched with straight lines and sharp angles that ended with smaller circles were carved into the stone between each throne and the lip of the pool. There was a time when the High Warders appointed to each Brysh village would meet here to discuss matters of importance to the Fifth Lord Martyr and the Brysh Sovereignty. As Crowe looked down upon the various symbols etched before each throne, he recalled the settlement that each represented; Ambermane, Sparrow, Subterranea, Ambly. He took his seat at the Ambly throne, feeling it appropriate given the circumstances surrounding his return here. Otep sat beside him on the throne where the High Warder of Sallow once sat during the conclave.

"So, what is it that brings you here my old friend?" Otep asked, looking idly down at the pool of clear water.

"Before we go into that, Otep, there is something that you must know." Crowe stared at Otep until he looked up, and then the two locked eyes. "I am no longer the Lord Martyr's tool, and truth be told, I am an outlaw, an enemy of the sovereignty. If you choose to help me, you will be helping a criminal."

Otep shook his head. "Pish posh, Asher. We are both much too old now to worry about the Lord Martyr's folly. If I choose to help you, I'll be helping a friend, to the Shadows with the Lord Martyrs."

"I thought you would feel that way, which is why I've come." Crowe placed a hand on his friend's knee and gave it a squeeze. He was glad that their bond of friendship ran thicker in Otep's veins than his loyalty to the Fifth Lord Martyr who had been dead for more than thirty cycles, or the Sixth, which had replaced him so long ago.

The two of them spent the evening discussing Crowe's past. Crowe began with the events preceding his discovery of the possession of Ambermane University Headmaster Collinhodge, the murder that made Crowe an outlaw, and Badden's Rock, where Crowe had hidden the demon's heart and the dagger used to carve it from its host.

Chapter 11

The two wizards walked with renewed purpose – Odderly's serum pulsing through their veins and making each feel as they had so many cycles ago when it was garuk that they hunted on these very slopes. It was not garuk that they hunted now, but men, bandits, but as before their prey would not elude them.

"That is where you found him?" Crowe asked, pointing to a blackened scar on the mountainside where flames had charred both grasses and trees the night before.

"Aye," Otep said. "And given that the road down below is the only one working its way through these parts they would have to have been traveling on foot."

"Which means they are close at hand," Crowe said, pointing across the valley.

Otep's gaze followed the path that Crowe indicated, and sure enough, even in the gloom of the early morning there was a light burning upon the neighboring mountainside.

"You would think that they'd be more clever than that," Crowe commented.

"Well, who have they to hide from out here? Stonehold is the closest settlement, and the wardens there seldom come this far north. Even the caravans from Lursh turn southward at the crossroad. If not for my watchful eyes these highwaymen would have gone completely unnoticed. And truth be told, if they'd not started the fire, they'd likely not have drawn my attention."

"So, they've simply preyed on the occasional stragglers from Market who chose the road less traveled," Crowe said.

Otep nodded. "They've been smart enough to leave the caravans alone, but I suppose that two old fools such as ourselves, alone on the road would be darn near irresistible, yes?"

Crowe smiled. "I would say so. And this looks like as good a spot as any."

Despite the knife-wound he had suffered in the fight with the blonde-haired brute, the night before had turned out to be good enough to fill Palis' head with pleasant dreams. Waking up to his brother's smelly breath and disheveled form hunkered over him, however, promised that the coming day would be a bad one indeed. Palis recoiled and kicked his brother away from him as he came up to his feet amid a volley of curses.

"There's people on the road," Anvis said. "Wick told me to come and get you."

"What?" Palis asked as he rubbed the sleep from his eyes.

"People on the road," Anvis said again before disappearing through the curtain that separated Palis' sleeping niche from the rest of the uneven secondary cave.

Palis found Wick and the others standing outside with his brother. They were all dressed and ready, each leaning on their sharpened wooden poles and taking turns passing around Wick's spyglass to get a better look at the road. The rising sun still had much work to do to dispel the shadows from the canyon road. Palis snatched the glass away and squinted into it, focusing on area around the campfire burning just off the road below.

"Looks to be just the two of them," Wick said in answer to the question no doubt swirling in Palis' mind. "They've been sitting there for about an hour. Two old men. Cooking breakfast by the looks of it."

Palis stared through the glass, but beneath it his lips turned up into a wicked smile cleft by the recent knife wound. "Well then lads, what do you say we go introduce ourselves?"

The highwaymen began laughing and nudging each other in turn, saying that they were all just thinking the very same thing.

———•●•———

Claudia woke when the morning light streaming through her window became too bright to ignore. At first, as she eased herself out of bed, she thought that the last few nights had been nothing more than a dream, but as the grogginess faded, she came to realize that she was not in her cottage bedchamber. The events that had transpired came rushing back at her. Still, after several days on the road, the soft bed had done wonders for her aching muscles. She felt truly refreshed.

She had bathed last night and dressed in ladies' bedclothes that Rusk had provided for her. When she opened the door of her room, she was surprised to find her traveling clothes washed, folded, and stacked neatly by her door. Taking the clothes and returning to her room Claudia changed into her own clothes and made a mental note to thank Rusk for washing them.

Odderly didn't' open his door when Claudia knocked so she let herself inside. She found him buried beneath his covers.

"Wake up," Claudia demanded.

Odderly barely stirred.

Claudia pulled back the cover from Odderly's rugged face. His hair was still matted from the storm, his face caked with grime, and he looked utterly exhausted.

"Wake up," Claudia repeated, "and go take a bath, you smell like a stiddleback's rear end."

Claudia sat Odderly's clothes down on the rocking chair by his bed and headed back to the door. Across the hall she began checking the other rooms for her grandfather, but one by one she found them empty. All except for the last door which stood ajar at the top of the stairs.

When Claudia pushed open the door to peek inside, she saw the traveler that Otep had spoke about the night before. The injured man was sleeping, and so Claudia quietly stepped inside. Now she knew why Odderly had not taken advantage of the warm bath. He had obviously been here most of the night tending to the wounded man.

Roak's hand, Claudia thought as she looked down upon the injured traveler. *Who would do such a thing?*

Claudia sat down beside the large blond-haired man and took hold of his hand. His color was fair and there was warmth in his skin.

"I don't know what happened to you," she said to the man, "but it is good luck for you that Odderly happened to be here. He could nurse a misborn robuck back to health, so don't you fret, you'll be feeling like yourself again before too long."

Claudia felt the man faintly squeeze her hand, and as she looked up, she saw two watery blue eyes turned to the side to look at her.

"You . . . you're awake," she said softly.

Another faint squeeze.

"Do you need some water? You must be parched."

Another squeeze.

Claudia sat the traveler's hand gently down on the side of the bed and poured water into a clean bowl from a pitcher that must have been left in the room by Rusk or Odderly. She knew that the man wouldn't yet be able to sit up despite the magical salves that she could smell in the air, so she wet a cloth in the bowl and rang it out over his cracked lips. He winced when he swallowed, but the thankfulness in his eyes was readily apparent.

Claudia repeated the process several times, and finally wiped beads of sweat from the man's brow. He licked his lips, and then tried at last to speak. Claudia leaned close so that she could hear.

"Ha . . . Hann . . . ah?" he asked weakly.

"Hannah?" Claudia repeated softly.

The man made an attempt to nod.

Wick and Anvis were the first to leap out of the trees onto the road before the two old men. If they had intended their sudden and intentionally dramatic appearance to inspire fear, they were sorely mistaken. The two old men hardly looked up, even as Palis casually strolled out of the brush with four other highwaymen behind them. Otep took a bite of something he had been roasting over the roadside fire and began to chew.

Palis spoke up, "that's right old-timers, you just go ahead and finish up there while we help ourselves to your bags."

"Bags?" Otep said to Crowe as he chewed. "Did he say bags?"

"He did," Crowe replied as he stood and brushed off his leggings. "I think that they believe us to be petty travelers."

"Petty?" Otep asked as he stood. "Such a rude thing for them to think about us."

Anvis looked to Wick. Wick looked to Palis. And Palis, not understanding the old men's calm demeanor did what any highwayman would do in such a situation. He shouted, "kill them!" and threw his makeshift spear at Crowe.

Crowe's wand appeared in his hand in that same instant that Palis' spear left his own. *"Lorroak Fury!"* Crowe shouted.

The spear splintered and broke apart in midair as the tip of Crowe's wand flared and a blast of force surged out toward the bandits. Needles blew off the nearby trees, which were then blown over as if caught in the grip of a hurricane's wind. Palis and the four scoundrels he stood with were blown back fifteen feet to land in a battered heap.

Otep's magic was no less devastating. He jabbed his gnarled staff toward Wick and blew the air out of his lungs as he spoke the words of his spell. From the staff erupted a cone of searing flame that sent Wick staggering backward on fire and rolling around on the ground. He was dead in seconds though the flames and smoke continued to rise from his burning body.

Anvis had been standing close to wick, and the flames had spread to him as well. He worked frantically to strip off his burning leathers, which had taken flame as if they had been soaked in oil. When he saw Otep swing the gnarled tip of the staff toward him Anvis forgot the task and broke out into a fiery run.

Otep stalked after him. "Fire, was it? You and your cohorts set *my* mountain on fire? Let me show you fire!"

Anvis screamed as a second blast of flame engulfed him. He fell to the ground burning, and Shadow took him.

Behind Otep, Crowe shouted magical words and fired spiraling contrails of green energy into the highwaymen as they scrambled up to their feet and attempted to flee. One by one the magical bolts ripped open armor and flesh, sending the highwaymen to their graves. But as the last of them scurried away Otep's wrinkled hand pulled Crowe's wand astray.

"Let that one go," Otep said calmly. "Let him return to whatever place it is that vermin of his kind go to hide and let him spread the word that these mountains are protected."

Crowe sighed. Something of the old times burned in his eyes, a long-dimmed glint of excitement that had suddenly been rekindled. He nodded and turned around to see what had become of the two bandits that Otep had faced. Satisfied with the results he said, "to the cave then. Let us see if the woman you saw in the traveler's mind was taken there. She met yet be alive."

———•·•———

Palis ran as fast as his legs would carry him. He followed the road at first, but when he came within sight of the Otep-Korah Crossroad he began to fear that other warders might be around. Warders, that is what the two old men must have been, but why they were not wearing the telltale orange and black cloaks of those in the Lord Martyr's service he could not say. It did not matter though. Palis knew that two things were undeniably true. The two old men were wizards, and everyone else, including his own brother, was dead.

Palis did not know what to do. He certainly could not risk going back to the cave again, which meant that everything he had looted over the last few weeks was also lost. Finding a sheltered place among some tall pines Palis stopped to catch his breath. There was no time to be wasted. It would not be long before the old wizards would come looking for him, and there weren't many routes that one could take out of the narrow canyons of Roak's Elbow, which was precisely the reason that Palis had led his band here to begin with.

If he was to survive the day and escape these cursed mountains, there was only one possible route open to him. He would have to take the Lursh Road and pray that he could reach the lowlands before any more of the Lord Martyr's men arrived. At least in the Hagstead he stood a chance of eluding the wizards.

Crowe and Otep had found the cave easily enough, and within it they discovered nothing less than they feared they would find. The bandits had accumulated a small fortune in the time that they had worked the area. There was a thick sack filled to the brim with golden flays. The stolen money was the life savings of everyone who had fallen victim to the highwaymen on the road. And there was a collection of goods ranging from household items and tools to cloth and herbs that would have fetched a fair price in the undercity. But the most heart wrenching discovery of all was the body left tied to the rocks in the back of the cave.

Otep covered her with a blanket and then turned to consult his friend. "She's dead then. He'll not take this news lightly when he awakes."

"Then he shouldn't be told," Crowe said curtly. "He'll need strength of spirit to recover from such a beating, magic or no. Tell him of her fate and you'll condemn him to grief. You'll condemn him to die right along with her."

"What do you suggest?"

"Give him hope," Crowe said. "Tell him that before one of the bandits died, he told us that she had been taken east. Don't say to where. He'll recover more quickly, and when he is strong enough to face the truth, you can tell him that you'd since come to realize that the bandit had lied in hope of saving his own skin. At any rate, do not speak of her being ravaged."

Otep considered this, and then nodded in agreement. "Let us take the flays then on his behalf and bring the mountain down to cover this place lest it ever be found again."

Claudia and Odderly had prepared their own lunch when they had been unable to find Rusk anywhere around the inn. The rest of the day had passed quietly enough with Odderly checking in on the injured traveler now and then and trying desperately to avoid Claudia's questions about the strange mountain inn where they found themselves. He told her again and again that she would find out soon enough.

When Otep and her grandfather returned later that evening they were both quiet and grim. Something had happened while they were gone that had deeply troubled both old men. Claudia kept quiet about it, however, deciding that now was not the best time to press the matter.

Rusk had appeared from nowhere not long after, and as they all sat eating their supper Claudia finally learned how a secluded inn in the middle of nowhere was going to help them on their way to the Black Rift.

"Rusk tells me that your boat is ready, Asher," Otep said during the meal.

"Boat?" Claudia asked. She had forgotten that Otep had said something about a boat when they had first arrived at *The Blue World*.

Odderly stopped eating. His nostrils flared as he took in deep breaths. "So, we're really going through with it then?"

"But there are no rivers near here deep enough for a boat, only the small streams that feed the valley," Claudia said.

"Oh, but child, you are thinking only of the waterways that you can see when you look down from the mountain," Otep said after washing down a bite with some blue wine. "Asher has told me all about what happened, and where you are headed . . . and why you would seek out the Black Rift. But by now the wardens have left Lursh in full and begun to disperse throughout the Brylands. There will be roadblocks on every road, and worse yet, the warders have no doubt left Ambermane and will be watching through eyes not their own. There is simply no place in the World Above that will be safe for the three of you."

"Will they not see us on a river then?" Claudia asked.

"Not on the river we will be taking," Crowe answered.

"You don't mean . . ." Claudia said quietly.

"Aye, they do," Odderly put in. "We're going by way of the World Below."

Chapter 12

Kobb slid down the steep incline and dropped into a lower tunnel that he knew all too well. This was the way to the fighting pit, and as he walked forward, he could make out the shapes of Pulgra's garuk standing in the dark recesses of the passage, just on the edge of his torch light.

When Kobb came to the end of the passageway he was greeted by silence as two garuk wearing Pulgra's brand scarred into their hands pulled the chains of the slave chute. The gate inset in the stone began to rise into the ceiling of the passageway. With Pulgra's people surrounding him so openly it became clear to Kobb that Pulgra's attack on Atta's stable had been total and complete.

Kobb stepped through the chute and found himself in the familiar confines of the fighting pit. Dozens of garuk shifted about on the lip of the pit. The gladiator had arrived at last, and the game was about to begin. Defiantly, Kobb walked to the center of the fighting pit, ignoring the warm muddy water that was being thrown down upon him by the garuk and the guttural shouts and taunts that echoed throughout the cavern.

It was not until Pulgra stood and raised a hand that the shouting of the garuk spectators fell silent. He stepped forward from the seat Atta had occupied before.

"Atta," Pulgra taunted as he played idly with the long gray tooth he wore around his neck on a leather cord, "is no longer alive to protect you, *Lor Sarkka Rah.*"

A terrible roar came from the larger chute at the opposite end of the fighting pit. Kobb maintained his stance despite the unnerving sound of the beast being routed into the pit to face him. His eyes moved slowly along the rim of the lava-forged arena. To Kobb, it was not a matter of how he would defeat whatever was about to come through the gate, but a matter of how he would escape the pit, kill Pulgra, and get out of Atta's stable and the surrounding caverns with Pulgra's garuk hot on his heels.

"And so, *human*, I will take great pleasure in finally watching you die."

Pulgra's statement signaled the raising of the gate. Kobb turned his attention to the black tunnel but prepared as he was to face Pulgra's latest champion, the sight of a sixty-foot garanu scurrying out into the fighting pit took the breath from Kobb's lungs.

The beast, a six-legged dragon-like lizard with oily green scales as thick as bucklers and a lashing, barbed tail, was beyond anything that Kobb had expected to face.

How did he catch such a thing?

The garanu was still tethered with the shackles that had once been used to restrain it, but the handlers were gone. All that remained of them was a severed garuk arm twisted in one of the chains. Kobb wondered how many of Pulgra's own people had died in the effort to subdue the beast and loose it into Atta's stable.

The din of the crowd returned as the garanu sprang forward and landed on its four rear legs. It arched its neck to the unseen darkness of the cavern's ceiling and roared again. The roar came back in a disturbing echo that played off the acoustics of the massive cavern.

Kobb began to slowly back away from the beast even as he brought the torch to bear before him and tightened his grip on *Enshalaan* until his hand was white knuckled around the hilt.

Charging forward with its mouth wide open, the garanu closed the gap in seconds. Its legs moved so quickly that it almost seemed to glide across the ground. At the last possible second Kobb thrust the burning torch into the garanu's jaws and leapt to the side. He hit the ground and rolled as the massive maw of stiletto-like teeth snapped closed at his heels three or four times in lightning succession before the garanu had to turn to realign itself for another strike.

All around the fighting pit the garuk shouted and threw warm muddy water down, as was their custom during the gladiatorial events. The garuk provided a momentary distraction, and the garanu arched up and snapped a group of shouting savages into its mouth for they had foolishly been leaning over the railing to get a better look at the fight. The garanu chewed a few times and worked the screaming garuk down into its throat where they finally fell silent. An instant later it turned its head to see Kobb running for the chute gate where he had entered.

But the chute was firmly secured and the points of garuk spears jabbed through the bars pushed Kobb away. Defiantly, Kobb slipped between spear poles and with a quick grab, he managed to wrestle one of the spears away. He turned and set the spear against the heel of his foot just in time to raise it against the garanu's charge. The spear caught the giant lizard under the jaw and pushed up through the thick scaly hide into its mouth. The impact lifted the front of the beast off the ground for an instant. But the garanu was hardly slowed.

Taking the only escape left open to him Kobb ducked beneath the snapping jaws and felt fragments of the spear raining down on him as it shattered. He drew the garuk sword he had taken from one of the dead guards and used both it and *Enshalaan* to hack away at the garanu's throat in turn.

The sword impacted dully against the garanu's armored underside, but *Enshalaan* bit deeply. Kobb felt the sudden alertness of the demon and a thirst for blood as the gore began to pour from the garanu's neck.

Just as Kobb thought that he might survive this battle after all, the giant lizard's front legs came up under it and raked Kobb away. He felt the razor-sharp claws slice into him, cleaving both flesh and bone, and then he was thrown out from under the garanu and sent flopping limply away.

Kobb rolled to a stop.

The pain was intense, worse than any he had ever felt in battle before. Between the throbbing pangs he thought he could feel his entrails slipping out of his abdomen. Weakly, he looked down, and saw that indeed they were. He knew that he was dying even as *Enshalaan's* healing embrace began to transform the pain to warm numbness. Though he had lost the sword, Kobb had somehow managed to keep hold of the magical dagger. But could even *Enshalaan's* magic heal the fatal wounds before they claimed Kobb's life?

Through partially opened eyes Kobb could see the garanu snapping its head back and forth in painful spasms. A shower of blood and gore ran out of the giant subterranean predator's neck. Perhaps he had dealt the giant lizard a lethal blow as well? But those thoughts were suddenly pushed from his mind and Kobb's attention was forced inward. In his weakened state Kobb felt something emanating from the magical dagger that he had never felt before.

Enshalaan was not only mending Kobb's horribly torn body; there was something else hidden beneath that magic. Kobb began to feel the weight of the demon's presence within him. It was as if *Enshalaan* had chosen this moment of weakness to assault Kobb's willpower.

"No . . ." Kobb whispered to himself as he tried to shake the strange sensation from his body.

Kobb held a hand tight to his belly to keep his insides inside as he staggered up to his feet. The shock of betrayal was evident on his face as he feebly tried to cast the dagger away, but he found his fingers clenched so tightly around the hilt that he could not let it go. His fingers cramped tightly against his will. He jerked suddenly and felt his ribs crack back into place.

Although *Enshalaan* was healing him, bringing him back from wounds he could never have survived, Kobb realized that he was fighting a second battle now. A battle far more dangerous than the one he had fought, and lost, to the garanu. Kobb was fighting for his very *self*. His willpower was fading.

He felt invaded. Betrayed. And though he began screaming madly and using every ounce of willpower to push back the overwhelming presence of the demon, he felt *Enshalaan's* tendrils of consciousness beginning to supplant his own. His legs burned with muscle spasms as he took a step forward against his will.

Kobb tried to focus on the chaos that had erupted around the fighting pit. He saw Pulgra there, looking down upon him in genuine confusion. And then there was darkness and the feeling of being submerged under water in inky blackness. His breath was suddenly taken away from him.

Kobb's force of will continued to fight against the possession, but now time and sensation were completely lost to him. One moment he thought he heard Pulgra screaming in pain, but then there was only muted sleep-like darkness. There was the faint sensation of his feet landing on the hard stone of the cavern floor. Was he running? Then, only numbness.

Kobb could feel the demon's consciousness inside of him. He knew that he was losing this battle. He heard himself laughing. And then he felt the sensation of drowning within himself.

Chapter 13

Yssa had never feared the forest, but she found herself doing just that with each quiet step through the woods. When she had come to a clearing and looked up to the sky, she saw the contrail of red smoke that hung motionless in the air despite the strong wind that rustled the leaves of the Hagstead's mighty ringbarks. It was a signal used by the warders in an effort for cohesion among a group. She knew that they had found the bodies she had left behind, and she knew that she had not covered nearly enough ground to forge for herself any sense of safety.

It was not until she reached the secluded lake later that afternoon that she found any sense of peace. This was a place that was incredibly special to her, or at least it had been in her youth before her naivety was shattered by the dark realities of the world. This was the place where she had fallen in love with Asher Crowe.

As Yssa came to the spot along the lakeside where she and Crowe used to sit together and stare up at the stars and the moons, she cast aside the last bit of romanticism that remained within her.

Now is no time to dream of a life that could have been when I was still young enough to harbor dreams.

There were tracks in the mud beside the familiar flat rock where she and Asher Crowe once sat and held each other. The boot prints were Crowe's, she knew, and as she looked down at them, she felt both sadness for him, and fear for both his safety and the safety of his granddaughter, Claudia. Yssa knew that the girl could never truly understand the events that changed her grandfather's place in history from that of a hero and prophet to that of a traitor and outlaw. And now Yssa's place too had somehow shifted to that of a criminal.

"Damn you, Asher," Yssa said to herself as she crouched in the mud and pried up the mossy rock.

As Crowe had promised, he had left something for Yssa there. A small wooden case had been hidden in a recess in the damp earth beneath the flat rock. Yssa retrieved it and sat there on her heels, not sure if she really wanted to open it and be pulled deeper into the chaos that had found her since Asher Crowe had returned. At long last, she accepted her fate and looked in upon the contents.

"I'll be damned," she said to herself.

Though the screaming had ended many hours before, the anger and pain in the air remained almost palpable. Warder Mankoff had been denied a mirror through the nights that followed his confrontation in the observatory. He waited for the burning pain that consumed him to end, for the numerous magics that had been evoked in an effort to heal him to take their effect. While he had survived the acidic burning of Odderly's magic, the maddening pain just would not go away.

He lay there, tied down to a table with thick braided ropes, gaining a sense of what remained of him only by the differentials of the agony that played on his skin. He could not feel his lips, and when he had slid his tongue over his teeth earlier in the day, he realized that this was due to the fact that he no longer had lips with which to feel. His teeth were dry, exposed, and the air that came into his lungs when he breathed through his nose came to quickly. He knew that his nose too was gone. And he could not blink. His eyes burned with the need to blink, but this too was denied him.

Warder Mankoff needed no mirror to know that he had been melted into a faceless monster, and though his screaming had stopped, his seething anger and hatred continued to grow to the point where sanity faded. He would have his revenge. It was only a matter of time. If he lay still, and remained calm, they would come and cut the ropes. And then he would be free. He would hunt down Odderly Flack and Asher Crowe. He would make them suffer as he had. He would do this, if it was the last thing that he ever did.

A sense of relief worked its way through Warder Solias' sore muscles as he and Warder Abrashi dismounted and felt solid cobblestones beneath their feet again. The ride from the Township of Ambermane to Lursh had taken the better part of two days, and as Warder Solias often said, "anyone who says that two days on stiddleback doesn't bother them should have their tongue stretched and their eyes put out!"

All around them, Lursh was a bustle of activity, and this was caused less by the fact that snowflakes had again signaled the coming of winter than due to the fact that word about the happenings in Ambermane had preceded the two warders. This was not unexpected. It was common these days for crows to be used to deliver messages quickly between the distantly separated settlements of the Brylands. Common crows were the birds of choice for common men, while larger crows with white feathers upon their chest were reserved for matters of importance to the Lord Martyr. Some might think that catching sight of a white-vested crow would invite an arrow, but the people of the Brylands knew better than to stick their nose into official matters. It was true that one would have a better chance of escaping the gallows for killing his neighbor, than one would for shooting down one of the large white-vested crows. And none dared face the mysterious obelisk in Subterranea where a fate far more dreadful than death was said to wait.

All afternoon as they rode, the two warders passed groups of armed wardens who were riding out of Lursh. They had learned that men-at-arms were being dispersed from the academy in record number to assist the wardens assigned to the reeves of the various Brysh villages. This alone confirmed that word had reached the stonetappers at

Stonehold, who had no doubt been in contact with the Lord Martyr or his highest-ranking officials, the High Warders. While it was not uncommon for fledgling wardens to be given reprieve from their duties in Lursh when a village was experiencing undue trouble at the hands of local ruffians, vagrant highwaymen, or would be usurpers, there was only one other time that Warder Solias knew of when fighting men who had not yet graduated the academy were deputized and directly involved with the hunt of a wanted man. Ironically, that incident, which Warder Solias had read about during his cycles in Subterranea, also involved Asher Crowe.

"I've never cared for this place, Master," Warder Abrashi said to Warder Solias as he followed him from the stables into the main castle-like structure of Lursh. "I can feel the animosity every time one of the wardens looks at me."

"Do you blame them for hating us?" Warder Solias said, his voice deep and resonant. "No matter what they achieve in life they will never attain even a fraction of the power wielded by a first cycle student of wizardry. They are commoners given the charge of policing their own. And they are a valuable tool, nothing more. You will do well to remember that."

Warder Solias looked away from his apprentice as the tall doors of the structure before them were pulled open by novice fighting men who wore orange and black striped sashes around their waists. This signified them as being mere students at the fighting school.

"We'll see how valuable they prove themselves," Warder Abrashi muttered to himself, his words dripping with venom. "I can't help but wonder how many of the fools will be killed should they be the ones to cross paths with Crowe and Flack."

"You forget, Morrinus, that Asher Crowe is no rabid hound out for the taste of blood. I've read the scrolls, and I believe that he believes himself entirely justified in having committed his crimes. There are records in the High Warder's archives that plainly state that he did go before them with his charges against Headmaster Collinhodge prior to killing the man."

"Then you think that Collinhodge was possessed?" Warder Abrashi stopped, forcing Warder Solias to stop and turn around to conclude the conversation. "You believe in the Ambra?"

"Of course, I believe in the Ambra. I've been to Roak's Grave and the entire island is abound with proof that the Ambra existed. Your question is, *do I believe in demons?*"

Warder Abrashi nodded.

"Yes, I do," Warder Solias began walking again, turning down the twisting halls and ascending several staircases, for he knew this place well.

"Then as a man of honor, how can you be so zealous in hunting Asher Crowe if you feel that his actions were justified?"

"Because, my young apprentice, Crowe is an outlaw. The Fifth Lord Martyr himself sealed the decree stating that Asher Crowe was to be apprehended at all costs, his body taken before the High Warder's Council so that it could be prepared for entombment in the Obelisk of Condemned Souls." Warder Solias stopped outside of the closed door that had been his destination. "It is not my place to challenge the Lord Martyr. Nor is it yours. I've been assigned a task, and I will see it done. Loyalty and obedience forge the path to a seat at the High Warder's Council." Warder Solias paused for a moment, lost in thought. "I truly hope that Crowe can be taken alive. I would so love to speak with the man before he is put to death. He is a rarity, you know, and it is not often that one finds the opportunity to speak with such a legend."

Yssa separated the contents of the small wooden case onto the surface of the mossy rock just as snowflakes began to fall around her. There were six syringes containing a bluish fluid that began to glow when the syringes were shaken. Crowe had also penned a letter that detailed the process of brewing the magical serum so that additional draughts could be made. He had left behind twenty golden crowns, each worth one hundred flays, which was about what Yssa earned each month from her position as a master at the university. She would not be wanting for money anytime soon.

All of this was less important, however, than the small silver charm that she found herself staring at. It was a colorful pendant that consisted of sixteen small round gems, each the brilliant color of one of the sixteen moons that orbited the World. In the center of the glittery circle was a softly glowing red heartstone, a rare gemstone that served but one purpose in terms of magical enchantments; heartstones were imbued with a trace of a person's essence, and with it she could find her way to Asher Crowe no matter where in the World Above, or the World Below he might be. It was said that one could even follow a soul into the World After with such a charm. The stone barely glowed as Yssa stared into it. If she chose to follow Crowe, it would grow brighter as she came closer to him.

As a wizard, Yssa could sense that each of the other sixteen gemstones on the charm also carried strong magic, though she wouldn't have the time to study them now to find out just what sort of enchantments Crowe had woven into them. They were trivial, however, to the fact that Asher Crowe had created a heartstone at all. He was a wanted man, the most wanted of men, and such a charm in the wrong hands would easily lead his enemies to him. There would be nowhere that he could hide. He had not only created it, but he had left it here, he had entrusted it, to Yssa. She was so touched that tears found her eyes.

———••———

Warder Mankoff heard the door open. He tried to turn his head, but the bondage kept him from looking over to see who had come inside. He waited, patiently, a machine that waited for each gear to lock into place before it could complete its function. Soon, several of his dearest friends hovered over him. He recognized the faces, though in his crazed state of mind their unimportance to his cause of vengeance rendered them all with similar features. Flack was not here. Crowe was not here. His wait had not yet ended.

"Loris?" One of the men said. "Are you awake?"

Warder Mankoff tried to speak, but his throat hurt too badly to let the words through. Instead, he nodded. It was a slight movement yet scabs broke open and he felt their throbbing sting.

"Loris, I'm deeply sorry for what has happened. You've been through so much already . . . and I'm afraid that we are going to have to do some things to help you that . . . well, we're going to put you to sleep now. When you awake, you won't feel as much pain. You'll feel much better, in fact. And you'll be able to get up and move around. Do you understand?"

Warder Mankoff forced the slight nod again. He was in no condition to refuse whatever aid these familiar faces might be able to give him. When they were done, the ropes would be cut, and if whatever they had to do to him helped him recover from his terrible injuries, then all the better. He only hoped that he would not be asleep for too long. Each hour that passed was an hour further away that the source of his pain would get. He was eager to begin the hunt.

Headmaster Penwigget, Reeve Griggory of Ambermane, and more than two-dozen university masters formed a ring around the six warders and physicians who had just arrived from Subterranea. Standing at the forefront was Master Darrowden, a necromancer and Dark Arts Master from Fire Falls. The tension could be felt in the air as they prepared to operate on Warder Mankoff. None of them knew whether or not the procedure would be successful, and while each and every one of them shared a great deal of genuine concern for Warder Mankoff, the disfigured warder had become something of a curiosity to them as well.

Here they had the chance to attempt something written of only in Ambraic hieroglyphs collected from the ruins of Roak's Grave during the time of the First Lord Martyr. It was old magic, and it was quite likely that the attempt would fail but knowing that Loris Mankoff would die if they did nothing meant that it was a chance that must be taken. If the spirit binding were successful, then all the better.

As one, the six warders and Master Darrowden began to chant the ancient phrases written on the yellowed scroll before them. Their fluency with the Ambraic language was lacking, but each took great care to sound out the words translated from the old hieroglyphs correctly. A single error, from any of them, might be the cause of tragedy.

As they chanted, starting over when they had sounded out the last words, the physicians went to work on Warder Mankoff. Although Headmaster Penwigget had intended to watch the procedure, his stomach began to churn as he watched his dear friend's eyes slowly being cut out of his head. Suddenly pallid and in need of fresh air, he found himself having to leave the room.

Chapter 14

Rusk led Crowe and Claudia through the kitchen and into the basement larder with Odderly creeping distantly behind. It was no secret now that Odderly was claustrophobic and deathly afraid of the World Below. He'd avoided any talk about the trip that lay before them, but his mood had notably soured after they had all said their goodbyes to Otep when the inevitable descent into the World Below could not be put off any longer by his insistence to check and recheck his medical case.

As they prepared themselves Claudia thought back to her traveling cloak and finally understood why so many cloaks had been left behind. They would not be needed underground, and the excursion ahead promised to be long and tedious. The kind of trip where only what needed to be taken could be packed along. Rusk had also made the comment that very few of those who go down ever came back up again. Whether this is due to them finding their path to whatever place it was that they were going, becoming lost in the winding subterranean tunnels, or falling prey to some unforeseen danger, Claudia did not know. She had never before ventured into the World Below and thinking of entering that alien environment gave her pause. She could certainly understand Odderly's unease.

Once in the dark cellar Rusk threw aside a moldy blanket and revealed a wooden trapdoor set into the stonework of the floor. He opened this by an iron loop fastened to the wood. Before them was a narrow and confining staircase that led down into total darkness.

"You're testing my loyalty here, Asher," Odderly said nervously. Claudia could not tell by his tone if he was being truthful or simply sarcastic.

Crowe smiled and put a hand on his friend's shoulder. "You don't have to go," Crowe said. "Claudia and I can make this journey on our own if you'd rather go back to Ambermane and see if you can work things out with the warders."

Odderly smirked. "We both know that there is no going back now. I'm with you to the end. I just hope that we don't find our end down there. I've heard enough stories about . . ."

"Stop your bellyaching before you scare Claudia," Crowe leveled his gaze at Odderly and gave him a wink.

Odderly, in turn, did not smile. He took a deep breath, brandished his iron rod, and spoke the words to a spell. There was a sizzling sound as the tip of the iron rod began to glow and the cold within the larder was replaced by a smoldering heat as the rod intensified as if it had been plunged into a forge. The larder was bathed in hot, orange light.

"What about the stiddleback?" Claudia asked.

"They'll be fine," Rusk offered. "I'll take good care of them until the traveler is able to ride. I'm sure that they'll help him on his way."

Claudia nodded and looked down the narrow staircase. She lit up her wand and was the first to follow Rusk, who raised a hand to shield his large all-black eyes against bright magical lights as he moved quietly down the steep stone steps. The stairs were unevenly cut into the stone for a while, but then, quite suddenly, the narrow and confining stairwell spilled out into a vast cavern that was thrice over the size of the boulder field that spread out above the Korah Valley. Claudia had never seen anything like it before. The light of her wand fell upon the bulbous stone shapes that pushed out of the cavern wall, and almost instantly her mind began playing tricks on her, rendering the natural formations of the dark stone as lurking monsters and leering wax-like faces.

With her next step she felt the stonework of the steps change to wooden planks that groaned in complaint as the four of them descended. She looked down and gasped. Catwalks had been constructed below. The lack of maintenance was obvious, and the entire structure looked as if it might fall any moment. The strange way that sound played off the giant pocket of air in the mountainside made Claudia's heart race. Each footstep echoed into the distance below. She walked with light, careful steps, afraid that the rickety wooden stairs would give out and send her plummeting into the darkness.

"Are you sure that this is safe?" She asked Rusk.

"As safe as such a place can be," he assured her. "There's nothing around here that will do you any harm. My people once called these caverns home."

The mention of *his people* took Claudia by surprise. Until now she had given little thought to how Rusk had come to live in *The Blue World* with Otep and she had somehow put the corpses that littered the area around the inn out of her mind. What was that which Claudia had detected in Rusk's voice? A distant pain or sadness? She found herself wondering why Rusk had been spared when the rest of the garuk, seemingly all the garuk, had been killed so very long ago. She would make a point to ask her grandfather about this, but as she watched Rusk descend the wooden catwalks and scaffolding that appeared below the stairs, she began to wonder if Rusk had betrayed his own people in exchange for his life. Her skin began to crawl at the thought of Rusk on his knees, bargaining for his life at the tip of her grandfather's wand. She shivered. Crowe's hand on her shoulder startled Claudia and she realized she had fallen behind their guide.

"Worry not, child, there is no danger here," Crowe said through a reassuring smile, and loud enough for Odderly, trailing behind them, to hear, he added. "The lake lies just below."

Crowe stepped around Claudia and continued down the catwalks until he met Rusk where he waited by a free-floating wooden platform suspended by a system of thick ropes and pulleys. Claudia watched as the two exchanged quiet words with each other and then shared the long embrace of two friends who would not likely see one another again.

She felt a sudden increase in temperature as Odderly, carrying the smoldering rod, stepped up beside her. "I suppose we'll both get used to it," he said. "The World Below that is, we're going to be down here for quite some time."

"Why are you afraid of it?" Claudia asked. "What isn't my grandfather telling me?"

"Afraid? No, I'm not afraid of it . . . I just, well I like to be able to see the sky over my head, that's all." Oddly looked up, his rod and Claudia's wand painting the uneven stone around them in a battle of strange orange and white patterns of light. Oddly dug his red handkerchief out of his pocket and wiped the sweat from his brow. He failed to answer Claudia's second question before he joined Crowe on the suspended platform.

When Claudia reached Rusk, she turned to face him, not sure of what she should say, but feeling that she should say something. They had not become friends in the short time that she had stayed at the strange mountain inn, but she felt a sort of kinship with him none-the-less. Perhaps this was due to the fact that she empathized with the wrinkled old garuk. He was the last of his people, utterly alone and no doubt longing for the company of his own kind. Yet here he was, moments before, his arms wrapped around the man who killed everyone that Rusk once knew. Claudia sighed. It was beyond her understanding.

"I have something for you," Rusk said to her. "This will keep you from harm and bring luck to your travels." From his pocket Rusk removed a braided knot of dry black roots.

Claudia accepted the gift and tried to hide her bewilderment as she looked at it thoughtfully. She wished that she had something to give to Rusk, some token of friendship, but this was so very unexpected. Instead, she smiled, thanking her garuk *friend*. Without another word she bravely stepped out onto the swaying platform.

On the scaffolding, Rusk began to operate a crank to which the ropes holding the platform aloft were connected. With a nauseating motion, the platform began to noisily descend into the depths of the giant cavern. The lake, which filled the cavern all the way to the point where it was swallowed by darkness, slowly came into view below them.

The boat was one of many floating in the calm water, and it was much larger than Claudia had thought it would be. Rather than the small fishing craft she had occasionally seen on the Goldwater River the few times that Odderly had taken her into Ambermane, this boat was a catamaran suspended on two parallel floats with a paddlewheel centered between them on the wide, enclosed deck. A system of wooden gears ending in a crank that allowed a single pilot to work the wheel and propel the boat forward or back. It was built beside a secondary wheel, which could be used to adjust the boat's course through the water.

Their bags, and Odderly's saddle basket, had been piled in the center of the boat along with several sacks of supplies, which would be needed for the daunting trip through the World Below. Extending out from each corner of the boat were long poles that held torches suspended over the placid water. Claudia dispelled the magic light from her wand and approached one of these. She got down on her knees to investigate the water and was amazed at how clear it was. Even with just the light cast from the ever-burning torch near her she could see the smooth, uneven stone at the bottom of the lake where a school of small eyeless white fish darted haphazardly through the water.

"It's deeper than it looks," Crowe said as he walked past Claudia and stepped up to the drive crank to which he raised his wand. The boat rocked slightly, drawing a grunt from Odderly as he quenched his magical rod in the water with a resounding hiss. Powered by Crowe's magic, the paddlewheel began to turn, and the boat came about.

Rusk's voice called out from the darkness overhead, "safe travels to you, my friends."

Warder Solias pushed open the door and strode into the well-appointed room with Warder Abrashi at his side.

"Ah, Allus, I'm glad that you've arrived," came the deep, gravel-throated voice of Reeve Boarwind, the highest ranking of the Lord Martyr's officials in Lursh. "Let me first express my most sincere condolences for the harm done to our friends in Ambermane. Most unfortunate."

"Yes," Warder Solias said coldly. "Most unfortunate."

Reeve Boarwind rose from behind his ornately carved desk of smoothly lacquered petrified wood. He gathered a few parchments and locked them away in a nearby cabinet before turning back to the warders. "I'm sure that you are both tired, but there is something important that I must show you. Your inquiry seems to have been answered."

Warder Solias nodded and the two warders followed Reeve Boarwind out of his office, down a long hall, and through a series of descending staircases. Before long they arrived in the dungeons. As they came to a solidly built door, Reeve Boarwind explained, "we've apprehended a highwayman who claims to have seen Asher Crowe."

———•———

Palis had been savagely beaten before he managed to say something that stayed the clubs of the wardens he'd stumbled upon. Banditry was a serious crime in the Brylands, and with a single glance it had been obvious that he was no casual traveler. Palis had immediately made a run for it, but while they hardly looked capable of reaching a speedy pace, the warden's stiddleback had little trouble running him down.

His guilt, of *something*, had been determined by his flight and he had been fortunate when his cries about having been attacked by two old wizards had stopped the wardens cold. The beating shifted toward interrogation, and when one of the warden's had referred to the outlaw, Asher Crowe, Palis knew that he had information that he could barter with. Knowing the wardens' reputation for lynching highwaymen after they had learned what they needed from them, Palis had wisely refused to divulge any further information about the old wizards, insisting that he be allowed to speak to a warder.

He had been immediately taken to Lursh and thrown in the dungeon, but not long after that a physician had arrived to care for his wounds and he'd even been given something warm to eat and fresh water with which to wash it down. Palis had been imprisoned before, twice for banditry, once for larceny, and between the three of these he'd spent more than six autumn cycles locked away in places far worse than this. As before, he knew that the secret to leniency was to sacrifice information about his associates. The warders were always interested in the biggest fish in the pond. Unlike last time, however, those bigger fish happened to be people he was only too eager to hand over to the authorities. He knew something important, and if he played his stones right, he might just see the light of day again.

The sound of keys rattling got his attention and Palis clambered up to his feet just as the door swung open. Three of the Lord Martyr's men stepped inside. He recognized one immediately as Reeve Boarwind, for Palis had served two cycles in this very dungeon. The other two men wore the black and orange cloaks he had expected the old men in the canyon to have been wearing. The warders had finally come for him. Palis finished his cup of water casually and sat it down on the ground before he walked over to the bars and bowed his head to the three men.

Warder Solias turned to Reeve Boarwind and asked him to wait outside. The reeve nodded, and left the two men alone with Palis, who smiled knowing that his opportunity had arrived.

"I told them that I wouldn't talk to anyone but a warder," Palis began.

"And what is it that you wish to talk about?" Warder Solias asked, folding his arms over his chest.

"I was senselessly attacked by two mages. They killed my friends, and my brother, and I think that one of them is of some interest to the Lord Martyr. How does the name Asher Crowe hit you?" Palis grinned despite himself. He knew he had piqued their interest.

"If you have information about a known outlaw, we have ways of encouraging you to speak of it," Warder Abrashi warned. It was all too well known that the more powerful warders could easily make true this threat.

"Pardon me of any crimes for which I am wanted, let me go, and I'll tell you where you can find him. I've been down this road before, you see, I know what you bastards can do, and I'll make you kill me to spite you, if you want it to go that way."

Palis was not sure if he could withstand magical interrogation again, it was the most painful experience he had ever endured, but his claim was the only chance he stood. As a betting man, he decided that it was worth the gamble. He glared at the two warders in turn.

"Very well," Warder Solias said. "You shall accompany us, and if your story proves to be true, you will be a free man. You will even have earned the Lord Martyr's gratitude."

A wicked grin spread across Palis' cleft lips.

"But if you are lying," Warder Abrashi added, "we will take you before the Obelisk in Subterranea and rip your very soul from your body."

Palis could see the sincerity in the young warder's face. The stakes of this game had just been raised.

No matter, he thought, *this was one gamble that he would win.*

Chapter 15

Lances shattered as two stiddleback charged past each other. The mounted wardens paused only long enough at the end of the lyst field to rearm themselves before turning and preparing to make another pass. Palis recoiled as they clashed a second time. One of the men-at-arms was thrown from his mount. He hit the ground hard, the metal plates of his armor rattling as he tried to get back up to his feet. Palis knew all too well the deadly precision with which the mounted wardens could strike. He had seen friends impaled before and only avoided the same fate the day before because the scrub around the road where he'd been found was too thick and cluttered with stunted trees.

Everything about being here, chaperoned by Warder Solias and Warder Abrashi as they met with various people around Lursh had Palis on edge. He was as nervous as a rabbit in a puma den. This place, more than any other in the World Above, was avoided by people like Palis who lived on the wrong side of the law. If only his brother could see him now, or Wick and the others, what would they think of him?

Well that hardly matters now, Palis thought, biding his time.

Once the wizards were dealt with, he would be free of his current company and able to go get his loot from the cave and head to the undercity. At least there he would be able to blend in again. In such a place, he could start over.

Yssa held her wand with both hands over her chest and the tip of it touching her bowed forehead. She spoke the words softly, repeating them over and over, "*illussory tenwathae, illusory tenwathae* . . ."

More than a dozen wardens, some riding stiddleback and others moving on foot, searched the woods around her and she dared not move. As Asher Crowe had always said, invisibility is best woven over that which does not move and should even one of the wardens notice her there among the thickets her end would be swift and merciless.

It was not surprising that they had come upon her at the lake. The wardens of these parts were skilled woodsmen and trackers, and Yssa had not bothered to magically conceal her footsteps until she heard the whinny of a stiddleback that signaled the approach of the lawmen. Fortunately, Asher Crowe had paved the way for her escape.

In the time that Yssa had studied the gem-encrusted pendant at the edge of the lake she had uncovered the properties of several of the smaller gemstones. They each held single-use enchantments of varying nature, but one in particular had captured Yssa's attention and made her believe that escaping the Hagstead was possible. Even with the warders and wardens in pursuit. With the heartstone glowing softly around her neck, Yssa had decided that she would find Crowe and join him in his quest for the Black Rift. What else could she do now that she had been uprooted from her work a second time? It was not as if she could ever return to Ambermane and pretend that none of this had happened.

A warden stepped up to Yssa and crouched to examine the ground directly in front of her. With her eyes squinted shut in concentration, she could not see him, but she could hear him and sense his closeness. She waited for the blow to strike.

But it never did.

After a moment, she heard footsteps moving away through the brush, and after awhile, she heard nothing at all but the wind through the trees. Yssa opened her eyes. The Lord Martyr's men were gone.

Crowe

Palis had been given a stiddleback to ride only because Warder Solias wanted to make haste on the road. Lursh was a little more than two days north of where Palis had encountered Asher Crowe, but upon swift mounts the trio would be able to close this distance in less than a day.

"With any luck," Warder Solias had said, "our business will be concluded by nightfall and you will be a free man."

Unfortunately, this was not the case. Less than an hour after they had left Lursh, the gentle flurry of snowflakes that had been falling all morning had become the first real blizzard to hit the Brylands in four generations. They continued to ride for as long as possible, heads down against the storm. When the temperature had dropped to the point that Palis' fingers had gone numb he began to grumble aloud.

"We have to stop!" Palis shouted over the blowing snow and howling wind. Seeing that both warders were pushing on, ignoring him, he yanked hard on the reigns of his stiddleback, halting the beast. "We stop now, or we freeze to death out here!"

The warders came to a stop and looked back at Palis before relenting and speaking quietly to one another. They were, all of them, unprepared for the sudden change in weather. But then, how could they have known what to expect. This was the first such storm of their lifetimes, and as fierce as it was, it was only the prelude of what was to come for the next twenty-five cycles. Winter would utterly change the face of the World Above.

"Over there, we'll shelter in those trees," Warder Solias pointed to a roadside grove over which could be seen the hazy shape of a rocky cliff-side.

Palis looked in the direction that the warder indicated and spurred his mount ahead of them, charging through the thickets and drifting snow. While the dense treetop canopy provided some degree of shelter from the falling snow, the wind whipping through the branches penetrated his clothing and he could not stop shivering.

They followed the cliff-side for another half mile, trying to find a cave, an overhanging ledge, or something that might provide some kind of shelter. What they found instead was a rockfall where giant slabs of stone had long ago crumbled away from the mountainside. Among the boulders and broken stone, they found a place where the shelves of stone formed a nook large enough to fit the three of them, but not the stiddleback. They were tethered to nearby trees, and as Palis ducked into the stone hollow a pack of dog-like barcoots scattered and went running out of the cave. At odds with losing their shelter, the small hounds lingered for a moment before surrendering and disappearing into the woods. Palis looked back at the stiddleback as the two warders entered the cave. The stiddleback hunkered low against one another. Palis did not think they would be alive when the storm finally ended.

If it ends.

Inside the hollow Warder Abrashi used his wand to heat a pile of rocks he'd stacked in a heap. They cast an orange-hot glow upon the roughly formed walls and illuminated the thick sheets of cobwebs that spiders had strung throughout.

Palis looked back into the hollow and saw the two warders stripping off their over-clothes and laying them out around the *fire* to dry. Palis was not allowed the luxury of making the choice, but he would almost have preferred freezing to death with the stiddleback outside as opposed to waiting out the storm in the warmth of the hollow with the two warders.

———•———

Yssa hunched over in pain as the magic took hold of her. She was on all fours now, her fingers dug into the snowy earth and though she tried to keep from screaming the pain of transformation became too much to bear. The bright yellow gem of the charm Asher Crowe had left for her began to glow intensely as his magic was called out of the stone. And then the gem cracked and fell as dust from the charm leaving behind a smooth depression.

The transformation happened quickly then, Yssa's body and all that she carried was pulled into itself as her mass was reduced by more than ninety percent. The white of her hair and the ashen-hue of her skin melded into the black of her academic robe, and from the gathered mass sprouted black-feathered wings. There was a sudden burst of light and Yssa took to the air as a crow.

This sort of magic was beyond her ability and totally alien to her. The sensation of flight was beyond anything she had experienced before, but along with the shifting of her form from human to bird came the instincts needed to survive in the new form. She cawed loudly, her wings beating furiously against the wind and blinding snow that blasted over the tops of the trees.

Yssa's felt the cold wind slipping through her feathers as she climbed above the trees, fighting through the raging snowstorm. In a matter of seconds, the green and white sea of trees and gathering snow was far below her, rushing by as she flew southeastward. She forced herself to go higher, above the storm and stared down in awe of the spectacle below her as the clouds rushed by.

The charm had become a part of her new form, in effect swallowed by the magical transformation, but Yssa had watched the heartstone grow brighter as she walked southeastward through the woods toward the distant peaks of Roak's Elbow. That alone was enough to guide her on her way. She had known Asher Crowe for a very long time, and she knew his ultimate destination. If Crowe had intended to travel to the Black Rift by way of the World Above, he would not have selected a course that would take him so far south. So close to the gates of Subterranea and the Lord Martyr's seat of power. With that in mind, Yssa had easily guessed the route that he must have taken. He was returning to *The Blue World*.

Crowe had told her once that the massacre of the garuk of the Korah Valley had been the point in his life when he realized that he could no longer mindlessly follow the edicts of the Lord Martyr believing in the sovereign ruler's omniscience.

When Crowe had returned from that mission, where he and Otep had played the role of assassins, Crowe had lied to the Lord Martyr and claimed that the way into the Korah Valley caverns had been closed. His official report stated that he and Otep had brought the very mountainside down upon the garuk they had been sent to kill. They *had* shattered the mountainside, but the ever-ambitious warders realized the potential gain in keeping such a place hidden from the eyes of the Lord Martyr. They had made a pact with each other that neither would reveal the secret remaining entrance to the World Below to the Lord Martyr, or even to the High Warder's Council.

It was an act of treason. To conceal this secret Otep chose to build his inn overlooking the Korah Valley when he stepped down from his office the following cycle. Crowe had taken Yssa to the inn on several occasions, and while she did not particularly care for Otep and his crude mannerisms, she knew that Asher Crowe was quite fond of him. She might not like the man, but she knew beyond any doubt that she could trust him.

It wasn't until several cycles later when the High Warders Council began meeting at *The Blue World* that Crowe confided in her about the true nature of the place and the passageway into the World Below that it was built to conceal.

After all these cycles, Asher Crowe, your little secret has finally paid off and I know just where to find you.

Yssa descended into the storm and watched the forest speed by below her until the dense woodland rose into foothills, which in turn climbed into low mountain peaks cut through by numerous canyons etched into the surrounding high country. She flew low, not knowing how much time she would have between when she felt the magic of the transformation ebb away and the moment that she would be returned to her true form.

When she came to a point where the canyon pushed up against the cliff-side she saw three stiddleback huddled together along a jagged boulder field. Knowing that she was close to the Korah Valley Yssa began to fear the worst. She landed in a nearby tree to have a closer look.

———•●•———

Palis thought nothing of the large black crow that landed in a tree outside of the hollow. He had refused to sit close to the *fire*, instead picking a place near the opening of the shelter where he could still feel the warmth coming from inside yet not have to make uncomfortable conversation with the two warders.

When he threw a stone at the crow it cawed loudly, which invited a few more stones to be thrown its way. The crow fluttered up into a nearby tree where it watched quietly. From deeper inside the hollow Palis heard Warder Abrashi approach. The warder looked outside to see what had attracted Palis' attention.

———••———

As the warder stepped into her line of vision Yssa's heart began to race. The mangy-looking fellow who had been sitting by the entrance to the makeshift cave shelter was a commoner with a rough look about him. The Lord Martyr's warders did not travel in such low company, not unless a commoner had to be retained as a guide. Worse yet, Yssa recognized the warder. It was Warder Abrashi, the svelte, dark-haired apprentice of Warder Solias, who happened to be among Warder Mankoff's closest circle of friends. That could not be a coincidence.

Yssa kicked off the branch and took to the air. She did not know how Warder Solias had followed Crowe's trail, but that hardly mattered. She knew Warder Solias' temperament and reputation. If he believed that Otep had seen Crowe, or helped him, as he no doubt would when he arrived at *The Blue World*, then Otep and Crowe in turn, were in grave danger. Once Warder Solias had gotten through Otep and discovered the passage into the World Below . . . Yssa shuddered at the thought.

She pushed herself to her limits covering as much ground as she could despite the raging blizzard that tried to push her down from the sky. When at last she crested one of the lower peaks of Roak's Elbow's eastern front she saw the broad Korah Valley come into view below her.

She circled as she descended, coming closer to the bright blue building that stood out in sharp contrast to the ruddy stone that surrounded it and the growing mounds of drifting white snow.

CHAPTER 16

They had slept on the boat, dropping anchor, and laying down on deck to rest only when they had all become too tired to press on across the endless underground lake. Odderly had given her grandfather another injection, but soon after, the two of them had both fallen asleep leaving Claudia alone in the foreboding silence of the World Below.

Claudia found it difficult to sleep under the light of the ever-burning torches, but her grandfather had assured her that in the World Below there were few things that moved willingly into the light. "Most predators down here," he had said, "do not need light by which to see, and they'll not willingly come too close to ours."

Despite the calmly uttered reassurances, Claudia drifted into sleep only after much distress. She had found the silence, broken only by the occasional dripping of water, disturbing. The very air she breathed tasted different, earthy. And the humidity made her sweat even though the temperature was comfortable. Beyond the torch light there was only darkness. Below the boat, still, clear water eventually faded to black.

Having drifted to sleep amid the silence of the vast underground lake, she awoke with a start in the realization that she could <u>hear</u> the once placid water churning around the boat.

"Grandfather," she whispered. "There's something in the water."

Claudia moved cautiously up to the edge of the boat and looked down into the water just as a long white snake-like shape slithered under the boat and disappeared from her line of sight. She rushed across the deck, drawing her wand as she leapt over Odderly, who was finally starting to stir. The creature sluiced through the water and came back into her sight on the other side of the boat. She judged its length at more than ten feet. And it was not alone. More than twenty of them swam under and all around the boat.

"Eels," Crowe said as he came up beside her.

"Eels?" Claudia asked skeptically. "They are gigantic, how can they be just eels?"

"The World Below has its own delicate ecosystem, Claudia. These are common enough down here, but unless you had planned to go for a swim in the open water, they are harmless enough as well."

"What's the matter?" Odderly called out groggily as he got to his feet and tied his wild red hair back behind his head with a leather thong. "It can't be morning already?"

Crowe patted Claudia on the shoulder and ruffled her hair playfully. "There's nothing to worry about, yet, I assure you." He moved around Odderly who had walked up to see what Claudia had seen in the water.

"Roak's hand," Odderly muttered looking down at the monstrous eels. "And I thought we grew them big back home."

"They're just eels," Claudia said with as much authority as she could muster. "Nothing to worry about. Yet."

Yssa had returned to her natural shape and she burst through the doors of *The Blue World* in a huff. "Otep! You old codger, where in Roak's Grave are you?"

Her sudden entrance and subsequent outburst had startled Amm, the fat old mool who had been sleeping by the fire once again. The mool snorted and ran through a curtain that corded off part of the room from a short hallway leading back into some other area.

"Otep?"

The old ex-warder came walking down the staircase with his staff landing forcefully on the wooden steps as he descended. "What is this all about?" he questioned.

"You've gotten old," Yssa said, grinning.

"As have you, Mistress Yssa. Asher said that you might be showing up here before long. His skills at predicting what is to come certainly have not faded over time."

"Then he *has* been here?" Yssa looked at the heartstone hanging around her neck. The stone had taken on a much brighter glow than it had in the Hagstead. "How long ago did he leave, Otep?"

"Less than a day ago," Otep answered.

Rusk entered from outside, leaving the door open behind him. "I heard shouting. Are you alright father?"

Yssa turned to see the familiar garuk, and then looked back to Otep to see him nodding.

"Aye, Rusk, though if my assumption is correct, I'm going to have to ask you to prepare another boat." Otep stepped closer to Yssa, "you do mean to go after him, do you not?"

Yssa nodded. "Aye. But there's something more. I've seen the Lord Martyr's men. Two warders led by a guide with a fresh scar across his face. I don't know the commoner, but I know these warders, Otep, and you will not be safe here. They are coming for Asher and Odderly, and it won't matter who you are. These warders are dangerous men. If you don't help them, then they'll turn their wands on you."

"Mistress Yssa, *The Blue World* is my domain, and I'm not afraid of any warders. They have no authority here. The Korah Valley was put under my protection by the pen of the Fifth Lord Martyr himself. I am the *only* authority here."

"That won't matter," Yssa said in a firm tone. "Odderly struck down Warder Mankoff in Ambermane, defending Crowe. In my own escape another warder and a warden were killed. Word has no doubt reached the Lord Martyr by now. They are coming Otep, and I hope you'll not be so stupid as to hide behind some brittle decree written fifty cycles ago."

Otep paused to consider Yssa's words. Rusk stepped away, throwing aside the same curtain the fat mool had disappeared under.

Otep and Yssa stared at each other for what seemed like several minutes before Otep finally surrendered. "Very well," he said. "I owe Asher Crowe my life, and I know your feelings for him. When these warders come, will you stand with me against them?"

Claudia had long since wondered if there would ever be an end to the mammoth subterranean lake. When the boat eventually came to the end of the cavern, she chewed her lip and looked at the stone pinching together around her through a series of naturally formed mineral columns and drooping stalactites. She began to wish that they had been able to stay on the open water a little longer. Through the tooth-like formations of dark stone she saw a much narrower flooded tunnel and any sense of safety she had begun to feel on the lake seeped out of her, leaving a cold chill that caused the fine golden hairs on her arms to stand on end. Claudia looked over at Odderly and her grandfather and noted that they too were more on guard. Her grandfather even had his wand at the ready.

"Pay attention now Claudia, the Chasmarrud Tunnel lies ahead," Crowe said.

Claudia repeated the name under her breath, committing it to memory.

"This is guskar territory," Crowe explained. "They are monstrous Neanderthals, and this passage passes far too close to Chasmarrud, a guskar village."

"Just what I wanted to hear," Odderly complained. He brandished his iron rod and started digging through the supplies that Rusk had packed for them for the large rectangular shield he had seen at the bottom of the pile the day before.

"If it comes to a fight, Claudia," Crowe said in an even tone, "you keep your head down. Guskar are a nasty lot."

Claudia nodded as she bit her lip. She took out her wand and gripped it tightly, watching as her grandfather steered the boat through the columns of wet, mineral-laden stone and into the mouth of the tunnel. Not for the first time since their descent, she felt the claustrophobic grip of the World Below. The stone around her bulged in some places, and sunk inward in others, leaving ample dark niches where she began to imagine enemies laying in wait, preparing to launch a stone or spear as the boat slowly navigated the twisting passage. Several times they passed places where the tunnel branched, but every path looked the same and at each branch her grandfather would stop the boat and spend several minutes thinking back to remember the proper course through this labyrinthine section of the Chasmarrud Tunnel.

Hours later, as they drifted under a low-hanging cluster of stalactites her grandfather spoke out, breaking the silence that had followed their course through the flooded tunnel. "The water is too high."

Both Odderly and Claudia looked back at him. A moment later, Odderly had to duck as the boat floated beneath a low spot to avoid pointed spires that pushed down from the tunnel's ceiling.

"The water is too high," Crowe muttered to himself, no doubt searching for the meaning of his own words.

"Too high for what?" Odderly finally whispered.

"Otep and I had come this way with Rusk several times before when we first began exploring this region of the World Below. I remember every tunnel, more or less, and the water is several feet too high here. Something has changed."

Odderly offered a logical conclusion, "well maybe the spring floods drain down into these caverns? You haven't been here in a long time."

"Possibly," Asher said, though he seemed hardly convinced.

They all turned their attention back to the path ahead as the boat maneuvered around a wide, but sharp turn through the solid rock of the earth around them. The bottom of the boat scraped across a shelf of stone as it came around the bend. The tunnel opened up into a cavernous chamber with a ceiling that was above the reach of the light shed from the ever-burning torches of both their own boat and another, similar craft, upturned and twisted into a wall of crumbled stone that cut the cavernous chamber in half.

"We're not alone," Claudia whispered.

"Aye." Odderly nodded.

When they crawled out of the hollow, they discovered that the storm had ended, but everything, including the frozen forms of the dead stiddleback, had been drifted in dunes of soft white snow. Palis swore under his breath as he walked, with much trouble, through the knee-deep snow to examine the dead animals.

"We'll not be going anywhere fast with this . . . snow," Palis said to the warders. "And I don't know about you two, but I'm not dressed for this kind of weather."

"Don't worry about the cold," Warder Solias said. "We've magic capable of keeping us all warm for however long we may be out here. But with the loss of the stiddleback we've no time to waste."

Both of the warders began to dig through the snow in search of various supplies that had been loaded on their mounts when Warder Solias stopped abruptly and looked to Palis, and then to the mountainside visible above the ringbarks around the boulder field. "A few hours, if we can keep a fair pace?" he asked Palis.

Palis followed the warder's gaze and nodded.

Warder Solias pulled a long, curve-bladed sword sheathed in a black leather scabbard from out of his saddle basket. "Your life is on the line here, Palis, as much as ours is. Do you know how to use this?" He threw the falcata blade to Palis.

Palis snatched it out of the air. "What, are you deputizing me?"

"Call it what you want to call it," Warder Solias said. "If Asher Crowe is nearby, and he is with Odderly Flack, then you just might need that. Put it into either one of them if you see them."

"Wait a minute here, that's not our deal. We agreed that I would lead you to them, nothing more."

"I'm changing the deal."

Warder Solias narrowed his eyes at Palis, and Palis was reminded once again why he hated dealing with the Lord Martyr's men. He unfastened his belt and strapped on the sword. "I don't suppose that you have anything to eat in there?"

Crowe

As they drifted up to the wreckage of the catamaran, Crowe stood at the bow of his own craft. Without looking back, he waved his wand over his shoulder and the crank stopped moving, cut off abruptly from his magic. The boat drifted up to the rocks, scraped against them, and came to a stop.

"It looks like one of Otep's," Odderly said, joining Crowe as he stepped out into the gravel-bottomed bank to examine the wreckage.

"Aye," Crowe said, paying less attention to the half-sunken boat then to the rockfall that had came down all around it. He began climbing out over some of the boulders.

Claudia watched them both nervously. Her grandfather had almost reached the edge of the light cast from the two ever-burning torches of the wrecked boat when he stopped suddenly. "What is it?" she called out to him.

Crowe studied something in the water, and then yelled back to her and Odderly. "This cavern has been intentionally collapsed. There used to be a column right over there," he pointed into the darkness with his wand. "They brought it down."

Odderly began to crawl across the boulders. Not wanting to be alone on the boat, Claudia hurried after him. They reached Crowe simultaneously and hopped down to a slick rock where he crouched.

"*Intium orohthem*," Crow uttered, bringing a bright point of white light to the tip of his wand.

In the light cast from her grandfather's wand, she saw the bones of a massive lizard-like creature beneath what looked like about six feet of crystal-clear water.

"What was it?" Claudia asked.

"Garanu," Crowe answered. "The predator to end all predators."

Claudia shifted and looked around nervously. "Are there more of them?"

"Let us hope not," Odderly said from behind her.

"They are solitary hunters," Crowe said. "But this presents another problem." He looked up to Claudia and Odderly. "With the passage blocked, we're not going to be able to go around Chasmarrud."

There was a long moment where the weight of Crowe's words hung almost palpably in the air. Claudia looked back to Odderly. And Odderly rolled his eyes and looked up as if in search for some god to curse for their continued bad luck.

They returned to the boat together. Crowe bewitched the paddle wheel and brought the boat around. They would have to backtrack through the tunnel for almost a mile before reaching the branch that would take them to the guskar village.

CHAPTER 17

Palis was the last of the three to cross the icy natural bridge. He moved slowly, carefully choosing his steps so that he would not slip and fall. He hated heights, as he hated most things, but he hated the warders ahead of him most of all.

When they had found the place where Palis had met Crowe and Otep, the warders spoke to each other quietly while Palis gathered the bodies of his friends. He piled them into a heap that the warders burned with fire from their wands. Warder Solias had decided by this time, that given the proximity of *The Blue World* to their current location, it was there that they would find Asher Crowe and Odderly Flack. It was well known that an old wizard named Otep watched over these lands from there. It was equally well known that he and Asher Crowe had been friends.

The trip up the mountainside had been difficult, and when Palis finally felt the reprieve of the Otep-Korah tunnel he was relieved that the warders had decided that they should rest there. Palis needed the warmth of the heated stones to bring back the feeling in his limbs. If he were expected to fight alongside these warders, he would do so, but only because the grim reminder of Wick's frozen face and Anvis' charred body were fresh in his mind.

Palis needed to be able to move swiftly so he idly swung his arms back and forth to get his blood moving again. When all this madness about Crowe was over, his business with the warders was done one way or the other. He was tired of being drug along on the hunt for the outlaw mages, and if Warder Solias had no intention of keeping his word, then Palis had every intention of running the warders through when the battle was over and the warders had been weakened by their expenditure of magic.

He judged that he would then be able to get his bag of golden flays out of the cave and be safely in the magma-heated lower tunnels of Subterranea before snow fell again. Having spent so many cycles among the scoundrels of Rish Hollow, he had made many friends throughout the Brylands, and he knew people in the undercity that he could fall in with. The sooner he established himself in Subterranea, the better.

Visions of him rising to power among the denizens of the undercity passed the time that they waited in the dark, bone-strewn tunnel. When Warder Solias had finally announced that he and his apprentice were well rested enough to face Crowe and Flack, Palis was the first on his feet. He was ready to be done with all of this.

The two stiddleback had been sheltered in a crude enclosure beside *The Blue World*, but they must have sensed the coming confrontation. Both began to stomp at the frozen ground, and one reared up on its hind legs and whinnied loudly as Palis moved up alongside the two-story mountain inn. The two warders had chosen a more direct approach. They walked boldly up to the doors of *The Blue World* and blew them in with a blast of magical force that reduced the door to shards of wooden debris.

They charged into the building, counting on the element of surprise, but what they found instead was Otep standing in plain sight. Otep and Yssa had watched the warder's approach in the scrying pool of the old council chamber, and thus they had known that there would be no pleasantries before the warders made an outright attack on the inn.

"*Juris maronette*," Otep shouted, jabbing the tip of his gnarled wooden staff in Warder Abrashi's direction.

As the warder tried to raise his wand to Otep, he went suddenly stiff. Otep had gained control over the warder's limbs. When Otep swung his staff to the side, Warder Abrashi was thrown in the same direction and smashed into Warder Solias forcefully, sending him crashing into and rolling over a round wooden table. A flash from Warder Solias' wand sent a contrail of golden energy off-target. It impacted the ceiling and blew a huge jagged hole in the once smooth stone.

Rubble fell into the common room, and before Warder Abrashi likewise crashed over the table, Otep swiped his staff in the opposite direction. Warder Abrashi reversed his fall instantly and went flying across the room. He hit a wall hard and crumbled to the floor in a dazed heap.

"*Carru deteonni!*" Warder Solias shouted as he rose from behind the toppled table.

A blast of golden energy streaked across the room trailing gold sparks as it closed the gap between Warder Solias and Otep. It hit Otep hard, knocking him backward. He spun to the ground, just as Yssa rose from behind the bar only a few feet away from Warder Solias.

"*Lorroak fury!*" she shouted, taking Warder Solias down with a blast of magical force that knocked him into a wooden pillar that supported the weight of the stone ceiling overhead. The pillar cracked. Dust rained down from above.

Warder Solias rose quickly, however, sending another bolt of golden energy in Yssa's direction. She ducked behind the bar and the glittering energy from the warder's wand shattered bottles and the long mirror that was affixed to the wall behind them.

Yssa stayed down and crept along the length of the bar. She braved to stand once, but as soon as her head popped over the bar, she was forced to duck to avoid another deadly bolt of magic. Twice more her attempts to survey the room were thwarted. "Roak's hand!" she cursed.

Yssa found a piece of the broken mirror and crawled to the far end of the bar where she used the mirror to peak around the corner and get an idea of what was happening in the room. She saw Otep right away. He was still down, lying on his stomach with his staff laying several feet from him. Warder Abrashi too remained sprawled out on the floor.

She couldn't see Warder Solias, who had found shelter behind an overturned table. She turned the mirror. Striding right through the blasted doorway of the inn came the commoner with the terrible scar across his face. He was headed directly for Otep twirling a gleaming falcata in his hand.

A blast of magic hit the mirror and golden sparks flew all about her. Yssa was forced to pull back behind the bar again. She heard footsteps dart across the room as Warder Solias drew closer, gaining an even more advantageous position behind another toppled table closer to the bar.

Palis kicked a chair out of the way and pulled the table that pinned Otep off the old wizard. He played idly with the curve-bladed sword. "Remember me?" Palis taunted.

"I do," came a deep, dry voice behind him.

Palis spun around just in time to catch the full force of a burning log pulled from the fireplace as it cracked him across his head. The blow snapped his head to the side so violently that the cranking of his spine carried over the entire room, and Palis went down hard. Haverstagg was still topless and bandaged, but his face was red with fury as he lurched over him.

Warder Solias turned on Haverstagg, raising his wand, but in that moment of error he turned his back to Yssa, who came up over the bar. A streak of glowing yellow energy hit Warder Solias square in the back, and it blew clear through him. Through the gaping bloody hole, Yssa could see Haverstagg raising the log for another strike.

Warder Solias' wand slipped from his fingers and clattered on the ground. A moment later, he fell forward, dead.

Palis, prone on his back, tried to scurry away from the blonde-haired brute towering above him, but Haverstagg bore down on him with the makeshift club, landing blow after violent blow on Palis' upraised arms, eventually breaking both of them.

"You . . . If you kill me, you'll never find her!" Palis shouted with panic shaking his voice.

This stayed Haverstagg's hand momentarily.

Yssa hurried to Otep and checked for a pulse. He was alive, but just barely.

"Where is she?" Haverstagg threatened feigning a strike at Palis' face. "Is she alive?"

Palis, never a good liar, let a smile form on his lips that told Haverstagg all he needed to know. With a howl of rage, the makeshift club came up, and then down into Palis' face, caving it in with a damp *thud*.

"We have to get out of here, Otep," Yssa said to the half-conscious wizard. She looked up at Haverstagg, not knowing who he was, but knowing that he was at least, not her enemy. "Help me move him," she pleaded.

Haverstagg spit on Palis' body and dropped the log. He bent down and easily scooped Otep up into his arms. As he looked at Yssa, his expression was mixed of anger, confusion, and shock.

"We have to get to a boat," Yssa said.

Warder Abrashi's eyes flew open as he suddenly came back to his senses. He scrambled up to his feet and quickly took in the damage around him. Several tables and chairs had been knocked over, and stones had fallen from a hole in the ceiling where the corner of a bed threatened to fall through. His eyes then came to Palis, which he recognized as Palis only by the dead man's clothes.

"Roak's hand," Warder Abrashi whispered. "Allus!" he cried out, his eyes searching for . . . "No, no . . ." he said. He hurried across the room to where he saw his master laying face down in a pool of blood, a mortal wound centered in his back.

Warder Abrashi looked down at Warder Solias' corpse and felt a wave of guilt and nausea wash over him.

It's my fault, he thought. *If only I'd been able to hit the old mage first, if only I'd been able to resist his control, then you would still be alive.*

He crouched and put a hand on his dead master's shoulder, the body was still warm. Warder Abrashi was devastated at the loss of the man who was more than just a master and his stomach turned from the loss. Warder Solias had been his only true friend.

"Crowe!" Warder Abrashi shouted when he was at last able to transform his grief into anger. "I'm coming to get you Crowe!"

Warder Abrashi heard movement downstairs and reached to his wand sheath for his wand, but the sheath was empty, his wand gone. He looked down and then bent over. Lying beside Warder Solias' body was his wand. Warder Abrashi picked up the wand, and held it tip down to the floor. A moment passed as he watched the blood ooze down and drip off it. His oath, his vow, was rent of his master's blood.

"So be it," he said to Warder Solias' body. "It will be your wand after all that takes the life of Asher Crowe and all those that he calls friends. I shall avenge you, Master."

Rusk's sensitive ears had heard the fighting up in the inn, but he had been working frantically to prepare another boat. With the arrival of the warders, he rushed to complete the final tasks. The boats had been built more than forty cycles ago, and had floated down here, mostly unused, since long before Rusk's hair had turned from black to gray. It had taken a good deal of work to get the boat that Asher Crowe had taken seaworthy. This one was in even more of a state of ill-repair.

Unlike humans, Rusk's eyes were well suited for life in the World Below. When he heard people coming down the catwalks and scaffolds, he looked up and he clearly saw Yssa and the injured traveler rushing down toward him. In the traveler's arms was Rusk's father. Rusk was alarmed at seeing Otep being carried thus, but he was not one to allow fear to cloud his judgment or lead him to hesitation. Before they were halfway down the wooden construction, Rusk was already using the ropes to raise the elevator platform back up to the scaffolding. He heard Yssa's voice cry out in the darkness.

"Rusk!" she shouted. "Get that boat moving!"

The light from Warder Abrashi's wand chased Yssa and Haverstagg down the scaffolding. Three times, Warder Abrashi thought he had a clean line of sight to the outlaws, but each time they disappeared beneath another layer of the catwalks just as the golden blast from his wand shattered the planks on which they had just stood.

Warder Abrashi jumped down to the lowest level, landing hard, but raising his wand again for a blast that showered Haverstagg with golden sparks just as the outlaws slipped out of sight and the free-floating platform descended noisily into the darkness.

When he reached the edge of the catwalk Warder Abrashi peeked his head over quickly and caught sight of a fire lit boat floating in a lake at the bottom of the cavern. He could make out the shapes of several people on deck. When he leaned over a second time, he was almost hit by a bolt of lightning that crackled past him, singing his hair and causing those on his arms to stand upright. It was a close call, but he soon realized that it was not intended to hit him.

The bolt of lightning crashed into the heart of the rickety scaffolding and sent wooden debris flying everywhere. The entire structure began to sway and creak. And then it all began to come crumbling down toward him. Warder Abrashi had but a moment to decide whether to ride the mass of tangled wood down to the bottom of the lake, or leap over the side and pray that the water was deep enough that he didn't hit the stone beneath it. He slipped Warder Solias' bloodied wand into his wand sheath and jumped.

CHAPTER 18

Chasmarrud drew ever closer as the boat slid quietly through the clear water that flooded the winding tunnel. Odderly crouched in front of Claudia and Crowe, his shield firmly planted against the deck and his rod smoldering in his hand.

More than two hours had passed since they turned down the wide, low tunnel. Like Odderly and her grandfather, Claudia was nervous in knowing that the waterway they had been forced down ended at the guskar village.

Chasmarrud had first been discovered when mining efforts launched out of Subterranea had broken through a cavern wall into the tunnels claimed by the guskar during the rule of the Second Lord Martyr. Most of the miners of that particular expedition were slaughtered, a few were taken captive, and single survivor who had hidden when the guskar revealed themselves returned to Subterranea and reported that he heard the guskar repeating guttural noises that sounded like *chass-mar-ud* before the captives were taken away.

It was presumed, by her grandfather at least, that the guskar, who had not yet developed a complex spoken language, were referring to the village that Asher Crowe and Otep had later discovered. Whether *Chasmarrud* truly referred to the name of the guskar village, the chieftain who ruled it at the time, or something else, had never been determined. In all the cycles that followed the famed mining encounter nobody had ever opened peaceable relations with the guskar.

The Second Lord Martyr ordered the tunnels leading from Subterranea to Chasmarrud sealed. They were not reopened again until the time of the Fifth Lord Martyr, only forty-two cycles ago, but in the cycles that passed between the regimes of the second and fifth Lord Martyrs the stories of the ferocity of the guskar had become common tavern-talk in the undercity. The primitive guskar had become the *monsters* in bedtime stories told to scare children. The ghosts of stories told by travelers of the subterranean tunnels, around their campfires. But they are no myth. Bands of guskar were sometimes encountered in the wild labyrinthine tunnels of the World Below, and seldom did the lizard wranglers and mining companies who happen across them return to the undercity without very real horror stories to tell.

There were few people who would willingly travel anywhere near Chasmarrud, but Crowe, Odderly, and Claudia had been left little choice. Had the collapsed tunnel not blocked the way, they would have been able to reach the caverns at the bottom of the Black Rift after only a few more days on the water. But now, the only route available to them came within a stone's throw of one of the most volatile races yet discovered in the World Below. Crowe, Odderly, and Claudia were all on edge.

Even if they were to somehow pass through Chasmarrud and the surrounding guskar territory unnoticed, they would then have to face the possibility of contact with their own kind, and this posed great danger in and of itself.

By now it was possible that word of the happenings in Ambermane had reached Subterranea and that they were now being hunted by the Lord Martyr's men in the World Below in addition to the warders that they knew were hunting them in the World Above. A single chance encounter could reveal their location, and there were few routes one could take through the subterranean tunnels to escape direct pursuit.

Claudia shook the thoughts from her head. Before she could worry about the possibility of facing the warders again, she had to address the current threat before them.

Warder Abrashi felt the wind explode out of his lungs when he hit the water. Breathless and gasping for air he rose to the surface and found himself alone in the absolute darkness of the underground cavern. The water was cool and deep, and all around him he felt the floating remains of the wooden catwalks.

He brought light to his master's wand when he was able to grab a hold of a section of wood large enough to support his weight. The cavern and the lake seemed to stretch endlessly around him, and he could no longer see the heights from where he had jumped.

Thrashing through the water, picking his way through the floating debris, he eventually identified the shape of another boat floating in the giant subterranean lake. Heaving himself out of the water and onto the deck, Warder Abrashi lay still for some time before he noticed the deck beginning to slant toward the water. His weight upon the boat had been just enough to push the floats down to where one must have been breached. It was taking on water now, and with every passing minute it began to sink deeper and more quickly.

It was not long before the boat capsized and went under, throwing Warder Abrashi back into the waters of the lake. For a moment he tread water, seeking out something else in the darkness that might work as a raft, but then something brushed up against him under the water and his wand was snatched out of his hand. He saw the light diffuse as the heavy wand, crafted of intricately carved petrified wood, sank like a stone to the bottom of the water some twenty feet below.

Something brushed against him again, and when he looked down, he saw a long white eel slither by under the water, illuminated by the glowing wand at the bottom of the lake. Panic filled him and Warder Abrashi swam frantically toward the main bulk of the catwalk wreckage that stuck up out of the water. But the eels had come from all over, drawn to the scent of Warder Solias' blood on the wand.

Warder Abrashi churned the water beneath him as he swam, revealing his location clearly to the hundreds of giant eels. He felt a burning pain in his calf when an eel bit a piece of meat from his leg. Within seconds his blood was in the water too, and within minutes, the last of Warder Abrashi's dying screams faded from the cavern.

Rusk smoothed his father's hair, running his fingers over Otep's gray tangles. Rusk's heart was heavy with fear and sadness, for if Otep died, everything that Rusk had ever known would die with him. Laying there, cradling Otep's frail form, Rusk began to recall the events that had brought him and his adoptive human father together.

The garuk lay dead and scattered all around the subterranean village. The buildings, once carefully stacked from long, crudely cut slabs of ruddy stone, had been destroyed. Many looked as if they had exploded from the inside, and others roared within the grip of burning fires as if they had been made of wood and not stone.

Rusk was only a small child of three cycles, not able to fend for himself. Soon after chaos erupted throughout the village, Rusk's mother had taken him to the western edge of the cavern where there were no shelters and hidden him among the giant mushrooms and moss fields where the garuk grew their crops.

"No matter what you hear," she had told him the in crisp, snarling language of the garuk, "you stay here. And don't you cry, not a sound."

She kissed her son and returned to the village where she died along with everyone else.

Long after the flames had died away and the darkness returned to his village, Rusk realized that he was alone. He began to cry. It was his sobbing that eventually turned into the pitiful wailing that attracted the two warders who had not yet left the village that they had just destroyed.

Rusk remembered the young warders standing over him. They spoke to each other, and though Rusk had been unable to comprehend what it was they were saying to each other, the words remained in his head through all the cycles that came after them. In time, he learned to speak the Brysh language, and Rusk had finally come to understand what had been said.

"This is madness, Otep," Asher Crowe had said. "The Lord Martyr has grown old and he knows that the end of his reign is drawing near. He wants to leave a legacy of bloodshed in his wake. These people could have been made to understand peaceful coexistence. This, what we have done . . . is savagery."

Otep looked back to the ruins of the garuk village. The air throughout the cavern was scented with smoke and burned flesh.

"What have we done, my friend?" he asked of Crowe while he stared down at the crying garuk child, the only survivor of the massacre.

Rusk remembered the way that they both looked down at him. He was never able to forget the pity and shame in their eyes.

It was Otep who kneeled and placed his head to the ground before the guskar child. When he at last looked up at Rusk, tears in his eyes, Otep threw down his staff. "No act of kindness can atone for the sins committed against you this day. You may not understand what has happened here, or why, or what it means to forgive. But one day, child . . . one day I hope that you can forgive me for what I've done."

Rusk leaned forward and placed his head against his father's chest. Otep had taken Rusk as his son that day, and not once from that day on did Otep show anything but love and kindness to the garuk boy.

In many ways, Rusk's childhood had been filled with more happiness than any human child could have hoped for. Otep and Rusk lived together in the peaceful seclusion of the Korah Valley enjoying the isolation, the streams, the shady forest, and the rolling green hills. When the Lord Martyr who had ordered the execution of Rusk's people began sending the High Warders to *The Blue World* for the council, Rusk would hide in the tranquil valley below. In time, the Fifth Lord Martyr died, and his heir moved the council to Subterranea. Rusk no longer had to hide.

Unlike any garuk before him, Rusk came to call both the World Above and the World Below his home. As was garuk custom, the bodies of the dead were not buried. The garuk believed that to bury the dead was to trap their souls and keep them from being able to find their way into the Light. It was not the garuk way to cast aside the memories that the sight of ancestral remains instilled in their living decedents, and so Rusk and Otep would often walk among the bones of Rusk's people. It gave the two the chance to each come to understand and accept what had happened.

But now, everything teetered on the edge of a knife. Otep had been touched by deadly magic, and though he had prepared to stand against the Lord Martyr's men by weaving several defensive magics around him, it had not been enough. His breath was shallow. And Rusk was for the first time since the massacre of his village, afraid.

Yssa had done everything that she could for Otep, but while Yssa was a powerful wizard, she knew little of healing magic. In an effort to give Rusk as much space as they could aboard the small boat for him to be alone with Otep, Haverstagg and Yssa sat together on the bow of the boat, speaking quietly about how each of them had come to be there.

"I'm so sorry," Yssa said to Haverstagg after he had told her about what had happened to Hannah. Yssa wanted very much to console the poor man by telling him the practiced oratory about how good souls will always find their way into the Light, but she had long ago renounced the last bit of faith that was common to the Brysh people. Instead, she asked, "what will you do now?"

To this, Haverstagg only shook his head and let out a heavy sigh. It seemed like only a few hours had passed since he and Hannah were making plans to start a family in Subterranea, to forge for themselves a good life in the undercity, but now everything had changed.

"When we find Asher," Yssa said, "you can go with Rusk back to *The Blue World*. It'll take more than a warder's wand to kill old Otep. Odderly's magic seems to have brought you back from a worse state, and Odderly is never far from Asher." Yssa looked back to see Rusk cradling his father in his arms. "He'll recover from this, don't you doubt, and he'll not forget that it was you who saved his life today. Nor will I forget that it was you who saved mine."

"Saved you?" Haverstagg asked.

Yssa nodded. "I know those warders, and had you not been there, Haverstagg, they would have killed me. I've no doubt of that. I'm just an old lady, no match for the youth and loathing of men like them."

"Then maybe I'll go with you. There is nothing left for me up there, and if you'll be traveling in the company of Asher Crowe, then I doubt we've seen the last of the Lord Martyr's men."

Through the night and day that followed the commencement of the ancient ritual, Warder Mankoff remained somewhere between sleep, life, and death. He heard every word spoken above him, and he felt every moment of pain as his body was cut open and probed. The removal of his eyes had only been the beginning.

He felt his organs being removed from his abdomen and the hollowness that was then filled with ashes gathered from the catacombs of the ancient Ambra ruins on the volcanic island of Roak's Grave. He felt distant from his mortal body as he was stitched back together and then embalmed while he still drew breath.

It was at this point when three of the six gathered warders began another incantation that seemed to blend forebodingly with the first. The Master from Fire Falls led the chant. Warder Mankoff listened, and in each new verse began to sense some familiarity within the words that even those who spoke them did not fully understand. He felt his body jerk and heard the gasps of the academia gathered around him to watch the ritual.

"It's working," he heard one of them say. "By Roak's hand, it's working . . ."

Chapter 19

The passage of time is difficult to discern in the lightless World Below. With no day or night, and no moons crossing the sky, it is often exhaustion that pulls subterranean travelers into slumber. The others had long since fallen asleep, and Yssa's only measure of the passing hours came in counting Haverstagg's rumbling snores. The rhythmic roar brought comfort and helped to break the monotony of the time spent crossing the seemingly endless underground lake.

While Yssa's body and joints ached with exhaustion, her mind was too busy to let her rest. Memories of the last week played in her mind's eye and she often found herself wishing that she had acted differently. If she had, perhaps nobody would have been hurt. She was now directly responsible for the deaths of three men. While she had acted only in self-defense, the old Brysh proverb of Herma the Seer kept echoing in her conscious: *"It is not what a man will do in order to preserve his life, but what a man will not do to preserve his life, that separates the souls destined for Light or Shadow."* Herma had written in one of his famed books of philosophy, *Immortal Wisdom*.

By Herma's reckoning, Yssa had condemned herself three times over. Although she was a woman who lacked faith, the thought of damnation chewed at her. Yssa began to think of whom she might run into in the realm of Shadow. Ultimately, she decided that at least she would have Asher Crowe there with her, and that was something. Her thoughts of Crowe, however, only led to a longing to be with him now.

Yssa looked down at the magical charm that hung around her neck. The heartstone was glowing steadily from within. She was close. But how close? Yssa began to run her thumb around the circle of smaller gemstones. One was missing, it had been consumed by the magical transformation that had allowed her to take on the shape of a crow and escape the Hagstead Forest. As she traced her thumb around the broken circle another one of the small stones broke away and turned to dust.

Chasmarrud was only a few hours away and there had been no sign of guskar or anything else that might present a danger to Crowe, Odderly, and Claudia. In several places Crowe noted that shelves of once-exposed stone could now be seen under two feet of water. Tunnels that the boat once fit easily through now scraped burning cinders away from the torch poles as the boat passed through them.

It was not only the rain of last spring that had caused an increase in the water level of these caverns, Crowe realized as he stared into the blackness ahead, but the cavern collapse that had trapped the water here. He was thinking about how the increased water table might have affected the guskar village when a wave of force washed over the boat from behind. It hit Crowe, and Crowe alone, with such force that it almost caused him to lose his balance and fall.

"Yssa?" Crowe said quietly when he realized that the source of the magical wave was his own spell woven into the charm that he had left for her at the lake.

"What's that?" Odderly asked, squinting into the darkness as if Crowe had noticed something ahead that he had failed to see. He picked up his shield.

When Crowe did not respond, Claudia rose from where she was sitting beside Odderly and said, "grandfather?"

Crowe raised a hand, palm-out to quiet them. He turned to regard the flooded tunnel they had been moving down for most of the day.

Odderly mumbled something under his breath and then Crowe felt the heat of the smoldering rod as the tunnel around them was thrown into the fiery orange glow.

"What is it?" Claudia asked.

Crowe pointed to some flat rocks at the side of the tunnel ahead. "Steer us over there, Claudia, we're putting down for awhile." Crowe waved his wand, retracting his magic from the paddlewheel.

The boat slowed as it ground up against the rocks. Crowe immediately stepped off and began tying the belaying line to a thick stalagmite to keep the boat from drifting away.

"This is as good a place to wait as any, and we should be safe here," Crowe said. He had already assured Claudia and Odderly that the guskar were poor swimmers.

Odderly jumped over the rail and landed steadily on one of the large flat stones before helping Claudia over. "What are we waiting for?"

"Yssa's found us," Crowe said with a smile.

"Yssa?" Claudia asked excitedly. "But how?"

"I left her a way of finding me," Crowe said evasively. He knew that Claudia would never approve of him having crafted a heartstone, so he was picking his words carefully. "She must already have gotten a boat from Otep, because she's not far away."

"How do you know this, Asher? These tunnels have gone on for days. They're like a maze. Even if she had gotten a boat . . ."

Crowe put a reassuring hand on Odderly's shoulder. "I felt her," he insisted, "and if she's taken it upon herself to follow us, then things must have gone sour after we left her. We owe it to her to wait."

After taking a short rest with solid land beneath her feet, Claudia helped Odderly prepare stew with some of the salted korum meat that Rusk had packed for them. The torch poles were securely mounted to the boat, and with nothing to use as tinder to start a *real* fire, Odderly's magical rod came in handy; it was left smoldering beneath the cooking caldron and quickly brought the stew to a boil. They were also able to season the meal with some mushrooms that Crowe found growing near the water on the far side of the landing.

"How many days are we going to have to be down here?" Claudia asked while she ate her meal. "It's so depressing, not being able to see the sky. It's suffocating."

"Told you," Odderly interjected, talking with his mouth full and pointing with his spoon.

"Another two weeks I'd imagine," Crowe said. "Once we're beyond Chasmarrud. The tunnels on the other side are well-kept enough because miners use them. Beyond that it will be slow going, and we'll not have the ability to travel the waterways. I'm actually not sure if they would reconnect to any tunnels I know."

"Maybe we should just go back up to the World Above," Odderly suggested. "We've covered a lot of ground, haven't we? I'd wager that we're as far as Market by now."

"Near there, aye," Crowe nodded, finishing his stew. "But therein lies the problem."

"What do you mean?" Claudia asked.

"We won't be able to surface again anytime soon. The only other route up between us and the Black Rift leads into the gem mines at Ambly," Crowe looked pointedly at Claudia, "And we're not going there."

"Grandfather!" Claudia pleaded.

"No." Crowe shook his head. "You saw the image in the sand, Claudia. Horace is alive, and alive somewhere in the Black Rift. Likely in a garuk slave pen or working some mine with a whip at his back. We won't know until we get there, and when we do get there, it will be hard enough finding him and getting out alive again. We'll have more than enough garuk to deal with, it would be unwise to be stirring up more trouble than we must. For all we know, the garuk could still be living in the mines."

Claudia wanted to argue, to see Ambly again, but she conceded the point and finished her stew in silence. Her grandfather was right, of course. She was not far from her father now, and with two powerful wizards standing with her, three counting Yssa when she arrived, then they just might be able to rescue him.

Sleep came easily that night for Claudia. While the journey thus far had been extraordinary in many ways, passing through Chasmarrud only marked the end to the first leg of her quest. For the first time in as long as she could remember, Claudia dreamed of her father and saw herself reunited with him. In the dream she rode happily beside him along the warm beach and steaming waters Seahaven. It was the first night since that horrible day so long ago, that Claudia's sleep brought her joy.

Yssa studied the charm, focusing on the heartstone for the subtle changes in brightness and clarity that helped her to navigate the labyrinthine tunnels around them. Otep had stopped breathing three times over the course of the night, recovering only after Rusk, Yssa, and Haverstagg had thought that he was beyond saving. With Crowe and Odderly now so close, Yssa had withdrawn her magic from the paddlewheel in favor of Haverstagg's brute strength. The gap was closing, but would it close fast enough to save Otep's life?

"Hold on just a little longer," Yssa said to Otep.

"His heart beats weakly," Rusk said quietly. "If we don't find Odderly soon . . ." He shook his head, dismissing the thought.

"Don't give up hope, Rusk," Yssa said.

A little less than an hour later, the heartstone flared brightly and bathed the corridor in bright red light. Yssa looked up suddenly and stared into the darkness beyond the edge of the red light.

Could it be?

"Mistress Yssa," Haverstagg said, "there's a light ahead!"

Crowe sat on the dark stone of the landing, his back against a dry mineral column with veins of red and white running through the otherwise dark stone. He had encouraged both Claudia and Odderly to take advantage of the time they would be waiting to get some much-needed rest, but shortly after they had fallen asleep, he gave up trying and took up a vigilant watch.

Crowe had consulted the knowledge stars the night before he set out to meet with Yssa. What he had seen was inconclusive. He knew that by returning to Ambermane there was a high likelihood that his past would surface again. He saw hardship ahead for both himself and for Yssa, and the knowledge stars showed them being torn apart violently.

Crowe had immediately crafted the magical charm as a precautionary measure. If he and Yssa were forced apart, the heartstone was linked to Crowe's essence, his very soul; there would be no place in this world or the next, that Yssa would not be able to find him. Into the first magical gemstone Crowe had woven an enchantment of shape-shifting so that Yssa would be able to quickly cross any distance to reach him. The second gemstone carried an enchantment of protection so that any single spell meant to harm her would be thwarted. The magic he had woven into the third gemstone of the magical charm had alerted Crowe that the heartstone was within a few miles of him, but he had not sensed the magic of the fourth gemstone, which would let him know if anyone if anyone other than Yssa was carrying it.

Crowe and Yssa had indeed been torn apart by the violence that night in the observatory chamber, but now, Crowe's foresight had brought Yssa safely back to him. Knowing that Claudia's quest would likely be the last of his long life, Crowe was happy to know that Yssa would once again be at his side. There had been a time, many cycles ago, before the massacre at Korah Valley and a dozen other events that led to Crowe's notoriety, when Crowe had thought that his destiny lay hand in hand with Yssa's. It was nice to know that even though they had been forced to spend so much of their lives apart, that they could be together again in the end.

When at last, Crowe saw the reddish cast of the glowing heartstone illuminate the flooded tunnel he knew that his wait was over. Crowe's knee popped as he got up to his feet, but such annoyances came with age. He now paid such things little attention. He pulled his long gray hair away from his face and walked up to the water's edge.

The boat slid around the bend and came fully into view. Crow's beaming smile faded. Yssa was at the bow. The once-injured traveler glistened with sweat as he frantically worked the paddlewheel. Laid out in the center of the deck was Otep, with Rusk hunkered over him. Tears streamed down Rusk's face. Crowe's relief melted away.

"Odderly!" Crowe shouted, bringing the dusky alchemist up with a start. "Get your medical cases and make haste!"

Her grandfather's shouting had abruptly pulled Claudia out of her pleasant dreams and thrust her into the chaos that ensued as Yssa's boat crashed up against the rocky landing. Both Odderly and the big blond man carried Otep to the center of the flat rocks where Odderly immediately began examining him.

"Otep," Odderly said as he held open the old wizard's eyes with grubby fingers. "Otep, keep your eyes open and blink if you can understand me."

No response.

"Claudia," Odderly said, "in my green bag on the boat is a thin wooden tube. Get it."

Odderly began uncorking small jars of various herbs and components as he dug them out of the wooden case, he kept in his saddle basket. He began throwing pinches of various substances into a large mixing dish.

"You there," Odderly called to Haverstagg, "take this bottle and fill it with water. Be quick."

Haverstagg returned a moment later and handed over the dripping bottle. Odderly tapped his mixture out into the bottle. With a thumb over the opening, he shook it and it soon took on a sickly green color. Claudia handed Odderly the tube and then gasped as Odderly opened Otep's mouth and roughly shoved the thin tube halfway down the old wizard's throat. He poured the sickly green potion into the open end of the tube. Though still unconscious, Otep gagged and tried to cough. Odderly paused a moment to steady Otep's head, then filled the tube and let the remainder of the fluid drain into Otep's stomach before he pulled the tube back out.

Claudia was pale as she watched, but when she saw Odderly begin to assemble a syringe she could take no more. She turned away and walked to the edge of the water where she crouched down and wrapped her arms around her knees. She tried not to think of the needle piercing Otep's skin and another magical concoction being injected into him.

Whatever Odderly had done took effect quickly. Otep stirred, and tried to speak, but the wooden tube Odderly had used to administer the potion left Otep's throat raw. His words came out as nothing more than an incoherent whisper.

"He's awake," Claudia heard Rusk say.

She clambered up and joined the others who crouched around Odderly and Otep.

"Don't try to speak, Otep," Odderly said as he prepared a second mixture for injection. "I'm putting you back to sleep now." Odderly drew fluid from another bottle into the syringe.

Otep looked at each face hovering over him. He had tears in his eyes, but he must have understood that whatever had happened at *The Blue World* was behind him now. He was here with Odderly and Crowe. Yssa was here, and Rusk. As well as Claudia and the traveler who Otep had saved on the road. Surrounded by friends, the concern on his face faded and Otep nodded weakly to Odderly.

Odderly smiled. "Don't you worry, you're going to be fine, I just need your body asleep so that the potions can work their magic. Just a few hours, Otep, I promise." Odderly put the needle up against Otep's skin just below the tourniquet wrapped around his arm. Claudia's stomach tightened and filled with butterflies, but she managed to watch Otep as he slipped back into a deep, magically induced sleep.

"That's four dead then," Odderly said after Yssa recounted what had happened during her escape from Ambermane and the battle at *The Blue World*. "And Mankoff?"

Yssa shrugged. It was a slight movement. She raised her bowl to her lips drank the broth she had taken from the stewing caldron.

"Five dead," Crowe shook his head sadly, counting Warder Mankoff among those who had died.

Claudia sat back away from the others, her head down and her shoulders slouched. *Five dead*, she thought, *and it's my fault*. She felt sick to her stomach.

"So, what are we doing then?" Odderly was the first to ask. "We can't go back to get Otep home, not if the catwalks are gone, and we can't risk going through Chasmarrud with him like this. He needs a place where he can rest and heal."

"No, we should go back, Otep and me," Rusk said quietly. "There are other tunnels that will take us back up to the Korah Valley, and I can see him home from there if you are sure that you've done enough for him to recover."

Odderly nodded.

"What about the warders though, surely it won't take them long to find out what happened at the inn," Yssa said.

Rusk shook his head. "It is you all that the Lord Martyr is after. They won't be looking for us."

"They will if Warder Abrashi survived the fall," Yssa rebutted.

"Not with eels in the water he didn't," Odderly said. Rusk nodding in agreement, and everyone seemed satisfied that the warder had not survived.

"Six then," Haverstagg said. "Warder Abrashi makes six." Until now he had remained as quiet as Claudia. All eyes turned to him.

"What about you then?" It was Crowe's voice. "Nobody knows that you were involved. You're not yet a wanted man. You can go back with Rusk and Otep. Our stiddleback are still at the inn. You're welcome to them."

Haverstagg slowly shook his heavy head. "Hannah's dead. My dreams are gone. There's no reason for me to go back, not if it's all the same to you. At least here there's still a dream, still hope. Her dream.

Her hope."

Claudia looked up and found that everyone's eyes were upon her. She felt naked under the solemn stares.

Crowe looked back to Haverstagg. "Then we are fortunate to have you with us, Haverstagg." Crowe said after a moment, breaking the awkward silence. "It is a long road ahead, and we've stirred up quite the hornet's nest. A strapping lad like yourself is most welcome here."

Crowe clasped a hand on Haverstagg's knee and gave him a reassuring squeeze. Haverstagg nodded. Claudia smiled at him, and the big man returned it as best he could, given the grief that was weighing heavily upon his shoulders.

"Well then," Odderly said as he stood up and brushed off his breaches, "let's get some rest."

Chapter 20

Claudia looked back as the two boats paddled away from each other not knowing if she would ever see Rusk or Otep again. The anxiety that had been growing with each day spent in the World Below was now becoming overbearing. There was a burning pain in her stomach, an acidic taste in her mouth, and she could not help but to be afraid.

She was standing behind Yssa, with Haverstagg at her side turning the crank of the paddlewheel as she steered the boat through the dark tunnel. At the bow, her grandfather and Odderly stood side by side. All of them had their wands out, except for Odderly who gripped his smoldering rod.

Claudia had lived a sheltered life, but all that was changing, and she was about to cross a barrier from which she could never go back. She had never killed anything before, nor had she ever seen anything killed. But there was so much death surrounding her. Her grandfather had taken many lives, though she had never witnessed him do so. She had seen Odderly's magic strike down Warder Mankoff, however. Odderly had done so without any hesitation. He had killed to defend himself. Just as Yssa had done. But Claudia wondered if she would be able to do the same thing. Two weeks ago, she would not have doubted her resolve in striking down a garuk. They were evil non-human beasts. And then she had met Rusk, who was perhaps the most kind and selfless *person* that she had ever met. Could she strike down a garuk so easily now? Could she strike down a guskar? Did they not have families and children, just like her people did?

Claudia was sweating, she realized. The boat ground to a sudden stop, but there was no shore in sight. It was then that Claudia realized that there would be no shore. The water table here had risen drastically since her grandfather was last here. Chasmarrud had been flooded.

"Is he alive?" Headmaster Penwigget asked as he looked down upon what had once been Warder Loris Mankoff.

"Yes, and no," Master Darrowden said as he stared at the mixture of science and the arcane that lay tied down to the table before him. "The man we knew as Loris Mankoff is certainly a part of him, but he's no longer alive in the same sense that he once was. And he's not alone. The Ambra spirit has been bound to the body as well. In a way, due to the spirit binding, he is both of them now."

All around them, the onlookers comprised mostly of members of the university faculty began whispering skeptically amongst themselves.

"The spirit," Headmaster Penwigget said, his voice low and filled with concern, "it retains free will?"

Master Darrowden nodded. "To some degree."

"Roak's hand, Tadris, you've created the very thing Asher Crowe claims to have destroyed, to destroy him? How are we to be sure that this . . . thing . . . that we are able to control it."

"No, it's not the same thing Headmaster, I assure you. Spirit binding is not quite the same as simply giving a shade a host body. We've been dealing with this particular spirit at Fire Falls for quite some time. Its limitations are well-known to us, and the Ambra ashes contained within the body are but half of the mortal remains. So long as we possess the urn containing the other half, we can control the Ambraic side of him. The shade that Asher Crowe claims had possessed your predecessor was an *unbound* spirit. Fully in control of the body it had taken, and all but indestructible. Further proof that Crowe's claim was false. His act, a simple act of murder."

"And this urn, where is it now?"

"It has never left the safe keeping of the Lord Martyr himself. I am sure that you continue to trust in the Lord Martyr's guidance. It was after all, the Lord Martyr who authorized this . . . experiment. I am sure you can understand the importance of bringing Asher Crowe and his allies to justice. In addition to the murder of Headmaster Collinhodge three officers are now dead, and Warders Solias and Abrashi have disappeared during the course of their pursuit." Master Darrowden smiled and looked down at his creation. "Where everyone else has failed, Warder Mankoff will now succeed."

"And if he does, what then will become of this abomination?" Headmaster Penwigget asked, his brows drawing downward in a scowl.

"That will be for the Lord Martyr to determine, Headmaster." Master Darrowden put a hand on Headmaster Penwigget's shoulder and stared him in the eye. "Do not worry, my friend. We will take Warder Mankoff to Stonehold, where he will be released. You can rest assured that nobody wants Asher Crowe dead more than Loris himself. And when I return to my laboratory in Fire Falls, I will be monitoring Warder Mankoff's every action clairvoyantly. When the deed is done, we will call Loris home, and all will be as it is meant to be. Perhaps you and I will even be honored for finally putting an end to the legacy of Asher Crowe."

Headmaster Penwigget put his hands on his hips and let out an exasperated sigh. This was not what he had in mind when he had agreed to allow the Masters of the Fire Falls Academy to perform the ritual here. He did not doubt that the desiccated thing Loris Mankoff had become would succeed in its task. But he was afraid of what would happen after the fact. Such an abomination should not be allowed to survive beyond its purpose.

Headmaster Penwigget recalled the story of Domma and Thom, two woodsmen from Sparrow who kept poisonous snakes as pets. Not only were both woodsmen killed by one of the snakes they kept, but the snake killed several other villagers before it was destroyed. *Peace has prevailed in the Brylands for six generations, since the very founding of the sovereignty. How easily would all that change if the Lord Martyr lost control of this pet, especially if this abomination retained enough of its own memory to bring others of its kind into existence.* The thoughts were disturbing.

"Very well," Headmaster Penwigget said. "Take your leave and take this monstrosity with you. The Lord Martyr is a wise man, my trust is with him."

Master Darrowden nodded and gave the signal for his people to remove Warder Mankoff. The crowd of spectators parted as Warder Mankoff, or whatever he was now, was rolled out of the room.

"Come, Telmar," Master Darrowden said to his son who stood quietly in the crowd. "We've a long road ahead of us."

The water was warm against her skin as Claudia followed the others toward the rocky shore. The water came up almost to her knees, and twice she felt something brush up against her. When she looked down, Claudia saw small white fish gathering around her. She was thankful that they were fish and not eels.

With the boat left behind, Claudia was given a fair share of supplies to carry. The backpack was uncomfortable on her shoulders. The load heavy. But she could not complain. This was *her* quest, and everyone had risked so much on her behalf. Fortunately, she did not have to go far before she forgot all about her discomfort. A nauseating, moldy smell filled the tunnel ahead.

The roughly hewn gray rock around them became increasingly veined with obsidian. This was the place her grandfather had once told her about. It was not far from where he had said he'd discovered the guskar settlement. She gripped her wand so tightly that her knuckles went white.

As they walked the obsidian became more and more pronounced. The volcanic glass played strangely with the bright white light of the three wands, and the hot orange glow of Odderly's rod. The obsidian seemed to swallow the light altogether at times, and then cast it all back at them at others. It was almost dizzying when the gray rock disappeared all together and her grandfather led them through a long obsidian-walled tunnel that opened into the cavern which housed Chasmarrud.

Claudia stepped into the cavern and doubled over. The smell of mold and rotting vegetation was overpowering, and it took all her force of will to keep from vomiting. Tears welled up in her eyes and she pulled the front of her shirt up in a futile attempt to filter the stench.

Spread out across the cavern were thousands of giant gray-brown mushrooms with stems twice the height of Haverstagg, and he was no small man. The ground became mushy beneath the murky, stagnant water, and each foot came up out of the water with a sickly sucking noise as she stepped forward. It was as if the cavern was a single massive underground swamp of the worst kind. Claudia could not discern if the smell was coming from the water, the mushrooms that towered over her, or both.

Odderly paused to dig his greasy red handkerchief out of his pocket and he held it over his nose. Claudia could see that his eyes too were teared up from the horrid stench. Only Haverstagg seemed unaffected by the smell. She wished that she had his constitution.

Claudia mumbled through her shirt, "what is this place?"

Crowe shook his head. He was bewildered. "This is the cavern, look there."

Claudia followed the tip of her grandfather's wand to a building stacked of crudely carved blocks of rough gray stone. The building was little more than a half-spherical ruin covered with slimy growth, with an opening in one side big enough for Haverstagg to have walked through with space over his head.

Claudia shined the light from the tip of her wand into the structure. There were no furnishings, and it looked as if there probably never had been, unless the three slabs of glistening stone had served as such. A central column of stone was braced in the center of the chamber to support the ceiling, but even it had cracked under the weight of the giant mushrooms that grew from the top and sides of the structure itself.

There were other such buildings, hundreds of them, but they had all but been buried by the fungal forest that had overtaken the cavern after it had flooded.

"This is a stroke of luck," Odderly mumbled.
And then something moved in gloom ahead.

The company of physicians and wizards had formed a protective ring around Warder Mankoff to keep the few students who still roamed the university grounds from seeing him being loaded into the back of a covered wagon. Snow was falling again, but Telmar Darrowden, the only son of one of Fire Falls Academy's most honored masters did not mind at all. Like everyone else, he had never seen the snow before, and like the other denizens of Subterranea, any trip to the World Above was one filled with wonderment.

He paid less attention to the zombie-like *thing* being loaded into the wagon than he did to the falling snowflakes. Lofty ringbark oak grew in the beautifully landscaped courtyard of the university, and these too captured his attention. Unlike his father, who was an anatomist and necromancer, as well as the Dark Arts Master at Fire Falls Academy of Magic, Telmar had a love for nature and *living* things. Instead of being allowed to accompany a trade caravan to the Hagstead Forest, which Telmar had begged of his father as a birthday gift, Telmar celebrated his twelfth cycle six weeks ago, watching his father work through the night in a dank laboratory. Instead of singing songs, opening gifts, and eating sweet cakes filled with fresh fruit, Telmar helped perform the autopsy of a man murdered on Magmorra Road just outside of Subterranea.

The trip to Ambermane had thus far more than made up for it, however. With his father being required to oversee the binding ritual for six consecutive days, Telmar had had free run of the university and the surrounding woodlands. Though late, his birthday wish had been granted. Some time spent above ground, in relative solitude, had been wonderful. Though he now found himself wishing that he would be able to pursue his education here at Ambermane University rather than at Fire Falls Academy.

Unlike Ambermane University, where students were able to begin their first term at twelve cycles, Fire Falls did not permit enrollment until a student was fifteen. Telmar had three more cycles before he would officially be mature enough to begin his studies. That meant three more cycles spending time around things that were, more often than not, dead rather than alive. Things like his father's latest curio, Warder Mankoff.

It isn't fair!

Telmar wandered as far away from the wizards as he could while remaining within earshot of his father. He soon found himself at the edge of the river that cut the courtyard in two. He crouched there on the riverbank and looked up at the observatory tower. Telmar knew what astromancy was, but he also knew that he would never have the opportunity to study nature or the stars in Subterranea. He hated that his true interests would be of little consequence to his future profession almost as much as he dreaded the thought of his entire life being spent in the sunless World Below.

"Telmar!" he heard his father shout.

Telmar quickly got up to his feet and ran across the courtyard enjoying the soft touch of grass, not stone, beneath his feet. Sky, not stone, above his head.

"Yes, Father?" Telmar asked. He was panting and out of breath.

"It's time to go."

Telmar nodded and climbed into the back of the wagon where he saw Warder Mankoff again. He retook his seat among the clutter of books and laboratory tools that his father was taking back to the undercity and leaned forward to get a better look at his new traveling companion. Warder Mankoff hardly looked human anymore. Humanoid, certainly, but hollow and dry in a way no living thing could be.

The ritual had consumed the fluids of Warder Mankoff's naked body, and as a result his flesh became drawn tightly around his bones. It looked brittle, though Telmar knew it not to be. A girdle of polished metal had been attached around Warder Mankoff's sunken abdomen to protect the Ambraic ashes kept inside. The black fluid that had been used to embalm him pulsed through his bloodstream with each beat of the undead heart. Telmar could see the veins bulge beneath the bluish-gray pallor of the warder's skin as the vile substance was circulated.

It was the warder's eyes though, upon which Telmar's gaze eventually settled. The orbits were hollow, the eyes gone, but in their place glowing magical orbs emanated a steady magical light. The interior of the covered wagon was bathed in a steady, soft green glow. It was staring back at him, Telmar realized. He could easily guess the thing's thoughts. He had been forced to watch the beginning of the procedure and had learned of the events leading up to the attack on Warder Mankoff. Such a thing, bridled with magic to control the ancient spirit, shared the warder's thirst for revenge and the Ambra's need for freedom. It waited for the moment that it would be free to pursue the warder's one consuming need, which would in turn sate the spirits restlessness. As Telmar studied it he realized that it in turn was studying him. It would kill him, Telmar knew, if he came between it and its prey. Of this, he had little doubt.

The entire mushroom forest seemed to waver for a moment and then several of the taller, more slender of the mushrooms near Claudia uprooted themselves and with long, lumbering steps, moved away. Claudia had not noticed anything different about them. Until they moved, the fungoids looked indistinguishable from any of the other giant mushrooms around her, yet the whole time that she had been standing there they had been watching. But now, seeing them move, Claudia could see that their long spindly stems split into spongy stick-like legs. Slender arms, bent at the elbows, reached out to cover the fungoid's big black eyes to shield them from the light of the wizard's wands as they fled deeper into the underground swamp.

Crowe, Odderly, Yssa, and Haverstagg too, were all turning around in wonderment as the forest thinned out around them. When one fungoid nearly stepped on Odderly, he raised his smoldering rod, but Crowe stayed his hand.

"Wait," Crowe said, watching the movement all around him until after the fungoids had disappeared into the growth on the other side of

Claudia. "They mean us no harm; they're running away from us."

"No," Haverstagg said. He pointed off into the mushroom forest just at the edge of the wand light where even more of the living mushrooms were uprooting and moving away in the opposite direction. "They're running, but they're not running from us."

There was a sudden stillness, a sudden silence, and a palpable sense of danger filled the dank, moldy air.

Chapter 21

Claudia saw something move out of the corner of her eye and she spun around just in time to see what had to be a dozen or more small gray bipeds come leaping from mushroom to mushroom. They were spindly, flea-like little things with long thin arms and legs that ended in clawed feet and hands. They had spines ridged with translucent sails that made them look even larger and more menacing, and their round, bald heads lengthened into fleshy beaked snouts. Claudia did not see eyes at all.

"Ings," Crowe said, seeing similar groups of the little creatures jumping out of the darkness all around him. "They are scavengers."

The group came together, back-to-back against each other, all facing outward. Claudia had her grandfather on one side, Haverstagg on the other, and both Yssa and Odderly right behind her. They all stared out into the mushroom forest as the ings began chattering to each other like the monkeys of Roak's Grave.

"Do you see anything?" Odderly asked.

Claudia could feel the heat of his rod behind her. To her left she heard Haverstagg grunt a *no*. And then, quite suddenly, the chattering of the ings fell silent. They clinged to giant mushrooms by the hundreds, watching.

Claudia squinted into the darkness. "I'm scared," she whispered.

There was a distant, muffled thud that caused a moment of

excitement among the ings. Another one followed a few seconds later and the brackish water all around the wizards quivered. Several more thuds followed, each a little louder than the first, as if some giant beast were lumbering toward them.

"Over there," Haverstagg said. He moved his shield aside and pointed into the blackness. Everyone turned to look.

"Do you know the way out of there?" Yssa quietly asked of Crowe.

"No," Crowe said flatly. "Otep and I never came further than this. But it stands to reason that the tunnels connecting to Subterranea lay in that direction." Crowe pointed with his wand.

"Then run!" Yssa shouted.

All at once everyone turned and began running through the mushroom forest, except for Haverstagg who backed slowly away from whatever was approaching. Without a wand or torch of his own, he was quickly being swallowed by darkness.

Claudia felt the mud of the swamp pulling at her feet and the slick undergrowth of moss and fungal pods caused her to slide and almost fall several times as she weaved around the mushroom stalks. She paused, grabbing a glistening mushroom for support, and turned around to see where Haverstagg was. The footsteps were getting louder, and any hope that they would be able to run and hide was thwarted by the incessant chattering of the ings that squealed all around her.

"Haverstagg!" Claudia shouted.

"I'm coming!" she heard him shout back.

Haverstagg stumbled through the swamp. Claudia waited until he was fully back within the radius of her glowing wand before she turned again and ran. She could hear his footsteps sloshing through the swamp behind her. Ahead of her she saw two bobbing white lights and a single orange one, making a generally straight course through the underground swamp. She followed the lights as best she could, but as she ran through a smoking patch of bulbous mushrooms her foot caught on something and she went down face first in the muck.

Her fall was just what the ings had been waiting for. Claudia had hardly gotten her face back up above the rancid water when she was landed upon by several ings. Her face was forced back down. She took a mouthful of the slimy black water and found herself pinned. They were heavy things and she was unable to get out from beneath the pile of the scavengers. The small claws pinched into her all over and she felt them pecking at her backpack, which was about all that was above the water. Claudia struggled in a panic to get a lungful of air but took on water instead.

As soon as Telmar's father climbed into the back of the covered wagon he made his way to his personal chest and tapped it thrice with his wand. The deep etchings in the petrified wood glowed for a moment and then the lid of the chest popped open.

Telmar turned his attention away from Warder Mankoff and watched as his father wrapped an urn carved from white marble in a black cloth and seated it carefully into the chest.

"Will we be staying long in Stonehold?" Telmar asked.

Master Darrowden closed the chest and tapped it again with his wand, re-empowering the wizard lock that kept his most prized possessions safe from the hands of thieves. Telmar had once seen the charred remains of a would-be thief who had tried to pick the lock on the magically protected chest. Without his father's wand first being tapped three times on the wood, and then the wizard lock dispelled, any attempt to open the chest would burn the burglar alive from the inside out. It was a ward that prevented even magically enabled thieves from stealing from the chest, for who else but his father himself would ever be in possession of his father's wand? His father had used such wards liberally throughout the most restricted areas of the Fire Falls Academy.

"Less than two days," Master Darrowden said, "and you'll not be allowed to wander."

Telmar was disappointed. He always enjoyed visiting the stone quarry and watching the stone carved from the side of the mountainside as it was carried down to the lowest tier of the village by way of the zip lines. More so than that, however, Telmar was disappointed that he would not be able to visit with the few *friends* he had been able to make in the World Above during his infrequent visits.

Stonehold was only a few miles away from Magmorra Road; the main artery that led from the World Above to the great undercity of Subterranea. As such, when his father's work required travel to the surface it was always Stonehold where they took their first night of rest. Still yet, it had been hard to make friends with any of the local children even when his father gave Telmar any degree of freedom. It was difficult to be the son of a necromancer and children are seldom anything less than cruel when it came to teasing. Now, his last few days in the World Above were sure to be spent at his father's side, and Roak only knew when they had come back to the surface with winter only just around the corner.

"Father?" Telmar said.

"Aye?"

"I was rather impressed by Ambermane University during this visit." After a moment without response, Telmar scooted closer to his father and continued. "I've been thinking that perhaps it would be advantageous for me to begin my schooling at Ambermane *this* cycle. Even if you would want me to transfer to Fire Falls when I am fifteen, it would allow me an extra three years . . ."

"To waste your time and energy studying things that have no bearing on your future," Master Darrowden said looking over the top of the book he had begun to read while his son was talking. "Besides which, the masters who remain at Ambermane through the winter do not accept students. It is an ill-thought-out suggestion that is well below you, and I'll hear no more of it."

Telmar forced himself not to sigh. How many times had he tried to tell his father that the dark arts were not where his interest lay, but stopped because he was afraid his father would be outraged? "Yes, father," Telmar said at last, turning his eyes again to Warder Mankoff.

Telmar looked back to his father after a moment. His frustration was tinder to his building anger about the life that had been laid out before him. It just wasn't fair; he had never been asked what *he* wanted to do.

"Why did you lie to the headmaster?" Telmar asked. He had

debated whether or not to bring it up, but with the anger building in him about being denied the chance to study in Ambermane, Telmar had decided to take the stab at his father, even if it meant punishment when he returned home.

Master Darrowden looked up over the top of his book, his deeply sunken features pulled up into an angry scowl as he said, "I told Penwigget what he needed to hear."

Telmar kept his eyes purposefully locked on the zombie-like warder. He knew that he would lose his resolve under his father's cold stare and so he avoided making eye contact. "Yes, but what if he checks with the Lord Martyr, or the high warders, and learns that they are completely unaware of what you've done? I mean, it was obvious that Headmaster Penwigget is afraid of Warder Mankoff now."

Telmar felt his father's gaze boring into him. As the seconds ticked by, he knew that his father was waiting for him to look his way. Telmar had no choice, but he kept his eyes as downcast as possible when he looked up at his father.

"I have complete control of my creation, son. Warder Mankoff is nothing more than an automaton now. A tool. As such, I will use him to bring Crowe and Flack to justice. When Crowe's head is delivered to the Lord Martyr, the means of that end will not matter, and I will have proved to the Lord Martyr the effectiveness of having bound Ambraic spirits at our disposal."

Telmar looked back down as he said, "but if it is nothing more than an automaton, that means that it can't do anything at all *unless* you command it to, right?"

"That's right."

"Then why is it looking at you like that?"

Claudia began to feel weak and lightheaded. Twice she felt the beaks pierce her flesh; once on the shoulder and another on the buttocks. But the painful sensation was beginning to grow numb.

And then she was jarred violently and pulled up out of the water. In that instant she spit out the water that had filled her throat and was heaving vehemently. Air returned to her lungs.

Haverstagg had pulled the vicious ings off Claudia and had his heavily muscled arm wrapped around her chest as he dragged her away from their snapping beaks. Claudia saw the mound of translucent sails behind her scatter suddenly. A loud thud came from just a short distance away followed by the sound of water raining down on the tops of the giant mushrooms.

Everything came back into focus. Claudia saw what was chasing them. She screamed as the colossal toothy maw of the ubering swung toward her. It looked like a giant, obese version of the ings, but it literally towered over the giant mushrooms. Everything shook and spore-filled clouds wafted down from the mushroom caps each time one of its heavy club-like feet hit the ground. With each lumbering step the ubering swept the mushroom forest out of its way with a clawed hand the size of Haverstagg himself. As Haverstagg dragged Claudia through the swamp the ubering opened its mouth and lunged forward for the kill.

"*Lorroak fury!*" Claudia heard called out by a trio of voices just ahead of her.

The blast of force was deafening as it roared over her head, but it did little more than cause the ubering's head to snap back to the side. It was the shock of being hurt by something that must have stunned the giant predator. The little ings chattered all around, dozens actually clinging like parasites to their giant cousin. The ubering slid to a sudden stop and just stood there quietly, not sure what to do. Perhaps if it had eyes, or facial features other than a mouth, Claudia might have seen confusion manifest on its face. Clearly, it was not the sort of beast that was used to being challenged.

"Are you alright?" Crowe asked, pulling Claudia out of Haverstagg's grip, and quickly looking her over.

She nodded.

"Go with Haverstagg, that way!" Crowe pointed with his wand. "There's a tunnel that this thing can't possibly fit into. Wait for us there."

"But Grandfather!"

"Go!" Crowe shouted.

Claudia felt Haverstagg's hand take her by the wrist and pull her away. She turned and ran with him, her wand lighting the way as they left Crowe, Odderly and Yssa behind to face the ubering.

Master Darrowden looked down at Warder Mankoff and felt his heart skip a beat, his body stiffen. Fear washed over him, and he was unable to find his next breath as he clumsily tried to draw his wand. The ropes that had bound Warder Mankoff snapped and the willowy revenant moved so suddenly that the next thing Master Darrowden knew his head was slammed against the side of the wooden wagon and he felt a vice-like grip around his neck.

The blow had dazed him, but as the shimmer in his vision faded, he saw that Telmar was pinned to the floor with Warder Mankoff's other hand covering his face. Telmar was not moving, and there was a spot of blood slowly dripping out of his left ear.

"Open the chest and return my ashes or I will crush your son's skull and wrench his very soul from his bleeding corpse," the voice of the revenant was bivocal, a sinister mix of Warder Mankoff's baritone and something that sounded entirely otherwordly.

Master Darrowden tried to speak, but he was being strangled. The grip around his neck released only enough so that he was barely able to draw air. Master Darrowden started to conceive a lie that might trick the Ambraic spirit into trying to open the chest itself and thus be destroyed by the protective ward, but he looked down at his son and thought better of this. As stern and shrewd as he was in parenting the boy since the death of Telmar's mother, he loved his son dearly and would not risk his life with a lie. "Ak . . . ahk . . . all . . . right," he finally managed to say.

The revenant's grip did not loosen as Master Darrowden shakily drew his wand and thrice tapped the lid of the chest. It popped open silently. Master Darrowden's mind began racing, waiting for the opportunity to strike down his creation, but the ashes were about to be out of his reach, and without them, how could such a demon ever truly be slain? He never had the chance to dwell on the subject. Warder Mankoff yanked Master Darrowden sharply to the side by the throat, and his neck snapped in two with a gristly cracking sound. The most honored Dark Arts Master flopped to the floor of the rumbling wagon beside his unconscious son.

How many years have I longed for this moment? Azarajji thought as he reached into the chest and removed the urn. He opened the urn and inhaled deeply, relishing in the odor of his last mortal remains.

Azarajji had been alive when Roak, the creator god walked in the mortal realm. He had been one of the great Ambraic heroes responsible for slaying Roak atop the lone mountain. He had been among the first to feel Roak's dying wrath. But that was a millennia ago. Roak's magic had long since begun to fade, and slowly, the cursed shades of the Ambra accumulated power enough to overtake mortal hosts. As shades, they had become an entirely new species, able to move in and out of mortal bodies as easily as their mortal hosts changed clothes.

Azarajji had been one of the first of his kind to taste life inside a mortal body. But long before the Bjoran Revolt and the founding of the Brylands that mortal body had been destroyed and before Azarajji could recover from that defeat his spirit was bound into the mortal's ashes. Now, those ashes were in the palm of his hand. Azarajji was flesh again. And this time, the foolish wizards had taken great precautions to protect that flesh on his behalf. There was great irony in that.

Warder Mankoff was indeed a part of Azarajji now, but the warder's will was weak. His thoughts were dominated by a thirst to kill Asher Crowe and Odderly Flack, and little else. Azarajji was not compelled to appease the mind that shared his new form, but he would do as Warder Mankoff wished of him. After all, the weak-minded wizard had given Azarajji so much, it really was the least that Azarajji could do for his host in return. Besides, Azarajji's spirit had been bound for such an exceptionally long time. He would greatly enjoy the hunt of a worthy adversary.

Asher Crowe was known even to Azarajji, for the demon had been imprisoned in the Fire Falls Academy from the day it was first constructed. He had listened to the gossiping wizards, and he knew that this *Asher Crowe* had slain and spirit bound Enshalaan. In a way, Warder Mankoff's vengeance would be Azarajji's vengeance as well, for the two ancient Ambra had known each other in life. Perhaps the legendary wizard would even reveal Enshalaan's location before Azarajji killed him. Then, as Ambra, together they could return their kind to power.

As Azarajji stripped the wizard he had killed and donned the dead man's clothes, he regarded the unconscious boy at his feet. He debated whether to kill him as well. In the end though, before Azarajji leapt out of the back of the covered wagon, he decided to let the boy live. Perhaps he would still be close enough to hear the boy's screams when he awoke to find that his father, and everyone else with the caravan, had been killed.

Chapter 22

Crowe raised his wand and released a volley of six little balls of brightly glowing red light. Each one spiraled through the air attached itself to the ubering's hulking form; three on the head, two on the chest, and the last hit the ubering's wrist as it swiped Odderly out of the way.

Odderly went flying and broke through the stalks of several giant mushrooms before he tumbled down into the muck as the caps fell upon him. The resulting black cloud of mushroom dust and spores glowed from within and Crowe could hear the frying hiss of Odderly's smoldering rod in the water. But Crowe had no time to check and see that his friend had not been hurt. The ubering stepped forward, lowered its head to the ground and charged Crowe with its mouth open wide.

Crowe saw the maw of massive, twisted yellow teeth coming for him and he wove circles in the air with his wand just as the ubering's mouth snapped closed around Crowe with speed unbecoming so large a beast. At that same moment, an invisible sphere around Crowe lit up with crackling, crawling tendrils of electric energy. The ubering recoiled from the protective shield with smoke pouring out of its scorched and blistered mouth. Angry chatter erupted all around as the ings shouted and snarled in protest. They were silenced by a terrible roar from the ubering.

Taking advantage of the distraction, Yssa thrust her wand at the giant predator and shouted, *"endra alisharra!"* A thunderous boom shook the cavern as a stroke of lightning crackled between the tip of her wand and the ubering's chest.

The magical blast of lightning staggered the foul creature. It stumbled in the muddy water as the six festering red points of light began to grow. Each became a large, open, bleeding ulcer as Crowe's magic ate holes into the ubering's flesh. Before it had even regained its composure from Yssa's lightning strike, the point of red light that had hit its wrist had chewed through the bone and the ubering's clawed right hand fell off and splashed into the murky water around it.

Odderly had returned. He was slick with rotten vegetation and his wild red hair tangled with muddy water. He wore a furious expression as he pulled his smoldering rod back over his shoulder and lobbed a ball of burning pitch into the bloody mess of flesh and bone that had become the ubering's face. Black smoke poured from the burning giant as it toppled forward into the swamp where the ings descended upon it. As scavengers, meat was meat.

"Are you alright?" Crowe asked of Odderly, who merely nodded as he wiped mud off his face with his red handkerchief.

"Let's get out of here, Asher," Yssa said as she looked back the way Claudia and Haverstagg had gone.

As they fled, the hundreds of little ings enjoyed the meat of their protector. It would likely be their last meal until some other predator discovered the mushroom cavern of Chasmarrud.

Telmar awoke slowly with stiffness in his body and a pounding headache. When enough of his senses had returned for him to realize what had happened, he rolled over suddenly and looked to where his father had been. A whimper escaped him.

"Father..." Telmar said quietly.

Tadris Darrowden's head lay flat against his shoulder and the bones of his spine pushed up against the flesh of his pale neck from the inside. The break was obvious. Telmar's father stared back at him with cold dead eyes that were still wide open with surprise. The body had been stripped entirely, leaving the once honored Fire Falls Master lying naked on the floor of the wagon. His wand, and even his signet ring, had been stolen.

Telmar crawled quietly to his father's body with tears streaming down his face. Everything seemed so trivial now, all the arguments, all the whippings. His father was dead. Murdered. And though Telmar hated the man, he loved him too. Now he was gone and Telmar felt his stomach twisting within him. He thought that he was going to be sick, but he did not vomit. Instead Telmar closed his fists together so tightly that his fingernails dug into the soft meat of his palm hard enough to draw lines of red. He arched his head back and screamed.

It was music to Azarajii's ears, the way the boy's voice carried through the canyon on the clean mountain air. It was those things, the feelings of personal accomplishment and mortal sensations that had driven Azarajii mad for the long cycles that he had been spiritbound and unable to enjoy the gifts of flesh. Now, with the cold winter wind blowing across his skin once more, those old sensations, mixed with the boy's pitiful wailings, brought the demon much pleasure.

With his unnatural strength and agility, as well as a body that could suffer no harm, Azarajii quickly ascended the canyon's ruddy cliff-side and reached the summit. With an unobstructed view, the new world spread out before him and he could see mountain peaks that brought back old memories of the time when the Ambra called this land home, before the great plague all but destroyed his people and they were forced to turn against their own creator.

Roak had been blamed for the pestilence and famine, of course. He was a god, after all, and such things were well within his dominion. But even gods could be slain when they walked the mortal realm, and the Ambra had pursued Roak's avatar across these very mountains and hills. All the way to the lone mountain of the south where Roak was made to pay for his treachery. But now Roak was gone, the God Times ended. The Ambra, however, remained. Azarajii was proof of that. And Azarajii could almost feel himself being called back to the lone mountain and the ruins of his people. He would rededicate himself to his ancient mission soon enough. When Asher Crowe and Odderly Flack were dead, Azarajii would revive his people and retake this world.

The Brysh had evolved greatly over the millennia. They were no longer scattered clans at war with one another as they had been before they were united under the First Lord Martyr. In the cycles that followed, the Brysh ultimately discovered the Ambraic ruins of Roak's Grave. Within the ruins they also discovered Ambraic magic, and while their skill in the traditional ancient arts was noteworthy, none of them, not even the most powerful of the Brysh wizards, could ever hope to challenge the power of the Ambra sorcerers. Ambraic magic traced its roots all the way back to glyphs discovered across the Easterly Sea in the tomb of Lavarinth. It was old magic, from the first days of creation.

"Nothing lasts forever," Azarajii mused as he thought about the many civilizations that had risen and fallen over the centuries. He looked out upon the Brysh plain and regarded the small villages he could make out from his high vantage point as he said aloud, "except for us." Azarajii's laughter carried for miles beneath the dark, brooding clouds.

Claudia and Haverstagg had watched the battle from the shelter of the confining tunnel. A wave of relief washed over Claudia when she saw the giant ubering fall before the wizards.

"Grandfather!" Claudia shouted when Crowe ducked into the tunnel. She threw her arms around him and pulled him into a powerful embrace. "I was so scared."

Crowe patted Claudia's back and spoke quietly, "we are unharmed, child."

"Odderly!" Claudia said as she moved to hug him as well, but he put up a hand to stop her and looked down at himself.

"Best not," he muttered and started to walk away. The expression on his face was one of absolute disgust at being covered with the muck of the swamp.

Claudia found this particularly amusing given that Odderly was never one who put much effort into personal cleanliness. She grabbed him and spun him around, pulling him into her embrace. She was easily as filthy as he, but that would not have mattered anyway. Odderly was family to her, if not by blood, then by kinship of spirit. She hugged him tightly.

"I'm glad that you're safe," she said.

Odderly nodded and walked alone down the passageway. The orange glow of his magical rod lit the way as he picked a path through the boulder-strewn tunnel.

"I'm glad you're safe too, Yssa," Claudia said when she turned to regard the old woman. Claudia hesitated and then finally threw her arms around Yssa too.

"What in Shadow was that thing?" Haverstagg asked.

Yssa shook her head.

Crowe looked back through the mouth of the tunnel to the darkness beyond. They could all hear the screeches of the ings as they fed on their fallen cousin. "I honestly don't know," Crowe said, "an evolutionary mutation?" He shook his head. "I've never seen anything like it. And I hope to never see such a thing again."

Claudia stared at her grandfather as he spoke. He was breathing heavily, and he did not look well. Perhaps it was just time for another injection. Perhaps the expenditure of magical energy had fatigued him. Either way, he looked older and more haggard than he should have looked, and she began to worry.

As if sensing her fears Crowe looked at his own hands before tucking them each into the folds of his robe at the opposite wrist. "Odderly," Crowe called as he hurried to catch up to him. "It's time."

Telmar stepped out of the wagon afraid of what he would find outside.

He knew that Warder Mankoff had escaped and fled, but what of everyone else? The snow was falling heavily now. Gray clouds hung in the sky blotting out the sun. There was no wind.

Telmar could smell blood as soon as his boots touched the road, but he saw nothing until he came around the front of the wagon where the bodies were scattered. It looked as if a war had been fought and lost there. The four other covered wagons of the caravan were either toppled over, burned into skeletal remains, or broken and shattered as if they had exploded. The stiddleback had been ripped apart. Debris lay scattered everywhere and a few of the roadside pines were still burning.

Five wizards, Telmar knew them all by name, had challenged the revenant his father had created. In addition to nearly a dozen hired mercenaries and the quartet of Subterranea wardens who were assigned to escort the caravan to Ambermane and back. They all looked as if they had been butchered and magically savaged.

Telmar was used to seeing death. To seeing blood. But not even in his father's laboratory had he ever seen anything such as this. The ferocity and violence that had taken place would forever haunt this place, and Telmar himself. He shuddered and put his back against his father's wagon not knowing what to do.

After taking a deep breath Telmar tried to sort out his thoughts. Judging by the mountain peaks that served as landmarks the caravan was somewhere between the Otep-Korah crossroad and the village of Stonehold. Stonehold was the most reasonable place to go for help, but it was likely still several miles away, and if any bandits lived in these hills, they would plunder his father's wagon and what remained of the caravan long before he arrived or could return. It was snowing, night was coming on quickly, and when the sun was gone altogether who knew what sort of animals would come down here to feed on the bodies of the dead. Telmar couldn't let that happen, not to his father.

———◄●►———

When night had descended on the Brylands the temperature dropped sharply. Shivering and with blood dried into the creases of his scraped knuckles, Telmar put the last heavy stone into place over his father's grave. It had taken him hours to dig the shallow hole, and all his strength to drag his father's body to the roadside grave, but now the deed was finished. And somehow, the act had strengthened Telmar. It brought closure and acceptance of the fact that his father was gone, and his own life forever changed.

"I'm sorry, father," Telmar said aloud as he crouched alongside the rocks that marked his father's grave. "I'm sorry that I was never the son you wanted me to be. And I'm sorry that your passing came this way. I . . . I . . . I can tell you, father, that I loved you. I still love you, even if I was nothing but a disappointment to you. I always loved you, and I was always proud to be your son." Telmar rubbed his dirty hand across his eyes, forcing himself to hold back the tears. He would not let himself cry again. "At least now, you will be spared the course of life I choose to take. I'm sorry that I could never tell you this before, but as much as I've always loved you, I don't want to be you. I don't want to end up like you . . ."

Telmar looked through the trees to the caravan on the road, to the mountains lurking under the dismal gray sky, and then back down to his father's grave. "Murdered by some *abomination*," he said, choosing Headmaster Penwigget's word for Warder Mankoff, "and buried by a son you never wanted, in a shallow grave on the side of a road." Telmar stood up. "No, father. It is here that our paths part, and we go our separate ways because of decisions that *you* made. You never let me be a boy. You made me grow up too quickly. Now I'm on my own. I'm alone."

Telmar spit on the ground, letting his anger ease the pain he was feeling inside. "I will go to Stonehold and I will tell them what happened here out of respect for you, father. But after that, I'll only be returning to Subterranea to speak with the Lord Martyr and settle your affairs. And then, I'm coming back here, to the World Above. I will spend winter *above* the ground with those who choose to stay here. I *am* going to Ambermane University, and after that, I don't know . . . but I'm not going to follow in your footsteps."

Telmar looked down at the grave and stared silently for a while until his attention was captured by the sound of something moving back at the caravan. Through the trees he could see some manner of small animal moving around the bodies. "Sleep well, father," Telmar whispered. "I hope that you found Light and not Shadow ahead of you."

Telmar returned to the wagon and selected a collection of personal items and some things out of his father's special chest. Before he climbed back out of the wagon, Telmar opened and drained one of the oil lamps that hung from a hook overhead. He poured it out evenly as he backed out of the wagon. He scraped his striker across the attached flint stone and sent sparks flying into the wagon. It took several tries, but when Telmar walked away from the caravan the scavenging dog-like barcoots scattered and his father's wagon went up in flames.

Chapter 23

Haverstagg rested with his back against the stone of the hot, humid, cavernous chamber. They had wasted little time in putting distance between themselves and Chasmarrud cavern. By the time they stopped to claim their first moment of rest everyone was exhausted. Crowe, more than any of the others, appeared worse for the wear. He had taken two small boosters of Odderly's magical serum as they moved through the uneven, winding tunnels of the World Below, but despite the frequent injections he looked older and gaunter than Haverstagg had seen him before.

Yssa sat with Crowe now, holding his head in her lap and soothing him by gently caressing his head as he slept. They had talked for a little while before Crowe had fallen into deep slumber and watching them filled Haverstagg with a deep sense of loss. Claudia had told Haverstagg that Crowe and Yssa had fallen in love when Crowe was about half Haverstagg's age, and even though they had spent so many cycles apart, she thought it nice that they were together now. Haverstagg, however, would never be with Hannah again. He did not even have the chance to say goodbye to her. One minute they were dreaming together, the next she was gone.

Vengeance had been hollow. Haverstagg had since learned that Crowe and Otep had killed the highwaymen who had taken Hannah, all except for the scarred man that Haverstagg had the pleasure of killing himself. Their deaths, however just, did not ease Haverstagg's pain.

And the memory of the scarred man's smiling face tormented Haverstagg even now. It was a lasting, taunting image, and one that would likely never go away. The sense of loss within him would never go away. Nor the guilt.

Had I been able to keep pace with the caravan, Hannah would stil be alive.

As they moved through the World Below, Crowe had assured Haverstagg that Hannah's death had been swift. Haverstagg had asked if she had been ravaged, which Crowe denied, but something in the scarred man's grin suggested otherwise. Anger at being rendered helpless while Hannah was likely raped and murdered by the highwaymen burned within Haverstagg.

Growling, Haverstagg stood up and walked across the smooth incline of the cavern. He paced restlessly and tried to push the horrid images out of his mind. At last, he caught sight of Claudia and Odderly crouched together behind a cluster of mineral columns and strange crystal formations. He needed to be around people to avoid the lurking loneliness within him, so he wandered over to them.

Haverstagg felt the heat of Odderly's smoldering rod as he drew near, and when he sat down near them, he caught the foul scent of the swamp. In what he estimated to be a full day's pace through the tunnels, they had not come across any water for them to wash. Both Odderly and the girl were covered with swamp filth and the heat of Odderly's magical rod only made the odor more pungent.

"There's another one," Odderly said, sticking a grubby finger out to point at a small gray-skinned lizard that crawled along a thin, sparkling column of stone and quartz. "Try it again on him."

Odderly looked over and nodded to Haverstagg, welcoming him to watch as Claudia raised her wand and pointed it at the little lizard.

"*Geosium transverte!*" Claudia said. When nothing happened, she looked back at Odderly, biting her lip. "It just won't work," she complained.

"The magic is there, child," Odderly insisted. "Do it again and *will* it to be. Don't just speak the words. Put the image of it happening in your mind and *will* it to be."

Claudia nodded to Odderly and looked over at Haverstagg. She smiled meekly and repeated, *"geosium transverte!"*

The tip of Claudia's wooden wand lit up for just a moment, and the lizard, perched only a few hands width away froze in place. Haverstagg raised a brow and leaned forward to get a better look. Claudia's gray eyes were locked intently on the lizard, and as she stared at it the lizard's sides stopped moving as it stopped breathing. Its gray skin darkened, taking on the deeper gray of the wall to which it held fast. The lizard's tissue began to transform with a grinding, earthy sound, and then all was silent. The little lizard had been turned entirely to stone.

Odderly smiled wide and plucked the petrified lizard from the wall. He examined it and showed it to Claudia who held the little lizard in her hand before smiling proudly and reaching over to hand it to Haverstagg to examine.

"I did it!" she exclaimed.

Odderly was nodding eagerly to Claudia as Haverstagg examined the lizard. It looked like an incredibly life-like stone carving, but it was solid stone magically hewn of the same rock that formed the surrounding cavern.

"Now how do I turn it back?" Claudia asked as she brushed her mud-tangled hair out of her face.

"Back?" Odderly asked.

"Aye," Claudia said eagerly, "how do I turn it back to flesh again?"

Odderly looked over to Haverstagg and the petrified lizard that he held. "You can't turn it back lass, its dead."

Telmar's fingers and toes were numb when he saw the lights of Stonehold come into view on the mountainside. The blowing snow had made every step tedious. Even wrapped in one of his father's extra academic robes, Telmar could feel the cold deep inside of him. Realizing that Stonehold offered shelter from the raging storm, he trudged on with renewed effort. He was almost there.

No gate marked the entrance to the village, but lamps lit with ever-burning flames burned outside of the peaked village hall. Telmar followed these beacons of hope until he crashed against the smooth wooden doors and fell to the marble-tiled floor inside.

When he awoke Telmar found that he had been changed into a clean linen night robe. Both his hands and feet had been bandaged with cotton wraps, and he could feel the intense warmth of sticky salve on his fingers and toes. A heavy blanket covered him, and the bed in which he had been sleeping was soft and comfortable.

The bedchamber spoke of wealth and status; it was not the home of a peasant. The walls were of smooth ruddy stone accented with moldings of rare petrified wood that was carved into the of images long-horned deer-like korum surrounded by beautiful knotwork. The only light came from the fire burning inside of a hearth so large that its stonework occupied an entire wall. The mounted head of a white korum was centered over the mantle. It looked at Telmar with eyes of polished black stone.

Before the hearth was a rocking chair that rocked silently on the ornate rug that was spread over the tiled floor. A lone figure was seated in the chair, a book held open before him. Telmar immediately recognized the man. He was in the home of Artimus Halton, the village reeve and a close friend of his father.

"Oh, good, you're awake," Reeve Halton said when he noticed that Telmar was looking at him. "I'll have to thank Magus Ferency for his efforts. It was he who healed you."

"How long have I been here?" Telmar asked.

Reeve Halton turned to regard the timepiece against another wall. It was a tall, wide cabinet with a myriad of spinning gears and swinging pendulums. "A little over six hours," Reeve Halton said, "though without the help of the good mage I'm not so sure you would be here at all. The cold had all but done you in. Curious time, winter."

"I need your help Mister Halton," Telmar said as he swung his feet over the side of the plush bed.

"I reckon that you do indeed. Something terrible has happened to your father?"

"Aye, but how do you know that?"

"Well, you arrived alone, half killed from exposure and wearing your father's robe. We were expecting the arrival of the wizards from Subterranea yesterday afternoon. Along with a special package of which I'm sure you are aware."

Telmar nodded slowly and said, "they're all dead."

Reeve Halton stood and crossed the room, taking a seat next to the boy. "We had assumed the worst. Why don't you let me get you a cup of sweet tea and you can tell me what happened . . ."?

———••———

"You can't let it get to you that way," Haverstagg said to Claudia after Odderly had wandered off to find a private place to relieve himself. "Killing that is."

"How can I not let it get to me?"

Haverstagg shrugged.

"I just never thought that things would turn out this way," Claudia lamented. "Its just madness, Haverstagg, all of this."

"Its not madness," Haverstagg said, "its love. Its love that has us all here."

Claudia scooted up and leaned forward putting her elbows on her knees. "What do you mean?"

"You're here because you love your father."

Claudia nodded.

"Asher is here because he loves you."

Claudia looked over to where Crowe and Yssa slept nearby. They held each other the way young lovers might. Claudia could not help but smile before she said, "and Yssa loves him."

Haverstagg nodded. "It sounds like she's given up everything to be with him. I would wager that she's always loved him."

"I know," Claudia looked down and blushed. "My grandfather told me about how they were when they were young."

"And Odderly loves him too. In a different way, aye, but he loves him."

Claudia stared at Haverstagg. "But what about you? You hardly know us all, but here you are."

"I'm here because of love too . . . because of the love I lost. Without Hannah there's no point to my life anymore. Being here with you all . . . well maybe I'm just being self destructive."

Claudia opened her mouth to say something, but then stopped herself and looked down at her boots. "I don't think that's all that has you here. I think you need us right now. And I think you care about all of us. I think you care about me."

"I do," Haverstagg admitted. "I look at you and see everything that was denied me. I see the daughter that I'll never have." Haverstagg let out a deep sigh. "It changes you, losing someone you love. But your father is still alive, Claudia. Unlike me, you have a chance to find him, and be happy with him again."

Claudia looked up with tears in her eyes. Haverstagg scooted over and put a comforting arm around her shoulder as he said, "that is why you can't let things like that lizard get to you that way. There's a lot standing between you and your father, Claudia, and you have to be able to do whatever it takes to get him back."

Claudia stared down at the ground.

"From what I understand," Haverstagg continued, "Rusk is a great exception among his kind. He was raised by that Otep fellow, and he was raised like a human. The garuk that we're going to find down here, well I don't think that they're like him. They are the same garuk that destroyed Ambly, and Roak only knows what your father has had to endure as their slave." Haverstagg gestured to Claudia's wand. "I don't know what all you can do with that thing, but when the time comes . . ." Haverstagg let his words hang in the air.

The sound of flopping feet on the stone spun both Haverstagg and Claudia around suddenly as if the moment to test both of their resolve had just come. But it was only Odderly; naked except for his wet, but clean black breaches. His hair was red again, his face the dusky tan color of his skin, and under his arm he clutched a bundle of his clothes and leathers that had all been recently washed free of the muck from the Chasmarrud cavern.

"I found water!" Odderly exclaimed, smiling broadly as he noticed the reaction of the other two.

Claudia and Haverstagg both looked at themselves. Claudia was certainly the worst off, being utterly covered in dried filth, but they both sorely needed a bath. Haverstagg stood and extended a large hand to Claudia, helping her up to her feet.

"Show us," they said together.

Odderly stuffed his magical iron rod into his breaches but left everything else spread out on the rocks to dry. While Crowe and Yssa slept, and while Claudia and Haverstagg had talked, Odderly had wandered ahead a little bit, feeling that it was a good idea to scout the area before he tried to rest. Less than a hundred paces from where they had stopped to camp, Odderly found a small crack in the cavern wall where he had to get down on his belly and crawl under an overhanging sheet of mineral-streaked gray stone and fragile white cider straws. The hollow on the other side opened into a cavern of significant size that connected to dozens of smaller tunnels. In the center of the cavern, the ground sloped up, and then dropped off suddenly into a small underground pool.

Odderly did not have to help Claudia through the crawlway, but the both of them had to grab Haverstagg's arms and give him a good tug to get the much larger man through.

"Oh, thank Roak," Claudia said when she crested the top of the slope and saw the clear water reflecting the light from her wand. "How do I get down there?" she asked of Odderly.

Odderly and Haverstagg climbed the slope and then Odderly pointed at a narrow ledge that winded its way down to the water. "Go down that way. And don't worry, it's an isolated pool, nothing that'll eat you," Odderly snickered.

Claudia started down the ledge, and stopped, turning around suddenly when she noticed both Odderly and Haverstagg were still standing at the top of the slope watching her. She blushed. "Are you two going to stand there and watch?" she asked facetiously.

"Oh . . . um, of course not," Odderly said before ducking down the slope. Haverstagg, red with similar embarrassment, followed.

A few minutes passed in awkward silence as Odderly and Haverstagg stood together by the crawlway. They began to pass the time while they waited with Haverstagg again thanking Odderly for his help when he was injured, but then Haverstagg stopped suddenly.

Odderly raised a furry red brow and asked, "what's wrong?"

"Have you explored any of these tunnels?" Haverstagg asked.

Odderly shook his head. "No."

"The magical fire you make . . . it doesn't make smoke?" Haverstagg asked.

Odderly straightened and took a deep breath. He drew his magical rod from his breaches and scanned the dark patches at the edges of Claudia's magical light that rose over the slope. "I smell it too."

Chapter 24

Haverstagg moved quietly through the darkness following the flickering torchlight moving down the roughly hewn tunnel ahead of him. Odderly was not far behind. They had chosen to move without the benefit of Odderly's magical light so that they could assess the threat before they revealed themselves to whoever was in the tunnel with them.

The tunnel curved sharply and gained elevation, but the stone was smooth and firm. It masked Haverstagg and Odderly's movement as they crept forward. There was whispering just ahead of them, and the light had stopped moving. Haverstagg paused and took shelter against the shadowy wall of the tunnel while he waited for Odderly to crawl up to his side. "They've stopped," Haverstagg whispered into Odderly's ear.

The two of them crept up into the torchlight that was cast around the corner, and when they peered around, they saw three men dressed in fighting leathers crouched at the opening of a tunnel which looked down upon the pool where Claudia bathed. The men were talking quietly to each other about all the fun they were going to have with her.

Odderly, who had been like a father to Claudia for the last six cycles instantly turned red and fumed with anger, but the conversation the scoundrels were having hit a particular cord with Haverstagg as well. These men were bandits just like the men who had raped and murdered Hannah.

There was a sudden flare of bright orange light and Haverstagg felt the heat of Odderly's magical rod wash over him. Before Odderly could raise the rod against the scoundrels, however, Haverstagg charged forward. Rising to his full height as soon as the tunnel allowed, he caught two of the men by the throat and lifted them clean off their feet. He twisted and slammed them both violently into the stone wall. The third man, larger and fatter than the other two, was stunned only for a moment by Haverstagg's barbaric charge. He raised a gleaming flanged mace and swung at Haverstagg, but Haverstagg's strength and fury was so that he actually used one of the scoundrels he had pinned against the wall as a shield, swinging the grizzled gray-bearded man into the path of the mace.

It was a fatal blow. The mace cracked open the gray-bearded man's skull. Gore flew everywhere, and the impact was so unnaturally powerful that it sent Haverstagg and the other scoundrel flying over the ledge before the mace clanged loudly into the surrounding rock. Metal chirped against stone, chipping a huge section of rock away.

In the pool below Claudia spun around, covering herself with her hands just in time to see Haverstagg come flying down toward her gripping a longhaired man by the throat. At that same moment, a fiery blast shot out of the concealed tunnel from which they had come silhouetting another figure that collapsed to the ground entirely aflame. Startled by it all, Claudia screamed.

Haverstagg and the longhaired man landed in the pool with a resounding splash. Haverstagg sank like a stone, and as he thrashed underwater trying to find footing, the man he held tried to pull free from his grasp. It was a futile effort with Haverstagg's large hand wrapped so tightly around the man's throat that his windpipe was pushed completely in on itself. Haverstagg was huge by comparison and having taken a deep breath of air the moment before hitting the water, his efforts were focused purely on keeping the longhaired man pinned against the stone at the bottom of the pool.

Frantic and drowning, the smaller longhaired man reached for his ankle. In the clear water, Haverstagg was able to see that there was suddenly a knife in the lesser man's hand. The attack was half-hearted, meant less to slash Haverstagg, than to drive him back. At this, it succeeded. Haverstagg found the ground beneath his feet and pushed up and out of the water. In one swift motion he threw his head back and dodged another swipe of the knife as his opponent came up out of the water slashing wildly and gasping for air.

The two circled each other, the small longhaired man feigning with the knife several times before suddenly changing his attack pattern and landing a deep blow that sliced into Haverstagg's chest near the collarbone. It was a painful cut that exposed bone for an instant before blood began rushing from the wound. Haverstagg winced back, grabbing at the wound and unknowingly giving his attacker the opportunity to lunge in with another slash aimed for the neck. The knife sliced quickly through the air and the small longhaired man's aim was true. But the knife stopped just short of the mark.

The water all around the longhaired man erupted up from the pool and tendrils of magically animated water wrapped around the hand holding the knife with a sound like the snapping of a wet leather whip. Two more animated tentacles reached from the pool; one taking the small man's other hand and pulling it back, and the other latching around his face and pulling him backward into the water.

Haverstagg watched dumbfounded as the man wrestled against the grip of the water itself. Below the surface of the pool, he appeared to be struggling against nothing at all. At one point when the longhaired man almost got his face back up above the water the pool swelled up into an almost humanoid form that howled with an unearthly watery sound before it pushed him back down into the pool.

The struggle continued for less than a minute, but when it was done the small longhaired man stared up at Haverstagg with lifeless eyes and an expression that betrayed total fear, profound confusion. The water churned and suddenly felt less dense around him. Haverstagg looked across the pool to where Claudia sat with her legs drawn up against her chest. She held her slender wooden wand extended with the tip hovering just above the surface of the water. She was trembling.

Claudia's scream had awoken Crowe and Yssa with a start. The two of them quickly scanned the area where they had been camped. Odderly's clothes were there, but there was no sign of him or the others.

"This way!" Crowe exclaimed as he rushed down the tunnel in search of the missing companions.

With all the noise, it did not take long to locate the crawlway. Light spilt out into the cavern from the low horizontal crack in the stone. Crowe and Yssa slithered under and crested the top of the slope just in time to see Odderly's fire dying down and Claudia settle herself against some rocks redressed in her wet clothes. Her wand glowed still, though it lay on the ground beside her.

It didn't take long to figure out what had happened. Claudia's eyes were locked on the body floating in the pool and something had changed about her. It was as if some degree of her innocence had suddenly been ripped away. Her eyes were narrowed, her brow creased with the same lines that formed on Crowe's own face when he was deeply troubled, and tears stained her face.

Crowe and Yssa made their way down to the pool, but Claudia did not look up as they pulled Odderly and Haverstagg aside.

"There were three of them," Odderly said quietly. "The one in the pool there, and two others up there on the ledge." He pointed to the charred tunnel. "Smugglers I'd wager, they have a wagon just down the third passage there where they'd been making their camp."

Yssa looked at Haverstagg with concern in her eyes. Blood seeped out from between his thick fingers. "You're hurt."

"Aye," Haverstagg said. He pulled his hand away from the deep cut and blood ran freely down his chest. "But it's nothing that Odderly can't mend."

Crowe looked to Yssa. "Come with me. Odderly, take care of Haverstagg's cut and then go break our camp. I want to have a look at this wagon."

Odderly was already working magic to close the wound as Crowe crouched down beside Claudia. "Are you alright, Claudia," he asked.

She nodded, but kept her eyes locked on the corpse. Crowe followed her gaze. "Don't you fret about this. Look at Haverstagg,"

Crowe commanded.

When Claudia did not avert her eyes from the body Crowe grabbed her by her chin and guided it over to where Odderly and Haverstagg crouched nearby.

"You see that cut?" Crowe asked.

Claudia slowly nodded.

"That man would have done far worse. Whatever you think you did, know that you did what you had to do to make sure that Haverstagg, and all of us, weren't killed by these men." Crowe narrowed his gaze. "You did a good thing, Claudia. These were not good men."

Crowe stared at Claudia for a moment longer and felt Yssa's hand touch his shoulder. When he looked up, Yssa gestured for him to leave Claudia alone. Crowe nodded, leaned forward, and kissed Claudia on her forehead. "You did good girl."

Crowe and Yssa found the bandit's tunnel camp exactly where Odderly had pointed them.

"Our luck is turning, Asher," Yssa said as she ran a wrinkled hand along the thick neck of one of the two robuck that were tied up to the wagon.

The animals were well-nourished, and typical of the subterranean oxen, they were docile and took easily to Yssa as she stroked their black hides. Each had thick curving horns that rolled back behind their ears and emerged again just below their jaws, and each was easily the weight of a stiddleback, even though robuck stood only half as high.

"Maybe," Crowe said. "The wagon is fully stocked, so we'll be able to resupply here. But this brings us to a point where a decision must be made. These scoundrels were most likely on their way to the tunnels below Rish Hollow. The main tunnel here, will likely take us that route, which is a stroke of luck, but I can't say what type of welcome we'll be given when whoever is expecting this shipment realizes that we've sacked the smugglers."

"You think we should leave it, and continue on foot through the less traveled tunnels?" Yssa asked.

"No . . . no, I think not. By now the warders know that we are down here, somewhere, and we should put as much distance as possible between us and Magmorra Road, which must connect to these tunnels somewhere south of here." Crowe regarded the sacks of stolen goods loaded into the back of the wagon. "Let's regroup, take what we need, and put this region behind us. We'll take our chances."

Yssa nodded. "I'll go get the others."

———•·•———

Telmar took little comfort in the sweet tea and warm soup that Reeve Halton had given him. He recounted the tale of the past few days spent in Ambermane while the wizards from Fire Falls performed the Ambraic ritual that bound a shade into Warder Mankoff's dying body. Telmar even told the good Reeve about his father's deception, and this caused the older man great worry.

"The thought that this . . . *thing*, is out there somewhere, Telmar. Well, it's frightening to say the least." Reeve Halton wiped perspiration from his forehead. "The Lord Martyr has to be told."

Telmar looked up but said nothing. He felt cold and empty inside. However frightened Reeve Halton was to know that an Ambraic demon walked the Brylands, the reeve would never understand the fear that the abomination had instilled in Telmar. Telmar had been face to face with the demon. He had felt its vice-like grip around his neck. He had looked into those glowing eyes and seen the evil that burned within them.

"I must go pass word of this through the stonetappers, and I must ask what your intentions are now, Telmar? The loss of your father, while terrible, it makes you the master of the Darrowden estate. Shall I arrange for you to have an escort to the undercity?"

Telmar stared at the reeve and after a long while of watching a bead of sweat run down the old man's cheek, Telmar nodded and said, "I want to leave as soon as possible."

With the bitter cold chewing at his desiccated skin and a blizzard raging all around him, Azarajii dug his clawed fingers into the snow and cleared a patch of raw earth. Old magic fused within him the ability to find his prey, to complete a task for which he had been selected hundreds of thousands of cycles before, and the stink of Asher Crowe was now directly below him. He pounded the ground and howled in fury.

His prey was in the World Below, and if not for the miles of earth and rock separating them, Azarajii would now be rending the wizard's flesh from his bones. The demon felt Warder Mankoff's excitement stirring within him, and he mentally subdued the warder who shared his mind.

Through the night Azarajii had prepared himself to face Asher Crowe and complete the warder's task. He needed to be free of Warder Mankoff's burning hatred of Crowe so that Azarajii could do what he had been created by the old curse to do. One remained. Enshalaan. He must break the cycle. Bound as he was, he remained unable to exact his wrath, and his anger reached a new height.

Azarajii rose and surveyed the snowy landscape. Across the frozen plains to the southwest lay the Brysh market town. He had passed it without taking a single life, so sure was he that he would be tasting Asher Crowe's blood this night. But the wizards had been denied him. Now, the demon debated returning to Market or pressing on in the direction that Asher Crowe was moving.

So much had changed since his kind walked these lands, but Azarajii knew that he could gain entrance into the World Below by way of the Black Rift. Once he had, it would not take long at all to stalk his prey through the lightless caverns. Should he bide his time and taste of mortal flesh once again, as he had at the caravan? Or should he make haste and intercept the wizards Crowe and Flack at the rift?

In the end, Azarajii ran onward to the northeast, eager for the moment that the wizards would again cross his path without the mantle of the world between them.

Chapter 25

Haverstagg and Odderly, being the two strongest of the companions, went about the task of unpacking the wagon while Crowe and Claudia picked through the overfilled sacks. Yssa had been charged with preparing the first *real meal* that any of them had seen since departing *The Blue World*. The bandits had a plentiful store of both flour and dried meat.

In addition to finally finding clothes, Haverstagg, who had been shirtless and barefoot since the battle at the mountain inn, took comfort in donning a suit of armor crafted from smoothly polished banded iron plates. No more would a brigand with a knife place him in mortal danger. He strapped Odderly's shield over his shoulder and collected a lantern and tins of oil from another bag. Having relied on the wizard's magical light all this time, Haverstagg grinned happily knowing he now carried his own source of light. And better yet, he now had a weapon that suited him. Haverstagg carefully examined the flanged mace that Odderly had taken from the bandit up in the tunnel.

"It's been enchanted," Odderly said matter of factly when he handed over the weapon. "You can feel how lightweight it is, yet you saw what it did in the tunnel. With this and your raw strength . . . well, I'm glad that you're standing with us and not against us," Odderly said with a smile.

"And I'm sure that I'll have the opportunity to put it to good use," Haverstagg said, slipping the mace into his new weapon harness alongside a series of throwing knives that he had no idea how to use. "I've felt a bit like a fifth leg on a roshea around all of you with no light and no weapon. I may not be a trained man-at-arms, but I think I'll be able to hold my own against whatever is out there now. Block and swing, or something like that. But I'm leaving the warders to you. I'll let magic fight magic."

"Well, let us hope that there are none of those ahead of us," Crowe interjected.

An hour later, the robuck pulled the wagon quickly through the tunnel with little direction. They were trained beasts, and this pair had likely run these tunnels a thousand times, if they had run them once, which only confirmed Crowe's suspicion that they were headed toward Rish Hollow. Thieves and smugglers often used the World Below to move goods stolen throughout the Brylands to the remote mountain village where the Lord Martyr had little sway and both warden and warder alike were afraid to go.

While Crowe had told Claudia that they would not go to Rish Hollow itself, it was a course that would take them within a few miles of the smuggler's village. With any luck they would not encounter any more bandits. They had enough to worry about. At the Black Rift waited an entire population of garuk which stood between Claudia and her father. Knowing this, all of Claudia's thoughts eventually began to turn toward the garuk, and Claudia, more than the others, began to worry. She had crossed a line, a point in her life from which there could be no going back. She had known right from the beginning that her quest would bring her to this very moment, but it did not make it any easier.

As the wagon rattled down the tunnel Claudia stared at Haverstagg. He hardly looked like the same man she had met at Otep's inn. With his eyes downcast and peering out from under the rim of a helmet that tapered up to a spiked point, and dressed in the mismatched suit of stolen armor, he looked more like some kind of gladiator or mercenary from Lursh than the gentle and kind hops farmer she knew him to be.

Have I also changed so much?

Claudia looked at herself. She still wore the same clothes that Rusk had once washed for her, but now she had a hooded cloak wrapped tightly around her as well. She had braided her hair into two pigtails that fell out of the hood, and she realized that she had picked the oversized cloak out of the bandit's spoils purposely. It allowed her to pull herself into it. It allowed her to hide. But who was she hiding from?

She was hiding from herself, she realized. For the last six cycles she had been adamant about how she wanted to return to Ambly and find her father. But through all those cycles she had failed to realize that to do so was to cast aside what remained of her childhood. A child could dream and make bold claims, but to actually embark on such a journey? That was a task laden with responsibility. She now carried a great deal of responsibility on her shoulders. She was responsible for what happened to all of her traveling companions, and she was responsible for the chaos that they left in their wake. She was responsible for the deaths that followed her quest.

The miles rolled on with little change in the dull gray stone around them. The days wore on uneventfully. At times the ground was smooth and the ride comfortable, and at other times the passages were so filled with rocky debris and stone columns that the robuck had to struggle to move onward. And as each cavernous tunnel twisted into the next, Claudia came to realize that she was no longer that frightened little girl with grand dreams and little resolve. She was a woman, a wizard, a force to be reckoned with.

Haverstagg had been right after all. She had a chance to be with her father again, and she *would* do whatever she had to do to ensure that he was rescued from the garuk, and that none of her *family*, for that is how she had come to think of her companions, came to any harm.

Claudia drew her wand and stared at it intently. She didn't speak aloud, but in her mind, she made a vow. Never again would she hesitate to raise her wand against those who stood against her, be they man or beast. She would strive to be just, and justice would be found in her heart without the bias of laws meant not to protect the innocent, but those of power and privilege. Woe be to any who stood in her way.

Claudia had always found that elemental magic came easily to her. Even though she struggled with the *geosium transverte* spell that she had used to turn the little lizard into stone, she knew doing so at all was quite the accomplishment. Such magic was well beyond her age, and she a mage lacking traditional training. But then, she had been mentored by Asher Crowe and Odderly Flack, the both of whom were quite fluent in the magical arts. She had been fortunate in having them as teachers. For while much of what she had been taught was often beyond her comprehension, it was all there in her head, committed to memory right along with her grandfather's countless yarns and tall tales. Just as had been the spell used to summon the water elemental at the pool. Claudia knew now that she had the potential to unlock all of it. What she had always lacked was the courage to do so. It had always been herself holding her back.

In a way, Claudia had found herself during this journey. She had somehow grown up without realizing it. She looked up at her grandfather. Yssa leaned against him and the two now talked softly to each other. Claudia knew then and there that the time had finally come.

When all of this is done, I'll no longer allow myself to be a ward or a burden to my grandfather. The sun is setting on his lifetime, and if ever I can give anything to him in return for all the love, knowledge, and care he has shown me, I can give him his final days without the worry.

She smiled despite the sullen mood she had been in since drowning the man at the pool. She wanted her grandfather to have his final days alone with Yssa. And in that, she knew he would be happy. She knew that in Light they would be together forever. When that day came, Claudia Kobb would stand strong, a young and self-confident woman with her entire life ahead of her. She would make him proud.

The days blurred together as they navigated the seemingly endless subterranean tunnels. At times, the elevation rose steadily only to plummet over the next handful of miles. Before long, none of the companions could realistically guess how deep underground they were. They knew only that each passing moment took them deeper into the

World Below. It was only with the steadily rising heat that Odderly wagered to guess that they were a lot deeper than anyone had imagined.

This proved to be true when the sweltering tunnel became hazy and the odor of sulfur all but unbearable. Yssa, unable to bear the heat any longer, cast a protective barrier over the wagon. This at least offered some relief. In places the gray stone of the caverns gave way to smooth obsidian, and all too often the robuck had to be guided around cracks in the ground that emitted both incredible heat and a fiery glow. These fissures became more and more prevalent as the wagon descended a steep decline as the cavern spiraled downward. When the wagon passed through a short tunnel beyond, it emerged onto a narrow ledge passing through a truly massive cavern.

Claudia stood up in the back of the wagon and looked over the edge. Extending for as far as she could see was a river of molten lava that fed a bubbling, black-crusted lake. She had heard tales about Fire Falls academy, the subterranean school of wizardry that was built overlooking a magmafall, but this was beyond her wildest dreams. She leaned out to look down the rocky cliff of the ledge, but immediately pulled her head back into the protective sphere of Yssa's magic. Beyond the cooling effects of her spell, the heat was simply unbearable.

"What is this place?" she asked her grandfather.

Crowe stared out in equal awe. He responded with a slight shrug.

Driven onward by the heat, the robuck quickened their pace, moving rapidly along the ledge and ducking into a side tunnel only a short distance into the cavern. The tunnel gained elevation quickly and it was obvious that the thickly furred animals were relieved to be away from the heat of the magma chamber. Through a series of short passages, the robuck ran with renewed purpose. The wagon shook and rattled under the stress. Each bump in the tunnel jarred all aboard. Crowe's attempts to slow them by pulling back on the reigns was fruitless. Something was driving them onward. Finally, the tunnel spilled into a large cavern where a broad, but shallow pool of water spread out across the stone.

As soon as the wagon entered the chamber Claudia and the others felt the temperature drop unnaturally. Her next breath came out in a cool mist. She shivered and wrapped the cloak she had removed earlier back around her. The change in temperature took them all by surprise, though it was certainly welcome.

"This isn't right," Odderly said, clanging his iron rod onto Haverstagg's cuirass as a signal for Haverstagg to make himself ready.

The two of them stood up together. Yssa and Crowe were on edge, each looking around curiously with their glowing wands ready at their sides.

"What kind of place is this, Asher?" Yssa asked nervously.

"I don't know, but the robuck are not afraid of it. They knew that it was here."

Everyone looked at the massive hairy animals. They had brought the wagon to a stop on a flat stone that sloped gently down to the pool and were stomping their cloven feet restlessly. Drool ran down from their mouths. They were clearly distressed about being hitched up to the wagon with cold water right there in front of them, just beyond their reach. Odderly and Haverstagg climbed out of the back of the wagon and began to unhitch the robuck. No sooner were the animals freed than they moved out into the pool to drink.

Haverstagg bent down and put his hand into the water. "It's cold," he said to Crowe.

"I don't like this, Grandfather," Claudia said as she readied her wand.

They all turned around slowly, searching the darkness, but it was not what they saw that brought alarm. Rather, it was what they heard. At first it was a low, continuous humming sound, but it soon grew louder and was joined by other, more melodic tones.

"Bagpipes?" Crowe whispered.

The song carried hauntingly through the cavern, playing off the natural acoustics of the stone.

"Where is it coming from?" Claudia asked.

"Over there," Yssa said pointing into the darkness with her wand.

Indeed, the sound was coming from somewhere beyond the range of her magical light, but then a second set of bagpipes began to play from the opposite direction, its song accompanying the first unseen piper.

"I'm with Claudia," Odderly muttered, "this isn't good. We're too close to Rish Hollow. It's an alarm."

Those words sent a chill down Claudia's spine. "An alarm?" she repeated.

"Look," Haverstagg said, holding his lantern up before him and pointing with the flanged mace. "Someone's coming."

Lights began to appear in the distance, illuminating previously unseen tunnels in the darkness. Seconds later, other tunnels lit up and it became obvious that not just *someone* was coming, but a lot of *someones*.

A wave of heat broke the genteel cool of the cavern as Odderly called upon the magical properties of his iron rod. The familiar orange glow spread out around them.

"No, Odderly," Crowe said, raising a hand. "Everyone lower your wands."

They all glanced up incredulously at Crowe as dozens of people began to surround them. It was a crowd of ruffians to be sure; men dressed in fighting leathers like the men that Claudia and Odderly had killed at the pool. They were armed, carried shields, and were clearly prepared for a conflict. Many faces were painted white with varying degrees of vertical red stripes swashed across them. But there were wizards among these common ruffians. Mages dressed not in robes or magical vestments but wearing light armor with their hands wrapped around magical staves that glowed with the same magic that the companions had used to light their own way through the World Below.

Haverstagg sat his lantern down and slung Odderly's shield down off his shoulder. He moved defensively to place himself in front of Claudia.

From atop the wagon where he stood, Crowe locked eyes with the figure that seemed to oversee this ramshackle force of scoundrels. From the back of the crowd, which was probably closer to fifty men than twenty, and growing continuously as more shapes appeared from the darkness, a bald, bearded man wearing nothing more than a weapon harness and a pair of cut-off breaches pushed his way through the crowd. He paused at the front line and looked from Haverstagg and Odderly up to Crowe and Yssa. And then he looked over at the robuck drinking in the cold pool. It was obvious that he recognized the wagon and the animals.

Claudia peered around Haverstagg, but kept her cloak pulled tightly around her. Within the folds of the cloak, she wrapped her fingers tightly around her wand and began to assess the situation. If not for the wizards standing within the ranks of ruffians, and she counted seven magi in all, then this would be a fight easily won despite the fact that the companions were greatly outnumbered. The wizards though, presented a much greater threat than common fighting men.

Claudia decided that the only hope rested in being able to bring down the wizards as quickly as possible. Her mind began racing in search of a spell that she could cast quickly, the moment Haverstagg charged into the fray, yet would allow her to disable as many of the wizards as possible in a single casting. She settled her gaze on where three of the wizards stood close together.

The bald, bearded man raised a hand up in the air, palm out, and signaled for the pipers to fall quiet. The bagpipes began to fade away as the bald, bearded man looked back up to Crowe. He folded his arms over his barrel chest waited until the cavern was absolutely silent. And then he did the most unexpected thing of all. He smiled and spread his arms wide open.

"Welcome to Roak's Forge . . . Asher Crowe," the bald, bearded man said at last. "We've been expecting you."

Chapter 26

Claudia and Yssa were led down a narrow corridor with countless assurances that they could feel safe here. As they walked, Claudia regarded the surrounding tunnels and noted that they had been tooled with chisels to strip the natural shape from the stone. Every surface they passed had been similarly transformed with knotwork designs and crude images that resembled winged garanu.

"Great wyrms," said their escort, a rugged dark-skinned figure with as muscular a form as Claudia had ever seen on a woman, said when she noticed Claudia looking at the monstrous carvings. "Roak crafted them once in the forge, eons before he created men."

"The forge?" Claudia asked. "You mean the magma chamber we passed through on the way here?"

Rimsha nodded. "It is where *everything* was created, before time began, when the world was barren and lifeless. Our legends tell us that Roak once stood in the firewater with a great anvil at his side and a hammer in his hand. He forged the great wyrms after he seeded the world with trees and grass, and all the beauty of nature. To protect those things from the other gods."

Yssa looked at Claudia and rolled her eyes. Claudia frowned. She had come to know that Yssa was a faithless woman, but Claudia believed that there had to be some truth to the existence of Roak, the creator god. She found it particularly fascinating to hear mention of *other* gods. It was a concept that Claudia had never really thought of before. To believe in Roak was one thing, but to believe that Roak was just one of a host of gods, well that was entirely another. It diminished Roak's individual splendor, but at the same time it made him part of something greater.

Claudia found Rimsha, her guide, to be equally fascinating. Yssa was typical in her beliefs. There were few people in the Brysh Sovereignty that maintained any degree of faith, but Rimsha was obviously a deeply religious woman and she was taking great pride in the telling of her tale.

"Where are they now?" Claudia asked. "The great wyrms? Have you ever seen one before?"

Rimsha stopped and bore into Claudia's eyes with a gaze that caused Claudia's breath to catch in her lungs. "Yes," she said flatly. "When I was a child, my mother took my brother and I to the forge and we sat together in the terrible heat, waiting, just watching the firewater boil. And after many hours, I saw a great wyrm rise up from the forge and stretch its wings."

"The heat had made her delusional," Yssa muttered quietly enough for Claudia to hear. She then nodded as if it were fact.

"We're here," Rimsha said.

They had come to a place where the tunnel opened into a cavernous pocket in the surrounding stone.

Haverstagg and Odderly looked back at Crowe with unease evident in their expressions. They were then led away from the cold pool by a sullen, bare-chested young boy with coal-black eyes and ashen skin. Haverstagg still had his shield in hand, though he had replaced the flanged mace in his weapon harness. He walked quietly behind the silent boy, wondering just what manner of ill-breeding the boy was. A half-breed, Haverstagg decided when he had determined that the boy's feral features could only be the result of garuk blood somewhere in his lineage.

Roak's Forge, they soon discovered, was actually a small but thriving village that had been hidden from the eyes of the Lord Martyr for more than twenty cycles. As a resident of Barnwall, the Brysh village boasting more drinking establishments than any settlement aside from Subterranea itself, Haverstagg was surprised that he had never heard so much as a rumor about the existence of this dubious little hideaway. Great care had obviously been exercised in maintaining such a secret.

There had been countless times that unsavory characters had come through Barnwall, and Haverstagg's only true combat experience before meeting Asher Crowe was the occasional barroom brawl where he had taken to fisticuffs to defend Hannah's honor from those loathsome travelers. More often than not, however, those he suspected as having ties to Rish Hollow were loud and boisterous. But not once, had anyone spun a yarn about this place.

Haverstagg recalled hearing his village reeve proclaiming that efforts were being made on the Lord Martyr's behalf to put an end to the criminal activity at Rish Hollow. He now laughed at the thought. Not only had those of ill repute seized control of the abandoned mining village following the last winter season, they had burrowed deep underground to ensure that they could never be uprooted from the place.

As the sullen boy led Haverstagg and Odderly through the fire lit village milling with ruffians Haverstagg saw all manner of things that were outlawed in the World Above. Stolen goods were being openly traded at stalls in the main market square. A group of no less than twenty men were being trained in swordplay and fighting bloody duels among each other in an open yard while dozens more armed warriors stood around cheering them on. And archers not far away took aim at straw-filled targets that wore the black-crested iron helmets of the wardens. Now Haverstagg knew what had become of the wardens sent to enforce the law in the isolated village.

When they passed another open yard, two mages were fighting a magical duel under the tutelage of a grizzled old wizard covered with burn scars. A dead body lay there, unattended and ignored.

"Roak's hand," Odderly commented, "they're training a small army down here."

Haverstagg nodded while his mind strayed to the slaughter that would await the Lord Martyr's men when these reinforcements surfaced to repel any threat to Rish Hollow. He was respectfully frightened by what was happening here. While there were mercenary companies here and there in the Brylands, such activity was strictly monitored by the Lord Martyr to prevent any one group from gaining enough of a following to present a threat to the sovereignty. The military force concealed down here was clearly such a threat. It was an army that could have only one purpose.

At last, they came to a building constructed of obsidian blocks that formed a tower from the smooth stone around it. The tower rose to the high, uneven ceiling where stalactites hung down like gigantic teeth. Haverstagg could see some sort of mechanical contraption sharing the ceiling with these and he reasoned that the entire top of the cavern had been rigged to collapse should the need ever arise.

The sullen boy pushed open the black wrought iron doors of the obsidian tower and stepped aside. His first and only words to Haverstagg and Odderly were spoken with a very guttural accent as he said, "we're here."

After the crowd had departed, Asher Crowe walked alone with the bald, bearded man who had politely introduced himself as *just* Kimbrak. Crowe had been led through a different tunnel than the others and Kimbrak's initial conversation regarded how Crowe and his party had come across the wagon. Crowe told the tale truthfully and was not surprised when Kimbrak dismissively changed the subject after learning that the three smugglers had been killed.

"Acceptable casualties," Kimbrak announced, "and well worth the loss to have you here with us."

They entered a natural cavern where wooden catwalks and bridges spanned obsidian ledges over a pit of black-crusted magma. The magma bubbled from time to time, but the heat of the forge was absent here; controlled no doubt by the many mages that Kimbrak had at his disposal.

"There were rumors, of course, but we didn't know that you were truly still alive. When word reached the hollow that you had resurfaced at Ambermane of all places, it quickly traveled here. We have spies throughout the sovereignty."

"Who is *we*?" Crowe asked, trying to gain some insight into what was going on here, and who was interested in him. "If I may be so bold as to ask."

"We," Kimbrak said, "are those who subscribe to the thinking that an enemy of our enemy is our friend."

"You mean the Lord Martyr?"

"Among others," Kimbrak confirmed. "You have more friends than you know, Asher Crowe. There are those of us who know your history and believe in what you did. Especially now that demons walk amongst us again."

Crowe stopped cold and the fine hairs on the back of his withered arms stood on end as he said, "what do you mean?"

"It wasn't long ago that a strange man arrived at the hollow, but we have our ways, and we know that this man was not a man. He was Ambra."

"You are certain?" Crowe asked.

"Of course, I'm certain," Kimbrak said. "We had our agents following him. After they went missing, we began scouring the canyons for them. We only found one of them alive. You see, Asher, it is no coincidence that you have arrived here at precisely this moment in time."

"Why?" Crowe asked.

"Because in all of recorded history, you are the only man who has slain a demon and bound an Ambraic shade."

"I don't understand," Crowe admitted. "What is it that you are wanting me to do?"

"What we want, my friend, is for you to do it again."

Crowe considered his response. "You understand, Kimbrak, that this is all rather unexpected. How can I be sure that what you are saying is true? In all the cycles since, not once has the claim of Ambraic possession proven to be true."

"I can offer you proof," Kimbrak said.

"What proof?"

Kimbrak led Crowe through a crack in the obsidian at the far end of the cooling magma chamber. They climbed a set of stairs carved into the side of the neighboring cavern so cleverly that Crowe had not seen it from the landing on the opposite side.

"After we found Rael," Kimbrak explained, "the tracker who was following the demon, I put my people on the demon's trail. Not just to follow it, but to discover where it came from."

Kimbrak opened a door concealed from the view below by a curtain of stalactites. He led Crowe inside.

"As you know, Rish Hollow is awfully close to the Black Rift, which is garuk territory. My mages were able to follow the trail all the way back to a cavern below the rift. They found that hundreds of garuk there had been massacred." Kimbrak paused to look Crowe dead in the eye. "Massacred by the demon they had been keeping as a pet."

The chambers beyond the concealed door were like those that would be found in any well-appointed home. There was virtually no trace of the natural cavern. Magical light brightly illuminated Kimbrak's quarters, and furnishings fitting to a man of wealth and power gave his quarters a pleasant appeal. Thick curtains hung along every wall softened the place.

"Please, be seated," Kimbrak said to Crowe as he walked over to a shelf of books and retrieved a small, long wooden box.

Crowe sat on the plush sofa and instantly felt the aching of his bones that he had been ignoring for all the days on the road return in full. He became painfully aware of his exhaustion and his need for another injection. He readjusted himself and tried to make himself comfortable.

"I'm told that many mages are able to hold an object of significance and get impressions from it. You possess such skills, yes?"

Crowe nodded and Kimbrak handed him the box.

"I believe that you will find this most interesting. It is the proof that I promised you."

Crowe took the wooden box and sat it in his lap. He needed no magic to get an impression from what the box contained. Crowe had seen the simple dagger before. It was the same one that he had used to kill Headmaster Collinhodge and cut the demon's heart from its host body. The leather thong he had used to tie the heart to the dagger remained, but the heart itself was gone.

"Roak's hand," Crowe muttered in utter disbelief.

CHAPTER 27

Claudia looked back over her shoulder and frowned. Since their arrival at Roak's Forge, Yssa had not been herself and Claudia had come to realize that Yssa's crabby behavior began when she was again separated from Asher Crowe.

When Rimsha had returned a little while after Claudia and Yssa had been shown to their quarters in the female's barracks, she had offered to show Claudia and Yssa around the village. Claudia had been eager to explore. Yssa, however, had plainly refused.

"Is she always like that?" Rimsha asked Claudia as the two of them walked away.

"No, it's just that all of this came so unexpectedly. Yssa has been through a lot lately, and I feel bad leaving her alone in there," Claudia said.

"Well, there are worse places to be, believe me," Rimsha said. "Kimbrak takes good care of his *valued* guests. It's no loss though, we'll move much quicker without her."

"Aren't we going to look around the village?" Claudia asked, following Rimsha down a torch lit tunnel that led the opposite direction from the way they'd entered the cavern that housed the unmarried women of the forge.

"Later. There is something that I want to show you first." Rimsha smiled and said, "I think you'll like it."

The two of them walked in relative silence with Rimsha in the lead and Claudia following closely behind her. When they reached a point in the subterranean tunnels where the torches ended, Rimsha pried one of them loose from a sconce and used it to light the way.

Unlike the obsidian-laced tunnels that had led the companions to the hidden village, the tunnels that Rimsha selected became increasingly dominated by crystal growth. In places, the stalactites, and stalagmites, which had become so familiar that Claudia ceased noticing them were replaced with sparkling columns that glittered beautifully in the light of Rimsha's torch. But all this paled compared to the sight that befell Claudia when she climbed down a sinkhole and dropped onto the edge of a spherical chamber where every surface glimmered with purple-hued crystal.

The light from the torch was reflected a thousand times over and the perpetual refraction of light illuminated the entire inside of the giant geode cavern with near blinding light. The geode was easily thrice the size of the observatory chamber in Ambermane.

"Roak's hand!" Claudia exclaimed before taking a deep breath and pausing to stare wondrously at the cavern around her. "In all my days, I'd never imagined such a place as this existed!"

Oddly laughed and clapped his hands together vigorously as Haverstagg was sent sprawling to the ground once again. "Well done, you almost hit him that time!" he shouted.

Laying prone with his face against the stone, Haverstagg let out a growl and pushed himself back up to his feet shooting Odderly a nasty glare before he turned to regard his opponent. The young boy didn't yet have hair upon his chin.

The boy, dressed in fighting leathers, held two short wooden sticks, one in each hand. Carved to represent curved daggers, the mock weapons had left more bruises on Haverstagg than he cared to count, and the way the boy taunted him with them was causing Haverstagg's anger to build.

"How long has he been doing this?" Haverstagg asked the beefy instructor that had been introduced to him as Hamish.

"All his life," Hamish laughed.

"Come now Haverstagg," Odderly called out. "How are you going to best a bloodthirsty garuk if you can't best a twelve-year-old boy?"

The added taunt from Odderly sent Haverstagg into frenzy. He raised his wooden club and charged forward. The attacks were clumsy, yet powerful enough for the boy to believe in their authenticity. The boy ducked under Haverstagg's arc and came in quickly with the wooden daggers. Both clanked loudly against Haverstagg's shield as he spun around.

Haverstagg noticed the boy's eyes flick upward, expecting him to come around with another swipe of his practice club, but the club had been discarded as Haverstagg turned. Instead, Haverstagg grabbed the straps of the boy's weapon harness where they crossed his chest. With a mighty grunt, he lifted the boy cleanly off the ground with one muscular arm and threw him in Odderly's direction.

The boy hit the ground frightfully hard and lost both of his daggers as his body rolled head over heels twice before coming to a stop at Odderly's feet. Haverstagg did not follow through with a mock killing stroke, which would have been easy enough considering that the boy was sufficiently dazed to warrant the attention of one of the mages who had been watching the spar.

The grin left Odderly's face and he nodded appreciatively as Haverstagg walked over and took a seat beside him. Haverstagg accepted a waterskin offered by one of the other melee students who sat in the crowd and drank thirstily.

Quenched, but exhausted, Haverstagg turned his attention back to the sparring area where Hamish was giving instructions to two other students. Beyond them, the ring of onlookers began to part. Through the crowd walked Asher Crowe, who quickly made his way toward Haverstagg and Odderly with Yssa at his side. Everyone bowed their heads to Crowe reverently, but he paid them no attention.

"I've been looking everywhere for you," Crowe snapped at Odderly, nodding to Haverstagg as soon as the words had left his lips.

"You don't look well, Asher," Odderly said, a sudden expression of concern creasing his brow.

Crowe waved a wrinkled hand dismissively. "We've other problems now. Have you seen Claudia?"

Claudia traced a thin finger along the edge of a long spur of crystal growth, letting her finger linger at the point of one of the beautiful shards. Her eyes moved thoughtfully across the berth of the geode and finally looked back at Rimsha, who was smiling widely.

"They say that places such as this were created when Roak's tears fell to the ground after he was betrayed by the Ambra," Rimsha said solemnly. "These crystals still, to this day, hold a touch of his ancient magic."

Claudia bit her lip and looked down at the crystals once more. She closed her eyes and concentrated, holding her hands out over them as one would when warming her hands over a fire. She calmed her breathing and focused on the beating rhythm of her own heart. Within seconds she felt a surge of magic push into her bloodstream as she opened herself to the magical web. Never before had Claudia felt anything so magically pure, and when she opened her eyes she could see the glimmering strands of magic as thick as her entire body strung all throughout the geode; swaying, shimmering, and pulsating with power.

Sensing magic was one of the most basic of magical spells. So simple in fact that Claudia no longer needed a wand to do so. But always when she had sensed magic and seen the web, she saw but single strands spanning the land or sky. Only once before had she seen a junction of the magical strands. Her spells, cast near it, had been two-fold as potent as they drew power from both sources. Here, she could not even begin to fathom how many tendrils of the web came together and conjoined in the star-like ball of light her magic-sensing eyes saw hovering the exact center of the geode cavern.

Claudia turned to regard Rimsha who watched her joyfully, her hands clutched together in excitement.

"Wish that I could see what you are seeing, child," Rimsha said. "A few of my people have *tried* to describe the node, but it is beyond my sight."

Claudia shook her head in disbelief. Her grandfather had told her of nodes, but even the great Asher Crowe had never discovered one. His knowledge had been second hand, passed down through the generations. To be standing within one, well, it made Claudia feel changed somehow and as she walked through the cavern, passing her hands and her body through the strands of magic, she could distinctly feel the residual presence of it lingering within her.

"Rimsha . . . I don't know what to say," Claudia managed after some time. "My grandfather, and Odderly, and Yssa . . . they won't believe me when I tell them!"

Rimsha's smile faded. "But you can't tell them, child."

"What?" Claudia asked. "Why not?"

"This place, it is incredibly special to my people. No outsiders are supposed to know of it. Should Kimbrak or the Lord Martyr know that such a place of power existed here, none of us would be safe. They would each fight and kill each other to claim it as their own. Such things are rare in this world."

Claudia looked back to the node and then to Rimsha as she said, "then why did you bring me here?" Claudia asked.

"Because I need you to trust me, Claudia."

"I don't understand," Claudia admitted.

"My brother is seer."

"A seer?" Claudia asked, referring to reclusive prophets of Seahaven.

Rimsha nodded enthusiastically. "And he is not the only one who has received visions of you, Claudia. We knew that you were being drawn to Kimbrak. And while we do not yet know why your destiny seems tied to his, we know that we cannot allow him to use you the way he intends to use your grandfather."

Claudia began to feel a knot growing in her stomach. Something was not right here.

"Kimbrak interests in your grandfather are selfish and he seeks only to see himself become more powerful," Rimsha explained. "He will use your grandfather to suit his own ends, you can be certain of that, but he knows nothing of visions save for his own delusions of grandeur. He would lead you all to your death in the hope that your grandfather might deliver to him a weapon powerful enough to challenge the Lord Martyr's rule. Kimbrak will lead you all to your deaths."

Claudia's concentration faltered and the web faded away around her. She stared at Rimsha, uncertain of her intentions and alarmed by what had just been revealed. "What do you mean he would lead us to our deaths?" Claudia demanded.

"There are things that I can tell you, Claudia, but this is neither the time nor the place. It won't take them long to realize that we've left the forge. They'll be coming soon, and we must be away from here. We must get to my brother in Seahaven, he will know what to do."

Rimsha reached into her belt pack and withdrew a long shard of violet crystal, just like that which grew all around the geode cavern. She reached out and gently tapped it against a nearby spur. The chime, clear, high pitched and resonate, echoed through the cavern despite the faintness of the strike.

It was a signal, Claudia realized, when a group of dark-skinned men appeared at the far side of the geode cavern.

"You must come with us, Claudia. You must trust me if you are to have any hope of saving your grandfather's life, and your own."

"You're lying!" Claudia shouted as she drew her wand. "What is it you want with me?"

In response, the six men who had entered all drew swords and began to spread out around Claudia.

"No, you fools!" Rimsha shouted, throwing her arms up and gesturing for them to back away. "She'll kill all of you! Put your weapons down, this is not the way to earn her trust. She is our ally against Kimbrak!"

"We've no time for delay, Rimsha. Crowe and the others are already on their way," one of the men spat. "We have heard movement in the tunnels, and it sounds like Kimbrak has sent a full company of his men with them. We take her now, or we don't take her at all."

Rimsha turned to face Claudia. "Please, Claudia, you have to listen to me. If you don't come with us, your grandfather is going to die. You will see it coming and not be able to do anything to stop it. It has been foreseen!"

Claudia raised her wand and backed away from the men who were moving to surround her. "Rimsha, I don't know why you are doing this, but I'm not going anywhere with you."

"But you must!" Rimsha shouted. "Your father . . . Claudia, you cannot face . . ." Rimsha's words were cut short by the sound of feet hitting the stone from the adjoining tunnel above the sinkhole.

Claudia braved a glance over her shoulder, and when she looked back Rimsha and the men were gone. She caught sight of them just as they disappeared into a tunnel on the far side of the geode cavern. Where Rimsha had stood only moments before lay the long crystal shard. Claudia grabbed this and stuffed it into the pocket of her cloak taking advantage of the fleeting light of Rimsha's torch to climb back up through the sinkhole. She didn't know if there was truth in anything that Rimsha had said, but she wasn't about to risk being found in the node, or risk leading Kimbrak's soldiers here.

Crowe's energy had been fully restored by an injection of Odderly's magical serum. Between this and the panic that filled him as he rushed through the subterranean tunnels, he was moving far more quickly than he ever did. He had picked up Claudia's trail in the tunnels outside of Roak's Forge and had been following Claudia's footprints, which now glowed brightly to his eyes, trusting in them to guide his way more than the light which was cast from his wand. Behind him were Crowe's closest companions, Yssa, Odderly, and Haverstagg. Behind them, moving with surprising stealth, were twenty of Kimbrak's foot soldiers who had been ordered to accompany Asher Crowe while he was outside of the forge.

With his eyes down, Crowe was not actively watching the tunnel ahead. When Claudia's wand suddenly flared to life at the edge of his own light, he jolted backward and would have fallen if not for Haverstagg's quick reflexes and long reach. Claudia had just scrambled up out of the sinkhole, and as she joined her friends, she made a point to push through them, turning their attention away from the place she had just come from. Crowe noted this and glanced back over his shoulder. He could see where she had touched the stone, but his relief at finding his beloved granddaughter unharmed outweighed his curiosity regarding where she had come from and what she had been doing there.

"Roak's hand, child," Crowe chided before pulling Claudia into a deep and for Crowe, powerful, embrace. "We've been worried sick."

"I'm fine, Grandfather," Claudia said. "But we need to talk." It was then that Claudia must have noticed the company of armed swordsmen who had come to a standstill behind Odderly and Haverstagg. Claudia looked to Yssa, and then back to her grandfather.

Rimsha's ear was to the stone. While she was no mage like Claudia, and no seer like her brother, she was in her opinion, one of the most skilled subterranean rangers in the World Below. She had been born underground and had never seen the natural light of the sun before her thirtieth cycle. Her entire life had been spent below ground, save for her infrequent jaunts to Seahaven in recent cycles to consult with her brother. As such, Rimsha was at one with the tunnels and the rock that formed them.

Her trained ears could hear the conversation faintly, but distinctly, for Claudia and Crowe were separated from her by only a few feet of stone over their heads.

"What do they say?" Porran whispered. He was silenced as Rimsha shot him a glare and swiped a hand at him angrily.

Rimsha pushed up from the ground with a noise that was somewhere between an angry growl and a sigh. "She told them nothing," Rimsha said.

"Then we've no worries, if they're not leaving the Forge then we can try for her tonight," Porran said quietly.

"She *is* leaving the Forge," Rimsha snapped. "Crowe's taking her and twenty of Kimbrak's goons down into the Black Rift. We're too late."

Chapter 28

Sixteen miles of lightless tunnels hewn from dark gray stone that twisted, and folded, and doubled back on itself led the party deeper and deeper into the World Below. With every step Claudia felt the weight of the danger that seemed to be closing in on her.

She had made the decision to tell her grandfather about her encounter with Rimsha, and her band of subterranean rangers when Arkhanades, the captain of Kimbrak's company of footsoldiers, called for their first rest break. Yssa purified a pool of stagnant water with a wave of her wand so that everyone might drink. As the soldiers did so, Claudia pulled her grandfather away.

Crowe was quite interested in Claudia's description of the node and interrupted her twice during her telling before she quoted Rimsha's warning about Kimbrak.

"I had figured as much," Crowe said quietly as he eyed Kimbrak's soldiers near the pool. "Men like Kimbrak see value in life only for as long as that life serves their purpose. They balance loss versus gain, and so long as the pendulum continues to swing in their favor . . ." Crowe let his words hang in the air. "His goals serve ours to some degree, but I fear that what we will find when we find the garuk, is not what we have come to expect."

"What do you mean, Grandfather?" Claudia asked.

"I am afraid that we may be too late, Claudia." Crowe looked at his granddaughter with an expression mixed of concern and pity. "Kimbrak had something, that has led me to believe that my own past has come full circle to haunt me. When we find the garuk, no matter what we find there, you must promise me Claudia that you will keep your faith in me . . . in my judgment."

Crowe could see a great many emotions swirling within Claudia's steely gray eyes. "What aren't you telling me? I've had it with your secrets, Grandfather. I'm not the little girl that I was when you took me in six cycles, now almost seven cycles ago. You don't have to try to protect me any longer."

"I'm afraid," Crowe began, but Claudia immediately cut him off.

"Yes, you are afraid. You are afraid that I cannot handle losing you, or my father, or probably even Odderly for that matter." They both looked sidelong at Odderly as Claudia drew her next breath. "But I can handle whatever comes my way, Grandfather. You need to realize that I love you, and I'm grateful for everything you have done for me, and that I will always trust in your judgment. But you also need to realize that just as you ask me to keep my faith in you, I must ask you to start showing your faith in *me* and *my* judgment."

Crowe stared at his granddaughter for a long while. She looked so much like her mother that it bit deeply at Crowe's soul as he remembered sharing a moment not so unlike this with his only daughter forty cycles before. "I'm sorry if I have sheltered you too much, Claudia. What you say is true enough, but you must understand that I always have a good reason for doing things the way that I do."

Claudia smiled. "I know, Odderly always reminds me of that."

Crowe put a hand on Claudia's shoulder and gave it a slight squeeze. Raised voices sounded back at the pool and Crowe and Claudia turned simultaneously to see Kimbrak's men calling to those that had wandered away from the pool. The men had assembled in a double-file marching order, but there was discord among the ranks as Arkhanades moved through them.

"What is going on?" Claudia asked.

Crowe and Claudia returned to the group and found Yssa, Haverstagg, and Odderly talking quietly amongst themselves.

"What's going on?" Crowe asked Yssa.

Yssa looked back toward Kimbrak's men. "They seem to be missing a few people."

Porran climbed up the craggy side of the cavern with little effort despite the fact that he carried the full weight of the dead man slung over his shoulder. He had bound the foot soldier's wrists to his ankles on the opposite hip to ensure that he would not drop his kill.

Though he looked slight of build, Porran, like the rest of Rimsha's band of rangers, had a strength that betrayed his meek stature. Beneath his thin lizardskin armor that helped him to blend into the surrounding rock, his corded muscles bulged as he dug his gloved fingers and tips of his booted feet into cracks and crevices. He pulled himself effortlessly up onto the ledge.

As he dropped his kill the others untied the dead man's bondage and slung him over onto the pile with the other three corpses.

Rimsha nodded approvingly and smiled. Her white teeth stood out against the dark earthy tone of her skin. This was always the part of her life that Rimsha enjoyed the most. It was not the killing, but the hunt that drove her. "Good work, Porran," she said in near whisper. "Were you seen?"

Porran shook his head and scowled, as if the question posed was something of an insult. "Of course not. But they are breaking and preparing to move. They know that they are not alone down here, and their guard will now be raised."

Rimsha nodded. She had known that the missing men would kindle a fear in Kimbrak's men, and the wizards as well. It was a needed fear, she had reasoned. The loss of four men who were all likely thieves or murderers, or both, was of little importance. Rimsha would see Kimbrak and all his men dead if it were up to her. The fact that she had to spend six months living with them and pretending to be one of them to get close to the girl had sickened her, but it was something of such importance that she had been left little choice.

Now they would be wary as they drew nearer to the Black Rift. Claudia's decision to accompany her grandfather into garuk territory was a foolish one, but Rimsha tried to understand that the girl simply couldn't fathom the danger waiting for her in the depths of the World Below, or the importance she would play in future events.

"We leave them behind," Arkhanades shouted to his men. "There will be no more rest until we return to the Forge. I want two of you with each of the wizards," Arkhanades paused to gesture toward Haverstagg, "and with that one. The rest of you with me . . . we walk point together."

Claudia did not like being surrounded by the painted ruffians, more than a few of which eyed her lecherously as they walked. Her grandfather and Yssa walked just in front of her; Haverstagg at her side, with Odderly trailing a couple of paces behind them.

"I don't believe that they aren't even going to go look for them," Claudia said quietly to Haverstagg.

Her grandfather must have heard her, for he turned around and nodded at her knowingly. She knew that he was telling her that this only proved Kimbrak's views of his men's worth, and she felt a chill on her spine. How safe was she supposed to feel when the loyalty of the men sent to protect them all was threadbare?

The remaining miles were spent walking in silence, lit only by the light of a single torch held in the front of the ranks and Odderly's smoldering rod behind them. On several occasions Claudia looked over her shoulder with the distinct impression that she was being followed. She had seen Rimsha's passion firsthand, both in the telling of the great wyrms and at the node when Rimsha had fervently pleaded with Claudia to go with her.

Rimsha was back there, Claudia knew. Kimbrak's soldiers hadn't just wandered away. Rimsha had killed them. It was not knowing Rimsha's true intentions that made Claudia so frightened. Almost more so than the fact that she would soon be walking into the hive of garuk territories at the bottom of the Black Rift.

Every so often, Claudia's group would catch up to where Arkhanades and his group waited so that the foot soldiers acting as the guards to the companions could be appraised of the path ahead and any dangers that might lie therein. When the light of the latter group's torches spilled around a bend, Claudia had expected another momentary exchange between Kimbrak's men. But this time, Arkhanades wore a grim expression.

"There are garuk ahead," Arkhanades announced loudly enough for them all to hear.

Claudia involuntarily grabbed hold of Haverstagg's wrist at the mention of finally having reached the garuk territories. Haverstagg looked down and smiled reassuringly. When Claudia removed her hand, blushing slightly and looking away, Haverstagg loosened his shield from his pack and prepared himself for whatever lay ahead. His knuckles whitened around the haft of his enchanted mace.

"They are already dead," Arkhanades continued. "A month at least, maybe two. And none of the bodies have been eaten by carrion beasts, which tells us to be ever vigilant. Scavengers are not quick to move in to feed when the predator still lingers."

Crowe turned around and gestured to his companions to huddle together. "There will be more dead garuk. Keep your wands ready and your wits about you. I fear that it is not predators that have been here before us, but a greater evil still."

"Are these the garuk that have my father?" Claudia asked bluntly.

"I don't know, Claudia," Crowe said honestly. "Let us hope not."

Both groups stayed together as they moved among the corpses of the garuk massacre. Bodies, and pieces of bodies, were everywhere. Claudia had seen the remains of the Korah Valley massacre, but what her grandfather and Otep had done could not be compared to the slaughter around her. The two old wizards had killed garuk, but not like this. Whatever had killed these garuk had been equally indiscriminant, but it had also ripped the garuk limb from limb in the killing of man, woman, and child alike.

Claudia covered her nose and mouth with her free hand and bit her lip to fight against the urge to vomit. Even Haverstagg who had the constitution of a wild boar, seemed pale. Oddly covered his nose and mouth with his red handkerchief to insulate himself from the stench and grumbled continuously about the smell.

"What in Roak's name could have done this?" Oddly finally broke the silence to ask. Nobody answered.

As they pushed further and further into the garuk tunnels, the surroundings changed from magma formed passageways painted in dried blood and dismembered garuk bodies to larger and larger natural caverns painted with dried blood and dismembered garuk bodies. The group continued in silence, working their way further and further into the garuk stable. Crude buildings stacked of roughly carved stone often filled the caverns, and everywhere the carnage was the same.

Claudia, like all the others, was aghast. Her mind searched for answers to what could have caused so much death and destruction. But it was when the group entered the slave pens that she finally broke out of her trance. There, directly in front of her, was her father's cage. There could be no mistake. Metal bars with a single gate had been stretched across the mouth of a natural niche within the stone opposite a tiered landing where a single table displayed an unfinished game of stones.

The cage itself was less than ten feet across and just a little deeper. A makeshift bed occupied the space behind two thick columns of stone bridged by a curtain of hanging stalactites and a formation of stone on the floor that resembled melted candles. It afforded little privacy, but it was the only place within the cage that offered any at all. What confirmed that the cage belonged to Horace Kobb was Claudia herself. Scratched into the wall with shards of bone were dozens of crude drawings of a young human girl . . . unmistakably images of Claudia.

Claudia's lip trembled and her glowing wand nearly slipped from her fingers as her eyes began to water. She wiped away the wetness before tears could form and choked up her emotions. "This is where they kept him," Claudia stated calmly. "Where is he?"

Crowe's withered fingers lightly touched Claudia's shoulder and she turned to face him. Anger was clearly visible behind the grief, yet she kept herself composed. Not knowing what to say, Crowe just stared at her. Behind him, tears gently ran down Yssa's cheeks.

Claudia pulled away and walked down the slope of the cavern toward a garuk-made tunnel.

Haverstagg began to move after her, but Odderly grabbed his arm to stay him.

"Let her have a moment," Odderly said gruffly.

"She shouldn't wander alone," Haverstagg said in protest. "Whatever did this may still be here."

"No," Crowe countered. "The demon is gone."

Haverstagg, holding his lamp in his shield hand, walked off after Claudia anyway. He was followed by the others who saw no point in remaining behind.

The tunnel led into the slave chute, which ultimately came to a locked gate that popped open and swung wide silently as Claudia swished her wand through the air before it. When Crowe, Yssa, Odderly, Haverstagg, and the others caught up to her Claudia was standing in the middle of the lava-forged arena before the massive rotting corpse of a sixty-foot garanu. The bodies of dozens of garuk also lay scattered in the arena. More lay around its edges. It was obvious that whatever had killed the garanu, had killed everything.

"I'm so sorry, Claudia," Haverstagg was the first to say.

"He may still be alive!" Claudia snapped from the brink of tears. When her grandfather approached her, she rushed forward to meet him. "You *knew* what had happened here!" She accused.

Crowe nodded. "I had been told as much, but we had to come to be sure."

"What did this, Grandfather?" Claudia demanded to know. "What manner of beast *could* do this?"

Crowe untied the leather straps of his side bag and reached inside to remove something wrapped in dirty white cloth. He handed it to Claudia and then walked away as she unwrapped the dagger.

Chapter 29

Pulgra lay dying at Kobb's feet, the hilt of the dagger pushed in under his double chins and the point protruding through the top of his bald head as the fat stable master's body quivered on the floor. The satisfaction for Enshalaan was two-fold. The demon felt vengeance on the part of Kobb who held a strange fondness for Atta, his murdered keeper. But more than that the demon simply lavished killing a garuk who had so pathetically groveled and begged for his life.

Chaos had erupted throughout the arena and the surrounding stands as Pulgra's garuk rushed in and tried to cut the aged human slave down, but they could not understand that for all practical purposes, Horace Kobb was already dead. While a touch of Kobb's consciousness struggled to survive, the demon had already tainted and claimed the human's soul. What Pulgra's garuk faced was an Ambraic demon fully in control of a host body for the first time since Asher Crowe had slain the last.

All the cycles of biding his time had finally proven fruitful. The binding magic had faded just enough. The moment of attack had been perfect. Kobb's ego had been easily suppressed. The shade that had once been bound into the mortal heart of its previous host had now passed into another mortal husk, and as long as the host lived, Enshalaan would remain a creature of flesh. The demon's magic could sustain the life of this mortal shell indefinitely. Just as

Enshalaan had healed Kobb's wounds a thousand times, the demon would now do so for its own benefit.

Garuk spears, little more than shafts of rare wood from the World Above fitted with obsidian points, pushed into Kobb's body and Enshalaan lulled his head backward to enjoy the sensation of pain. All such sensations; pain, heat, cold, even the experience of taking in a breath of air, had been kept from Enshalaan for so long that he relished the mere fact that he was able to experience such a thing before he ripped the spears out of his new body and used them against their wielders.

Not a single one of Pulgra's garuk was spared as Enshalaan worked his way through Atta's stable. When weapons were made available, they were used to cut down the garuk who were not quick enough to get out of arm's reach. And those that ran faced Enshalaan's ancient magic as the demon used spells of fire and ash against them. It went on for hours until not a single garuk remained to stand against him.

The dagger clattered to the ground as it slipped from Claudia's fingers. She had not realized that she was crying until she was suddenly forced out of the images that flooded her senses and back into the real world around her. Kimbrak's men stood staring, as did her own friends. Crowe, who had sensed the history of the dagger in even greater depth than Claudia, stood some distance away with his back turned and shoulders sagging.

Claudia looked back down to the dagger before she wiped away the tears on her cheeks. She looked up first to Odderly, the most familiar face in the crowd gathered around her, but no sooner had her eyes met his did he look away and settle his gaze on his boots. Yssa wore a look of concern, she was visibly shaken.

"My father . . ." Claudia began to say, but then lost her own words, unable to describe the horror that she had seen.

"We heard you," Haverstagg offered when Yssa herself could not find her tongue. "You were screaming and telling us what you were seeing."

"Screaming?" Claudia asked.

"Aye, lass," Odderly said. "It was your father that did this. Or what is inside of him rather. We're too late."

Claudia wiped away her tears. And then a loud, slow clanking echoed over the arena. All eyes turned to see the massive black iron gate at the far side of the arena begin to lift. It was a surreal moment. With all the carnage they had seen in the garuk complex, nobody had expected anything to come walking out of the slave chute to challenge them directly. But that is exactly what happened.

Rimsha watched from her high vantage point on the narrow ledges of the cavern's outer wall as Kimbrak's men organized and formed a defensive line between Claudia and her friends, and the lone figure that approached them. All along the edge, Rimsha's rangers held their hands back to their ears ready to release nocked arrows to protect their quarry, all except for Porran who had been ordered down the ledge.

"Hold your aim," Rimsha commanded, "and save your arrows to protect the girl. Her friends, and Kimbrak's cronies are fodder."

Without another word Rimsha turned and ran. The light from the torches and wands was not enough to reveal her presence, and so she moved with all haste. She had hoped that this confrontation would take place elsewhere in the garuk stable where she would be able to separate Claudia from her allies and make her escape while the *thing* did what Rimsha's brother had warned her it would do to everyone who journeyed to this place between the dark phase of the third moon of Seraph and the light phase of the sixth.

Rimsha's only comfort as she descended the switchbacks of the cavern ledges was that in knowing the future, it was sometimes possible to change it.

Shouts of "Demon!" and "Revenant!" split the line of Kimbrak's men. Some turned to flee. Some joined Arkhanades and drew weapons. Trained fighting men, they spread out into a wide single-line formation and began to circle the demon.

Claudia had but a moment to contemplate the fate that had befallen her father, and now it seemed she would have to face him. She could barely get her mind around the fact that when she saw his face looking back at her after all these cycles, that it wouldn't be *his* soul looking out her.

Would my own father strike me down?
Could I strike him down?

But it was not her father that approached. The figure, wrapped in black academic robes trimmed in orange, was a gaunt and deathly thing; near skeletal and with a complexion blued by death. Its face a bubbled mess of melted tissue.

"Loris?" Yssa whispered.

Claudia did not recognize the name, but Odderly obviously did as he pushed forward and immediately let out a string of muttered curses.

"Mankoff?" Odderly muttered.

Azarajii stopped only five short paces ahead of the line of foot soldiers and locked his glowing green eyes upon Claudia. There was hesitation and the demon took a single step back from the girl. Asher Crowe stepped between Yssa and his granddaughter then, coming fully into the demon's line of vision and at that moment what was left of the melted wax-like surface of Loris Mankoff's face twisted up into a lipless smile.

Crowe drew his wand and whispered over his shoulder, "Haverstagg, get Claudia to the surface. Do not go back to the forge."

Claudia stared for a moment at the abomination before her and recalled Rimsha's warning. It was a warning not just based upon Rimsha's fear or her own malicious intent, but upon the visions of a seer. Her brother must have seen everyone die here. He must have seen this very moment. Claudia was afraid.

"We must get to the surface, to Seahaven. Right now!" Claudia shouted. "This is what Rimsha was trying to warn me about. We cannot kill this thing. Not here, not now!"

"Go with Haverstagg," Odderly and Crowe said together.

"No! If you choose to fight, I'm fighting with you."

It was at that moment that Azarajii thrust his hands out to the side. Bony fingers wrapped tightly around Master Darrowden's black wand and the tip began to glow with a bright white light.

The demon was immediately set upon by Kimbrak's men with Arkhanades leading the charge. Having been trained around, and in many cases, by wizards, they all knew that their only chance for victory against one lay in being able to cut down it down before it was able to unleash a volley of magic against them.

Three of the thirteen who charged forward never made it to Azarajii. The demon casually pointed his wand in their direction, uttered a word of power, and then laughed as their bodies blew away like gray ash caught in a powerful wind. Men with no connection to the web had no innate resistance to magic. Their clothing, armor, and weapons scattered to the ground as the others sliced and hacked at Azarajii.

Each strike hit with the sound of metal connecting to stone. Flashes of white light and sparks flew from each impact, but not one of the blows damaged the demon in any way save for sheer inertia staggering him a step or two.

Arkhanades' eyes went wide as he came fully into the demon's glare. Two quick strikes knocked Azarajii's head from side to side before the demon caught the blade within the claws of a single hand and overpowered the veteran's strength.

Azarajii twisted the blade back up and into Arkhanades' own stomach ever so slowly, ignoring the continued assault of Kimbrak's men. The blade caught against the metal, but the demon's sheer strength overwhelmed the iron and pushed the blade through as if it was little more than stiff leather.

Crowe, Odderly, and Yssa, ever-so-confident in their abilities, had begun to move forward to meet the demon when Claudia grabbed Yssa and pulled her backward to the ground.

"We *cannot* win this battle, Yssa!" Claudia pleaded. "Listen to me! Rimsha's brother is a seer, he has seen us all die here!"

The sincerity in Claudia's eyes must have rung true to Yssa, for when she stood back up, she shouted at Crowe, "Asher, we must trust in Claudia! Asher!"

The tactic worked. Haverstagg and Claudia were already running back toward the slave pens. When Crowe saw that Yssa was half jogging behind them, he grabbed Odderly's arm and pulled him away from his advance.

"Another time," Crowe said, admitting, "we are not prepared for this foe and a seer's visions are against us."

Odderly snarled. He had never liked Warder Mankoff when he was alive. Having survived Odderly's magical acid attack in the observatory, Loris Mankoff was now host to an Ambraic demon. However irrationally, Odderly blamed himself for this. Only four of Kimbrak's men remained fighting against Azarajii and their continued attempts seemed futile. Odderly looked back to Crowe, who was now following Yssa and the others back toward the pens.

"Roak's hand!" Odderly shouted. As stubborn as he might be, he was not about to face the demon alone.

Within moments, Kimbrak's men were no more. Those who had tried to flee were brought down by contrails of golden glittering light that streaked across the arena. And then Azarajii turned his wand toward Claudia and her companions who had not yet reached the protection of the slave chute as he systematically eliminated those who stood between himself and his quarry.

Streaks of softly glowing green light flew from the cavern's edge. Whereas Azarajii had been unharmed by the mundane weapons of Kimbrak's men, the enchanted arrows of Rimsha's rangers' bit deeply into the demon's body. Azarajii howled! An instant later, a second volley bit into the demon before he was able to fully circle his wand around him and weave a spell that would protect him from the arrows.

When the third volley came from the unseen archers, Azarajii was able to pinpoint their location high along the cavern wall. A bony, clawed hand was outstretched in their direction as Azarajii spoke ancient words of power. When he closed his fist and shouted the final word in the low, ominous language of the Ambra, the stone of the cavern wall folded in on itself as if it was made of clay; the archers were crushed within it.

Claudia and Haverstagg had stopped in the cavern that housed her father's cage both to catch their breath and to wait for the others. Yssa was not far behind them, nor was Crowe, but Odderly came running into the cavern from the adjoining tunnel only after the rest of them had begun to worry that he had decided to face the demon after all.

"How could they have spiritbound Mankoff?" Odderly asked between gasps for air as he tried to catch his breath from the frantic run. "That *thing*, Asher, it couldn't have come to be through possession, it was created deliberately."

"Indeed. It wears the academic robes of Fire Falls academy. The Lord Martyr must be desperate to see us dead to have risked the creation of such a thing. One does not join an Ambra shade to a living soul lightly."

"That *thing* is alive?" Haverstagg asked.

"Not as we would define life," Crowe answered. "Come, let us get into the tunnels beyond the rift. It will be more difficult to find us there."

"Too late," Yssa whispered.

Everyone turned to follow her gaze as Azarajii strode into the cavern. He had been wounded by the ensorcelled arrows, but the injuries were superficial at best. While magical weapons could hurt an Ambraic demon and perhaps destroy the host body, the Ambra's shade could never truly be destroyed. In the cases of natural possession, the spirit could theoretically be exorcised and then imprisoned, but Enshalaan's escape from such entrapment proved only that even such a binding did not last forever. In the case of this abomination, which was the willful creation of man, who then could say if such a thing could be exorcised at all. Its creation was a mystery to the companions, and if those who had created it had prepared for the contingency of its destruction and prepared a phylactery for the shade's spirit to return to in the event of the host's destruction, it could very well be impervious to spiritbinding.

"Run!" Rimsha shouted as she and Porran revealed themselves from within the shadows of the stone formations near the tunnel.

Porran's first strike took the demon's wand, and the hand that clutched it, cleaving through dried tissue and bone alike before the blade of his sword carried through to the ground hard enough to divot the stone below. Rimsha, wielding an identical ensorcelled blade, also caught the demon unawares. Her blade bit deeply into the niche of the demon's neck. There was a brief instant of resistance before the falcata cleaved through the collarbone. Bright white light flashed from the wound. It began to close again even before the blade could be pulled free.

Wasting no time, the companions save for Claudia turned to flee. In her hesitation Claudia saw Porran's head torn from his shoulders by a swipe of Azarajii's clawed hand. Lifeless, the ranger's body toppled to the ground like a rag doll. Only a moment later, Rimsha screamed as the demon reclaimed its black wand and used it like a stiletto to pin her to the ground through the stomach. Her blade clattered down beside her.

Rimsha looked back to Claudia, her eyes pleading with her to run as the demon cruelly twisted the wand. Rimsha struggled to get her hand into her pack. She removed a shard of violet crystal and fought to control her pain long enough to get a firm grip on it. Rimsha mouthed the word *run* to Claudia, and as her final act of defiance she smashed the geode crystal into the ground.

Chapter 30

It was an explosion rent not of fire and smoke, for such things are the way of men, but wrought from the very magic of creation. A shimmering bubble of light blinded Azarajii as it expanded from the point of the crystal's impact and pushed outward enveloping everything it touched. Time stopped within the bubble, if for only a moment, as the power of the creator god's ancient magic gathered strength.

And then everything began to change.

Rimsha and Porran's bodies, and Azarajii with them, fell down a growing abyss as the stone beneath their feet grumbled with the roar of an avalanche and was pulled away into darkness. The stone walls of the World Below blurred by too quickly for Azarajii to focus, but then from the walls sprouted grass, and trees, and thorny vines as thick as giants; odd shapes that grew wildly and far beyond the constraints of nature. Unable to find a center of gravity the burgeoning forest became a tangled thicket of wooded cliff-side lit suddenly by a blinding flash of light from below.

Azarajii shielded his eyes against the god-light and as it faded, he watched as the bodies of the dark-skinned rangers burst into fleshy shapes that bulged and twisted as they fell. They looked as if some divine hand was actively molding the clay of life with an uncertainty as to what it was trying to create. One of bodies, Azarajii could no longer tell which, suddenly burst into a downpour of misshapen mounds of blood and tissue that took a somewhat humanoid form before a strong gust of wind took them away from the demon.

Snow began to form in the air, replaced moments later as he plummeted by extreme heat and dust. Twisting tornados swirled into being and spiraled upward from a lightning filled vortex, which stretched across the shifting landscape below. The fear, not of death, but oblivion, washed over Azarajii. For the first time in his ageless existence the demon was afraid. Azarajii tried to use his wand, frantically searching both his own mind and Loris Mankoff's for magic that would propel him away from certain destruction.

A blast of energy shot forth from the wand toward the vortex, but long before the beam reached the swirling mass Azarajii was caught by a giant wave of water that came from the darkness that precedes creation. There was an impact that jarred the demon to the core, and then he was disoriented and underwater. Stunned, he drifted with the current of the murky depths.

Claudia screamed. She had hardly put any distance between herself and Rimsha when the geode crystal was shattered. The roar that chased her up the tunnel was deafening and heralded the coming of a blinding wall of force that passed through her and continued up the tunnel ahead. Claudia was knocked forward by the blast. The light evoked a feeling as it passed through her that was not unlike the strange sensation she felt when she walked through the strands of the magical web inside the node, only a thousand times more potent.

In that instant, time itself seemed to stop, and then jerk forward suddenly. Claudia had almost made it back to her feet when she was thrown forward again by a second wave of pressure. She hit the ground hard enough to daze her. It seemed like hours passed, as she lay there, unable to move and barely aware of the landscape as it twisted madly all around her. Dark shapes rose impossibly high, the very land on which she lay changing shape beneath her.

She heard Crowe and Yssa calling for her from the darkness, but it was impossible to discern from which direction their voices came. Her hand searched the cracks and crevices in the stone and Claudia breathed a sigh of relief when she felt the familiar shape of her wand.

"*Intium orohthem*," Claudia uttered. The tip of her wand flared to life and cast light across a barren expanse of sharp and jagged stone.

It was an alien landscape. Claudia sensed that she was still underground, yet the air smelled of flowering pine and rain fell upward into the waiting darkness overhead as it seeped out of the solid ground. The tunnel was gone, replaced by plateaus topped with clusters of unfamiliar red-leafed trees and immense raging waterfalls that gathered into vast lakes spotted with frothing whirlpools. Vertigo nauseated her as her mind took in the opposing forces of gravity.

Claudia looked back the way she was certain she had come from, but the landscape there had also changed. A tangled mass of thorny trees clung to the sides of a ravine that rivaled the stories she had heard of the Black Rift itself. For a moment Claudia wondered if she had somehow been moved by the magical surge to the rift, but this she dismissed almost instantly. Rimsha had told her that the crystals of the node were said to hold a touch of the creator god's magic, and Claudia had seen for herself that it was one of these crystals that Rimsha destroyed to cover Claudia's own escape.

The node, Claudia thought. She could tell that everything for miles around had been changed by the creator's stone, was the node far away enough to have survived? Claudia's thoughts turned to Rimsha, the ranger who had urged her not to come to this place. The woman who had saved her life. Claudia had thought Rimsha wanted her for some sinister purpose, but the ranger woman had sacrificed herself to *protect* Claudia. Her death was now another that weighed heavily on Claudia's consciousness. It was another dead *friend* for whom she was responsible.

"Claudia!" Crowe's voice called out from the darkness.

"Can you hear me? Claudia?" shouted Odderly.

Claudia turned an ear toward the voices, trying to pinpoint them, but this proved no easy task for each echoed strangely in the twisted, magically forged cavern.

"I'm over here!" she shouted.

This went on for several minutes until she at last saw the orange glow of Odderly's rod push back the darkness ahead of her. She ran toward the tube-like pillars that rose to the unseen subterranean sky and threw herself upon Odderly, giving him a vehement hug.

"I found her!" Odderly shouted.

"We are lucky to be alive at all," Crowe said as the companions, united once more, walked through chest high grasses that finally gave way to where the bubble had popped. Crowe studied the stone wall before him under the bright light of his wand. The cavern was sheered smoothly with a concave curve that marked the edge of the creator's stone's sphere of influence. "Such an event . . . I cannot even imagine what the God Times must have been like."

"Aye", Haverstagg said as he crouched against the wall, "but seeing this . . . it is encouraging."

"What do you mean?" Odderly asked. "We don't know that Mankoff, or whatever he is now, was destroyed back there. We survived. He might have too."

Haverstagg shook his head and said, "that's not what I mean."

"You're thinking about Hannah?" Claudia asked, and for the first time since she had met the hops farmer, she saw the glimmer of hope in his eyes.

"If what happened here *was* divine, and what else could it have been but god magic, then it proves that Light and Shadow are not just metaphor. They must be real, and that means that my Hannah is not gone, but waiting for me in the Light."

Yssa stared at Haverstagg and soon drew Claudia's eye. "Yssa?" Claudia asked, but Yssa turned away.

"I remember this place," Odderly said hours later when the

companions strode into a cavern not far from where they had united with Arkhanades and the group that walked point earlier that day.

Crowe nodded, and deliberately took a tunnel that they had not been down in their journey from Roak's Forge.

"Asher?" Yssa questioned.

"We're not going back to Kimbrak," Crowe said. He turned his back to the others and began a vigorous march despite his growing fatigue.

"What's going on?" Odderly asked Yssa as if thinking she might have some insight into Crowe's sudden urgency.

"Kimbrak is not to be trusted," Claudia said in answer. "We must make for Seahaven instead. Rimsha spoke of this happening, and of my father. I believe that her brother has had visions of him." She then turned to follow her grandfather.

"Seahaven?" Haverstagg and Odderly said in unison.

———•———

The hours dragged ever onward, and the group only found rest when Crowe could no longer hide his distress. He was given an injection from Yssa's store, for Odderly's supply of the glowing serum was quickly depleting. Crowe's tolerance was growing, and a single booster was no longer enough to get him through the day.

As Crowe slept, the others sat together in a cavern that echoed with the sounds of dripping water. The humidity was intense. They had drawn water from the nearby pool and found both mushrooms and fish to make soup. It was over this meal that Claudia confided in the others about what had happened when she was alone with Rimsha, and about Rimsha's warning. Claudia did, however, leave out mention of the geode and the fact that she had a similar shard of crystal in her cloak pocket.

"What in Roak's name is so special about you?" Odderly asked. He quickly corrected, "not that you're not special, but . . . that . . . you know what I mean."

Claudia nodded and then shrugged. "I don't know," she answered honestly.

"She has power in her," Haverstagg said. "It could be not that the rangers wanted her for their own ends, so much as they wanted to keep her away from Kimbrak and his men."

Everyone turned to look at the usually quiet farmer.

"You said it yourself, Odderly. He's readying an army down there. And Yssa, you said that he wanted Crowe to bind a demon. But nobody has asked why?"

"It is a demon," Odderly said, "it must be bound. Such things are not meant to walk these lands in flesh. They are too powerful . . . too dangerous."

"Exactly," Haverstagg said. "And what a weapon such a thing would make if it could be controlled. We all heard Claudia's recount of what her father did when he was taken by spirit, and we all saw the carnage that was left behind. That was one man, one spirit."

"And now we know that there are two," Yssa added.

Haverstagg nodded. "If not more."

"Asher would never allow Kimbrak to do such," Odderly said sharply in defense of his old friend. But even as he spoke the words he began to see where Haverstagg was going with all of this. "He meant to have Asher bind the demons, and then use Claudia to control them?"

"Could you bind a demon, Odderly?" Haverstagg asked. "Or you, Yssa?"

Both shook their heads.

"I'm no a wizard, but us lay-folk know that power runs in the bloodlines, all the way back to the days of the clans long before there was a Lord Martyr. The whole sovereignty knows the yarn of Asher Crowe binding a demon. And you can bet that Kimbrak believes that the same strength of magic still runs in Claudia's veins. Kimbrak wouldn't be so naive as to think he could control the legendary Asher Crowe, but you can bet that if Crowe had bound a demon for him, that we would all be dead and Claudia would be forced to serve Kimbrak's own goals."

It was difficult for any of them to believe what Haverstagg was saying could be true. Yet it was the only fitting explanation.

Odderly had become red-faced and shook his head. "I won't let it happen," he said. He then stood up and swiped his smoldering rod through the air before beginning to pace back and forth, muttering to himself.

"To what end?" Claudia asked. "If that is what Kimbrak was planning all along . . . what end is he seeking that he would do such a thing? He is already a powerful man. He has everything."

Haverstagg looked to Yssa and then to Odderly to see if they were drawing the same conclusion as he. He then looked back to Claudia. "Powerful men are always in want of one thing, more power. He has an army down here, right under the nose of the Lord Martyr. Fighting men, magus, and he seeks to bring demons under his command? He has high ambitions, that one. He wants control of the sovereignty itself."

"Wage war on the Lord Martyr? Attack Subterranea? It would be folly!" Claudia exclaimed.

"It could be done," Odderly muttered. "Any one of us could blast our way to the Lord Martyr's doorstep with little to fear but his wizards. But an army could overcome wizards, and with as many wizards as Kimbrak has rallied, he would stand a fair chance at the High Warders with or without an Ambraic demon at his disposal. And I'd reckon that the man is crazy enough to try it at that."

"Then what are we to do?" Yssa asked. "It is not as if <u>we</u> of all people can stroll into Subterranea to warn the Lord Martyr of a coup."

"Nor do we have the time," Claudia said drawing all their attention. Her eyes were transfixed on her grandfather as she spoke. "I'll not believe that my father is lost to the thing he carries inside of him. I'm not going to give up on him. And I'm not going to let Kimbrak be the next to enslave him." Claudia looked up, and then around from face to face, finally settling on Yssa as she said, "my grandfather's part in all of this has come to an end Yssa. When we reach Seahaven, I need to speak to Rimsha's brother, and then I intend to set out again to find my father, and Grandfather cannot come with me."

There was a heavy, awkward silence as everyone was taken aback by Claudia's statement.

"Of course, we'll be going with you," Odderly said.

"No. I cannot ask it of you, Odderly." Tears began to well up in Claudia's steely eyes, but she refused to let them fall. "Grandfather is waning, you said so yourself. We can all see it. He has given so much of himself to me, and I cannot . . . I will not, allow him to give any more of himself on my behalf." Claudia turned to Yssa. "He loves you Yssa, he has told me so a thousand times, long before you and I met. I want you to stay with him in Seahaven, and I want you two to enjoy being able to be with each other there for the rest of your lives. Everyone else is turning to the World Below for the winter. You will be safe there, it's beyond the Lord Martyr's reach."

Yssa had begun to cry. She looked down at Crowe realizing his mortality and all the lost cycles that they had been forced apart by his self-exile. She lovingly stroked his gray hair. She looked up as a tear rolled down her cheek and surrendered with a weak, trembling nod.

"And Yssa," Claudia said, "Haverstagg is right about what we've seen here. The God Times were real. Light and Shadow are real. You must hold faith in that."

"You're not ready to be alone, child," Odderly said gruffly, a hint of sadness evident in his voice.

"I have Haverstagg to protect me," Claudia said before she smiled and turned her head to look at him. "Don't I?"

Haverstagg blew out a breath and smiled. "You do."

Odderly took out his red handkerchief and turned so that he could wipe his eyes without the others seeing him do it. He threw the red strip of cloth down on the ground as he turned back toward them. It was obviously a difficult moment for the dusky alchemist. He and Crowe had been friends since before Odderly was Claudia's age. Everyone was looking at him expectantly. There was a choice to be made and Odderly clearly was not prepared to make it.

Chapter 31

So much had changed since the day that Claudia had fled down the rickety catwalks below *The Blue World*. Snow had only just begun to fall at that time, and though Claudia knew that those light snows were but a prelude of the season to come, which would carry her well into middle-age, she was completely unprepared for the bitter cold that had sank even into the tunnels of the World Below.

"We're near the surface," Crowe said as he laid his thin, wrinkled hand against the stone wall of the tunnel through which they traveled.

Claudia had her black cloak pulled tight around her. Like Haverstagg she walked close to Odderly whose smoldering rod not only provided light to see by, but also the added warmth that helped to keep the chill at bay. She had become comfortable in the ever-steady temperature and humidity below ground and her thoughts began to drift to what the surface must be like now if the cold had penetrated the tunnels through which they all walked. Less than an hour later they chose a tunnel that smelled of pine and was filled with both the haunting howl of the wind and the snow that it carried inward. They had returned to the World Above.

It was daytime on the surface, and the bright light was blinding. Claudia's eyes had become used to the dim light of their wands and Odderly's smoldering rod during their weeks below ground. The sun glaring off the snow, which blanketed everything, made it even more difficult to adjust.

The cave they had reached came up to the surface from under a landslide of rock, and it was in the shelter of those rocks that they regained their strength before heading out across the rocky mountainside. None of them talked to each other. Yssa and Crowe sat quietly together. Haverstagg and Odderly regarded Claudia with solemn faces. The tension in the air was palpable.

Haverstagg finally rose and walked to the mouth of the cave where he took in the snowcapped mountains as the frigid wind blew inward caking him with snow. "Please tell me that traveling in the company of wizards means you are prepared to deal with this. I'm not dressed for travel in this weather."

Claudia came to stand beside him and squinted as she looked down the snow-laden crag. Perhaps a thousand feet below the cave the snowy boulder field was replaced by a forest of mountain pine. The trees grew close together. At least there would be a windbreak there.

"How far are we from Seahaven, Asher?" Yssa asked as she, Crowe, and Odderly joined the others.

Crowe looked at the land contours of the mountain peaks visible from the cave and studied them for a while as the others waited. At last he extended a finger to the eastern peaks. "I believe that is Mount Uerulius there," he said.

Claudia leaned around him to see and nodded. "It is, you can see the tip of Badden's Rock right there."

Crowe nodded and put a hand on Claudia's shoulder. She looked up at him, and seeing her grandfather looking down at her with that same smile he had in the days before they began this journey together, she felt her heart catch in her chest. But things were not the same now. Everything that could have changed had changed, and Claudia's smile quickly melted away. She turned so that her grandfather could not see the tears welling up in her eyes.

"So, we're what, thirty, maybe forty miles east of Ambly?" Odderly asked, cutting in between Crowe and Claudia before Crowe could question the girl's behavior.

"Aye," Crowe said.

"Then that puts us due north of Rish Hollow. You're sure that you want to head to the coast? We could outfit in the hollow and secure stiddleback for the road to Seahaven. We'd make much better time without risking travel in the hinterlands."

"We cannot go to the hollow," was all that Crowe said before taking that first step down the slope to break trail.

A sudden heat washed over the area as Odderly gently tapped his smoldering rod on a good-sized slab of rock that lay nearby. He picked it up and handed it to Haverstagg. "It won't burn you, but it will keep you warm. Hold it to your chest." He repeated the process, warming several other stones. Two he gave to Yssa, who was the first to set out after Asher Crowe.

———••———

Euum giants, fourteen in all, watched the companions from high atop the mountain peak. They were hunters, immune to the cold as they were to the heat and dressed only in the furs of mighty wolf-hulk as testimony to their hunting prowess.

The discussion among them was quick and ended with no debate. Under ordinary circumstances the euum were peaceful hunter-gatherers, but like all the other races of the world that had never before known winter, they had been caught unprepared. The mountain game had fled with the first heavy snow several weeks earlier, and their bellies ached with hunger, particularly the young who had not the constitution for fasting.

To the euum giants, the companions were food. But the giants, while far less evolved than men, were not stupid creatures by any means. They were keen and perceptive hunters, and the humans reeked of magic. Crestfallen, the giants averted their path down the trail they had been following. They deliberately headed back down the north slope toward the Black Rift which spread east and west across the mountain range, a three-mile-wide crack in the world itself.

———••———

The third day of walking and camping in the frozen wilderness brought a great and much needed victory. At the end of each day's travel Haverstagg and Odderly worked diligently at knocking down short pine with Haverstagg's enchanted mace and then piling the fallen trees in such a way as to provide a windbreak and overhanging shelter for the night. In so doing, a rabbit had fled from under the low-hanging branches of a bushy evergreen and sped across the snowy forest floor.

Unlike the previous occurrences, Haverstagg had been both quick *and* accurate. His knife had flashed toward the rabbit and lodged itself deep into the rabbit's central mass. It died instantly and meat was made available at the campfire that Claudia had stacked and brought to life with a simple wave of her wand.

It wasn't much, the rabbit, but with the weather turning worse day by day and many miles still between them and the coastal village, a few mouthfuls went a long way toward giving the companions the nourishment they needed to complete the trek. They ate in silence and had talked little as they walked. None of them were used to the cold, the snow, or the altitude. Crowe's growing fatigue wore at them all. Each of their faces were etched with concern for the fading old man.

The fourth day of crossing the highlands forced them to take shelter in a shallow cave while a blizzard raged outside. For two days they were forced to hide and wait out the weather. The time passed slowly, and though the companions all welcomed the first long rest in the warmth of the cave, the close quarters and lack of provisions soon led to irritation and claustrophobia. Claudia's decision to leave her grandfather and Yssa in Seahaven created an almost palpable tension in the air. Crowe had not yet been told, but with his condition worsening, her resolve had only been strengthened.

There had been several occasions while waiting in the cave when Claudia had thought about telling him, but a single glance outside to the storm made her hold her tongue each time. It was a decision that she knew he would not willingly accept and being closed in with him in such tight quarters would not allow for any degree of privacy in the argument that would inevitably ensue. She would tell him when they reached Seahaven, she had decided, but reaching Seahaven was important for other reasons as well.

"How much is left?" Crowe asked meekly as he lay back against the uncomfortable walls of the cave.

"Enough," Odderly answered with a scowl.

Crowe's hand touched Odderly's. "Be honest with me now, Odderly, I know that the store is getting low."

"There is enough," Odderly said again as he removed the needle from Crowe's wrinkled, jaundiced skin. "The storm will break soon, Asher, and I'll start a batch as soon as we reach Seahaven. It won't be pleasant rationing what we have left, but there will be enough."

Crowe closed his eyes as the serum began to burn within him. He lulled his head back and bit his lip as he slipped into a fitful slumber.

Claudia could not watch this any longer. They had come so far and been through so much. She knew well her grandfather's stories about winter in the World Above, and she stared out of the cave not knowing if the storm would ever end. "Something must be done," Claudia whispered to Yssa.

Yssa examined the syringes in the case that Crowe had left for her beside the lake. It was now all that remained of Odderly's rejuvenating magical serum. She closed the case and said in a near-whisper so that the sleeping Asher Crowe would not be awakened, "we cannot continue to wait out the storm, Odderly. You know this. With what is left now, there is a chance that he might still be alive by the time another batch of the serum is ready, but not if we wait any longer. Can you guide us to Seahaven?"

Odderly let out a heavy sigh. "I can, we're only a day, maybe a day and a half north, but he'll not be strong enough to walk through this weather."

"Then I'll carry him," Haverstagg offered.

———◆ • ———

Azarajii watched the orange glow burning within the cave just above him. The demon had awakened at the bottom of the newly born subterranean sea with no idea how long he had been adrift among the languid undercurrents. It had taken him a great deal of effort to find his way back into tunnels where he was again able to pick up his quarry's scent, and those tunnels had inevitably led him back to the World Above.

On two occasions Azarajii thought that he had found his prey, but each time the fire pits were cold. And then the storm had picked up, transforming into a blizzard that had hidden the trail entirely. *Ironic*, Azarajii thought, that in the end it would be blind luck that led him back to Asher Crowe and Odderly Flack.

Clawed hand, by clawed hand, the demon pulled himself up the craggy slope with his one remaining arm. The cold chewed at his flesh, but this mattered little now. The cave was just ahead and Azarajii's keen senses could hear movement within even as the blizzard winds raged around him. When the demon at last stepped into the cave he found them sleeping before a raging fire – the party of euum giants who had taken refuge from the storm.

Odderly ran with Haverstagg, who carried Crowe, hot on his heels. Claudia and Yssa trailed a short distance behind. All of them ran with their heads down against the fierce winds that swept up the hill. The cold was numbing their feet and legs, but the magically heated stones kept their blood warm and their sheer desperation kept them moving at as quick a pace as they could muster despite their growing exhaustion. Yssa in particular, was having trouble keeping up.

They stopped to rest only twice; once among a windbreak of boulders where the snow had drifted over and frozen smooth to form a natural ice shelter. The second time deep within a forest of pine where the wind still blew, but finally brought with it the faintest touch of warmth. At this second break, Crowe was given another injection, double the ration that Odderly had been administering. His wrinkles faded, his color returned, and his eyes slowly opened.

"Where are we?" Crowe asked in a gravel-throated voice once he had returned to his senses.

Claudia leaned over him and spoke quietly, "Odderly says that Seahaven can't be more than an hour or two away. We can feel the warm sea breeze, Grandfather. We're almost there."

Yssa gave Crowe some water by wetting her fingers and letting the water drip between his cracked lips. "We all decided that you would probably want to walk into Seahaven on your own two legs," Yssa said.

Crowe nodded and took Yssa and Odderly's offered hands to help him get back up to his feet.

———•—

Azarajii's glowing eyes flared with anger as he came to realize his mistake. It was not Crowe and Flack, but brainless giant savages that he had come upon. The demon drew his wand and then stalked over to the largest group of the giants where three particularly large specimens slept close around the fire to keep warm.

Azarajii swiped his wand over the flames and then raised it upward with a series of dancing strokes. The flames crackled and grew higher, following in the air, the same movements that Azarajii signaled with his wand. In a final motion, Azarajii set the flames down upon the three sleeping giants and the fire suddenly burned ten-fold as fiercely. The screaming was deafening, but short lived as the giants wailed and rolled around frantically on their furred sleeping hides, setting them aflame as well.

The initial confusion bought Azarajii enough time to bring several more giants down with blasts of dark, almost black energy that crackled with purple lightning from within. When each was hit the giants froze in place, and then burned away into ash as the growing impact hole spread and consumed them. The giants stood no chance against him. Those that still survived armed themselves with massive clubs and throwing stones; one of which took Azarajii from his feet and crashed his desiccated gray body into and then through a column of stone before he went crashing into a bed of stalactites that almost reached the cave floor. But the demon was unfazed. The successive stones shattered in mid air; blasted apart by Azarajii's magic.

Several of the giants, fearful of the thing that had come upon them in the night to begin this slaughter, fled to the mouth of the cave to escape. In the end, however, only one of the giants escaped the wrath of the Ambraic demon. He would return alone to the tribe and tell them of the disaster that had befallen them. With the hunting party lost, Azarajii had doomed the euum giant that escaped him to a slow and terrible death along with the rest of his tribe.

Chapter 32

Claudia raised her eyes from the ground when she heard Odderly calling from atop the forested ridge ahead. The snow was at last behind them, though the air was still thick and damp with storm clouds brooding overhead. Yssa and Claudia both had walked arm and arm with Asher Crowe as the last miles between the companions and the coast were left behind them.

"Seahaven!" Odderly shouted, his arms raised over his head and waving side to side.

Midway between Odderly and the rest of the group, Haverstagg's pace picked up.

"We've made it, grandfather," Claudia said to Crowe. "Just a little further now."

As they joined Odderly and Haverstagg atop the ridge Yssa, Crowe, and Claudia looked down upon the little village nestled on the northernmost coast of the Bryland's eastern edge. A warm wind that smelled of the salty sea blew up at them as they gazed down upon the blue-roofed white buildings and the pale green cobblestone roads that ran between them. A white sand beach was visible along the bay whose quiet waters were protected by a finger of forested land at the end of which could be seen the silhouette of an ornately sculpted building.

"Seahaven," Crowe whispered, almost as if saying the name himself confirmed the existence of the village he had not seen for more than fifty cycles.

"It's true then," Haverstagg said, shaking his mane of unruly blonde hair and letting it blow in the warm sea wind. "Winter does not touch this place."

Crowe nodded. "There is a magma chamber beneath the bay."

The companions worked their way down the pine-shaded decline walking in single-file with long strides and a renewed sense of vigor. But to Claudia Kobb, each step brought not only relief, but another feeling as well. Her steps came less assured. She had purposely fallen behind the others so that she could watch them. This was the last time that she would ever see them all together. Oddly had always seemed like family, but Claudia now felt the same bond with Yssa and Haverstagg as well.

Perhaps more with Haverstagg than with Yssa, because Haverstagg was the first friend that Claudia had ever made on her own. She was thankful that he would be going with her when they left the others behind, even if she still did not fully know where it was that she was going. Her father was out there, somewhere, and Claudia was determined to find a way to bring him back from the darkness that had taken him. She had been through too much, both in losing him as a child, and the journey to find him lost to the dark menace of an Ambraic shade.

Claudia knew little about the Ambra, or Ambraic possession, but she had the wisdom of Asher Crowe, one of the few men in the world to have ever drawn out and bound a shade. Her hope rested in a man she had never met. Rimsha's brother was a seer, a prophet, and thus Seahaven offered her a chance to discover where her father had gone. Rimsha had spoken evasively about Claudia and her father, her brother no doubt knew something of value.

Claudia began down the hill with her thoughts on Rimsha, the ranger woman who had in such a brief time, taught her so many things. In a way, Rimsha defined many of the metaphors and morals present in old children's tales. Rimsha was not a book that could be judged by its cover. She blended easily into the scoundrels of Roak's Forge, yet she was never one of them. She had been passionate about her beliefs, and a strong, vibrant, and noble woman all the way to the end. She had unknowingly inspired a great deal of strength in Claudia. While this leg of her journey was coming to an end, a new journey with new trials and challenges stood immanently ahead of her. She would need all the strength she could muster.

Gulls flew to and fro over the quiet, and seemingly abandoned streets of Seahaven as the companions walked between the three- and four-story buildings. The village architecture resembled Ambermane in many ways, though without the dark and ominous tones and layers of intangible mystery. In fact, everything about Seahaven seemed to be filled with hope and beauty from the white statues of children playing around the small market fountain to the boxes of blooming flowers that hung under nearly every window. Yet for all the peace the village pervaded, there was not a villager in sight. Seahaven appeared to be abandoned.

"Where have they all gone? Evening beckons, but surely it is not so late as to take every living soul from the streets," Yssa spoke aloud.

"The village is empty?" Claudia said quietly to herself. All the hope that Seahaven might offer her grandfather and Yssa safety began to fade. Something was wrong, and Claudia sensed danger drawing near.

Just then Haverstagg grabbed Crowe's shoulder to get his attention and pointed up to a third story window where several children's faces were pressed up against the foggy glass. As they watched, curtains were drawn over the window and the faces disappeared.

The companions continued to walk down the strangely silent village road. Several times they saw curtains drawn or shutters pulled closed as they approached. Once, a man stood looking out of a door that was slightly ajar, but as Haverstagg stepped toward him trying to get his attention the door was slammed shut.

"I'm beginning to think that we're not welcome here," Haverstagg said as he pushed on the door to test the lock. "Why are these people afraid of us?"

"It is not you that they are afraid of," a voice sounded from behind and caused them all to spin around.

There was a man standing there in the middle of the road. He wore a clean white robe trimmed with a pale blue that matched his eyes. He was balding and well-aged with long white hair hanging down past his shoulders from the spots where it would grow at all. He must have walked silently up behind them.

"We have foreseen your coming," the man explained. "I welcome you to Seahaven, even if it is only ill tidings and trouble that you bring here."

"Rimsha," Claudia spoke out.

"You are here, and thus Herres' sister is dead." The man nodded to Claudia. "It is not your fault, child, for it was not meant for things to come to pass any other way."

"Who are you?" Crowe asked.

"My name is Mirowan," the man answered, bowing low. "I am the Reeve of Seahaven, and I am your friend, Asher Crowe, for as long as it is meant to be that we are such. You must forgive the others, we do not often see strangers here, let alone those we have had visions of."

Odderly's brow furrowed. "Well then, *friend*, if you knew that we were coming, then you know why we are here and what we need."

"I do," Mirowan confirmed. "If you'd care to follow me, I can show you to the house of Herres, for he has offered to provide for you both food and shelter. As we do not often see traders or travelers here, we have no inn, so I do hope that you will take Herres up on his offer."

Crowe looked to Yssa and then to Claudia. Both nodded.

"Take us then, to the house of Herres."

Mirowan led the companions through the winding streets of Seahaven and up a long case of stairs to a neighborhood of small homes where he gently rapped on a door. When the door was opened, Claudia and the others found themselves looking at a slender dark-skinned man who was clearly related to Rimsha, for their features, gender aside, were nearly identical.

"Your guests have arrived, Herres."

Herres' expression was difficult to read. He neither cringed nor smiled, but there was a trace of sadness that Claudia could see in him and she believed that it was due to more than just the loss of his sister.

"Please, come inside," Herres said.

Crowe and Yssa were the first through the door, Claudia the last. The entryway of the home was much larger than any of them had expected. The furnishings were simple and sparse, but what there was had the touches of excellent craftsmanship.

"Thank you all for accepting my hospitality," Herres said as soon as the door was closed behind him. "I am sorry for my sister's failure, which is my failure as well. I had hoped that Rimsha would be able to change things."

"Is that supposed to make us feel welcome?" Odderly muttered to Haverstagg.

"You *are* welcome here Master Flack, and I do hope that you will remain my guest for some time to come. We are to have a grand friendship, you and me. But there will be time for us to discuss these things later." Herres looked from Claudia to Crowe, and then to the others one by one as he continued. "If I may show you to your rooms, I believe that Mistress Kobb and Master Crowe have much to discuss. So little time remains."

Claudia paled at Herres' words and looked immediately at her grandfather. She *had* planned to tell him of her decision, but she had certainly not expected Herres to force her hand only moments after what she supposed was an introduction.

"Claudia?" Crowe asked, raising his brow.

Knowing what was coming, Yssa touched Crowe's shoulder and whispered to him, "be easy on her, Asher."

Claudia's jaw dropped open, and Haverstagg, Odderly, and Yssa followed Herres upstairs.

"I have only this room to offer," Herres said when he opened the door to his guest room and led the trio inside. "There are only two beds, but after the journey you have endured, I am sure that they will provide much needed comfort. Please take your rest Master Haverstagg, Mistress Yssa."

"What about me?" Odderly complained.

"While I am quite sure that I have anticipated everything correctly, I must first show you something Master Flack," Herres said.

Odderly followed Herres into a room directly across the hall. Before they had passed through the threshold, Asher Crowe's voice carried up from downstairs; Claudia had no doubt just told him of her decision. The ensuing argument was one that Odderly was glad to be missing.

The room was divided in decor between a study and a workshop. One half of the room held a floor-to-ceiling bookcase filled with numerous old texts and a table where other voluminous tomes were laid out beside whittled scraps of wood and a small model of a ship that had a sewn bag for a sail. The other half of the room held a long low table the length of a man, which was covered with medical supplies. Beside the table was a second, smaller table dedicated to laboratory equipment just like that which Odderly had set up in the basement larder of Crowe's woodland cottage. Jars of various herbs and extracts cluttered the little available table space.

"Perfect," Odderly said, looking over the equipment. He regarded Herres for a long moment, quite impressed with the man. It seemed that the legendary seers of Seahaven were forces to be respected.

Crowe's back was turned to Claudia and his face was tightened up, color painting his typically pallid complexion as he tried to calm himself.

"Grandfather," Claudia said, touching his shoulder from behind, "it is my decision to make."

Crowe shook his head and spun around suddenly, yelling, "You are too young to do this."

"You were a *warder* at my age, in the service of the Fifth Lord Martyr, and doing things far more dangerous. I've been to *The Blue World*, grandfather, you told me yourself."

"I was twenty cycles then," Crowe defended.

"Which means you had passed your trials long before! And do not forget, Grandfather, that you have spent the last six cycles making me commit your version of history to memory. You may have tried to keep your secrets, but I know what the Lord Martyr puts the hopefuls through, and the Fifth was even more cruel than the Sixth," Claudia protested. "I love you, Grandfather, and I have made my decision. You are not well enough to travel with me, and you have Yssa now. Hunting my father is no longer your burden." Claudia tried to calm herself and lower her voice. "I . . . am no longer a ward to be sheltered. I've grown up, Grandfather, and now the time has come for me to see this through to whatever end I may find." Claudia grabbed hold of her grandfather's chin and made him look into her steely eyes. "The time has come for you to let me go."

CHAPTER 33

"She's right," Odderly said to Crowe as they stood together in the seer's sanctuary which looked out over the tumultuous waters of the open sea.

"And what about you, Odderly?" Crowe asked. He stood on the smooth, spiraling pattern of blue and white stonework and looked out to the open white-capped waters of the turbulent Easterly Sea as Odderly leaned against one of the supporting pillars. "If I do as she asks, then what will you do? Will you go with her?"

"Would you ask me to stay, knowing more than any other what it is she is hunting?"

Crowe shook his head. "No, of course not. She'll need you at her side more than ever. But it is a fool's quest, Odderly, and you know it. In all my cycles as a wizard even I did not have the power to exorcise a demon. Collinhodge had to die for me to get the damned thing out of him."

"But you also had no emotional tie to Headmaster Collinhodge, Asher. You told me yourself, all those cycles ago, that it *was* possible, that it *could* be done. Collinhodge simply did not have the will left to fight back against the shade. This shade is in Horace Kobb now, and the bond between parent and child, Asher, that gives her power that you did not have. She may very well be able to do it."

"It pains me, Odderly," Crowe admitted.

"Aye, I know that. It pains me too my old friend, but I cannot let her do it on her own. Haverstagg's a good sort, and he means well, but he's more inexperienced than she is. They're going to need me more than you do."

Crowe sighed and looked down at the stones used to pave the sheltered area of the sanctuary. He was about to say something more when a long shadow fell over him.

"You didn't expect him to give in easily," Yssa reminded Claudia as they sat with Haverstagg and Herres in the parlor of Herres' home. "That is why you waited so long to tell him."

"Yes, but none-the-less, he needn't be so stubborn. You and Grandfather can have a happy life here. And Odderly and Haverstagg are going with me, I'll be fine."

Herres took a heavy breath and held it as he sadly shook his head. When he looked over at Claudia, he had tears in his eyes. He had spoken little as Claudia had told him about Rimsha's death in the World Below, and Claudia had attributed his continued silence to be Herres' way of dealing with the grief of that loss despite his repeated proclamations that it could have happened no other way. Now, Claudia felt that it was more than that.

"Herres?" She asked.

Herres stared down at his feet.

"Herres?"

"I regret being the one to tell you this, Mistress Kobb. You failed to heed my sister's warning, and there is nothing that can be done to stop what has been put in motion. Perhaps I was foolish to think that sending Rimsha to find you might be able to change what I had already seen." Herres looked up but seemed at a loss for words.

Claudia sat bolt upright. "What are you saying?"

Herres looked at Claudia for a long moment before speaking. "Everything has thus far come to pass exactly as I foresaw it. Rimsha is dead. Here you are, in my home, having barely survived your encounter with the Ambraic demon yourself . . ."

"No, we survived." Claudia interrupted. "Rimsha's warning..."

"... was that if you wanted to save your grandfather's life you would go with her *then*," Herres said.

"My grandfather did not die in the World Below. Rimsha traded her life for ours," Claudia said.

"My vision was not that Asher Crowe would die in World Below, only that once encountered there, the demon would follow you all here, to Seahaven. It is here, that..." Herres' voice trailed off and he looked down at the floor.

Claudia paled, Yssa's mouth fell open, and Haverstagg stood up abruptly.

"Yssa, where did they go?"

Azarajii stepped around one of the supporting pillars, his long, backlit shadow falling directly across both Flack and Crowe. He felt the excitement of the weak-willed warder that shared his mind peak as the moment of Loris Mankoff's vengeance approached.

Neither Crowe, nor Odderly, had expected anyone to interrupt them at the seer's sanctuary, not when the people of Seahaven were going so out of their way to avoid them. The sight of Azarajii's naked, desiccated form stepping into the sanctuary caused both Crowe and Odderly to do a double take. The demon had found them, alone and unawares.

"*Magus cadavus!*" Azarajii shouted at the same moment he raised his wand toward Crowe.

A bolt of blackish-purple electricity crackled from the tip of Azarajii's wand and hit Crowe full in the chest before he could so much as reach for his own wand. The bolt spun Crowe around three times as he toppled out of the sanctuary and into the bushes that grew down the dais steps. His wand flew up into the air and landed mid-way between Odderly and Azarajii just as a wave of heat washed over the shelter of the seer's sanctuary.

"*Ac araddisi enmorr!*" Odderly shouted, weaving together the exact same two enchantments that he had first used against Warder Mankoff in the observatory.

A wet *gloop* sounded as the jelly-like ball of acid was flung across the and hit Azarajii straight on as he turned away from where Crowe had stood to face Odderly. The ball of acid exploded and forced Azarajii to stagger back until he impacted one of the supporting pillars hard enough to crack and break the stone. Dust fell from above.

A resounding *hiss* came from the demon's body as the magical acid began chewing through his dried form. Steam rose from him, and the potent acid left a large hole in the demon's chest, even exposing a hollow cavity within the metal girdle around his abdomen, but almost as soon as it stopped burning through, the acid wound began to knit itself back together.

"Impossible," Odderly muttered.

———•———

"Grandfather!" Claudia screamed as she ran up the long, paved road that led from the village proper to the sanctuary at the top of the hill.

Haverstagg was in equal panic and quickly closing the distance between himself and Claudia, but Yssa, without the vibrancy of youth, struggled to catch up.

Claudia crested the top of the hill and rounded the curve in the road. As soon as she was around the trees that blocked her vision, she saw two figures standing beneath the onion-shaped roof of the sanctuary. Magical energies, one orange and wreathed in flames, and one dark and crackling with electricity, arched together in the center of the sanctuary. She recognized Odderly's unmistakable short and wide stature at once, and she recognized the corpse-like silhouette of the Ambraic demon, but her grandfather was nowhere in sight.

The power struggle within the sanctuary sent fire and deflected bolts of electricity shooting out from between the many of the pillars that supported the massive roof. Twice, powerful strokes of purple lightning blew away chunks of the pillars, the roof of the sanctuary shifted, and with each surge of power the demon's magic overtook more of Odderly's own.

"*Carru deteonni!*" Claudia shouted when she was close enough to the side of the sanctuary for her magic to reach.

Golden energy shot like a fireball from her wand and left a glittering trail behind its path as it streaked toward the open-sided structure.

Odderly saw the demon's magic surge once more and felt himself weakening. His knees began to buckle, and it took all of his strength and energy to keep his rod held up before him in an effort to keep the demon's deadly magic at bay. He could not hope to last much longer, but at the very moment that his strength wavered, golden sparks erupted from the demon and the dark lash of magic went astray as the demon's wand flew from Azarajii's hand. Rubble blew away from the roof of the sanctuary. Odderly went down to both knees, his smoldering rod clanging loudly against the stone tiles of the floor as he hunched forward in momentary exhaustion.

"Odderly!" It was Claudia's voice.

But he realized the danger too late. There was the sound of rock cracking and rubble fell all around him. The pillars behind him cracked and toppled away, buckling under the weight of the collapsing structure, and kicking up a choking cloud of dust and debris. Odderly looked up just in time to see a huge chunk of the roof come crashing down upon him.

"Odderly!" Claudia shouted as she saw the roof of the sanctuary crumble to the ground. "Odderly!"

She had reached the cloud of dust, but it was too thick, and Claudia was forced to step back as another pillar toppled over in front of her.

She waited in silence. Her stomach twisted inside of her. Nausea and fear filled her every shallow breath. As the dust began to settle, she saw a figure rise and come forward stepping out of the cloud. The demon had survived.

"*Sen urrumm!*" Azarajii shouted with a long, bony finger pointed

Claudia's way.

Claudia screamed and raised her wand to counter the three brightly glowing pinpoints of energy that spiraled at her, but in that moment of fear and surprise her mind had gone blank. She was helpless as the demon's magic flew toward her to claim her life.

And then Claudia felt the impact of Haverstagg as he slammed his shoulder into her. Claudia was sent flying out of the way of the spell as Haverstagg continued charging forward directly into it.

The pinpoints of light blasted into Haverstagg's shield, but even though the light quickly began eating through the metal it did little to slow the huge man's momentum.

The shield was thrown aside. Azarajii's spell consumed it entirely before it hit the ground, and the demon was met head on by a powerful strike from Haverstagg's enchanted mace.

There was a bright flash and then another, and another as Haverstagg assaulted the magical barrier that the demon had used to protect itself from such weapons. But even despite the magical barrier, the mace was still piercing the demon's defenses to some degree. Chunks of dry, dead flesh had been torn from Azarajii's left shoulder and a corner of the skull was crushed inward.

Claudia was back on her feet just in time to see Haverstagg raise the mace up over his head with both hands ready to bring it down in full force on top of the staggering demon's body. But before the strike could be made, Azarajii dropped to a crouch and thrust his remaining hand upward with his clawed fingers fanned outward. A blast of fire screamed up at Haverstagg. Even with his magic limited by the loss of his wand, Azarajii was a powerful Ambraic sorcerer, and a dangerous foe.

Claudia could not tell how badly Haverstagg had been hurt, but it looked devastating. Haverstagg was, for a moment, lost within the roaring flames and then Claudia saw him drop his mace and stagger backward holding his face as he screamed. He fell backward onto the ground and began to writhe around in pain, rolling in an effort to quell the flames.

Claudia raised her wand. *"Lorroak fury!"* she screamed. She saw the distortion in the air, but Azarajii waved her magic away before the blast of magical force could reach him.

"*Carru deteonni!*" Claudia shouted, and a shower of golden sparks erupted in mid-air as that spell too was countered.

Azarajii came forward with blinding speed and Claudia felt the demon's cold dead hand latch onto her throat as she was hoisted into the air. Her feet hung a full foot off the ground as Claudia fought to think of any spell that might save her, but as she raised her wand to Azarajii's melted, wax-like face the demon shook her violently. Claudia's wand slipped from her fingers and was kicked over the cliff into the steaming waters of the bay. Claudia felt the thing's vice-like grip tighten around her throat and she fought for enough air to breath. She tried futiley to pry away the demon's fingers.

"I remember you," Azarajii spat at her. "Foolish little girl," his glowing eyes bore holes into her soul. "What is it you think you can do to stop it all from happening?"

Claudia turned her eyes and saw Haverstagg laying face down on the road. He was no longer moving, and smoke streamed up from his body. Behind the demon she saw dust still hovering around the ruin of the seer's sanctuary, but there was no sign of her grandfather or Odderly. She fought hard to stay conscious, but without being able to draw a breath she was suffocating, and her vision was growing blurry and dim. Her thoughts were coming to her chaotically, memories and dreams flashing before her mind's eye among the terrible image of the demon's glowing eyes boring into her.

Her childhood.

Ambly.

Her father's last stand against the garuk.

Asher Crowe and their long and difficult journey.

Rimsha sacrificing her life so that Claudia could live.

It all seemed to transpire at once, but then in those last moments of consciousness Claudia remembered something. Her eyes popped open widely and she focused on the Ambraic demon before her. She tried to speak.

The demon must have wanted to prolong its torment, the way a cat plays with a helpless mouse before eating it. For it loosened its grip just enough for Claudia to take one deep breath, and with it the images in her mind's eye vanished and everything came back with striking clarity.

Claudia slipped her hand into her cloak pocket.

"I . . . said . . . *Geosium transverte!*" And at that moment she pulled out the long crystal shard that Rimsha had left for her in the node. Claudia thrust it at the demon's face as if the shard *itself* was a wand.

It was a last hope, and Claudia didn't know if such a thing could be used to channel conventional magic, but before she could even doubt her own wisdom, she felt her body surge with power. Power like that she had felt within the strand of the web. Power like that which had pushed through her when Rimsha shattered a similar crystal.

Claudia was forced to turn her head as the crystal flared with a blinding internal violet light. She felt the demon's hand recoil from her throat, and she dropped to the ground hard, but as she looked up everything began to fade back into focus, and she saw the demon stagger back. Quickly at first, but then with slowed motion as its naked body began to change into dark gray stone.

By the time Claudia had fully regained her senses, Yssa was there, cradling her.

"I'm alright," Claudia said.

Yssa moved to check Haverstagg as Claudia got up to her feet. Claudia slowly moved forward to examine the diabolic-looking statue of the demon that had been only seconds from killing her and who had, in all likelihood already killed her grandfather, Odderly, and Haverstagg as well. The demon's face was locked in a scream of intense agony, its remaining arm held up as if to shield it from some unseen foe, but even so, Claudia was afraid the magic would suddenly wear off and the demon would lurch forward and finish her off.

She reached down and picked up Haverstagg's enchanted mace. With a single angry stroke, she shattered the statue. Black ash wafted into the air and was carried away by the warm sea breeze. Azarajii's metal girdle, the only thing that had remained unchanged, fell to the ground at Claudia's feet.

Haverstagg moaned as Yssa rolled him over, but he was alive. He had taken a direct blast of intense fire but had somehow managed to quell the flames before they could kill him. Yet he would never be the same. Much of Haverstagg's arms, chest, and neck was blackened, blistered, or raw from the magical fire which had also taken a vertical stripe of skin up the left side of his face. Luckily, his eyes had instinctively closed.

Yssa put her wand to Haverstagg's face and uttered a spell that would numb the pain, but he would be forever scarred from the terrible wounds. Like wounds burned from acid, the touch of fire was not something that even conventional magic could heal. Yssa then helped the big man to get back on his feet and did what she could to steady him until he was able to stay standing on his own. He was somewhat dazed and oblivious as to the seriousness of his own injuries. Yssa looked to Claudia who stared in horror at the half-toppled ruins of the seer's sanctuary.

"Asher?" Yssa whispered in terror.

They all ran as fast as their legs would carry them.

"Grandfather?" Claudia screamed.

"Asher!" Yssa called.

"Odderly?" Haverstagg yelled as he began moving and shoving blocks of rubble away.

"Here!" Claudia shouted to Haverstagg. "Help me!"

One of Odderly's hands stuck out above the rubble. It was cut and torn; two fingers bent backwards. Haverstagg worked vigilantly at pulling the blocks of stone away.

Remarkably, Odderly was alive and muttering every curse he knew. The roof had fallen in such a way that from the waist up he'd hardly been hurt at all, but Haverstagg looked grim when he moved one large block and found that Odderly's legs were pinned by the bulk of the structure's debris. It would take Haverstagg and a dozen other men hours to dig Odderly's legs out and free him from the rubble.

Odderly turned and winced in pain as he looked back at his pinned legs. He could see the blood on the stones. Too much blood. He swallowed hard as he realized that he would not be alive by the time they freed him.

Odderly took a deep breath and tried to stop shaking. "Yssa, Claudia," he said. "The demon?"

"Claudia destroyed it," Yssa said proudly, even though she was on the verge of tears. "Where is Asher?"

Odderly shook his head. "I don't know. It took us by surprise. Asher was the first to be struck."

Yssa walked away in tears to search the ruins.

"We'll get you out, Odderly," Claudia said.

"Haverstagg can get me out. Help Yssa find Asher," Odderly said as calmly as he could. As soon as Claudia had walked away Odderly locked his eyes on Haverstagg and took a deep breath. "I'm bleeding out, Haverstagg. I'll be dead long before you can get me out of this mess."

Haverstagg, still weak himself, crouched on the rubble, holding Odderly's hand. He said nothing.

"I can heal myself," Odderly said weakly, "that damned prophet must have seen this coming. But not pinned in here like this. You have to get me to Herres' house. I need you to . . ." Odderly gestured to the knives Haverstagg wore on his belt. "You're going to have to *cut* me out."

Claudia found Yssa standing in the grass beside the ruins with her hands over her face. She approached with slow, fearful steps.

"Grandfather!" Claudia screamed.

She ran and fell to the ground beside her grandfather and wrapped her arms around him as she let out a sobbing wail. He lay pale and unmoving on the ground. Asher Crowe was dead.

EPILOGUE

Haverstagg waited a way back from the shaded grove with Yssa and Odderly while Claudia said good-bye to her grandfather. He thought that the grave of such a legendary man deserved to be marked by more than a bush of red roses planted at the top of a nameless hill, but Haverstagg understood why Claudia had chosen not to have her grandfather's name carved into a stone. Word would eventually travel throughout the Brylands that Asher Crowe had died, and there would be some who learned of the events in Seahaven and came here to see if the rumors were true.

While winter had driven most of the Brysh underground to Subterranea, the Lord Martyr would send his agents here. Should the body be found, it would no doubt be taken to the undercity and entombed in the Obelisk of Condemned Souls. Claudia would not let the Lord Martyr defile her grandfather's grave, nor steal his soul from the Light when he had finally found peace.

When Claudia stepped back to the others, she wiped away her tears and looked long and hard at her friends.

"I'm going to miss you, girl," Odderly said to Claudia when she bent down to his wheeled chair to give him a hug. "I wish that I could be going with you." Odderly wiggled the stumps of his legs.

"I'll be fine," Claudia told him. "Yssa needs you to keep her company more than I do."

Yssa smiled as best she could. "More like he needs someone to keep him out of sight if the warders come, and out of trouble in general. He's already taken over Herres' workshop."

Claudia smiled and almost laughed at the thought of Odderly ranting and bickering with the introspective seer.

"Just be safe, lass," Odderly said before spinning himself around. He wheeled forward and then stopped suddenly and looked back. "I expect to see you back here again before spring."

"You've my word," Claudia smiled. "Just don't get yourself killed testing out that flying contraption of Herres' in the meantime."

Yssa gave Claudia and Haverstagg each a hug and then bit her lip as they mounted their stiddleback. Yssa turned and hurried to catch up to Odderly who had already rolled down the hill.

When she reached him, Odderly looked up and furrowed his brow. Yssa's necklace, the heartstone that Asher Crowe had made for her, her most treasured possession, was not around her neck.

Yssa noticed Odderly's stare and smiled, touching the place where the jeweled charm always hung. "She's got a long road ahead of her," Yssa said, "and you never know when you might need a bit of magic."

The Subterranea Saga Continues In

CLAUDIA

Wade Gustafson

PROLOGUE

The weight of the kag increased with every step, threatening to overwhelm the runner's stamina. With his final reserve of strength, the runner lobbed the torturously heavy leather ball forward, sending it arching over the heads and outstretched arms of two line guards only a moment before he disappeared beneath the bulk of a third defensive man.

Up the mossy field, the now feather-light kag landed in the waiting hands of a fresh runner who made a short and effortless dash forward before throwing the ensorcelled ball through the unattended goal ring.

The crowd gathered in the Lord Martyr's arena howled and cheered, for the goal meant victory. There would simply not be enough time left in the game to turn favor. For Minowe, a small and meek-looking man with dark leathery skin and slick gray hair, the goal brought on a sense of utter disgust.

"Another fifty flays down the chute," Minowe spat as he got up from his seat and worked his way through the throng of spectators.

He hated these *civilized* games and had suffered nothing but ill fortune gambling on them. And he was not alone. There were others like him, bitter and angry as they filed out of the three-tiered arena with no need to watch the final seconds of the game play out to mock them.

Minowe moved quickly down the steep stone steps and was soon outside with the great undercity of Subterranea spreading out before him.

Crammed within a bowl-shaped cavern six miles wide and nearly three miles at its most narrow point, Subterranea, the Brysh capitol, was aglow with magically conjured fire light that painted the undercity in dancing shades of yellow and orange.

For more than one hundred and fifty cycles, a full year and a half by Brysh Reckoning, the great undercity had been expanding to fill the colossal cavern. Even in his grandfather's time Subterranea had stretched from cavern edge to cavern edge, and when the undercity could no longer expand outward it began to climb upward.

From his vantage point atop the great central flowstone upon which the arena was built, Minowe could see the tall, sprawling flat-roofed buildings interspaced with clusters of exotic towers further connected by a web of bridges. Some of the more impressive structures rose even higher until their tops disappeared into the perpetual gloom of this naturally lightless place and presumably connected to the scalloped cavern ceiling the way stalactites and stalagmites sometimes meld together into columns of stone.

The only light to break the gloom overhead was the reef, a region of jagged coral that snaked along the distant ceiling. *The Painted Reef*, as it is often called, an ancient remnant left over from the world's distant past when the cavern was flooded with seawater. The millennia that have passed have seen the water drain, leaving behind several salt lakes in the lower regions of the cavern, and the reef itself which glows green, yellow, blue, and red from the colorful lichens that paint it.

Minowe turned his attention away from the familiar sights of the undercity when he heard the deep horn and synchronous cheer erupt from the arena.

He waited.

Not far away from him and clearly visible despite the milling crowd of people emerging from the arena was the first of a ring of twenty-foot statues that surrounded the massive structure. The statue was that of *Tyrl the Lizard*, a long dead gladiator who had gained a great deal of fame during the time of the Fifth Lord Martyr when it was bloodsports that were played out in the prestigious arena.

Minowe was a much younger man back then and he had always

enjoyed the brutal and bloody duels. He longed for a return of the games, for the return of a Lord Martyr who would dispel the decadence of the once great sovereignty and return the Brylands, and Subterranea itself, to its former glory. That time was drawing near.

He had been given a simple, but important task. It had taken the better part of a month for him to verify that the boy existed, and even though he doubted that the rumors could contain even a shred of truth it was not his place to dabble in the work of his master's wizards.

After several minutes had passed, he caught sight of a familiar face. A man who shared the burnt color of Minowe's skin stood by the statue with his arms folded over his chest.

"Eddis," Minowe muttered beneath his breath.

The two made eye contact for only an instant before he turned and vanished into the crowd. The Lord Martyr had spies throughout the undercity. It was not safe to send written messages here, and one never knew when a warder might be watching from behind a shroud of invisibility or listening clairvoyantly for signs of conspiracy against the Lord Martyr's rule. It was made all the more complicated by the old slaver's increasing paranoia.

But Eddis *was* the message. Any one of Minowe's three associates in the undercity could have appeared at the statue following the game of kag, and each would have signified a different place where Minowe was to meet the slaver.

Forcing himself to walk at a normal pace so as not to attract any undue attention, Minowe navigated his way through the crowd. When he reached the bottom of the glistening flowstone, he chose a narrow road that led into a more squalid neighborhood where refugees from the winter raging in the World Above had come in droves.

The road was shoulder to shoulder with dirty people and countless makeshift shelters were pressed up against the walls of the surrounding architecture. No lizard-drawn carriage or mounted warden could hope to come this way without a great deal of effort or the trampling of the refugees who had come to Subterranea two cycles ago to forge a new life for themselves and found instead overcrowding and poverty.

Minowe ducked into an alley that smelled of sweat and urine and waited for several painfully long minutes to make sure that he had not been followed. Satisfied, he stepped over a homeless vagrant who slept there and opened a door set into the filthy alley wall.

He cast one last look over his shoulder and closed the door behind him. He had not even turned back around before he felt a powerful hand clamp down on his throat and pull him into the room. He was immediately slammed face first into a nearby wall.

"Were you followed?" A man's gravel-throated voice.

"No," Minowe gasped. "Of course not."

Minowe was spun around suddenly and pushed back against the wall a second time so that he could see the face of his assailant. The man before him appeared nothing short of deadly. Powerfully muscled, blade-scarred, and wearing a mismatch of battered armor. The mercenary raised the point of a leaf-bladed dagger even with Minowe's face.

Sweat began to bead on Minowe's dark, heavily creased skin. He turned his eyes to the side to where a grizzled old man sat coolly in a chair, which was the room's only furnishing. Behind the slaver was a white-skinned boy of no more than ten cycles. He cowered in the corner of the squalid apartment. A full minute passed in nervous silence as the slaver appraised him. Finally, there came two quick taps on the door followed by three slow knocks. The vagrant, he realized, was no vagrant at all, but one of the slaver's mercenaries who had hopefully just signaled the all clear.

Following the signal, the mercenary looked over at the slaver and then dropped Minowe roughly to the ground.

Relief surged through him as he finally drew an unobstructed breath. He wiped the sweat from his face and neck then stood up to try and salvage his composure. He cast a scowl at the smiling mercenary, but he merely sheathed his dagger and moved to stand by the door. Minowe was used to dealing with mercenaries, but he loathed their entire lot. Ally one minute, enemy the next, always on the side of the man who had the heaviest purse.

Pushing his contempt aside Minowe turned to the old slaver. "This is him?" he asked, indicating the boy.

The slaver nodded. When Minowe walked past him the slaver

caught his arm by the wrist. "There is the matter of payment."

Minowe pulled his arm free and untied the purse he had looped under his tunic to protect it from thieves. He tossed the heavy purse over and continued toward the boy as the slaver began to count the paper currency.

Crouching down beside the boy he listened for a moment to the child's muttered whispers spoken between fits of soft crying.

"We're done here," the slaver said as he finally rose from his chair and stuffed the money into his pocket.

Minowe heard him walk toward the door. He touched the young albino and the boy jerked with a start, spinning around to face him. The boy looked absolutely terrified as if he lived in a constant state of fear. His eyes were milky and white. Sightless.

"He's blind!" Minowe shouted, bringing the slaver to a stop by the door.

"And deaf," the slaver added. "Give Kimbrak my regards."

Made in the USA
Columbia, SC
01 November 2022